The Case of the Sharaku Murders

THAMES RIVER PRESS
An imprint of Wimbledon Publishing Company Limited (WPC)
Another imprint of WPC is Anthem Press (www.anthempress.com)
First published in the United Kingdom in 2013 by
THAMES RIVER PRESS
75–76 Blackfriars Road
London SE1 8HA

www.thamesriverpress.com

Original title: *Sharaku satsujin jiken*
Copyright © Katsuhiko Takahashi 1986
Originally published in Japan by Kodansha, Ltd.
English translation copyright © Ian MacDonald 2013

A CIP record for this book is available from the British Library.

ISBN 978-0-85728-129-6

This title is also available as an eBook.

This book has been selected by the Japanese Literature Publishing Project (JLPP),
an initiative of the Agency for Cultural Affairs of Japan.

D1261101

THE CASE OF THE SHARAKU MURDERS

THE CASE OF
THE SHARAKU
MURDERS

KATSUHIKO TAKAHASHI

Translated by
Ian MacDonald

THAMES RIVER PRESS

Prologue

A PAINTED scroll hangs on the wall.

The backing looks very old but the painting itself is in excellent condition, suggesting the scroll has rarely been unrolled. There is little sign of flaking or insect damage. Two silk bands attached to the rod that the scroll is hung from match the silver brocade mounting above and below the painting. It undoubtedly cost a pretty penny when new.

The predominant tone of the painting is brown. Executed on a rectangle of silk about a foot wide and a yard long, it shows an enormous lion, head lowered, face twisted into a ferocious snarl, with deep furrows running from its brow to the bridge of its nose. Its long, sharp claws are sunk into the ground and the hairs on its back, which are clearly discernable, stand up in great waves. One can almost hear the beast's labored breathing; it appears poised to pounce on the viewer.

This is not one of those stylized Chinese lions so common in early modern Japanese painting, it is something far more unusual: a lion in the style of the Naturalist School imported to Japan from the West in the late eighteenth century.

Though it appears to be painted with Japanese watercolors, the surface has a tactile quality and a luster like an oil painting. Upon closer inspection, it appears coated with some sort of varnish. Before oil paints were widely available in Japan, varnish was sometimes used to imitate the look of Western paintings.

The artist must have modeled his lion on a Dutch copperplate engraving or the like. The background features an Oriental landscape. The original probably had no background so the artist must have felt compelled to provide his own. The result is a lion who looks as though he has stepped out of the African savanna into a landscape of gnarled Japanese pine trees and craggy Chinese peaks. One has to admit it is a rather bizarre juxtaposition.

Putting aside the painting's thematic incongruities, it is clearly the work of a master. There is no denying the extraordinary brushwork.

In small lettering in the upper left-hand corner the painting is signed, *Chikamatsu Shoei, formerly known as Toshusai Sharaku*, and dated, *Month of Rebirth, Dog-Ox Year of the Kansei Era*. According to the old Japanese calendar, which was based on the Chinese zodiac, the Dog-Ox year corresponded to the tenth year of the Kansei Era and the Month of Rebirth to the second lunar month.

In other words, the picture was painted in March 1798 by an artist who changed his pseudonym from Toshusai Sharaku to Chikamatsu Shoei.

1

A Chance Reunion

October 10

THE NARROW BEAM of the small flashlight the man held in his hand petered out before reaching the ocean some two hundred feet below and melted into the inky blackness of the night. He heard only the heavy and persistent lapping of waves, whose sound, mingled with the howling of the wind, seemed to travel along the beam of light.

The man let out a deep sigh.

Even if his flashlight had been twice as bright he could have found nothing that night amidst the dark sea and the black barren cliffs. Still, the flashlight's beam swept stubbornly back and forth over the jagged coast, from time to time becoming swallowed up by the darkness.

It was three o'clock in the morning.

Though still early October the temperature hovered around freezing. A sudden strong gust of wind rose from the sea. The man instinctively turned up the collar of his suit. He was not wearing a coat. On the northeastern coast of Japan winter was getting ready to set in.

His frozen fingers still clutching the metal flashlight, the man at last turned his back to the sea with a look of resignation and began to walk away.

He gradually quickened his pace because of the cold, puffs of white breath emerging from his mouth. After about five minutes he came to a narrow road. The car he had come in, a silver BMW, sat parked with its powerful engine purring away. Another man sat in the back seat. He had heard the man's footsteps approaching.

"You've been gone a long time," the second man said as he opened the door. "How'd it go?"

The heater was switched on and it was warm inside. Cigarette smoke filled the interior.

"No luck," replied the first man, sliding into the driver's seat. "Not surprising at this time of night. I take it you didn't find anything either?"

"Nope. I looked all over. But I'm not familiar with the area… Oh, I found a restaurant a little further up the road…"

"I know the one. I doubt anyone's there."

"It was completely dark. I shined my flashlight inside to make sure."

"The owner obviously doesn't live there. I can understand why; it must be difficult seeing how few houses there are around here."

As he spoke, the man held his frozen fingertips up to the vent of the heater. Noticing this, the second man quickly took out a thermos and poured some coffee into a paper cup and gave it to him. The aroma of coffee filled the small car. The man took it and held it in both hands, savoring its warmth. For some time he said nothing.

"Well, I guess we ought to be getting back to the cottage," he finally muttered. "We won't accomplish anything by hanging around here. Better get some sleep… We've been on the road for over ten hours since Tokyo. Not that I mind; he's my brother-in-law after all, but I can't ask you to do more than you already have."

"Don't worry. I can live without sleep for one night… But I wonder if we're jumping to conclusions."

"I don't think so. He definitely came up here to the cottage. Plus there's that phone call I received this morning," the man sighed dejectedly.

The wind blew more fiercely than ever, rocking the car from side to side. The two men stared uneasily out the windows into the darkness. Overhead, the sky was shrouded in dense cloud. Not a star was in sight.

The man lowered the car window and tossed out the paper cup he had been drinking from. It was immediately swept away by the wind and vanished into the inky blackness of the night. There was still a little while to go before dawn.

Body Found off Cape Kitayama Identified as Saga Atsushi
Tokyo Calligrapher Disappeared Four Days Ago—Police Suspect Suicide

OCTOBER 14—At around seven thirty yesterday morning, Sato Hideharu (27), a deckhand on the Daihachi Eikomaru—a squid fishing vessel owned by Sakata Eizaburo of Ofunato city—discovered the body of a man floating in the ocean two-and-a-half miles off the coast of Cape Kitayama near Tanohata in Shimohei County. The crew recovered the body and transported it to the nearest police station, in the town of Kuji.

Shortly after two p.m. the same day, as police were attempting to determine the man's identity, an inquiry from the police substation in Fudai led to the body being identified as that of Saga Atsushi (56), a Tokyo-based calligrapher for whom a missing person's report had been filed.

Mr. Saga owned a vacation cottage near Tanohata and had not been heard from since the night of October 8, when he left his apartment building in Miyanishi-cho, Fuchu, Tokyo, without telling anyone where he was going. Concerned for his safety, his brother-in-law, Mizuno Keiji, filed a missing person's report with the Fudai police substation on the morning of October 10. Mr. Mizuno and an acquaintance of Mr. Saga's had visited the cottage the previous night and found only his luggage. Mr. Mizuno remained in the area alone to continue his search. He was notified of the discovery of the body on the afternoon of October 13. He proceeded directly to Kuji, where he identified the body as that of his brother-in-law.

At six p.m. the same day, Mr. Saga's body was taken via police ambulance to Iwate Medical University Hospital in Morioka where an official autopsy was performed. The investigation by the Kuji Police Department suggests that

Mr. Saga committed suicide at about five o'clock on the evening of the October 9 by jumping from the cliff at Cape Kitayama near his cottage. Though no suicide note was found and his exact motive is still unclear, Mr. Saga was a widower who lived alone and was reportedly suffering from mild depression. He recently expressed his intention to resign as chairman of the Tokyo Bibliophilic Society.

Mr. Saga enjoyed great acclaim as a calligrapher. His work won several awards and he was widely regarded as the leading designer of Chinese seals used by collectors of rare books. He was also a renowned expert on ukiyo-e and the author of numerous books and articles on the subject. His passing will be deeply mourned.

—*The Daily Morning News*, Iwate

October 17

TSUDA RYOHEI was in a hurry.

When his Japanese National Railways train pulled into Tokyo's Hachioji Station, he stepped out onto the platform the second the doors opened and bounded up the stairs two at a time. Thin and lean, Ryohei was also light on his feet.

Exiting the fare gate, he noticed the area around the station had changed considerably from his university days. Even the station itself, which was in the midst of renovations, looked different than how he remembered it. Ryohei looked around for the nearest police box. Before, there had been one immediately to the left of the fare gate. He looked, but saw it was no longer there. Then he noticed a temporary one had been set up behind the stairs. Ryohei breathed a sigh of relief. He only had twenty minutes. He wanted to make sure he knew exactly where he was going.

Upon inquiring at the police box he learned Koan Temple was less than a five-minute walk from the station. The policeman explained it was not far from the public library. As a college student, Ryohei had used the library several times. With a nod of thanks he set off in that direction and as he walked, he suddenly felt his steps grow heavy.

Ryohei, wearing his everyday suit and tie, had come to Hachioji on behalf of his art history professor to attend the funeral of the renowned calligrapher and woodblock print expert Saga Atsushi.

"WHAT A SURPRISE running into you here of all places, Yosuke."

The funeral was over and Ryohei was sitting in a café not far from the temple, smiling amiably at Kokufu Yosuke.

"Same here," responded his companion, gazing nostalgically at Ryohei. It was five o'clock in the evening. Outside dusk was already falling. There were only a handful of other customers in the café. "How long has it been—about two years?" he asked, doing a quick calculation in his head.

"Must be. I haven't seen you since the professor's book party."

Ryohei paused and glanced in Yosuke's direction. The last time the two had met was at a party held by Professor Nishijima, who taught art history at their alma mater, Musashino University—a private university near Kichijoji—to celebrate the publication of his latest book. Yosuke had gotten into a heated argument with another alum by the name of Yoshimura Kentaro. It had ended with Yosuke punching Yoshimura and leaving the party in disgrace. Ryohei had not seen him since.

But Yosuke's face betrayed no emotion. Relieved, Ryohei went on:

"Let's see... That was over two-and-a-half years ago."

"That long? Time flies, doesn't it?" Yosuke smiled and lit a cigarette.

Yosuke had graduated from Musashino ten years before Ryohei. In college, both Ryohei and Yosuke had majored in Japanese art history and taken Professor Nishijima's seminar on Edo art. Though they had never met on campus, they had come to know each other through the reunions the professor held several times a year for his former seminar students.

Most of those who attended these gatherings were connected in some way or other with the world of ukiyo-e. Professor Nishijima had been teaching at Musashino for ten years when Ryohei took his seminar, and while the full roster of Nishijima's former students—at least on paper—had almost sixty members, not all of these attended the professor's reunions.

Nishijima Shunsaku was widely regarded as Japan's foremost expert on the ukiyo-e artist Toshusai Sharaku. The professor's early groundbreaking book on Sharaku had made his name and was still in print twenty years later. On the strength of this book Musashino had recruited Nishijima to come and teach there sixteen years ago.

At the time Musashino was still a relatively new university and the decision to woo him had been motivated more by a desire for publicity than to have an ukiyo-e expert on the faculty, which was weighted toward Japanese literature; indeed, there had been stiff opposition within the university to offering courses on so narrow a subject as ukiyo-e. The upshot was that Nishijima had been forced to broaden his scope to include all of Edo-period art. Even so, the numbers of students signing up for his courses were not as great as his fame might have led one to expect.

On average, about six students a year enrolled in Nishijima's seminar. But instead of being discouraged, Nishijima took this rebuff—if that is what it was—as a call to action. He abandoned his half-hearted attempt to cover the entire Edo period.. Keeping the name of the course the same —*Japanese Art of the Edo Period*—he revamped his lectures and focused exclusively on ukiyo-e. At the same time, he threw himself into his research and began churning out articles and reviews for scholarly journals and newspapers alike. As a result, he climbed steadily up the academic ladder; within five short years had reached the rank of full professor, an almost unprecedented achievement for someone whose lectures attracted so few students.

Nishijima's enhanced status earned him greater respect within the ukiyo-e community. At the time, ukiyo-e still had not gained full acceptance in Japan as a bona fide academic discipline; only a handful of universities in the country offered courses on it. Only two other ukiyo-e scholars held university positions apart from him.

It was not long before the name Nishijima Shunsaku came to carry great weight.

As his influence in ukiyo-e circles grew, more of Nishijima's former students began finding jobs with museums and publishers of art books and journals. His power grew such that no publishing house or museum that dealt with ukiyo-e would dare refuse to employ a student he had recommended. And the more students he placed in such institutions and organizations, the more his power grew. It was through Nishijima's influence that Yoshimura—the cause of Yosuke's expulsion from the alumni group—had obtained the position of curator at a private art museum.

This was how things stood when Ryohei graduated from university four years ago. Lately he had heard that even students with no particular interest in ukiyo-e were trying to get into Nishijima's seminar because of his reputation on campus for helping his students get jobs in the mass media.

This sort of talk disconcerted Ryohei; upon graduation he had turned down a job offer from an art publishing house in order to stay at Musashino and work as Nishijima's research and teaching assistant.

That had been four years ago. Time had passed quickly; Ryohei was now twenty-six. *That would make Yosuke thirty-six*, thought Ryohei, doing a quick mental calculation.

Yosuke had enrolled in Professor Nishijima's seminar the first year it had been offered. After college he had taken a job with a trading company rather than working with ukiyo-e. But until the incident with Yoshimura, Yosuke had religiously attended the professor's reunions, almost as though he felt some deep connection to his student days which he was reluctant to sever. Yoshimura and the other alums had treated Yosuke with the deference Japanese students typically accord their seniors, but in private they kept their distance, disdainful of his career choice.

Only Ryohei had seemed to hit it off with Yosuke.

"SO HOW DID you know the late Mr. Saga?" asked Ryohei, voicing the question that had been on his mind.

"Strangely, it's got absolutely nothing whatsoever to do with ukiyo-e... I'm sure I'd never get back into the professor's good graces if he heard me say that... The fact is, I just happened to join Mr. Saga's book club when I moved from Nakano to Fuchu."

"So you live in Fuchu now?"

"Yeah. I've been there almost a year."

Now Ryohei understood. He had been wondering why on earth Yosuke had gone to the funeral.

Anyone with any connection to ukiyo-e was familiar with the name Saga Atsushi. Ryohei had read his books and seen him at exhibitions on several occasions, though he had never been introduced to him.

But for the past five years, Nishijima and Saga had been engaged in what one might call a feud over differences of academic opinion.

This feud was taken up by Ryohei and the other students in Nishijima's seminar. Whenever Saga came out with a new article, they would compete with one another to point out its flaws, rarely taking any of his arguments seriously. Despite their common love of ukiyo-e, Nishijima's students treated Saga as though he was from another planet, they dismissed him completely.

And yet there was Yosuke, standing behind the reception table at Saga's funeral.

At first Ryohei thought it must just be someone who resembled Yosuke. But then Yosuke had called out his name. Even now, as he sat in the café talking to Yosuke, Ryohei still couldn't shake the astonishment he felt when he realized it really *was* him.

It never occurred to me he might have known Saga other than through ukiyo-e, thought Ryohei, realizing he had jumped to conclusions. Then he picked up the conversation where he had left off:

"The book club you mentioned—did you mean the Bibliophilic Society? At the funeral I noticed they had donated a large floral wreath."

"Don't be fooled by the size of the wreath; the club has less than twenty members."

"So that's why you were at the reception table?"

"Yeah. I was on tenterhooks standing there thinking I might run into the professor. You see, since the incident at the party I haven't seen him... At one point I even thought of asking someone else from the club to take my place. So I was glad it was you who came to the funeral instead of the professor."

"You didn't really think the professor would come, did you?"

"Why not? He and Mr. Saga had known each other for thirty years. It's only natural to expect he'd show up... I mean, given the

way things had been between them over the past few years, I can
see why he sent you, but I have to say, I'm somewhat disappointed
in the professor."

"Were they such good friends once?"

"Yes. They used to share an office at Shokodo, apparently."

Ryohei could scarcely believe it. Of course, he had heard of
Shokodo—a well-known publisher of art books before the war,
now defunct—and he also knew Nishijima had worked there at
one time. But the professor had never mentioned Saga had also
been with the company. Given how improbable it seemed, neither
he nor any of the other students had ever thought to ask, but all the
same, Ryohei couldn't help feeling somewhat hurt.

Saga had been an independent scholar unaffiliated with any
university or museum. He hadn't even been a member of the Edo
Art Association, or EAA for short, an academic society of which
the professor served as a trustee. Moreover, Saga had been a central
figure in the Ukiyo-e Connoisseurship Society, a group formed
in opposition to the EAA. The simmering feud between the two
men had its origins in the rivalry between these organizations.
And as each rose in prominence within his respective organization,
the rift between them widened. It was a rivalry that lasted twenty
years.

Since Saga and Nishijima were both scholars of ukiyo-e, initially
each had followed the other's research closely, but as time went
on differences of academic opinion resulted in an irreparable split
between their two organizations.

One of these differences concerned *nikuhitsu-ga*, or hand-
painted ukiyo-e. The two organizations had clashed bitterly over
the question of how much importance to place on nikuhitsu-ga.

The Edo Art Association held that ukiyo-e consisted essentially
of woodblock prints. That is to say, it considered woodblock printing
key to ukiyo-e's development within Japanese popular culture due
to its low-cost and reproducibility. Of course, the EAA did not by
any means dismiss the importance of nikuhitsu-ga, which, after all,
were painted by ukiyo-e artists. But when one thought of ukiyo-e
one thought principally of woodblock prints; nikuhitsu-ga were
merely supplemental.

The Ukiyo-e Connoisseurship Society, on the other hand, asserted that ukiyo-e could not have existed without nikuhitsu-ga. The definition of ukiyo-e is "art that depicts scenes and objects from everyday life," and in this sense there had been ukiyo-e-style nikuhitsu-ga long before woodblock prints came along. While one cannot deny that woodblock printing contributed greatly to the development of ukiyo-e, a woodblock print was simply a mass-produced work calculated to appeal to popular taste. While the original line drawing was the work of an artist, the reproduction was the work of a block carver. How, then, did one judge an artist? How much of the final work was attributable to the artist's skill and how much to the block carver's? It stands to reason that the only true basis for judging an ukiyo-e artist is to go directly to a work from his own hand; that is, a nikuhitsu-ga.

Sometimes, when looking at a nikuhitsu-ga from the late Edo period, one is surprised to find that it is by a famous ukiyo-e artist even though it appears rather clumsy. One could take this as proof that when the artist's crude sketches were turned into a woodblock print, the block carver and the printer compensated for his inadequacies.

This is especially apparent when it comes to the depiction of hair. When an artist does a preliminary sketch for a woodblock print, he does not draw each individual strand of hair. Instead, he only depicts the coiffure in rough outline and inks in the rest before handing it over to the block carver. It is up to the block carver to use his ingenuity to fill in the rest. Therefore, it is natural that slight variations should occur among woodblock prints by the same ukiyo-e artist depending upon the skill of the block carver who executed the final product.

Hokusai is one ukiyo-e artist known not only for his many superb nikuhitsu-ga but also the care he took in ensuring the high quality of his woodblock prints. He would sometimes go so far as to write to his publisher specifying that a trusted block carver be used for a certain job. A woodblock print was not the work of a sole artist but a collaborative effort between artist, publisher, block carver, and printer. It is for this reason that studying nikuhitsu-ga is critical to understanding ukiyo-e.

This was the view held passionately by members of the Ukiyo-e Connoisseurship Society.

To an outsider, it must seem that there are merits to both arguments and that the rift between the two camps is no more than an amusing academic squabble fueled by scholarly passions. But below the surface of this conflict, the so-called Shunpoan Affair of 1934, which shook the Japanese ukiyo-e establishment to its core, still casts its long shadow.

Nearly half a century has passed since then, and though no one talks openly about it any longer, the truth is that the conflict over nikuhitsu-ga first flared up in connection with this incident.

It all began with an article published in *The Asahi News* on April 26, 1934 announcing an upcoming auction of nikuhitsu-ga from a private collection whose owner was identified only as "Shunpoan." The article quoted Sasakawa Rinpu, an expert on ukiyo-e and scholar of Japanese literature, who praised two of the works in the collection by Sharaku, thereby generating considerable public interest in the auction. In part, the article read as follows:

Rare Sharaku Paintings Discovered

Following the tragic destruction of the only known Sharaku nikuhitsu-ga in the Great Earthquake of 1923, the discovery of two such masterpieces in the collection of a former daimyo has been hailed by Sasakawa Rinpu, who appraised the paintings, as the "find of the century." According toProfessor Sasakawa: "The paintings are from the collection of a nobleman who wishes to remain anonymous. Having examined the nineteen paintings in the collection, which are all extremely rare, the two works by Sharaku foremost among them, I would put their total value at between 150,000 and 290,000 yen."

That comes to over 500 million yen in today's currency. Such a sale was unprecedented for its time. The art world was abuzz.

But on the day of the auction it was revealed that it had been an elaborate scam perpetrated by a criminal gang. The paintings were forgeries and the name Shunpoan was a complete fabrication.

As for the ukiyo-e experts who had become unwitting accomplices in the fraud—above all Professor Sasakawa—who not only appraised the paintings but also wrote the explanatory notes for the auction catalogue and publicly proclaimed their value—the affair showed up their incompetence before the entire world. Fortunately, being innocent of any wrongdoing, they did not have to face criminal charges, but the scandal effectively ended their careers.

Ever since, ukiyo-e scholars have steered clear of making pronouncements on the authenticity of nikuhitsu-ga.

The Shunpoan Affair was a perfect illustration of the proverb, "Fools rush in where angels fear to tread." Professor Sasakawa had been the foremost ukiyo-e expert of his day. It would not have been surprising if the sudden downfall of so towering a figure had been seen by other ukiyo-e scholars as the result of hubris. But what is undeniable is that the affair had a devastating effect on the value accorded to nikuhitsu-ga, which up until then scholars had regarded on a par with woodblock prints.

From then on, they adopted an extremely cautious attitude toward nikuhitsu-ga. Whenever a previously unknown work turned up, no one dared declare it genuine until a hundred other scholars had done the same. In this way, newly discovered works could languish in obscurity for years without any determination of their value being made.

This only led to greater confusion.

At last, fed up with the situation, a group of experts came together and formed a society for the sole purpose of studying nikuhitsu-ga: the Ukiyo-e Connoisseurship Society, or UCS for short.

That was twenty years ago. To this day, the rift in the art world has persisted. In the meantime things have gone from bad to worse; now everything comes down to academic egos. It should probably not be surprising then, even after all this time, that Nishijima had never mentioned his former friendship with Saga to any of his students.

Even so, the news came as a shock to Ryohei.

Whenever he got together with Yoshimura and the professor's other former students they always started bad-mouthing the Ukiyo-e Connoisseurship Society , or—as they only half-jokingly referred to them—"the enemy." What on earth must be going through Nishijima's mind as he listened to such talk? Ryohei could not imagine.

"By the way," said Yosuke, changing the subject since Ryohei remained silent. "I hear the professor is planning to publish his collected papers."

"Yeah. The editor from Shugakusha is breathing down our necks about it…"

"Is he going to include his early stuff?"

"Yeah. Right now he's got me and Iwakoshi busy organizing it all. He's even planning to include some research papers from his student days."

"Just as I thought," said Yosuke, frowning. "It doesn't surprise me in the least. But is any of it worth reprinting? When I was in college I remember him having us read some of those old papers of his. That was when he still ascribed to the theory Sharaku had been a Noh actor from Awa. Even *he* disowned that long ago, so won't reprinting them just generate confusion? I think the field would be better served if he used this opportunity to sink his teeth into Sharaku again. I mean, he hasn't produced any new research since that book of his came out twenty years ago; he's just been rehashing the same material over and over again. I'd like to see him take up Sharaku again for real, not just write the explanatory notes for art catalogues."

Ryohei was speechless. Yosuke had put into words exactly what he, Ryohei, who worked directly with Nishijima, had been feeling.

"Oh, I almost forgot," continued Yosuke. "Speaking of Sharaku, I read your own contribution to the subject."

"Really?" said Ryohei, taken aback.

The paper Yosuke was referring to—"Sharaku: The State of the Debate"—had appeared in *The Edo Art Association Journal*, which Professor Nishijima was instrumental in publishing. Primarily a vehicle for his own students' research, it appeared at irregular intervals and was distributed free to publishers, libraries, and museums. Some people snidely referred to it "Nishijima's publicity rag" behind the professor's back. It was especially unpopular with members of the Ukiyo-e Connoisseurship Society. Since it was not commercially available, Ryohei wondered how Yosuke, now ostracized from Nishijima's circle, had gotten hold of a copy.

"It impressed Mr. Saga too... He asked me about you, you know. He said it was a fine piece of research for someone so young."

"Are you serious?"

"Why would I lie? It's not like the UCS doesn't have its ear to the ground."

Ryohei was touched. His article was nothing groundbreaking—just a survey of all the scholarly literature on Sharaku published up to the present. But it had taken him two months to write; it felt good to hear it praised. And by none other than the Ukiyo-e Connoisseurship Society's own Saga Atsushi! Nothing his university colleagues might have said could have pleased him half as much.

"Mr. Saga was an interesting man," Yosuke went on. "You know, at first I was wary of approaching him, worried that if he found out I'd been a student of Nishijima's he'd suspect I'd been sent as some sort of spy, which might have made the professor look bad. But he did find out, and you know what? It didn't bother him at all. If anything, it seemed to ingratiate me with him. Later I heard the professor himself had told him about me, back when they were still on speaking terms. I can just imagine what he must have said—just thinking about it makes me break out in a cold sweat!"

"But you were one of the professor's star students."

"That's a joke! I didn't publish a single paper; that hardly makes me a star student."

"But that's how Iwakoshi always talks about you."

"Hah! I always used to boast around him," Yosuke snorted. "So is he still working for the professor?"

"Yeah. It's just the two of us, but we're managing."

"That must be rough—eight years as a teaching assistant! I don't know how you do it. I take my hat off to both of you for hanging in there."

"Well, it's only been four for me."

Yosuke nodded. "Anyway, perhaps we should get going." Looking around, Ryohei noticed the café had become quite crowded. "How about going someplace else?" asked Yosuke. "It's been a while since we had a drink together. There's a bar in Fuchu I go to a lot. You're free, aren't you?"

"Sure… But shouldn't you to be getting home?" Not having seen Yosuke for so long, it occurred to Ryohei he might have gotten married.

"That's very thoughtful of you, but I'm still single. No wedding bells yet, I'm afraid," replied Yosuke with a cheerful laugh.

"DON'T TURN around," Yosuke suddenly murmured to Ryohei. They had gotten off the train at Fuchu Station about five minutes ago and were now in the midst of a busy shopping and entertainment district. The nearby racetrack had closed for the day but there were still lots of people out and about.

"What is it?" asked Ryohei.

"Just keep walking and act natural."

"Is something wrong?"

"There's a guy who's been following us since we left Hachioji. You probably didn't see him—he was sitting behind you in the café—but I'm positive I recognize his face. When I saw him on the train I thought it was just a coincidence. But to come this far? It can't be a coincidence. I'm sure he's tailing us."

"Sure it's not someone who knows you from somewhere?"

"In that case he would have greeted me in the café."

"What does he look like?" asked Ryohei, beginning to tremble. He'd never experienced anything like this before.

"Short hair, somewhat scrawny, stoops, needs a shave. He's a bit shorter than you, looks a few years older than me; seems to be from out of town: he's carrying a coat, so it must be colder where he comes from."

"Boy, you don't miss anything, do you?" said Ryohei, taken aback by Yosuke's powers of observation.

"I was watching him on the train. It was obvious he was pretending to be asleep, which struck me as odd seeing as the train wasn't even crowded."

"I see. Well, what do you think we should do?"

"Why don't we confront him? I doubt he'd try anything here, not with all these people around. Anyway, there's two of us and only one of him."

Ryohei nodded. At the same time, he and Yosuke stopped and turned around.

The man, who had been walking about ten yards behind them, came to a sudden halt. A look of confusion momentarily flashed across his face, but it quickly transformed itself into a smile. Then, making a slight bow, he approached Ryohei and Yosuke.

"What do you want?" Yosuke asked menacingly.

"Did you notice me following you? I thought as much," said the man, flashing an embarrassed smile. "I didn't mean to—honest. Sorry if I caused you any distress."

Having delivered this apology, the man made a deep bow.

Ryohei and Yosuke turned and looked at one another.

"YOU SURE gave me a start back there when you flashed your badge at us and said, 'Inspector Onodera, Iwate Police,'" said Yosuke, grinning as he poured the detective a shot of whisky. The three men were seated in *More*, Yosuke's favorite bar. A bottle of White Horse with Yosuke's name scribbled on it sat on the counter in front of them.

"Yeah. Sorry 'bout that," said Onodera, scratching his head sheepishly. "It's the only ID I've got." His eyes had a warmth about them that Ryohei hadn't noticed outside in the street. He began to feel more at ease.

"Say, why didn't you approach us in the café?" asked Yosuke.

"Good question. It's kind of hard to explain. You see, when I'm on duty I don't care where I am or who I'm dealing with; I just do what I have to do to get the job done. But this is unofficial business, you see. I'm always causing people grief in my line of work, so I wanted to spare you two all of that. I was just trying to be tactful for a change."

Ryohei and Yosuke burst into laughter. Tactful was the last word one would have used to describe the detective.

Onodera continued: "Most people don't like it very much when someone like me comes up and suddenly starts bombarding them with questions. Now, if the person's a criminal I could care less about his feelings. But I try to go easy on innocent folks… To make a long story short, I was looking for an opening to approach you in the café but I blew it."

At this, Ryohei and Yosuke erupted into renewed laughter.

"Say, is it already snowing up in Iwate?" Yosuke blurted out as though suddenly remembering something.

"You must be joking. It's way too early for that. Anyway, I live in Kuji, which is in the warmest part of the prefecture."

"You call that warm?" retorted Yosuke. "I was up there just last week and it felt pretty damned cold."

"You were in Iwate recently?" broke in Ryohei, whose hometown, as Yosuke was surely aware, was Morioka, the capital of Iwate Prefecture.

"Yeah. I drove up with Mr. Saga's brother-in-law to look for him after he went missing… We didn't have time to stop in Morioka though. Anyway, I expect that's why Inspector Onodera is here. Isn't that right?"

"Correct. But right now there's something else I want to ask you about."

"Something else?"

"How shall I put it? Maybe I should begin with Mr. Saga… You see, I think I know why he killed himself."

"You found a suicide note?"

Ryohei and Yosuke both leaned forward in their chairs. Yosuke was considerably better acquainted with the facts of the case than Ryohei, who only knew what he had read in the newspaper about Saga's supposed suicide.

"The night before last," Onodera went on, "I got a call from a clerk at the lost-and-found office at Kuji Station. It seems among the lost articles brought to the office on the ninth was something apparently belonging to Mr. Saga."

"Something he left behind on the train? Not a suicide note, then."

"No. I rushed straight over to the station. It turned out to be a small parcel addressed to a rare book dealer in Sendai. No return address, just Mr. Saga's name. And no stamps on it either. He'd probably intended to take it to the post office after getting off the train."

"Where was it found?"

"In one of the overhead luggage racks on the 10:46 a.m. train from Hachinohe to Fudai. One of the cleaning ladies found it while the train was stopped at Fudai Station before turning around and heading back to Hachinohe. The train arrived in Fudai at... let's see..." Onodera paused to check his notebook. "At 1:25 p.m. That's the train we thought he must have taken. Now, if he arrived in Fudai at one thirty in the afternoon he would have reached his vacation cottage near Kitayama around three. So now we had a better idea of Mr. Saga's movements on the day he died, but the parcel raised a whole new set of questions. The autopsy report pointed to suicide, but would a man planning to end his life really go to the trouble of mailing a parcel?"

Yosuke and Ryohei left the question unanswered. Onodera continued:

"To be honest, I started to have my doubts... That's how I ended up here in Tokyo."

"So you found something here to confirm those suspicions?" asked Yosuke.

"No. It turns out it really *was* suicide," said Onodera, dejectedly. "But let's back up. First we needed to know what was in the parcel. One of my colleagues rang up the rare book dealer in Sendai. No answer. 'The shop must be closed today,' he said. 'We'll have to wait until tomorrow.' You see, we couldn't open the parcel without the permission of the addressee. I decided to go to Sendai and check out the shop myself. I arrived there around noon yesterday and telephoned from the station. This time I got through. The shop's called Hirose Books. I went straight over and showed the owner the parcel. Fujimura Genzo's his name—said he'd never heard of Mr. Saga, so why would he mail him a parcel? He refused to accept it, saying there must be some mistake."

"How strange," said Yosuke, shaking his head.

"Strange indeed. Why send a parcel to someone you don't know? And on the day you were planning to commit suicide, no less. It doesn't make sense. Anyway, there was no mistake it was addressed to Mr. Fujimura, so in spite of his protests I talked him into opening it in front of me."

By this point, Yosuke and Ryohei were hanging on Onodera's every word.

"What do you think was inside?" the detective asked, his eyes fixed on them. Then with a grin he answered his own question: "Two old books, wrapped up ever so carefully in newspaper. Now, I'm not one for books myself. To me these just looked like moth-eaten old tomes. But Mr. Fujimura was beside himself."

"What were they?" Yosuke pressed him.

"Let's see..." Onodera paused to consult his notebook again. "Fujimura said they belong to a series of one hundred Noh plays—called 'Suminokura Books' or something like that."

"By Koetsu!" exclaimed Yosuke.

"That's right. That's the name he mentioned."

"Koetsu... You mean *that* Koetsu?" asked Ryohei, looking incredulously at Yosuke.

Today, Hon'ami Koetsu is remembered as one of the so-called Three Brushes of the Kan'ei Era (along with Konoe Nobutada and Shokado Shojo). In the early 1600s he was commissioned by a wealthy merchant and shipping magnate named Suminokura Ryoi and his son Soan to produce a series of deluxe, hand-printed editions of Japanese literary classics—hence the name "Suminokura Books." A sword-appraiser by profession, Koetsu also happened to be a versatile artist with a highly refined aesthetic sense who dabbled in pottery and lacquerware design. But nowhere did his genius find fuller expression than in this series of books. His calligraphy served as the template for the woodcuts and the paper was underprinted with his own designs.

"Now that you mention it, I do recall that Mr. Saga was collecting that particular series of plays," said Yosuke. "He even showed me a few. I reckon he had about half of them."

"Half! Then his collection would easily have been worth a cool ten million yen," said the detective, whistling.

"Where did you come by that information?" asked Yosuke, smiling.

"Mr. Fujimura," replied the detective. "He told me all one hundred volumes together would fetch about twenty million yen."

"Ah, I see. But that's only for a complete set. Individually the books aren't worth nearly as much as they are together. You have to have them all. I don't know exactly how much it would affect the price, but my guess is even if you were missing just one volume, you could only get half that much."

"Is that right? So that last volume alone would be worth ten million!" Onodera's eyebrows shot up.

"In theory. In every series there's usually at least one book that eludes collectors. Sometimes that's because only a few copies of that particular volume were printed. Or it could be that it was banned by the authorities. Whatever the reason, without that last volume it's impossible to assemble a complete set. That's what collectors a 'trump card.'"

"A 'trump card,' huh?" His interest aroused, the detective scribbled this down in his notebook.

"If I'm not mistaken," added Yosuke, "there are two or three trump cards in Koetsu's One Hundred Noh Plays."

"So perhaps," broke in Ryohei as though struck by a sudden thought, "those two volumes in Mr. Saga's parcel were the trump cards."

"If they were, Fujimura didn't say so."

"So why was he so surprised when he opened it?"

"Ah, now this is where it gets interesting. He said the books had been stolen from his shop."

Yosuke and Ryohei were speechless.

"You see," the detective went on, "for some time Fujimura's been collecting the same series of plays, though so far he's only tracked down about twenty of them. Eventually he intends to collect them all. Rare books are as much a business as a hobby to him, you see. Apparently, the ones he had he kept on display in his shop window. They weren't for sale, of course. Anyway, this past February two of them were stolen. That's what bothered him even more than the shock of being robbed: Why only two? Fujimura was certain it was the work of a fellow bibliophile, maybe even one of his regular customers, who had succumbed to temptation. So he didn't report the theft to the police. He thought if he waited, the books would eventually be returned. He waited and waited, but nothing happened. Finally, he lost patience and last month he took out this ad…"

From the inside pocket of his jacket, Inspector Onodera removed a folded piece of paper and handed it to his two companions.

"Here's a copy of the ad Fujimura ran in *Japanese Antique Book News*. Frankly, it doesn't strike me it would do the trick. But Fujimura seemed confident the thief would see it."

The ad gave the name of Mr. Fujimura's shop and the titles of the two missing volumes. It didn't mention they had been stolen, just that he was looking for them.

"And?" Yosuke looked uneasily at the detective. "You think Mr. Saga saw this ad?"

"It's possible," replied Onodera, nodding his head. "Saga stole the books, then when he saw the ad, he had a pang of conscience. It fits, doesn't it?"

"But in that case," Ryohei countered, "why not just return the books and keep quiet? Why go to the trouble of writing his name on the back of the parcel?"

"You got me there," said the detective with a puzzled look, refolding the piece of paper and slipping it back into his pocket.

"Maybe it *was* a suicide note after all…" mumbled Yosuke.

The other two men caught their breath.

"Everyone knew Mr. Saga was collecting Koetsu's Noh plays," Yosuke went on. "It's possible he showed the two stolen volumes to someone. Maybe they were even among the ones *I* saw. You see, collectors are a bit like children: they love to show off their toys. They can't help it—it's something about the way their brains are hard wired. He probably showed them to any number of people. Of course, these are books after all. It's not like there couldn't be others exactly the same, so having them wouldn't necessarily make him a thief. But looking at it from his point of view, he might have thought someone would see the ad and turn him in. He was a man of very high principles, so I think he would have taken his own life sooner than suffer public humiliation. Writing his name like that on the back of the parcel must have been his way of taking responsibility."

When Yosuke had finished, Onodera nodded. "Sure is a shame to take your life over a book," the detective said pensively.

"I don't think Mr. Saga would have been troubled by it if he hadn't felt his position in the art world carried a great deal of responsibility. It wasn't something he could sweep under the rug.

If the theft had come to light it would have been a huge scandal, bringing discredit not only on himself but anyone associated with him. I think writing his name on the parcel was his way of saying, 'I'm paying with my life for what I did, so please don't pursue this any further.'"

"Spoken like a true samurai," muttered Onodera. "Not that I'd ever condone stealing, but I understand where you're coming from. As a policeman, though, it's hard to go against one's gut instinct. To an extent, I could accept Saga had committed suicide over stealing the books, but the question of why his name was on the parcel was still nagging at me. That's why I came for the funeral—to verify it was really his handwriting. I showed the package to Mizuno Keiji, Saga's brother-in-law. He confirmed it beyond any possible doubt... So I guess that settles it. If the verdict is suicide, so be it. It's a bit late to quibble over Saga's motives. I'll ring up Fujimura and ask him to overlook the theft of the books. No need to go stirring up more trouble."

Yosuke bowed to the detective and thanked him.

"So was that what you wanted to ask us?" prompted Ryohei.

"What? Oh, no, actually it was something else. But it doesn't matter. I don't think it's relevant any longer."

"Not relevant?"

"It's nothing really. Just an odd remark I overheard at the temple while I was talking to Mizuno which bothered me a bit..."

"What sort of remark?"

"That Professor Nishijima is responsible for Saga's death."

At the mention of Nishijima's name Ryohei and Yosuke gave a start.

"Don't worry. I'm sure it's just malicious gossip," the detective hastened to add, seeing the looks on their faces. "There's no evidence to suggest anything of the kind. People are just saying if Saga's death would make anyone to be happy, it's the professor. Mizuno dismissed the idea as ridiculous. Still, it bothered me, so I asked around at the funeral to see if anyone might know something. That's how I learned about you two and well, here we are. But now I know for sure the writing on the parcel does belong to Saga, so it doesn't matter anymore. Anyway, tailing you wasn't a *complete* waste of time—I got a good drink out of it!"

With a chuckle the detective tossed back another shot of whisky. Watching, Yosuke and Ryohei at last began to relax.

"Boy, am I going to sleep well tonight," said Onodera, gazing fondly into his empty glass.

2

A Tantalizing Discovery

October 23

IT WAS SATURDAY, one week after his meeting with Yosuke and Ryohei was walking down the long hill from Surugadai in Kanda toward Ogawamachi. He was on his way to the Tokyo Antique Book Association's exhibition hall at the bottom of the hill.

That Friday and Saturday the Association was holding its weekly rare book fair. Ryohei had learned that Kojima Usui's *Late Edo Ukiyo-e*—his personal Holy Grail of rare books—was to be offered up for sale, at an unbelievably low price, no less.

A catalogue had come in the mail. At first, when Ryohei saw the title of the book with the asking price next to it, he thought it must be a mistake. There was no way it could be so cheap. Someone must have left off a zero. But the more he thought about it, the more he began to think it might *not* be a mistake. A multi-volume anthology of Kojima's work was currently in press. Ryohei had learned that *Late Edo Ukiyo-e* was among the titles chosen for inclusion in the forthcoming volume. As soon as it was published, the value of the original edition would plummet. If someone wanted to unload it, now was the time. When looked at this way, the price was not so incredible. Ryohei's pulse quickened.

Once he had calmed down a bit, Ryohei managed to run his eyes up and down the page. He noticed a number of other titles relating to ukiyo-e, all of them rare editions which hardly ever came up for sale. He could barely contain his excitement. They were all offered at knockdown prices. Some collector must have died and his entire collection fallen into the hands of a rare book dealer. Ryohei checked to see who the seller was. He knew most of the dealers specializing in books on ukiyo-e. Catalogues from rare bookshops were always coming to the professor's office. Whenever there was something of interest, it was Ryohei's job to go and take a look, so he had come to know many of the shop owners personally. But this was someone he had never heard of. Seeing as the prices of the books were less than half what he estimated their current market value to be, perhaps this particular dealer didn't know much about ukiyo-e. Ryohei had filled out the reply postcard provided, indicating the book he was interested in buying and dropped it in a mailbox later that day.

If no one else requested the same book, it would automatically go to Ryohei. But if the seller received multiple requests, a lottery would be held to choose the purchaser.

For Ryohei, Friday could not arrive soon enough.

When it finally did, he put in a call to the Association from Professor Nishijima's office. As he had expected, there had been a drawing. By a stroke of luck, his postcard had been chosen from among the many received, which was music to Ryohei's ears. Now he could relax.

Promising to come one Saturday afternoon and purchase the book, Ryohei hung up.

The exhibition hall was crowded, though not, as one might expect, with students, as the Association rarely sold comic books. Ryohei made a beeline for the checkout counter. He could see that the books placed on reserve had been stacked on shelves behind the counter. The book dealers sponsoring the event were standing in front of the shelves whispering among themselves. Ryohei knew one of them well. Catching his eye, Ryohei greeted him.

"Hey, if it isn't young Tsuda! How's the professor these days?" A slightly built man in his fifties, the book dealer smiled affably at Ryohei from behind thick glasses and led him behind the counter. Ryohei bowed to the other men.

"Now here's a real bookworm for you," the first man said, introducing Ryohei to his colleagues. Ryohei suddenly felt very small. "So, what brings you here today? University business?"

"Actually, I came to buy a book I requested. My name was chosen…"

"Oh, really? What's the title of the book?"

"Kojima's *Late Edo Ukiyo-e*."

"Oh, that was *you*, was it? Aren't you the lucky one!" the man said as he ran his eyes over the shelves, piled high with books. "Now, where did I put that?"

"In the back and to the right," answered one of the other book dealers, a young man. The first man shifted his gaze and quickly pulled a book from the shelf. A slip of paper with Ryohei's name on it was attached to the book with a rubber band. Checking the name was correct, the man handed the book to Ryohei.

"The books Mr. Mizuno sent us this time have been a big hit. *A Social History of Edo Colored Woodblock Prints* alone got over forty requests! Thanks to him the book fair's been a huge success. We're thrilled."

"Where is Mr. Mizuno's bookshop?" Ryohei asked as he handed the man his money.

"Oh, he doesn't have a shop. He only sells through book fairs like this one," the man replied, putting the money Ryohei had given him into a moneybox. "He takes part in ours once a month. Say, why don't I introduce you? He's in the back right now restocking the shelves."

The man whispered something to the woman at the reception desk and she quickly disappeared into the back. Soon, a well-built man emerged and walked over to the counter. Though he only looked to be about forty, Ryohei surmised he was actually somewhat older. He wore a somber blue suit with silver pinstripes and had impressive features—not at all one's typical image of a rare book dealer. Ryohei had the feeling he had seen Mizuno somewhere before, but try as he might, he could not place him.

Then, once the introductions were over, Mizuno smiled at Ryohei and said, "It was nice of you to come all the way to Hachioji the other day."

Suddenly, Ryohei remembered. Of course, Mr. Saga's brother-in-law!

Mizuno thanked Ryohei at some length for taking the trouble to attend Saga's funeral. For his part, Ryohei apologized for not having recognized his name.

"Saga Atsushi was my late sister's husband."

Ryohei nodded and proceeded to tell Mizuno about his and Yosuke's recent encounter with Onodera. Mizuno looked surprised.

"So that detective actually tracked Yosuke down? Now that's what I call persistence!"

"But now he seems convinced it was suicide. By the way, how did you know that Mr. Saga had gone to Cape Kitayama that day?"

"Didn't Yosuke tell you? That morning Atsushi placed two calls, one to me and one to the Fuchu Public Library. He didn't seem his usual self—a bit down in the dumps. It sounded like he was calling from a train platform. Later, when I inquired at the library, the man there said the same thing. Fortunately, while he was speaking to Atsushi, he happened to overhear a station announcement for Hachinohe. That's when it hit me—Atsushi must have been heading for his cottage on Cape Kitayama. He would have had to change trains at Hachinohe to get to Fudai."

"But why did Mr. Saga place a call to the library?"

"The Bibliophilic Society was due to meet at the library that day, you see. Atsushi called to tell them he wouldn't be able to make it. I just happened to remember they were supposed to have a meeting that day. I'm glad I did. Otherwise, who knows how long it would have been before I found out that Atsushi had been in Hachinohe? That's why Yosuke and I drove up to Iwate." Mizuno proceeded to give Ryohei an amusing account of his trip with Yosuke.

When he was finished, Ryohei decided to change the subject.

"By the way, Mr. Mizuno, I take it you don't usually handle books about ukiyo-e." The fact was that Ryohei still couldn't get over how cheap the book he had purchased had been—he would have expected Mizuno, as Saga Atsushi's brother-in-law, to be more familiar with the ukiyo-e market.

"As a matter of fact, I do. But before, whenever I found something good I always took it straight to Atsushi. He knew a lot of people in the art world, so it was simpler than selling it through the Association."

"I see… Only, it's unheard of for so many ukiyo-e books to go on sale like this all at once. I could hardly believe it."

Mizuno laughed. "Is that so? Well, the people in the Bibliophilic Society know me pretty well. As for Professor Nishijima, on the other hand, I can't say I've had any dealings with *him* in the past."

Ryohei nodded. *What a shame*, he thought. To Mizuno he said, "By the way, it's a bit late to be saying this after I've paid and all, but I hope you made some profit on this book."

"That's alright," Mizuno replied. "You just let me worry about that."

"I mean, I'm happy to have gotten it so cheap but…"

"To tell the truth, I'm planning to get out of the market for ukiyo-e books after this. I was mainly buying them at Atsushi's urging. But now he's gone and… well, to be honest, there's not much profit in it for me. As a matter of fact, many of the books I put up for sale here this weekend were his."

"Ah, that explains it," said Ryohei. "Some of these titles are really quite rare."

"If I were more altruistic I would have donated them to a library somewhere. But I'm a businessman, and anyway, I like to think I'm honoring Atsushi's memory more by selling them at cut-rate prices to young scholars like you. But I guess that's just a rationalization. He's probably rolling over in his grave right now!"

The men behind the counter all burst out laughing. At this unexpected cacophony, everyone in the hall turned and looked in their direction, curious about what had happened.

"Your shelves seem to be getting pretty empty, Mr. Mizuno," the first man said as he surveyed the room.

"You're right. I forgot all about them." As though suddenly remembering something, Mizuno disappeared into the back and returned shortly with an armful of books.

"Here, let me help," Ryohei said, taking half of the pile from him.

"I guess people really know a bargain when they see one. This is the third time today I've had to restock," Mizuno said with a satisfied smile as he placed the books on the shelves. Nodding, Ryohei handed the books he was holding to Mizuno.

"Say—" Mizuno said abruptly, "Kiyochika also spent time up in Northern Japan, didn't he?"

"You mean Kobayashi Kiyochika? Yeah, I think he spent about a year in Tohoku toward the end of his life traveling from town to town exhibiting his work."

Kobayashi Kiyochika—as everyone familiar with ukiyo-e knows—was among the best artists of his generation and is considered one of the last great ukiyo-e masters of the second half of the nineteenth century. He produced much of his best work in the late 1870s and early 1880s, taking over where Utagawa Hiroshige left off, injecting a new sense of realism into Japanese landscape painting. Sometimes called "the master of light and shadow," Kiyochika was way ahead of his time in his skillful use of shading. Tradition has it that his fortunes—along with ukiyo-e's popularity—declined during his later years, but even today he enjoys considerable fame in some parts of Japan. "Not much research has been done on Kiyochika's life," explained Ryohei, "but it appears he spent about ten months——from July 1906 through May 1907 touring Tohoku while based in Hirosaki in Aomori Prefecture. Hence previously unknown paintings of his still pop up from time to time in that part of the country. But why do you ask?"

"Oh, it's just that I came across a book you might be interested in. The paintings in it aren't especially good, but I noticed Kiyochika had written the introduction," Mizuno replied as he rummaged through the pile of books he was holding. He pulled out a large but not very thick folio-sized volume. It had a stitched Japanese binding and appeared to be quite old. A white strip of paper had been wrapped around the cover and on it someone—presumably Mizuno—had written, *Painting catalogue with preface by Kiyochika*.

"Well, they're not ukiyo-e, that's for sure," said Ryohei, flipping through the pages. If Kiyochika had written the preface, he assumed the book dated to the Meiji period—that is, sometime between 1868 and 1912.

A photographic plate had been pasted onto each page. The paintings were done in the Naturalist style imported from the West;

even though the plates were in black-and-white, Ryohei could tell the artist's use of shading was quite good. But despite the skillful use of Western techniques, the paintings had an old-fashioned Japanese quality to them. *How strange*, he thought.

"I think they're what are called Akita School paintings," Mizuno said matter-of-factly.

Ah, no wonder they look old-fashioned, thought Ryohei. Based in Akita Prefecture in Northern Japan, the Akita School of Dutch (which meant Western) Painting—*Akita ranga* in Japanese—had flourished in the 1770s, around the same time the pioneering ukiyo-e artist Torii Kiyonaga had been active in Edo two hundred years ago. As an art historian, Ryohei felt he should have been able to identify the paintings on his own just by looking at them. But his attention had been focused on Kiyochika, who, as far as he knew, had no connection to the Akita School.

"Anyway, I didn't buy the book for the pictures," Mizuno went on. "If they'd been by Shozan or Naotake instead of some unknown artist that'd be different. It was only Kiyochika's preface that piqued my interest."

"That makes sense," Ryohei agreed. As any expert knew, Satake Shozan and Odano Naotake were the best-known painters of the Akita School.

"But then when I read it I was disappointed. I doubt I'll be able to sell it. I just put that label on out of desperation..."

Ryohei looked at the price. It was eight hundred yen.

"If you're interested you can have it," Mizuno offered, reading the look on Ryohei's face. "Maybe it will come in handy for your research."

"That's very nice of you but I couldn't..."

Ryohei was indeed interested. For Kiyochika to have written the preface to a book of paintings unrelated to ukiyo-e must mean he had some connection to either the author or the publisher. *Who knows—it might yield something interesting*, he thought.

"Don't worry. You bought a book from me already," Mizuno said with a smile, taking the book from Ryohei. Then, removing the label, he handed it back to him. "Please accept it as a gift."

Great Paintings from the Collection of the Master of Mountain Lake Villa

Preface

In these abundant times there is no shortage of books, and each passing month brings more and more. But most appeal to popular tastes and passing fancies. They are mere trifles that contribute nothing to our field. This is something scholars like myself greatly regret.

Thus it is that we welcome the publication of this catalogue of paintings from the collection of the late Sato Masakichi, a.k.a. Master of Mountain Lake Villa, which I have been eagerly awaiting for some time now.

I came to know Sato when I was living in Shizuoka Prefecture. He grew up in a small village in the mountains and at one time aspired to make his name in the world as a scholar. But due to circumstances beyond his control he was forced to abandon his formal education without finishing middle school. Coming from an old and well-respected family, with many art connoisseurs among his friends and relations, he acquired an extensive knowledge of painting from an early age and through self-study nurtured a great love of art. When he came of age, he was conscripted into the army and thereafter had to make his own way in the world, for family reasons. He eventually found his way to Akita Prefecture and spent a number of years in Kazuno County, working in the mining town of Kosaka.

After I left Shizuoka I did not see Sato again for over thirty years. When we at last reestablished contact with one another I began to visit him often. I still remember fondly my stay with him from November 23 to 28 of last year.

On September 17 of this year, Sato was killed in the historic flooding that hit the Kosaka area. I was deeply saddened when I heard the news.

Fortunately, the flood spared Sato's paintings and I heard that his widow intended to collect them into a book. I was delighted. In this way I know his love of painting will never die. On his behalf, I pray that many people will now be able to see his paintings and not just those of us who had the privilege of knowing him.

December 1907

RETURNING to his apartment in Kunitachi where he lived alone, Ryohei ate a simple dinner and brewed himself a large pot of coffee. Only after starting on his second cup did he at last unwrap the paper parcel he had brought back with him from the book fair. As he did so he caught the unmistakable musty smell of old books. It was a smell he was fond of.

His hand went first to the painting catalogue Mizuno had given him.

The title on the cover read: *Great Paintings from the Collection of the Master of Mountain Lake Villa.* The book was surprisingly heavy for its size, dried up and brittle though the pages were after the passage of so much time. This was no doubt due to the nearly one hundred over-sized photographic plates pasted inside.

Ryohei began reading Kiyochika's preface. At first the verbose Chinese-style prose was difficult to follow. His eyes had to pause on each Chinese character, making it hard for him to grasp the overall meaning. But as he read along haltingly in this way, the sense slowly began to sink in. Never before had he read anything quite like it. Leave it to the Japanese to come up with such an overwrought prose style to conceal the fact one was saying absolutely nothing! He recalled how once Yosuke had said much the same sort of thing.

Mizuno was right, thought Ryohei. The preface was disappointing, but at least it mentioned the dates Kiyochika had visited Akita. That might come in useful sometime.

Ryohei turned the page. There, staring out at him was a photograph of a distinguished-looking gentleman which had turned sepia with age.

He was about forty, with a round face and a handlebar moustache, and was seated in a chair wearing a suite and a pinstriped tie. His lips were pursed and his clenched fist conveyed a sense of tension.

The photograph had clearly been taken in a studio. Behind him hung a painted backdrop out of which a window had been cut. Through it one could see clouds floating by outside. In this era of snapshots, it seemed a bit peculiar, but Ryohei had no doubt it was nothing unusual by the standards of its time. The Western-style lamp that stood ostentatiously to the right of the chair was obviously brand new, but to Ryohei it recalled a bygone age.

Beneath the photograph appeared a caption: *The late Sato Masakichi, Master of Mountain Lake Villa—1905.* According to Kiyochika's preface, the gentleman in question had met his untimely death two years after the photograph was taken. Of course, nothing about the photograph gave any hint of the tragic fate that awaited him.

The paintings began on the next page. As Ryohei flipped through the pages something fell out of the book and fluttered to the ground. At first he thought one of the plates must have come unglued from the page, but when he picked it up he saw it was an old postcard. No doubt the previous owner of the book had been using it as a bookmark. Ryohei placed it on the table and turned his attention back to the book. The plates were all different sizes; some were tall and narrow while others were short and broad. But without exception all of the paintings in the photographs were mounted on Japanese scrolls.

Each plate bore only the title of the painting and in some cases a short profile of the artist. There was no explanatory text. That in and of itself was rather odd. *Perhaps after Sato died there hadn't been anyone who knew enough about the paintings to write something about them*, thought Ryohei. Or perhaps the book had been put together by someone who didn't know anything about art catalogues and thought it was enough just to publish the paintings. Typically, books of this kind were full of commentary that went on and on ad nauseam about how the collector had acquired each work, how great the artist was, and that sort of thing. By comparison, Ryohei liked the minimalist style of this catalogue.

There were seventy-four plates in the book, fifty-two of them by one artist in particular. Apparently, Sato had been a fan of his work. Indeed, from the moment Ryohei had first set eyes on these particular plates while at the book fair, he had recognized the artist was someone of no mean ability. Now that he was able to study them at his leisure his opinion remained unchanged. But the name of the artist meant nothing to him. Apart from ukiyo-e Ryohei did not know a great deal about Japanese painting, but he did have a basic knowledge of the other major artistic movements. Moreover, since he was from Iwate Prefecture the Akita School had always interested him—Iwate and Akita being right next door to one another—and he was familiar with the names of many of its major artists.

There's more to this than meets the eye, thought Ryohei, ignoring for the moment his own lack of knowledge on the subject.

How remarkable that so formidable a talent should have been completely forgotten. But in one sense, to be remembered simply meant that one's work was still seen by people. An artist might create any number of masterpieces but if they were never put before the public, how would his achievement ever be recognized? No doubt there was any number of great artists from remote parts of Japan who languished in obscurity.

Perhaps I'm on to something...

It was the lifelong dream of every art historian to discover an unknown artist and bring him to the attention of the world.

Ryohei felt an unexpected rush of adrenaline. It was still too early to say anything for sure, but it would be worth his while to do a bit of research. If the artist in question really was a complete unknown, Ryohei held the key to establishing his reputation.

He continued flipping through the book, looking for the page that gave the artist's biography. He found it next to the last plate in the catalogue. It read:

Chikamatsu Shoei—Born in 1762 into a samurai family in Kakunodate, Akita fief. Having demonstrated an interest in painting from an early age, he took up studies with Odano Naotake in 1780. In the early 1780s he went to Edo [now Tokyo] in the service of Lord Satake Yoshiatsu of Akita. When Yoshiatsu died in 1785 Shoei left his lord's house and took up with Shiba Kokan. After his return to Akita in the 1790s he settled in Odate, later moving to Honjo. He died in the 1820s.

Ryohei was somewhat taken aback by the terseness of the biography. It was not even a hundred words. But at least it contained some essential information. It gave Ryohei a place to begin his investigations. While it was not surprising that Odano Naotake's name should be mentioned in connection with Chikamatsu, Ryohei was intrigued by the reference to Shiba Kokan. The foremost Western-style painter of his day, Kokan's name was familiar to many people today because of his copperplate engravings. But surprisingly few knew that earlier in his career Kokan had been an ukiyo-e artist. The thought that Chikamatsu might be connected, however tenuously, to Ryohei's own field of expertise made him seem less remote a figure.

Ryohei's curiosity was piqued. He turned his attention back to the paintings, which before, he had only glanced at casually. He began pouring over them one by one, scouring them for additional clues to the artist's background and looking for any inscriptions in the corners.

Before long one of the paintings caught his eye—a picture of a lion that seemed to jump out at him from the canvas of a hanging scroll. It was a powerful work of art.

His gaze became riveted to the painting, but not because of the power of the image. He had noticed an inscription in one corner of the painting. He began reading. When he got to the end, he could hardly believe his eyes. It was signed, *Chikamatsu Shoei, formerly known as Toshusai Sharaku.*

Ryohei read the words over and over again. There was no mistake. He felt as though here were dreaming.

TOSHUSAI Sharaku.

Of the more than two thousand or so ukiyo-e artists who ever lived, no name is as recognized today, save perhaps those of Utamaro, Hokusai, and one or two others. But it is not simply a question of being famous. Compared to other ukiyo-e artists, there was something unique about Sharaku. Considering the very short period of time during which he was active, he produced an astonishingly large number of works. Moreover, all of his prints were issued by a single publisher. Over a period of just ten months, he published more than one hundred and forty prints. Then he suddenly vanished. Exactly who he was is still unclear. In short, Sharaku is a riddle wrapped in a mystery, inside an enigma.

Even in *Ukiyo-e Ruiko*, widely considered the most reliable source for information on Japanese ukiyo-e artists, there is only a cursory entry under his name:

Sharaku—Lived late eighteenth century. Commonly known as Saito Jurobei. Resided in Hatchobori in Edo. Employed as a Noh actor by the lord of Awa province [modern Tokushima Prefecture]. Made portraits of kabuki actors, but these were too true to life for contemporary tastes and his career lasted less than a year.

This brief description has come down to us from the notebook of one Sasaya Hokyo, written sometime in the 1790s, and provides the best glimpse we have of Sharaku from his own time. It forms the basis for the view, widely held today, that Sharaku was not well regarded as an artist in his own day. His contemporaries, so it is claimed, were incapable of appreciating his modernist style. But if so, how did he manage to publish over 140 works in just ten months? Nobody knows.

Today, the notion that Sharaku was a Noh actor from Awa province on the island of Shikoku has been thoroughly discredited. Most scholars instead ascribe to the theory that Sharaku was the pseudonym of some other artist. How else, they say, can one begin to explain the riddle of Sharaku's identity?

Apart from the appeal of his art, it is this riddle that continues to fascinate art historians.

October 25
ONE EVENING two days later, Ryohei set out for Ginza.

At seven o'clock Fujisawa Hiroshi, one of the core members of Nishijima's alumni group, was hosting a party at *Sakamoto*, a restaurant on Namiki Street, to celebrate the publication of his new book. It was just a small private affair, but the professor was certain to be there.

As Ryohei approached his destination his pulse began to race wildly. How ought he to explain the painting catalogue he had found to Nishijima? Would the professor be interested in what he had to say? These questions had been causing Ryohei a great deal of unease. He had hardly slept for two days. He had perhaps stumbled upon a discovery that would shake the field of ukiyo-e studies—indeed, the entire art world—to its very foundations. This realization left Ryohei in no state to sleep. Today, he had again gone to the university early in the morning and spent most of the day in the art history department and the library. If it were not for the fact that Professor Nishijima planned to be there that evening, Ryohei might even have skipped the party with hardly a second though. That was how engrossed he had become in his new project.

As Yosuke had pointed out, over the past ten years Professor Nishijima had moved away from the study of Sharaku. But he was still the leading scholar on the subject.

This was the scenario Ryohei envisioned: he would tell Nishijima his new theory about Sharaku and the professor would respond with his honest opinion. There was no room for power politics. This was what research was all about.

But when Ryohei reflected on how, over the years, Nishijima had attacked every scholar to come along with a new theory about Sharaku, he grew less sanguine.

He could understand the professor's position. As the leading authority on Sharaku, endorsing a new theory was an implicit admission of its truth. This had enormous implications. In the absence of incontrovertible proof, it was only natural that the professor should adopt an ambivalent position or come out against such a theory. Rather than singling out some scholars for praise, the wisest course of action was to criticize everyone. Though Ryohei had always understood this tactic of Nishijima's, he never in his life thought that he might find himself on the receiving end of it.

"RYOHEI, dear, you're late!"

Stepping into the restaurant, Ryohei immediately heard the voice of the proprietress, Yurie, calling to him. From her position behind the counter she playfully put her fists on top of her head with her index fingers pointing up in the air like horns, as though pretending she was jealous. Having been to the restaurant, one of Professor Nishijima's favorites, on numerous occasions, Ryohei's face was a familiar one. It was past seven o'clock.

"Where's the professor?" Ryohei asked hurriedly.

With her eyes, Yurie motioned toward a private room at the back of the restaurant. Laughter spilled out through the closed sliding doors; Ryohei recognized the voices of Yoshimura and Iwakoshi.

Ryohei slid open the doors and stepped inside. About ten people were already there. The professor sat at the head of the table away from the door. The others were arrayed on either side; all were former students.

"Hey, you're late!" Yoshimura reprimanded Ryohei. Though not yet forty he was already developing a middle-age paunch.

"Sorry. I had some work to attend to at the department."

"He's been acting strange all day," Iwakoshi cut it. "He's had his nose buried in reference books and painting catalogues."

During this exchange, the professor sat talking to Fujisawa, pretending not to notice.

"It's not polite to keep people waiting," added Yoshimura for good measure, clucking his tongue in disapproval. Then, seemingly satisfied, he turned his attention back to the professor and resumed his conversation.

"I apologize," said Ryohei with a polite bow, sliding into the space that had been left open for him near the door next to Iwakoshi. Being the youngest person there, Ryohei's seat was the one farthest from the professor.

"Hiroshi's finished his speech. Here—" Iwakoshi whispered to Ryohei, handing him a copy of the book Fujisawa had just published. The book was inside a paper bag, on the front of which was written Ryohei's name. Ryohei removed the book and glanced at it. It had been put out by Geichosha, a major publisher of art books where another of Professor Nishijima's former students, a man by the name of Yamashita, worked as an editor.

"Yamashita's proposed we put together a journal and get Geichosha to publish it," said Iwakoshi, his body shaking with laughter. "He says now's our chance: it seems Saga's death has thrown the enemy into disarray. He's been ranting about how it's time to crush *Ukiyo-e World*."

Ukiyo-e World was an art journal put out by the Ukiyo-e Connoisseurship Society. It focused mainly on nikuhitsu-ga and *shunga*—erotica—and lately had seen a surge in circulation.

"But their approach is fundamentally different from ours. We can't compete with them." Scholarly articles did not sell magazines.

"True. That's why, Yamashita says, we should write about shunga. That'll knock their socks off. The enemy would never expect us to do that, not in a million years. And if we can undercut their price they'll go out of business within a year. That's the plan, anyway."

"Has he talked to Professor Nishijima about it yet?"

There's no way the professor will sign on to that, thought Ryohei. Nishijima's contempt for shunga was famous. He never missed an opportunity to argue that, but for the existence of shunga, ukiyo-e would have been recognized as a legitimate field of academic study long ago. He was always going on about how shunga was the source of all manner of ridiculous misunderstandings about ukiyo-e.

"Of course," replied Iwakoshi. "The professor says if that's what it takes to exterminate the true believers in shunga once and for all, then that's what we'll have to do."

Astonished, Ryohei stole a glance in Professor Nishijima's direction.

"'Exterminate the true believers,' huh?" he mumbled. It was such a bizarre, antiquated notion that it didn't even make Ryohei angry. All he felt was how pathetic it was to have to work for someone who could voice such thoughts without batting an eyelash.

Iwakoshi continued talking but Ryohei had lost interest. He just sat there, mechanically lifting his sake cup to his mouth and drinking more than he should. The party went on until nine o'clock. All pretense of celebrating the publication of Fujimura's book had long vanished and the only thing anyone talked about was Yamashita's proposal. For the most part, Ryohei stayed out of the discussion. He had lost the desire to broach the subject of Sharaku with Nishijima. It no longer seemed the time or place.

As soon as Yoshimura had called the proceedings to a close, Ryohei got up and made to leave. He was feeling quite drunk.

"Ryohei, one moment."

It was Nishijima. The professor motioned with his chin in the direction of the bar. Presumably he wanted Ryohei to wait for him there. Leaving the room ahead of the others, Ryohei went over and took a seat.

"YOUR USUAL, professor?" asked Yurie, the proprietress, as Nishijima slid into the seat next to Ryohei's.

"Thanks," Nishijima replied, taking off his silver-rimmed spectacles and wiping his face with the wet hand towel she had placed in front of him. His face was oily. *If you ask me, he's had a few too many*, thought Ryohei. He wondered what the professor could want to talk to him about. Just then, Yurie reappeared with a flask of sake. Without saying a word, Nishijima held out his cup. Ryohei picked up the flask and began pouring. The sake overflowed the cup and spilled onto the counter.

"I'm terribly sorry," Ryohei mumbled, wiping up the spill with his hand towel.

"Quite alright—don't worry about it. Now tell me, Ryohei, do you want to go to Boston next year?"

"Huh?" Ryohei could hardly believe his ears.

"To the Museum of Fine Arts, that is," Nishijima repeated, a big grin on his face. "The Agency for Cultural Affairs wants me to recommend a few people to send over there to have a look at the MFA's collection of Japanese art. There's room for one ukiyo-e specialist. The only thing is, it's government work—no telling how many years it will take. So it has to be someone who's not married."

Ryohei thought he might have a heart attack then and there. The museum was famous for its ukiyo-e collection, which contained well over sixty thousand prints. Even the Tokyo National Museum had fewer than ten thousand. It was one of the best museums in the world. What's more, from Boston, Ryohei would be able to visit the Metropolitan Museum of Art in New York, the Art Institute of Chicago, and the Freer Gallery in Washington. All had large collections of ukiyo-e; easily more than four hundred thousand prints put together. In Japan it would take over fifty years to see half that many. This was his big chance. Ryohei looked into the professor's face with a feeling of disbelief.

"I haven't spoken about this to anyone except Yoshimura," the professor went on. "He looked pretty disappointed when I told him it had to be someone who wasn't married." The professor smiled amiably.

Ryohei did not doubt for a moment that Yoshimura had been sorely disappointed. He was an ambitious man. He was not one to be satisfied spending his entire career working for a small private museum. But the fact that it might take several years had probably given him second thoughts. If it had been a fixed period of six months or a year, Yoshimura would surely have got the job by hook or by crook.

"You and Iwakoshi are the only ones who are still single. The others are all too young. If I'm to recommend somebody it has to be a person who will impress the Americans. My reputation is on the line, after all."

"Then you've also spoken to Iwakoshi…"

"No. Yoshimura's suggested I recommend him for a job at a museum in Kyoto. I think that'll suit him better—emotionally, he's a bit unstable if you ask me. I don't want him going psycho on me in Boston. No, if someone's to go, it has to be you."

"Thank you, professor, I'm flattered. But I can't help feeling bad for Iwakoshi…"

"That's not your concern. It's my decision. If he's going to gripe about it I don't need him as my research assistant. Forget about him. Now that's out of the way, I assume you accept?" asked Nishijima with a rather menacing look.

"Of course," replied Ryohei shrinking. "That is, as long as my absence won't inconvenience you…" It seemed a win–win proposition.

"It's settled then. Of course, it won't be official until I've heard back from the Agency for Cultural Affairs. Your parents won't mind, I suppose."

"No, that shouldn't be a problem."

"Good. Let's drink to it." The professor filled Ryohei's sake cup. "By the way," he went on, loosening his necktie. "I hear you've been doing some research." Having settled the matter of who to send to Boston, Nishijima appeared more relaxed. "Iwakoshi says you were at the university since early this morning."

"Yes. You see, I came across an interesting book recently."

"Really? What kind of book?" asked the professor with obvious curiosity. Ryohei hesitated for a moment before deciding to go ahead and tell Nishijima everything.

"It has to do with Sharaku."

Ryohei proceeded to explain at length how he had come across The painting catalogue. When he mentioned Chikamatsu Shoei, the professor looked thoughtful for a moment. "Never heard of him," he replied. Then Ryohei reached into his backpack, removed the book and handed it to Nishijima.

The professor read Kiyochika's preface and began slowly perusing the catalogue. Eventually, his eyes fell on Shoei's painting of a lion. Noticing this, Ryohei sat up and pointed to the inscription. "This is what I was talking about," he said. The professor's eyebrows flickered and his gaze took on an unexpectedly intensity. Ryohei's heart beat faster. In all the time he had known the professor, he had never seen him look this way.

Nishijima kept his eyes riveted on the page. For a long time, he said nothing.

"Well, what do you think?" Ryohei asked eagerly.

"Hmm…" The professor finally looked away from the book and sat silently sipping his sake. He seemed to be searching for words.

Is there something to it, or is he just trying to let me down easy? Ryohei's doubts came flooding back as he thought about how the professor was usually quick to give his opinion.

"It's…" began Nishijima, at last opening his mouth, "…difficult to say. To be honest, the lines are completely unlike his usual work. It doesn't have any of the characteristics of Sharaku's painting."

Ryohei's heart sank. *Just as I feared*, he thought.

"On the other hand," Nishijima went on, "this painting is clearly based on a copperplate engraving. That would suggest the artist consciously adopted a different style from his own. It's meaningless to compare a Western-style painting like this to a woodblock print; they're apples and oranges. Just because the lines are different from one of Sharaku's actor portraits doesn't mean it's definitely not by him."

How stupid of me! thought Ryohei. For the past two days he had been pouring over the painting, placing it next to Sharaku's prints and scouring it for points of similarity, intent on trying to prove to the professor it was by Sharaku.

"Up until now," continued the professor, enunciating each word slowly, "theories about Sharaku's identity have been based entirely on perceived similarities between Sharaku's work and woodblock prints or Japanese-style paintings by other artists—the way he's drawn these ears is like Hokusai; the pleats of this kimono are reminiscent of Buncho; those eyebrows are exactly the way Okyo would paint them… Taken in isolation, each of these theories has points I find convincing. But when it comes right down to it, in each case the styles are different. You can't say something about a painting based on one detail. It doesn't matter how closely the ears or the eyebrows resemble Sharaku's style if the rest of the work doesn't. Sharaku's work has a distinctive look. If another artist's work doesn't have that look you'll never convince me he was Sharaku. But this painting here doesn't fit into that model. The style of painting isn't comparable in the least. If it weren't for this inscription no one in the world would ever think of connecting this work to Sharaku. That's what makes it difficult to say for sure." The professor folded his arms, leaned back and closed his eyes. "Now, it's also possible the artist who painted this picture forged Sharaku's signature…"

The thought struck Ryohei like a thunderbolt.

"But that seems unlikely," continued Nishijima. "It's dated 1789, three years after Sharaku stopped producing ukiyo-e. Now, if it were signed 'Utamaro' that would be one thing, but at that time there'd have been no reason why another artist would want to forge Sharaku's signature. You've probably heard this story before, but toward the end of Tokugawa rule in the mid-1800s, one of Utagawa Toyokuni's apprentices left Edo and was traveling through the countryside. Somewhere some yokels asked him what he did. When he replied he was an ukiyo-e artist, they asked, 'Oh, are you a student of Utamaro's?' This despite the fact that Utamaro had been dead for decades! 'No, Toyokuni,' the artist replied huffily; naturally so, since at that time Toyokuni was the brightest star in the ukiyo-e universe and had hundreds of apprentices. To his astonishment, none of the yokels had ever heard of his master.

"This story is always told to illustrate how Utamaro's fame echoed far and wide long after his death. But it also shows that people outside of Edo knew nothing about other ukiyo-e artists. One might be a household name in Edo, but step outside the capital and one became a complete unknown. This was all the more true for an artist like Sharaku who specialized in actor portraits. Why would people who had never seen a kabuki play in their lives give two hoots about a picture of an actor? By the way, the punch line of the story is that those country bumpkins told the artist that they had never heard of Ichikawa Danjuro either, the most celebrated kabuki actor of them all! In Edo, it was said that children as young as three knew his name. In short, we can conclude that there would have been no incentive for this Chikamatsu Shoei up in Akita to forge Sharaku's signature. We can also rule out the possibility that there were two artists living at that time with exactly the same name."

"In that case," said Ryohei, struck by a sudden thought as he listened to Nishijima's story, "could Shoei have been a protégé—you know, a former apprentice of Sharaku's?"

"His protégé? Well, I suppose it's possible but…"

"That would explain why the style of this painting is so different from Sharaku's."

"Well, until a woodblock print turns up clearly identifying Shoei as Sharaku's protégé, I'm afraid it's only a theory. Plus it's highly doubtful Sharaku was in a position to have apprentices. I think if he'd been in such great demand as a teacher we'd know more about him than we do. And if that information existed, then the riddle of Sharaku would have been solved long ago."

"I see what you're saying, but it would lend support to the Sharaku Workshop hypothesis."

The 'Sharaku Workshop hypothesis' held that Sharaku had not been a single individual but a group of artists. Sharaku was active for just ten months between May 1794 and February 1795. In that brief span of time he produced over one hundred and forty woodblock prints. That works out to a new print every other day. Could one artist really have accomplished such a feat? The Sharaku Workshop hypothesis arose to explain this apparent impossibility. In short, it proposed that Sharaku's prints were created by a group of people, each responsible for a specific task, like an assembly line. Taking this theory one step further, it was not unreasonable to think that 'Sharaku' might have had a protégé. Or so Ryohei thought.

"The Sharaku Workshop, huh?" snorted Nishijima. "That's never progressed beyond mere speculation. The question of Sharaku having a protégé just complicates matters unnecessarily. To begin with, I don't think Sharaku's output is such a big issue. Harunobu produced over a hundred prints a year, while Kunisada churned out several times that many."

"But in Kunisada's case, weren't many of his prints actually made by his apprentices under his name?"

"Yes, but so what? That was normal for the time. Just because artists didn't openly admit to the practice doesn't mean there was anything wrong with it. What's more, publishers preferred having Kunisada's name on a print rather than some unknown artist. It's as simple as that. If Sharaku had employed the same *modus operandi* no one would have criticized him. In those days people didn't talk about woodblock prints as 'art.' Rather than worrying about whether any given work from that time can definitively be attributed to a single artist, one ought to assume that if an artist had apprentices then his work was not entirely his own. But I've never seen any evidence Sharaku had apprentices. This so-called workshop hypothesis is just a way of saying Sharaku couldn't have done it all on his own. That's why I can't subscribe to it. There's no mystery to Sharaku's prolific output. If there is a mystery, it's not *how* did he produce so many prints but *why* did he publish them exclusively with Tsutaya Juzaburo?"

"That certainly seems to make sense," replied Ryohei, won over by Nishijima's argument. Never before had he heard the professor talk about Sharaku in this way.

Nishijima continued: "So the signature isn't a forgery; it's not by Sharaku's protégé; the artist didn't just happen to have the same name… That leaves just one conclusion: this painting is by Sharaku."

A slight shiver went down Ryohei's spine.

"That is, provided it's not an out-and-out fake."

"Do you think it might be?"

"Didn't the possibility occur to you?" asked the professor, looking somewhat surprised.

"Yes, that was my immediate reaction when I first saw it. But this catalogue was published in *1907*," said Ryohei, emphasizing the date. Nishijima said nothing. His mind seemed to be processing what Ryohei had said.

"*Before* Kurth..." he mumbled at last, as though seeking confirmation from Ryohei. He was sweating slightly.

"Yes, that's right," replied Ryohei, flipping to the back of the book and showing the professor the copyright page—it read, "December 25, 1907." It left no room for doubt.

The professor sighed. "*Before* Kurth..." he repeated again and again.

It was not so long ago that Sharaku had been all but forgotten in Japan. That changed in 1910 when Julius Kurth, a German art historian and scholar of ukiyo-e, published his seminal work, *Sharaku*. In it he declared the Japanese artist to have been one of the world's great caricaturists, and he placed him alongside Rembrandt and Velazquez as one of the three great portrait painters of all time. Kurth's book catapulted Sharaku to fame in the West and received an ecstatic reception in Japan, where it provoked a reassessment of his work.

Sharaku quickly became a household name in Japan. Everyone was talking about him, even people who had never seen an ukiyo-e print in their lives. All because some foreign scholar had singled him out for praise. That was what made all the difference. At the time, the opinion of one foreigner was worth that of a thousand Japanese. Those were the days when the Japanese were burdened by a sense that culturally speaking theirs was a backward country.

Before Julius Kurth came along, Sharaku had been virtually unknown in the land of his birth. The 1903 edition of *Who Was Who in Japan*, for example, lists Hokusai and Hiroshige in the section on artists but makes no mention of Sharaku. His name was only whispered among a small number of art dealers and connoisseurs.

And even *they* only thought of him as a second- or third-rate artist. He certainly was not an artist that an art dealer could have hoped to make any money off.

"So if the catalogue was published before Kurth's book," said Ryohei, pressing Nishijima, "the possibility that it's a fake—"

"Is nil," the professor conceded. Then changing the subject he asked: "Have you managed to find out anything about Shoei?"

"No, nothing." Ryohei had spent two days looking through every biographical encyclopedia and book on art history he could find in the professor's office and the university library, but he had turned up absolutely nothing about Chikamatsu Shoei. He gave the professor a detailed account of his efforts.

"Well, I couldn't have done any better," Nishijima said encouragingly. "If there's nothing on Shoei in any of the published literature, then the bio of him in this catalogue must be based on some old manuscript or an inscription on a box used for storing one of the paintings. I guess the only thing you can do now is go to Akita and do some research."

"To Shoei's hometown, Kakunodate?" asked Ryohei, trying to conceal his pleasure at the swiftness of Nishijima's unexpected response.

"Yes. Of course, while you're there you should go to Kosaka and try to find out something about this Sato fellow Kiyochika mentions in his preface."

"Good idea. But that'll be difficult; it was written in 1907 after all."

"You may not turn up anything. But it's important to find out for sure. Where exactly is Kosaka anyway?

"Near lake Towada—on the border between Akita and Iwate."

"Is that right? Fancy Sharaku living in a backwater like that!" Ryohei watched in silence as the professor reached for his sake cup, a look of disbelief on his face. "Well, well, well... the world is full of surprises!" Then under his breath he added, "Saga's suicide for one."

A slight smile appeared at the corners of his mouth.

October 26

THE TELEPHONE rang and rang but nobody answered.

When he had counted fifteen rings, Ryohei gave up. He'd been told it wasn't a big apartment. Yosuke must be out. He was just about to put the receiver down when suddenly the ringing was interrupted.

"Hello?" It was the voice of a young woman. Ryohei was taken aback.

"Er… is Yosuke there? My name is Tsuda. I'm a friend from university."

"Ryohei, right?" replied the woman giggling. Her voice had a note of familiarity.

"Huh? Saeko, is that you?" Ryohei felt his heart begin to flutter.

Saeko was Yosuke's younger sister. He had met her many times back when she was going to college in Tokyo and he was in the habit of hanging out at Yosuke's apartment. Though a bit willful, she was pretty and charming, and Ryohei had secretly had a crush on her. *She must be twenty-four now,* he thought; she's probably married. In fact, he had wanted to ask Yosuke about her the other day, but in the end he hadn't been able to summon up the courage to broach the subject.

"How are things? How long has it been, anyway?" asked Ryohei, trying to sound nonchalant.

"I hear you haven't changed, Ryohei."

"Huh? What do you mean?"

"My brother was talking about you. He said you haven't changed a bit."

"Same ol' Ryohei, is that it?" he said laughing.

"Actually, I was relieved…"

"About what?"

"That you're still single."

Ryohei felt himself getting flustered. It was not the sort of remark he expected to hear over the phone. He was at a loss for words.

"Er, is Yosuke there?" he asked at last, ignoring her remark.

"He'll be right back. He's just gone out to the store for some cigarettes. My brother's such a poseur; he smokes Gelbe Sorte or something like that. You can't buy them from a vending machine. Oh, I think that's him now. Don't tell him what I said."

Ryohei heard the sound of the front door being opened followed by Yosuke's voice. Shortly Yosuke picked up the receiver.

"Hey, good timing. Saeko's just arrived from Sendai; we've just returned from lunch."

"Oh, is Saeko living up in Tohoku now?"

Yosuke explained that when his sister had finished college two years ago their parents had wanted her to return home to Okayama, but instead she had taken a job at a public library up north in Sendai. Once or twice a month she came to Tokyo to clean his apartment and hang out.

"Cleaning's just a pretext," he quickly added, lowering his voice. "She really comes to hit me up for pocket money." Yosuke laughed. "Anyway, what are you calling about? Anything urgent?"

"Not really. I just have something I wanted to show you."

"I see. Where are you now?"

"At a café in Shinjuku."

"Well, how about coming straight over. Saeko's here; I'm sure she can whip us up something to eat."

"Are you sure that's okay with her?"

"No problem. She'll be delighted," Yosuke replied with a loud laugh.

AN HOUR LATER, Ryohei alighted from a train at Fuchu Station. Yosuke was waiting for him at the exit clutching a large bag of groceries from which a bundle of green onions protruded. I hope he didn't go shopping on my account, thought Ryohei, feeling bad for putting his friend to such trouble. Yosuke began walking. Ryohei walked beside him thinking only of Saeko.

"Your beloved Ryohei is here!" Yosuke called out as they entered the apartment.

"Stop that! You'll scare him away," replied Saeko, appearing from a back room. Of a robust constitution during her student days, she seemed to have lost a bit of weight since she began working. But she was as beautiful as ever. Back then long hair had suited her, but she looked just as pretty with it cut short. When she smiled a dimple appeared on her right cheek, just as Ryohei remembered. He felt he alone had aged while Saeko had remained exactly the same.

"I thought I might not recognize you, but I see you've hardly changed," he said.

"What do you mean 'hardly'?" shot back Saeko. "That's not the way to flatter a girl."

"'Girl'? I don't see any girls around here," teased Yosuke.

Saeko burst out laughing.

"Anyway, what does the professor think?" asked Yosuke, once he had finished grumbling that the whisky and water Saeko had mixed for him was too weak. In front of them on the table lay the painting catalogue, which they had just finished looking at.

"He refuses to commit himself either way, but he says it's within the realm of possibility."

"'Within the realm of possibility,' huh? For the professor, that's a rare admission," responded Yosuke, his eyes flashing.

"I think it helps I'm his student."

"That's irrelevant. The professor's not that considerate."

Ryohei recoiled slightly at the vigor of Yosuke's tone. If Nishijima were more considerate, Yosuke wouldn't be in the position he was in; that was how Ryohei interpreted his remark.

"If the professor accepts your theory, things could get interesting," went on Yosuke. "After ten years, Nishijima awakes!"

"It sounds like you are talking about Godzilla," laughed Saeko.

"What do you know about Godzilla? That was before your time."

"You took me to see it at the Meigaza in Shinjuku, don't you remember?"

"The Meigaza? Don't be ridiculous! They don't show movies like that," snorted Yosuke before turning his attention back to Ryohei.

"At any rate, as I see it, there are several questions to consider: First, does the bio of Shoei in this catalogue check out? Second, is there a connection between the Akita School and ukiyo-e? Third, is there any evidence of a relationship between Shoei and Tsutaya's publishing house? Fourth, can you link Shoei to the riddle of Sharaku's identity? If you can't answer at least these questions, your theory won't hold water."

Ryohei was speechless. Granted, he had only spent two days doing research, but so far he had not uncovered a shred of new information. In particular, when it came to the question of a possible link between Shoei and the publisher Tsutaya Juzaburo, the situation seemed hopeless. Ryohei had read all the available literature on Tsutaya while writing his article on Sharaku for *The Edo Art Association Journal*; needless to say, he hadn't come across any mention of Chikamatsu Shoei. He said so to Yosuke.

"Well, what do you expect? You'll have to go back and look at the question again with a fresh pair of eyes. Up until now, everyone's been focused on trying to solve the riddle of Sharaku's identity. But they've always run up against the same obstacle, lack of historical evidence. Evidence is the key that unlocks the door to the next level of research and will eventually lead to the answer. But now the situation is reversed. Before this painting catalogue fell into your lap, neither you, nor the professor, nor I would ever have imagined that Sharaku was an Akita School painter. You already have the answer. Do you doubt it's the right one?"

"That's the problem; I don't know what to believe. It seems so far-fetched."

"That's because you're an expert on ukiyo-e like the professor," Yosuke shot back matter-of-factly. "For the uninitiated, ukiyo-e and Akita School paintings look pretty much the same. They're both Japanese. Haven't you ever looked at one of Kokan's Western-style copperplate engravings and been reminded of ukiyo-e?"

"Well, I don't know…"

"Your problem is you can't get the image of Kokan's ukiyo-e out of your mind. But if you ask me, if Kokan himself hadn't confessed in his memoir, *Shunparo Notes*, to having published ukiyo-e under the name Harushige, no one would ever have thought of linking the two."

Ryohei groaned. Yosuke made a valid point. True, the ukiyo-e Kokan had produced using the pseudonym Harushige did incorporate Western three-point perspective. But apart from that, Harushige's prints were stylistically more or less the same as those of other ukiyo-e artists. They were a far cry from the hard, naturalistic style of his copperplate engravings.

"If the only thing bothering you is the difference between Sharaku's style and Shoei's," Yosuke went on, "then on that account at least I can only say it's well within the realm of possibility. But there's one more thing that struck me." Yosuke paused to gulp down the rest of his whisky before continuing. "Doesn't the name 'Shoei' suggest anything to you?"

Ryohei thought for a moment. Yes, of course! Ryohei was floored by Yosuke's insight. He felt his blood rush to his head.

"Shoeido Eisho," muttered Yosuke, as though reciting a mantra.

Eisho had been a contemporary of Sharaku's. He was famous for his prints of beautiful women, particularly close-ups. Like Sharaku, nothing was known of his actual identity except that he had been an apprentice of Chobunsai Eishi, a wealthy samurai and shogunal vassal who also happened to be an ukiyo-e artist. Although Eisho usually signed his work "Chokosai Eisho"—in tribute to his master—he sometimes used the pseudonym "Shoeido," or "Shoei's Studio."

"It just popped into my head a minute ago while you were talking," explained Yosuke. "Now, let's just suppose Shoei *was* Sharaku. That means Shoei would have to be connected in some way to the ukiyo-e scene of the 1790s. But how can we prove there's a link? The most obvious clue is his name—reverse the Chinese characters in Shoei and what do you get? Eisho! We know Eisho sometimes signed himself Shoeido. You can only make this connection if you're working backwards from Shoei to Sharaku. Even if some scholar were struck by the similarity between Sharaku and Eisho, he'd never think of linking Sharaku to some obscure Akita School painter called Chikamatsu Shoei. That's all I'm saying. The same goes for linking Shoei and Tsutaya—you can't start by looking at Tsutaya. You have to approach if from the opposite direction. If Shoei was Sharaku then that connects him to Tsutaya, *ipso facto*. The conclusion is inevitable."

"Good point. I hadn't thought of that. So my methodology was flawed."

"Not exactly. No scholar has ever found positive proof of Sharaku's identity, which this catalogue provides, so the problem never came up before. It's only natural you would have taken the position you did."

"I don't know about that," replied Ryohei. "Connecting Shoei to Eisho is quite an achievement. The ramifications could go way beyond simply establishing the fact that Shoei had links to ukiyo-e."

"I assume you're referring to mica printing?" Yosuke said matter-of-factly.

Ryohei was amazed at Yosuke's perceptiveness. "Exactly," he said. "The only artists using mica in the 1790s, were Sharaku, Utamaro, Eishi, Shoei, Choki and… That's about it, I think." Mica printing, otherwise known as sparkle painting or *kira-zuri*, was a technique whereby glue mixed with flakes of mica, or sometimes mother of pearl, was applied with a brush to the surface of a woodblock print. This made the paper sparkle like a mirror, hence its name. Not only did it involve extra labor but the mica itself was quite expensive, meaning that only the top artists could afford to use it in their work. "Plus," continued Ryohei, "both Sharaku and Shoei specialized in close-ups. Granted, Sharaku's portraits were mainly of kabuki actors, while Shoei's were of beautiful women." Close-ups, or *okubi-e*, referred to portraits drawn from the waist up. Until Sharaku's time, ukiyo-e artists had always depicted full figures. "Linking Shoei and Eisho is a major breakthrough," he concluded. "It can't simply be a coincidence."

"Now, now—let's not get carried away," said Yosuke, trying to restrain Ryohei's enthusiasm. He refilled his whisky glass.

"Listening to my brother, one would think scholarship was all about twisting the facts to fit one's conclusion," put in Saeko, laughing.

"Now hold on a minute. I'm not twisting the facts. The police build entire cases on less circumstantial evidence than what we've got to work with. Anyway, don't just take my word for it. My theory's got the seal of approval of the protégé of the world's premier Sharaku scholar!"

"Okay, enough joking around," said Ryohei. The mischievous smile on Yosuke's face was making him feel self-conscious. "Yosuke's right, Saeko. In this instance, I don't think we'll get anywhere unless we start from the hypothesis that Shoei *was* Sharaku. It's not a question of twisting the facts to fit the conclusion. It's just that, like your brother says, I think we'll find the answers to a lot of important questions if we assume Shoei was Sharaku. But if we don't find those answers then it means our hypothesis was wrong. Just because Sharaku's name appears on a painting in this catalogue doesn't mean we'll be able to convince anyone else of our theory unless we get more answers."

"I couldn't have put it better myself," said Yosuke, vigorously nodding his approval.

"You know, personally, I'm not all that into ukiyo-e. But I wonder about Kiyochika," said Saeko enigmatically, looking up from the pages of the painting catalogue. She had just finished reading Kiyochika's preface.

"What do you mean—'I wonder about Kiyochika'?" prodded Yosuke.

"Well, if he were an ukiyo-e artist himself, you'd kind of think he'd be into ukiyo-e."

"What are you trying to say?"

"Well, take this lion painting signed by this Sharaku guy. Why doesn't Kiyochika mention it in his preface? Didn't he know who Sharaku was? Was he as obscure an artist as all that?"

It was true that by 1907 Sharaku had been largely forgotten. The truth was, no one in the late nineteenth century considered ukiyo-e to be "art." As incredible as it may sound today, in those days an old print by Utamaro would have fetched less than a new one by some third-rate hack simply because Utamaro's style wasn't fashionable any longer.

Ryohei was about to explain this to Saeko when Yosuke said flatly:

"I bet Kiyochika never saw this painting. You see, Sharaku might have fallen into obscurity, but if anyone had heard of him Kiyochika would have. Thanks to Saeko I just realized something... I should have picked up on this sooner. If you read Kiyochika's preface carefully, you'll notice he refers to the paintings as 'great works' but he doesn't mention any of them in particular. What's more, his tone is a bit pat and dry. If you ask me, Kiyochika wasn't as close to Sato as he claims in his preface. I think he simply wrote it as a favor to someone else. Besides, Sato and Kiyochika are too far apart in age. He says he first met Sato in Shizuoka, what... thirty years before? Let's see, when did Kiyochika live there?"

"Around 1872," answered Ryohei.

"Okay. And he was already in his thirties at the time. But, judging from Sato's photograph, which was taken in 1905, he was only about forty when he died. So in 1872 he'd have been a child of ten, if that. Well, I suppose he could have been the *son* of one of Kiyochika's friends in Shizuoka. It's probably true Kiyochika visited Sato in Akita, but I bet Sato didn't show him his art collection. Kiyochika died in 1915, so if he'd seen this painting and remembered seeing Sharaku's name on it, I'm sure he would have written about it somewhere."

"You're right. Kurth's rediscovery of Sharaku's work happened while Kiyochika was still alive," said Ryohei, breaking out in a cold sweat. That was another thing he had missed.

"But at the very least, Kiyochika must have owned a copy of this catalogue, right?" chimed in Saeko. "Wouldn't he have noticed the painting sooner or later?"

"I doubt he would have bothered to read it," replied Yosuke. "As far as Kiyochika was concerned, the Akita School was a relic of the past. He probably wasn't all that interested. Sure, he might have flipped through the pages when he first received it, but then he probably put it away somewhere and forgot about it... Hey, don't look at me like that! I'm not twisting the facts this time. I'm just making a logical inference based on the fact that Kiyochika never mentions Sharaku's name. Even if he hadn't known who Sharaku was at the time he wrote this in 1907, he *must* have known who he was by 1910.

"I see..." Saeko replied. "Perhaps I judged you too quickly. You can be surprisingly persuasive when you want to be."

"Spare me the 'surprisingly.'"

"Just remember, you'll never get hitched if you're *too* persuasive," shot back Saeko, giving Yosuke a meaningful smile as she rose from the table.

"Joking aside, I assume you plan to go to Akita right away to look into this," Yosuke asked Ryohei, turning serious again as soon as Saeko disappeared into the kitchen.

"Yeah, I was planning to go up on Saturday. The professor was nice enough to say he could manage without me at the university for a while."

"Too bad. I'm afraid I've got to work this Saturday…"

"You mean you'd be willing to come with me? If so, I could go a bit later if that's better for you," suggested Ryohei hopefully.

"Thanks a lot… but on second thought, it's impossible. As much as I'd like to go, there's no point going up for just one day.

"In that case, maybe I could go," said Saeko, who had just come in carrying two steaming cups of coffee. She spoke as though the idea had just popped into her head.

"Don't be ridiculous," retorted Yosuke, flustered. "You'd just get in Ryohei's way. Anyway, don't you have work to do?"

"That's no problem. Unlike you, I've got plenty of vacation time saved up."

"Yeah, but… You see what I'm up against, Ryohei?" said Yosuke, giving him a pained look. "This is what I have to deal with all the time." Then, to Saeko he said: "You need to get your priorities straight. This is not a game, you know."

Taken aback by the unexpected turn the conversation had taken, Ryohei sat lost for words.

"But I *do* understand. You want to go but you can't, right? Well, I can go in your place and report back to you every day. That's okay with you, isn't it, Ryohei?"

"It's fine with me," Ryohei blurted out before he could stop himself.

"There. See? Ryohei says it's okay with him. Don't worry, I won't get in his way."

"Yeah, but… He doesn't have much of a choice, did he? You're so damned persistent."

"That's not so."

"What's not so? You just never give up… I don't know where you get it from," said Yosuke, crossing his arms and heaving a deep sigh.

"Ryohei, I won't be in your way, will I?" Saeko asked again.

"Not at all," replied Ryohei, less than thrilled about the idea. "As long as it's okay with you, Saeko, I—"

"There, it's settled!" she said, snapping her fingers as she looked at the two men.

Yosuke grudgingly relented.

3
The Sharaku Enigma

October 31

IT WAS SUNDAY. Ryohei was waiting for Saeko at the exit to Morioka Station. She was due to arrive on the 11:02 a.m. Shinkansen from Sendai. As the minutes ticked by, Ryohei felt his pulse quicken.

I wonder if she'll really be on the train.

Saeko had said she couldn't get away from work until Sunday at the earliest, so they agreed to meet up in Morioka because to get to Kosaka one first had to go to Morioka and take the Hanawa Line, then change trains again at Odate. It was better for Ryohei, since he wanted to stop off at his parents' house in Morioka in any case. Still, he was a bit anxious about Saeko traveling separately. There was no telling if somewhere along the way she might suddenly change her mind about making a trip like this, alone with a man. Ryohei grew impatient.

At last the Shinkansen from Sendai arrived. A stream of passengers began descending the stairs from the train platform. Ryohei scanned the crowd looking for Saeko.

"The whole time on the train I was wondering what I would do if you weren't there," said Saeko calmly, once they had sat down at a café inside the train station building. They still had a bit of time to kill before they caught the train bound for Kosaka.

"But of course I would come. This is *my* work, after all. As for you not coming... Well, that's another matter altogether."

"I talked to my brother on the phone last night and got bawled out again," said Saeko, smiling as she sipped her chai. "He said,

'Remember, you're not a tourist, so don't spend all your popping into souvenir shops.' What does he take me for? 'I'm not a kid anymore!' I told him."

Despite her grumbling, Saeko was in high spirits. She wore a beige jacket with orange herringbone embroidery and a pair of matching corduroy slacks.

"By the way, what's up with that?" she said, looking at the large suit bag Ryohei had next to him with curiosity.

"I thought I better bring it just in case."

"But we'll only be gone three days, right?"

"You never know who we might meet. I didn't think I could walk around like this all the time." Ryohei was wearing a heavy gray cardigan over a while turtleneck. The color scheme was sober but it was a decidedly casual outfit.

"I see… I guess I was approaching this all wrong. I'd been thinking of it as a fun little excursion. Boy, you must think I'm totally clueless," replied Saeko, playfully shrugging her shoulders.

"Not at all. You're doing me a favor. When I'm on my own I tend to jump to conclusions. You can help keep me on track. Plus you'll be able to sound out Yosuke's opinion."

"Oh, speaking of which, I need to give my brother a call." Saeko stood up and walked over to a red payphone in one corner of the café and dialed a number but Yosuke was not in his office so she soon returned to the table. Ryohei proceeded to ask her advice on their plans for the day.

"You've got me. I'm not familiar with this neck of the woods. I'll leave everything up to you."

"At this rate we should get to Kosaka by evening. The question is, where do we spend the night? I talked to the brother of an old high school friend of mine who lives up in Odate. He said Kosaka has two or three old-fashioned ryokans. Since it's Sunday, we should be able to get a room, but I imagine that doesn't appeal much to you…"

"A ryokan, huh?" Saeko looked thoughtful.

"On the other hand, Odate has a number of modern hotels. Even if we left immediately, we wouldn't reach Kosaka in time to start our research today. Besides it's Sunday, so the town hall will be closed. It's probably best if we stay in Odate tonight and continue on to Kosaka early tomorrow morning—it's not far."

"When you say 'not far,' how long does it take?"

"My friend's brother said it's about thirty minutes by train. The trip from Odate to Kosaka is apparently quite scenic."

"Is it? In that case, I think that's what we should do. I have to say, it *would* be rather fun to stay at a ryokan and lounge around in yukatas sipping sake…"

"Don't be silly. If Yosuke heard you say that he'd be *really* mad."

Saeko giggled. Apparently Ryohei's earnestness amused her.

"So, it's settled then," continued Ryohei, pretending to ignore her. "We'll stay in Odate tonight."

Saeko nodded. Ryohei stood up, took out his address book, and walked over to the telephone. Saeko watched him, looking pleased with herself.

"Okay, I booked the hotel," Ryohei said when he returned to the table. "I just spoke to my friend's brother in Odate who works for a travel agent. He's taken care of everything. It seems there's a hotel next to the train station, though I'm afraid our rooms will be a little far apart," he said with as much nonchalance as he could muster.

BEING THE MIDDLE of a Sunday, the Hanawa Line train bound for Odate was fairly empty. Ryohei and Saeko sat down next to a window facing each other on a pair of cushioned benches designed to seat four people. The trip from Morioka to Odate would take three hours.

"Boy, we're going to be stuck on this train until four o'clock," said Saeko looking up from her railway time schedule.

At Koma the train branched to the left away from the Tohoku Main Line and began running through paddy fields. Off to one side, across the fields with their cut stalks left over from the rice harvest, rose a range of mountains dyed the colors of autumn. The sun shone all around. Inside the train, warm air blasted out from the heaters beneath the seats. Some of the other passengers had pulled the blinds down over the windows and were resting, stretched out on the seats.

"That's strange…" said Saeko, frowning, as she pointed to far-off Mount Iwate. She had been staring out the window for some time. "That's the same mountain I saw from the platform at the station, isn't it?"

The first thing to greet one's eyes as one alighted from the Shinkansen in Morioka was the majestic peak of Mount Iwate rising in the distance. At six thousand seven hundred feet, it was the highest mountain in Iwate Prefecture and, like Mount Fuji, was an almost perfect cone-shaped volcano. Its beauty was slightly marred by the fact that one slope had collapsed long ago during an eruption. People sometimes referred to it as "Fuji viewed from the south."

"You're surprised its shape looks so different, is that it? You see, the Hanawa Line skirts the side of the mountain. This side is called the 'back of Iwate.' From Morioka you were looking at it from the opposite angle."

The serene impression one got of the mountain from Morioka station had vanished. The "back of Iwate" was bare and rugged where lava had torn away the side of the mountain as it gushed from the mouth of the crater.

"Look over there." Ryohei pointed about halfway up the mountain to three jagged overhangs. "That looks like an eagle, doesn't it? The rock in the middle is the head and the two outcroppings on either side are its outstretched wings. People around here sometimes refer to Mount Iwate as Eagle Rock Mountain," Ryohei explained proudly. Ever since he was a child, the mountain had held a special place in his heart, and he had climbed to the top any number of times.

Though the fields down below were bathed in warm autumn sunshine, the peak of the mountain glimmered with newly fallen snow.

BY THE TIME Ryohei and Saeko arrived at Odate Station it was already getting dark, a thick layer of cloud having blocked out the setting sun.

For a city of some eighty thousand people, Odate's train station was surprisingly quiet. Though Odate was the meeting point for two train lines—the Hanawa Line and the Ou Main Line—the station was some distance from the center of town. The closest station to downtown Odate was actually East Odate, which they passed one stop back. Apart from passengers changing trains to the Ou Main Line, few people got off at Odate Station. Moreover, being Sunday, there were hardly any schoolchildren about. The station felt desolate and lonely.

The hotel, which was just visible from the station, was an imposing seven-story building which towered above the mostly two-story dwellings that lined the street in front of the station.

Inside, Ryohei approached the front desk and gave his name. Just then he heard someone call to him from the back of the lobby. He turned to see a young man, who bowed first to him and then to Saeko.

"Say, you didn't have to come meet us," said Ryohei, raising a hand in greeting.

"I waited at the station for a while but it was too cold, so I came here. I figured this was where you'd end up anyway." The man approached, and Ryohei introduced Saeko to him.

"This is my friend Kudo who booked our rooms for us."

"Nice to meet you," said Kudo. He had large clear eyes and wore his hair in a short perm. He was three years younger than Ryohei.

Saeko bowed and thanked him for his help.

"Boy, you really surprised me just now. Ryohei told me there were two of you, but he didn't say anything about one being a beautiful woman."

"Is that so?"

"If he had, I certainly wouldn't have come down here to invite him out for a drink. I assumed he was just with some university pal of his."

The three of them were seated in the lobby chatting. Kudo had come to the hotel intending to take Ryohei out on the town and show him a bit of the local nightlife. Working for a travel agent, he knew all the hot spots. But having met Saeko, he did not pursue the matter any further. *No doubt*, thought Ryohei, *he's holding back because of her.* Instead Kudo asked them about their plans.

"By the way," he said. "I've got a drinking buddy who works at the Kosaka mine. I'll get him to show you around. How 'bout I give him a ring and have him meet you at the station?"

"But tomorrow's Monday," said Ryohei. "He must have to work."

"Nah, he's free during the day. The mine has three shifts, you see. I went ahead and checked with him when I heard you were planning to visit Kosaka."

"We shouldn't, really. I'm sure we'd be putting him to a lot of trouble."

"He won't mind. In fact, he's looking forward to it."

"Well, in that case, he'd really be helping us out."

"So you'll be going to Kakunodate the day after tomorrow?"

"Yeah, we're planning to take the first train."

"You know, I could take Tuesday off. I'd be happy to give you a ride there—that is, if you don't mind going by car." Ryohei and Saeko looked at one another. "It takes about six hours by train," Kudo added. "By car, it's a little over two."

"We'd appreciate that a lot," responded Ryohei. "But I'm not sure I want to be so indebted to you." He gave Kudo a mischievous smile.

"Don't mention it. Wednesday's a national holiday so I'll get two days off. I hardly ever get an excuse to use up my vacation time, so you'll actually be doing me a favor," Kudo replied, scratching his head.

Ryohei and Saeko decided to indulge themselves and accepted Kudo's offer gladly.

When they had finished discussing the details, the two walked Kudo to the hotel entrance and said goodnight to him. Outside it had become completely dark and the wind had picked up. Ryohei and Saeko abandoned the idea of going out and decided to eat in the hotel instead. It was still too early for dinner. Having left Sendai early that morning and spent all day riding trains, Saeko looked tired. They agreed to go to their rooms to rest and meet up again in the lobby in two hours.

The rooms were on the fifth floor. Getting out of the elevator, Saeko was about to head off in the direction of her room when

Ryohei asked her to wait. Then he took a thick manila folder out of his bag and held it out to her. Before leaving Tokyo he had made copies of all the research material he had collected on Sharaku.

"What? All this!" gasped Saeko.

"Well, there's also some stuff in here about the Akita School... Anyway, weren't you the one who said you wanted to read up on Sharaku?" Ryohei asked with a sadistic smile. "This just covers the basics but it should be enough to be getting on with."

"Well, if it's just the basics, I did my homework before coming, you know." Smiling, Saeko took the heavy folder, put it under her arm with some effort, and turned and headed toward her room.

Ryohei took a shower, changed, and went down to the lobby a bit ahead of time. He had discovered there was a small café near the front desk. While alcohol wasn't among his vices, Ryohei was rather a caffeine addict.

Having ordered, he took a seat so that he had a clear view of the lobby. Then he took out the research notebook he was carrying with him and opened it before him on the table. He had planned to draw up the following day's schedule, but he suddenly found his mind was blank.

As an art historian, Ryohei was not accustomed to doing fieldwork. He felt somewhat at a loss. In the past, while working on various research projects, he had gone to visit the grave of some ukiyo-e artist or talked to one or another expert. But that was only to take pictures or confirm what he already knew. He had a clear idea of where he was going from the outset. This time things were different. He had absolutely no idea where to begin.

The logical place to begin is with the town hall. Then I'll go to the local historical society—if there is one—or the public library. Or maybe I should start by interviewing someone associated with the mine...

Ryohei jotted down these ideas in his notebook. It would probably be hard to find someone connected to the mine back in Sato's time. That had been seventy years ago. If there *was* anyone whose memory stretched that far back, they would be nearly ninety by now. What's more, Sato had only worked at the mine for a few years, so it was unlikely the person would remember him.

Another possibility was to try to trace him through the town's death registry. But Ryohei thought the chances of that were pretty small. Sato had been from Shizuoka originally. He had only come to Kosaka for work. When he died, his remains mostly likely would have been returned to his hometown for burial.

Maybe coming all the way up here was a waste of time.

Ryohei chaffed at his predicament. The fact that Saeko was with him only made his frustration worse.

She'll laugh at me for being inept.

If the situation became too bleak, Ryohei would have to say something to Saeko. He had become less and less sure of himself since leaving Tokyo and he was starting to feel discouraged.

But that catalogue is for real. That's one thing I can be sure of.

Ryohei repeated this refrain over and over again in his head.

Just then, he heard a tapping sound on the large pane of brown-tinted glass to his right. He looked up to see Saeko standing on the other side, smiling. She had tracked him down in the café. She wore a dark-red blazer over a white blouse and skirt. The folder Ryohei had given her was tucked under her arm.

She looks like a movie star!

The tinted glass was like a movie screen with Saeko's image projected onto it. It was already twenty past seven. Ryohei waved, then got up and left the café.

"Sorry to keep you waiting," Saeko apologized, placing the palms of her hands together in a gesture of apology.

"That's okay. I was just getting ready for tomorrow."

"Oh, in that case, I needn't have hurried."

"I see you changed."

"Of course. You didn't expect me to walk into a restaurant wearing *that* getup, did you? This hotel is a bit swanky," she replied, pushing her hair away from her shoulders. Ryohei caught a whiff of makeup mixed with soap.

THEY SAT DOWN at a table and Ryohei ordered a veal cutlet. Saeko choose poached salmon in cream sauce.

"Care for a drink?" Ryohei asked. Saeko nodded, and Ryohei added two glasses of dark beer and a chicken salad to their order.

"Mmm, this salad is delicious!" exclaimed Saeko, still holding her fork in front her mouth.

"This area's famous for its chicken… Hinaidori, it's called. It's supposed to be as good as the Cochin variety from Nagoya."

"I wish you'd told me; I'd have ordered the sautéed chicken," lamented Saeko, looking like she really meant it.

"I can add it to our order if you like."

"No way. This beer already puts me way over my calorie limit for the day."

On the table, a candle sat floating in a glass, its flame flickering silently and casting a warm glow on Saeko's smiling face.

"Now, then. How about that folder I gave you? Did you get a chance to look through it?" asked Ryohei as the two sat sipping coffee at the end of their meal.

"More or less."

"So what do you think?"

"How should I know? I skipped the difficult parts. And you didn't include any pictures, so it was hard to follow some of the visual analysis."

"You mean of Sharaku's work?"

"Gimme a break! *That* much I know. I mean the parts about other artists who might have been Sharaku. Like Hokusai… Well, I've got a pretty good idea what *his* work looks like. But Maruyama Okyo? I haven't the foggiest."

"No, I guess you wouldn't."

"Does Okyo's work resemble Sharaku's?"

Come to think of it, Ryohei himself didn't really know.

Okyo had lived in Kyoto and founded what has become known as the Maruyama-Shijo School. He is also said to have popularized depictions of ghosts as a new genre within Japanese painting. Ryohei had seen photographs of the sliding doors Okyo was commissioned to paint for the subtemple of Enman'in at Miidera in Otsu, but until now he had never given serious credence to a possible link between Okyo and Sharaku. It was only in 1957 that it was first suggested the two were one and the same. Okyo had been an expert draftsman and staunch proponent of Western realism, so in that sense his attitude toward art had certain points in common with Sharaku. What's more, Okyo had no "alibi," so to speak, for the ten-month period from 1794 to 1795 when Sharaku was active. According to the historical evidence, Okyo experienced a bout of lameness and put down his brush during that time, but it was not clear to Ryohei why being unable to walk should prevent someone from painting.

At any rate, the theory that Okyo was Sharaku had already fallen out of fashion by the time Ryohei began to study ukiyo-e. There was no evidence that Okyo had ever been in Edo, and no connection between him and the publisher Tsutaya Juzaburo had ever been adequately proven. It was only natural, therefore, that the Okyo hypothesis was written off as merely an intriguing theory. That was why Ryohei had never actually sat down and compared the two artists' work.

"I can't imagine their work *does* look at all similar," he explained to Saeko. "But for that matter, neither does Shoei's and Sharaku's. Anyway, it's hard to compare paintings to woodblock prints... But come to think of it, I *have* seen prints attributed to Okyo."

"Attributed? What do you mean?"

"You know, prints said to have been drawn by him. I'm not entire convinced myself, but I suppose if they're labeled 'attributed to Okyo' even now, they must be sufficiently characteristic of his style."

"What kind of prints?"

"Well, not actor portraits... anyway the brush strokes looked nothing like Sharaku's."

Ryohei was not being entirely straightforward with Saeko. Though he had forgotten the title of the work in question, what he had seen was a series of twelve oversized erotic prints. True to Okyo's adherence to realism, the private parts of the figures in the images had been depicted in almost nauseating detail. But Ryohei had no intention of mentioning all this to Saeko. At any rate, it was true that the style had not looked anything like Sharaku's.

"And didn't he make any other prints?"

"I doubt it. And even in this one case, you have to take 'attributed to' with a grain of salt. There's no actual evidence that Okyo ever tried his hand at making woodblock prints."

"So you mean we can rule out the Okyo hypothesis?"

"Most probably."

Saeko leafed through the folder Ryohei had given her, pulled out several pages and spread them out on the table. They contained a list of all the theories concerning Sharaku's identity proposed since the end of World War Two. The list was in chronological order according to the year they were proposed. On the left were the artists alleged to have been Sharaku, on the right the proponents:

1957	Maruyama Okyo	Taguchi Ryuzaburo
1962	Katsushika Hokusai	Mogami Saburo *et al.*
1962	Tani Buncho	Ikegami Kosanjin
1966	Apprentice of Iizuka Toyo	Nakamura Masayoshi
1967	Torii Kiyomasa	Kimikawa Yasushi
1967	Utagawa Toyokuni	Ishizawa Eitaro
1967	"Sharaku Workshop"	Segi Shin'ichi
1968	Sakai Hoitsu	Mukai Nobuo
1969	Eishosai Choki	Fukutomi Taro
1969	Tsutaya Juzaburo	Enomoto Yusai
1969	Negishi Ubasoku	Nakamura Masayoshi
1969	Tani Sogai	Sakai Tokichi
1981	Santo Kyoden	Tani Minezo

Of course, there was also the theory that Sharaku, as stated in *Ukiyo-e Ruiko*, had been the Noh actor Saito Jurobei from Awa province. But since this was the prevailing view up until the war it was not included in the list. Until the late 1930s no scholar had ever questioned *Ukiyo-e Ruiko*'s veracity, and to this day there is still a tombstone with Sharaku's name on it at Hongyo Temple in Tokushima Prefecture (formerly Awa province). However, later research revealed there was not a shred of evidence for the Saito Jurobei Hypothesis. The tombstone, it turned out, as well as the temple's death registry—which during the rediscovery of Sharaku's work in the 1910s had been accepted more or less at face value as the sole basis for the theory—dated to long after Sharaku's death. Thus this long-held belief crumbled and many alternate theories rose up to take its place.

Also, not included in the list were many minor theories proposed in works of popular fiction and the like that amounted to little more than wild speculation. If one were to include those as well, the list would run to well over thirty names.

Such was the long line-up of suspects that had been assembled to track down the culprit known as Sharaku. Not one had a firm alibi for the ten-month period from 1794 to 1795. In the course of his research, Ryohei had come to realize that even though it was just one hundred and ninety years ago—not much in the overall scheme of things—the world of Sharaku's time was very far removed from the present day.

"Say, doesn't Professor Nishijima have his own theory?" asked Saeko, looking up from the papers spread out in front of her.

"The professor believes Sharaku was Sharaku."

"What's *that* supposed to mean?" asked Saeko, astonished.

"He thinks Sharaku was a superb artist but he's not interested in finding out who he was. It doesn't matter to him. It's enough simply that his works exist for us to see. Sharaku was just Sharaku; we don't need to look any further... That's *his* philosophy, anyway."

"I see... That's one way of looking at it, I guess. So he thinks all these other theories are a lot of nonsense, is that it?"

Though it pained him to hear Saeko say it, Ryohei did not deny there was something appealingly straightforward about Nishijima's contention that "Sharaku was Sharaku." Yet given how complex the problem had become, it was perhaps inevitable that the professor's view should be interpreted—as the members of the Ukiyo-e Connoisseurship Society might put it—as simply a cop-out. It was certainly true that Nishijima was in the odd position of being the foremost authority on Sharaku despite not having his own theory about Sharaku's identity.

"So what's the current prevailing theory?" asked Saeko.

"Well, it's hard to say exactly. Each one is convincing in its own way. The problem is the absence of any definitive proof. It's getting to be like the controversy over the location of the ancient Japanese kingdom of Yamatai; everyone's having fun playing detective."

"But there's something I don't get. There can only be one Sharaku, so almost everyone is wrong. Can't you just eliminate those?"

"The problem is, it's too far in the past. Sure, there are a few theories I'd like to rule out on the face of it. But then I'd be asked to produce evidence to the contrary. You can't rule something out simply based on gut instinct."

"I see... But I still don't get it."

"Get what?"

"Why did you come up here in the first place? Because there's a possibility that Shoei was Sharaku, right? If that turns out to be the case, then *everyone* was wrong. You say you can't rule out anything based on gut instinct, but isn't that what you'll be doing if you go ahead and publish your theory? 'Those other theories are all persuasive and I can't rule them out, but in my humble opinion Sharaku was Chikamatsu Shoei'... Is that what you intend to write?"

Ryohei groaned.

"Call it gut instinct or whatever you want," Saeko went on, "but if you ask me, there was no point embarking on this research trip unless you plan to prove all those other people wrong."

"All right, you win. Bias is the ultimate sin in academia. I guess I was confusing that with what I'm doing. But you're right. Even without mentioning those other theories, I'd be denying them just by proposing my own," Ryohei admitted meekly.

"ANY convincing theory of Sharaku's identity," Ryohei mused out loud, "has to meet a number of basic conditions and answer some basic questions." He began writing in his notebook:

1. The person in question was not producing any other significant work between May 1794 and February 1795.
2. There is evidence—or at least a reasonable probability—of a direct link to the publisher Tsutaya Juzaburo.
3. The person was an artist.

4. Why was a pseudonym necessary, and why did he choose the name Toshusai Sharaku?
5. Why are there no contemporary accounts, by Tsutaya or anyone else, of Sharaku's identity?
6. Why did Sharaku stop producing prints? Was he forced to?
7. Why did Tsutaya employ an unknown artist?

"I think that about covers it, though I could perhaps add a few other minor points."

Ryohei showed the list to Saeko.

"Isn't number three pretty obvious—that he was an artist?" She looked at Ryohei dubiously.

"Actually, that's a sticking point with some of the other theories."

"Really?"

"The Tsutaya hypothesis is a classic example. Except on that one point, Tsutaya Juzaburo seems to pass the test—with flying colors, in fact. He's a publisher of woodblock prints so he works closely with lots of artists and can pick and choose the best features of each. It would also explain why he had to use a pseudonym. If he'd used his own name no one would have taken his work seriously. So he created an artist out of thin air: Sharaku. It's quite a compelling theory. If there was any evidence Tsutaya actually had some artistic ability, it would be very convincing."

"Hmm… It seems pretty audacious to choose someone who wasn't even an artist and claim he was Sharaku."

"Actually, a number of prints signed by Tsutaya were published in a catalogue prior to the theory being proposed. But chances are they were by someone else; a ghostwriter, so to speak. Kyokutei Bakin—the bestselling author of *The Eight Dogs Chronicle* who for a time worked as Tsutaya's head clerk—wrote in his memoirs that his former boss was in the habit of publishing works by other artists under his own name even though he couldn't draw to save his life."

"Why did he do that?"

"No one knows. Maybe he thought it made him seem more cultured." Ryohei chuckled. "Anyway, if those works aren't really by him, the whole theory collapses. Still, a lot of people support it. It's convincing because it's logical."

Saeko was listening attentively. Ryohei continued:

"Funnily enough, the person who proposed the Tsutaya hypothesis has completely disowned it, probably because there simply wasn't enough evidence."

"What? You mean we're crossing that one off the list?" said Saeko, glaring at Ryohei like a child whose balloon had just been popped.

"Not at all. That's just one person's opinion. The Tsutaya Hypothesis is alive and well. In fact, it recently featured prominently in a NHK documentary."

"How complicated," said Saeko looking bewildered.

"Then again, seeing as the original proponent of the theory has abandoned it, I'm inclined to adopt a similar view," concluded Ryohei, removing a cigarette from a pack of Mild Sevens and lighting it. "Let's see," he went on, "we already discussed Okyo. Next up is Hokusai. This theory is currently very fashionable. When you take a larger-than-life character like Hokusai and combine him with a fascinating artist like Sharaku, it's too much for people to resist. Hokusai used over thirty different names over the course of his career, so it wouldn't be at all surprising if he'd signed his work 'Sharaku' at one point. The only thing is, we don't have many actor portraits by him. Hokusai simply wasn't particularly interested in drawing actors—assuming he *wasn't* Sharaku, of course. Then again, as proponents of this theory point out, in terms of style, there's a distinct similarity between Hokusai and Sharaku. As for the other points—such as why Hokusai would have assumed the name Sharaku, and why would he have stopped using it in 1795— there's no plausible explanation. What's more, around the same time Hokusai was producing lots of other work under his own name. In short, although it's an intriguing theory the chances of the Hokusai hypothesis being the correct one are pretty low."

Saeko nodded as Ryohei rattled off each point.

"Now, the Tani Buncho hypothesis has never gotten out of the realm of pure speculation. Buncho was one of the most popular painters of his time. He was also a samurai, a vassal of Matsudaira Sadanobu's—the man behind the Kansei Reforms—which addressed social and fiscal problems and imposed stricter censorship of the press—and a sort of a painter-in-residence to the powerful Tayasu clan, which Sadanobu headed, one of the three junior branches of the ruling Tokugawa family. If the shogun were to die without a male heir, a successor would be chosen from among the six senior and junior branches. In short, the Tayasu wielded immense power. Buncho's fame was extraordinary, thanks in no small part to his status as Sadanobu's official painter, for until 1793 Sadanobu was chief counselor to the shogun. Buncho had something like three hundred apprentices and his paintings supposedly sold for about five ryo each, a small fortune in those days. There's no plausible reason why someone like Buncho would have moonlighted as an ukiyo-e artists under a fake name, even assuming Tsutaya could afford to hire him. But if so, why hire an artist of Buncho's caliber if you're not going to put his name on the prints? Without it Tsutaya couldn't have hoped to turn a profit. The only intriguing part about this theory is that Buncho specialized in human portraits and he sometimes signed his work 'Shasanro,' which bears a faint similarity to 'Sharaku.' That's about it."

Again Saeko nodded and waited for Ryohei to continue.

"Let's see, who's next—Iizuka Toyo? He was the official lacquerware painter to the daimyo of Awa province. This theory holds that Sharaku was one of his pupils, but again his connection to Tsutaya isn't clear. The basis for the theory is that the background scenery and kimono designs seen in Sharaku's prints are suggestive of the techniques used in lacquerware painting, but personally I don't see it. The scholar who proposed the Toyo hypothesis has switched to a different theory, so I think it's safe to disregard it. The same goes for the next one on the list: Torii Kiyomasa. Kiyomasa was Kiyonaga's son, so no doubt he was a talented painter, but only a handful of his woodblock prints survive—too few to serve as a basis for comparison, in any case. Then there's the question of why not use his own name; that part doesn't make sense. The Torii School was renowned for its actor portraits, so Kiyomasa had no reason to publish under a pseudonym. As Kiyonaga's son, his own name carried considerable cachet. Anyway, there's so little historical evidence on Kiyomasa that I don't expect any further developments in this theory."

Saeko said nothing.

"You must be tired," he said.

"Not really… shall we have some tea?" she suggested.

Ryohei suddenly felt thirsty.

"Let's see… we discussed the Sharaku workshop hypothesis the other day," recalled Saeko.

"In that case, there are six more to go. That's quite a slog."

"You know, Ryohei, you're kind of funny."

"Huh? Where did that come from out of the blue?"

"I mean, you said each theory was convincing in its own way, but then as soon as you start talking you eliminate them one by one."

"That's because I'm talking to you. If I were writing an academic paper I couldn't dismiss them so easily."

"It must be hard being a scholar." Saeko smiled gently to herself and reached out for the cup of black tea with lemon which the waitress had just brought over.

"Okay," said Ryohei. "Next up is Toyokuni."

"He's a nonstarter, right? If I remember correctly, I read somewhere that Toyokuni was Sharaku's main rival."

"Correct. Just months before Sharaku appeared on the scene, Toyokuni released his debut work, a series called *Views of Actors on Stage*. The publisher was Izumiya Ichibei, one of Tsutaya's main business rivals. It's common knowledge among art historians that Tsutaya published Sharaku's works in order to compete with Izumiya. The idea that Toyokuni might have been playing two roles at the same time is pretty farfetched. Then again, the guy who came up with the theory is a mystery writer, so what do you expect?"

"Yeah," agreed Saeko. "No matter how interesting art history is, it's not like writing fiction."

"That's true. But to be perfectly honest, I'm somewhat taken with this particular theory. The more you look into it, the more interesting it gets. For example, Sharaku has a series of actor portraits in which each print is inscribed with the actor's *haimyo*. Have you seen it?"

Saeko nodded. A haimyo was a kind of penname that people in Edo times used when they composed haiku. Back then, haiku was all the rage among kabuki actors, and almost every actor had his own haimyo. For example, Baiko—meaning "plum happiness"— the given name of modern-day kabuki actor Onoe Baiko, started out as the haimyo of his great-great-great-great grandfather, Onoe Kikugoro, the founder of the Onoe acting dynasty.

"Now, one of the portraits in Sharaku's series is the actor Segawa Kikunojo," Ryohei continued. "Interestingly, it contains a mistake. Kikunojo's haimyo was Roko, meaning 'the way of contemplation.' But instead of 'contemplation,' Sharaku wrote the Chinese character for 'piety.'"

Ryohei wrote the two characters down in his notebook and showed it to Saeko.

"This is a big deal for art historians," he went on. "Some people say Sharaku couldn't have known very much about kabuki. If he'd been well acquainted with the actors whose portraits he was drawing, he'd never have made such a rookie mistake. I guess you can't blame them for saying that."

"Even though he did nothing *but* actor portraits?" asked Saeko incredulously.

"Okay. But here's the thing: Toyokuni also did a portrait of Segawa Kikunojo around the same time and..." Ryohei paused and gave Saeko a meaningful smile.

"Come on, stop teasing me—out with it!"

"Well, his print has the same mistake!"

"What does that mean?" asked Saeko, her eyes flashing.

"It's impossible two people made exactly the same mistake."

"So, Sharaku and Toyokuni..."

"Were one and the same? Possibly. Or perhaps for a brief time Kikunojo really *did* write his haimyo with the character for 'piety.'"

Ryohei grinned. Saeko sat gazing at him with rapt attention.

"If you ask me," he went on, "I think that's probably what happened. But I had a shock when I discovered the exact same mistake on both prints because I couldn't believe Toyokuni and Sharaku were one and the same. Still, it's an interesting theory. If it inspires even one person to go and check out an exhibit or read a book on ukiyo-e, then it's a good thing."

With obvious delight, Ryohei took a sip of tea before continuing:

"Now, Sakai Hoitsu was the younger brother of the fabulously wealthy Sakai Tadazane—lord of Himeji Castle—though he actually lived in Edo. He mastered every school of Japanese painting imaginable: Kano, Rimpa, ukiyo-e… Plus, he was a first-class poet who wrote both haiku and comic *kyoka* poetry. Since his brother was a daimyo, he never had to worry about money. He was easily one of the most—if not *the* most—cultured men of his era. The reason he's been linked to Sharaku is because of the latter's staggering output. Putting aside the question of whether Hoitsu could or couldn't have drawn them, it would have been a major undertaking for Tsutaya to publish so many prints in just ten months. What's more, according to historical accounts, Sharaku's works weren't that well received at the time. It's not surprising therefore that some people have suggested they weren't published to make a profit, in other words, that they were published at the artist's own expense. Now, a few prints is one thing, but over a hundred? It would have cost a small fortune. That's how Hoitsu's name was put on the list of suspects; he had both the artistic skill and the financial means—a rich man's vanity press, if you will. The theory goes that he had to change his name so as not to bring dishonor on his family by painting portraits of actors, who at that time were contemptuously referred to as "people of the wastes." But if Hoitsu *was* Sharaku, I don't see why the prints should have been published in batches over the course of ten months. I mean, it wasn't fame he was after, he had plenty of that already. If the prints were a flop commercially surely he would have stopped after the first batch. Don't you think? After all, there was no incentive for him to continue because his name wasn't on them. On the other hand, if the prints were a big hit, he would have continued churning them out without stopping…"

"But wait," objected Saeko. "Aren't there plenty of scholars who believe Sharaku's prints *were* a success?"

"Yes," confirmed Ryohei. "There are various reasons for believing the historical documents are wrong and Sharaku's prints actually sold quite well. Personally, I agree with that view."

"In that case, it's not surprising Hoitsu continued."

"But hold on a minute. That's putting the cart before the horse. The premise of the Hoitsu hypothesis is that Sharaku's prints weren't commercially viable—remember? Tsutaya continued publishing them even though they weren't selling because Hoitsu was footing the bill, isn't that right?"

"Oh, yeah," conceded Saeko. "I'd forgotten that."

"If you're working from the assumption that Sharaku's work was well-received, then the Hoitsu hypothesis never comes into play. Either way, the theory doesn't hold water."

Saeko finally seemed convinced.

"Okay," Ryohei went on. "Next up is Eishosai Choki. First I should explain that according to this theory Choki didn't act alone but was put up to it by Shiba Kokan. In other words, Kokan was pulling the strings."

"Shiba Kokan… you mean the guy connected to Shoei?"

"That's right. So let's put this theory aside for later until after we've dealt with the remaining three."

"Why's that?" asked Saeko.

"You'll see. Now, Negishi Ubasoku is something of an enigma. All we know about him for sure is that he illustrated one book published by Tsutaya. This theory rests entirely on the fact his style is very similar to Sharaku's. Actually, it's slightly an exaggeration to say he's an enigma. His real name was probably Kitao Shigemasa. Shigemasa was a close associate of Tsutaya's and at the time he was living in Negishi, hence his pseudonym. Shigemasa illustrated a number of books for Tsutaya."

"Is that all?"

"Patience, please. You'll see the relevance of this later. Okay, next is Tani Sogai. To explain this theory, first I have to talk about Sharaku's fan paintings."

"Fans… like the ones made out of paper that you hold in your hand? He painted those too?"

"Yes. There are just two such works of his known to exist. One is a picture of Otafuku scattering dried beans in spring to bring good luck. The other one shows a naked boy trampling a woodblock print by Toyokuni as a bald old man stands nearby, looking on sadly."

"That's bizarre."

"Yes, this is something that's perplexed art historians for some time. What's it supposed to mean? Some people claim the old man is Tsutaya, others say he's Toyokuni. But Tsutaya wasn't *that* old in the 1790s and Toyokuni was only around thirty. Assuming Sharaku did make this particular fan painting, then the old man depicted in it must have been someone he knew well. This is where Tani Sogai comes in. He was a highly esteemed teacher of Danrin poetry and a tremendously influential figure. He numbered many kabuki actors and ukiyo-e artists among his students and even boasted a few daimyo and other high-ranking samurai. Now, the person who proposed this theory happened to own a portrait of Sogai. When Sharaku's fan painting first surfaced and was in the news, he saw a picture of it and thought the old man looked familiar. Then he remembered his portrait of Sogai. He got it out and compared the two—it turned out they were practically identical. Now this is where things get tricky. His portrait of Sogai was unsigned. So *it* could have been by Sharaku, too. As he was staring at the portrait, his eyes fell on an inscription—a poem purporting to be in Sogai's own hand—which he had never paid much attention to. He noticed it was titled, somewhat enigmatically, 'Ode to a Painting by Me.' So it *was* a self-portrait, the man concluded. And if Sogai painted it he must have painted the fan also. Thus the Sogai hypothesis was born."

"Hmm… sounds a bit too good to be true," said Saeko, with an entranced look on her face.

"Exactly. And there's something else. This theory glosses over one very important point: though the fan picture is signed by Sharaku, it's never been definitively authenticated. If it's a fake then the whole theory falls apart. Also, if the picture of the old man *is* Sharaku, why does he look so sad? It'd be more natural if he were smiling, since the boy in the picture is trampling a print by his archrival Toyokuni. It doesn't make any sense. Then there's the question of how you interpret the title of the poem. It seems to me the most straightforward reading of 'Ode to a Painting by Me' is that the *poem* is by him and the *picture* is by someone else. If it were a self-portrait, wouldn't he have titled it, 'Ode to a Painting *of Me*'? Sogai made his living with his pen, so he'd never have used such an ambiguous expression."

Ryohei paused to take a breath. Saeko was looking at him in wide-eyed astonishment.

"I guess," he said, sounding somewhat reluctant to continue, "all that's left now is the Kyoden hypothesis."

"Is it as complicated as that?" asked Saeko, noting his change in tone.

"Well, it's a recent theory," explained Ryohei, "developed with an awareness of the weaknesses of those that came before it, so it's going to be a bit harder to refute. I have to admit my own first reaction when I read it was why in the world hadn't anyone ever thought of Kyoden before? It must just have been a blind spot. Santo Kyoden, as I'm sure you're aware, was one of the most popular and prolific fiction writers of the Edo period. He had an especially close relationship with Tsutaya, and later Tsutaya's son; between the two of them they published over eighty of Kyoden's works. Now, it's commonly believed that while the rise of Toyokuni was part of the reason for Tsutaya's decision to publish Sharaku's work, his main aim was to recoup the money he lost during the Kansei Reforms. In fact, it was Kyoden who was responsible for Tsutaya's loss of fortune. In 1791, Kyoden was arrested for writing *The Kimono Chest* and other works dealing with prostitution. He was put in chains for fifty days and his publisher, Tsutaya, had half of his assets confiscated."

"Wow, talk about harsh."

"It wasn't the first time Tsutaya had a run in with the authorities for publishing banned material, but this time it seems they wanted to make an example of him. Anyway, the result was that now Kyoden owed him one—big time. In addition to being a writer, Kyoden was a pretty good artist. He'd been an apprentice of Kitao Shigemasa— we talked about him earlier—and even published woodblock prints under the name Kitao Masanobu. When Kyoden started writing popular fiction, he illustrated most of his books himself. If he hadn't happened to be an even better writer than artist, he'd probably have rivaled Utamaro as the great ukiyo-e master of his day. Anyway, if Tsutaya thought to exploit Kyoden's talent by asking him to make prints of kabuki actors under the name 'Sharaku,' Kyoden would have been in no position to refuse."

"So," chimed in Saeko, "all our ducks are in a row. He's a good artist, he knows Tsutaya well, has plenty of reason for wanting to conceal his true identity… Looks like it must have been Kyoden, doesn't it?"

"So far so good, anyway."

"How about his alibi?" asked Saeko. "Does it check out?"

"Well, he certainly was in the right place at the right time."

"So you mean he *really* was Sharaku!" Saeko looked at Ryohei in shock. Ryohei laughed.

"Okay, I'll confess… Of all the theories, this is the one that convinces me the least," he said bluntly.

Saeko was speechless.

"Sure, Kyoden had the motive, the means, and the opportunity. But why should he have changed his name to Sharaku?"

"Because," suggested Saeko, "the authorities were keeping an eye on him…"

"That's what the person behind this theory believes. But actor prints weren't the least bit subversive. Remember, mica printing hadn't yet been banned under the government's sumptuary laws. That wouldn't happen until several months *after* Sharaku's prints were published. Anyway, even supposing there was a chance the authorities might decide to crack down on such extravagance, the responsibility lay entirely with the publisher. The authorities would never have gone after an artist for something like that. No, at the time Sharaku's first print appeared, Kyoden had nothing to fear from the law. If the argument is that he had been scared off publishing work of any kind, then he wouldn't have published *anything* after 1791. But in fact by 1792 he'd already published several books under his own name. In other words," concluded Ryohei, "Kyoden had no need to conceal his true identity."

He paused before continuing:

"Now, what about Tsutaya?" he asked rhetorically. "Might he have had a reason for wanting Kyoden to change his name in order to create an unknown artist named Sharaku? This scenario seems even more improbable. Kyoden was a huge celebrity. Other publishers were clamoring for his work. There's no way Tsutaya would have had Kyoden make over a 140 actor prints and then kept quiet about it. Quite the opposite—he would have put Kyoden's name front and center and publicized it heavily. In terms of name recognition, Sharaku and Kyoden were night and day. As long as Kyoden didn't object, Tsutaya would never have taken his name off his work. And there's hardly any conceivable reason why Kyoden might not have wanted to use his real name. No, I don't care if he's a perfect match in every other respect. For this reason alone I can't buy into the Kyoden Hypothesis. People are seduced by it simply because today Sharaku is much more famous than Kyoden."

Ryohei had become impassioned. Saeko sat watching him, looking somewhat amused. After a brief pause she asked, "Say, what kind of person was Tsutaya anyway? Listening to you I get the impression he was pretty heavy-handed."

"Heavy-handed or not, he was a shrewd businessman. He started out as just a small bookseller. Within a decade he'd built one of the biggest publishing houses in Edo. He must have had a good head for business."

"Wow, only a decade!"

"Not only that, but by forty-one he'd elbowed his way past his competitors to become head of the publishers' guild. Since he was about twenty-four when he opened his first bookshop, in just fifteen years he'd risen to the top of his profession."

"He must have been incredibly driven," observed Saeko.

"Driven, yes, but also a man of vision. When comic poetry became all the rage in Edo he befriended the leading kyoka poets and got them to order books from him for all their students. He also took in promising young artists and looked after them. If you wanted to be cynical you might say he liked to incur people's gratitude. Utamaro was one of the many artists Tsutaya nurtured. But when Tsutaya bet on the wrong horse it sometimes ended up costing him a pretty penny. Fortunately, Utamaro turned out to be the most popular ukiyo-e artist in Japan, so on balance you'd have to say Tsutaya had a good eye for talent: Eishosai Choki, Kyokutei Bakin, Jippensha Ikku… They all owed their careers to Tsutaya. When it came to business strategy, he was head and shoulders above his competitors."

"It seems he was quite a character," said Saeko, "but I can't help feeling a bit sorry for him."

"For Tsutaya?"

"Yes. I mean, most people today have heard of Utamaro, Sharaku, Bakin, and Ikku, but hardly anyone's heard of Tsutaya."

"Well, that's life. Anyway, Tsutaya probably wouldn't have minded; after all, he was the one making all the profit. Plus, I think he must have taken a lot of satisfaction in seeing the artists he nurtured grow up and be successful."

"I suppose that's true. But why would a shrewd businessman like him have taken a risk with an unknown artist like Sharaku?"

"Ah, now there's the rub. No matter how talented Sharaku was, someone as shrewd as Tsutaya wouldn't have continued publishing his work if it didn't sell. He'd have pulled the plug on the project without a second thought. But he didn't. He kept it up for ten months. Now, there are scholars who say the shock of losing half his fortune sent Tsutaya a bit off his head, or that he was so desperate to get his business back on its feet that he didn't know when to stop. But if Tsutaya had been as fainthearted as that, he'd never have built his empire in the first place."

"Good point," said Saeko, deep in thought.

"That's why I think Sharaku was a success from the very beginning," went on Ryohei. "In fact, his prints must have sold so well Tsutaya pushed him to churn out more and more. Look, he starts off with deluxe, oversize color prints, right? Gradually they get smaller and smaller and cheaper and cheaper. The prevailing theory about this is that the earlier prints were a flop, despite all the money Tsutaya lavished on them, so he scaled back and kept plugging away, waiting for Sharaku's popularity to take off. But I think it was the reverse: Sharaku was a phenomenal success from the very beginning. When an artist is hot, people will snap up anything with his name on it. Mica printing was very expensive, so Tsutaya switched to something cheaper to produce. There was more profit in that. For the better part of a year, Tsutaya put just about everything else on hold and devoted all his attention to Sharaku. He wasn't running a vanity press. He had a family to support and employees who needed to be paid. He had to put food on the table. For that reason alone, I can't imagine he would have continued publishing Sharaku's work if it didn't sell. But let's suppose he was so enamored of Sharaku he wanted to publish him regardless.

In that case, he would at least have found a more commercially viable artist to publish alongside Sharaku so as to make enough profit to scrape by. That's just common sense. But Tsutaya didn't do that. Why? Because Sharaku was bigger than any other artist at the time—that's the only possible conclusion based on what we know of Tsutaya's character. But either Sharaku fell into a rut and Tsutaya ditched him, or Sharaku realized Tsutaya was using him and decided to call it quits. Anyway, I imagine the reason Tsutaya stopped publishing Sharaku's work after ten months was something along those lines."

"Not that I don't doubt your interpretation for a moment, Ryohei, but how do you explain *Ukiyo-e Ruiko*'s claim his work was unpopular?" asked Saeko curiously.

"You mean about his work being 'too true to life' and his career lasting 'less than a year' and all that? Those things were written years after Sharaku had come and gone. By then I don't think anyone knew the real reason why Sharaku stopped painting. Plus, when someone rockets to stardom overnight people either love him or hate him. It usually takes years for an artist's reputation to settle down. You can't establish a reputation in just ten months. People go on about how 'the documents say this' and 'the documents say that,' as though it were holy writ! Remember, originally *Ukiyo-e Ruiko* was just someone's personal notebook; it wasn't published in book form until much later. Now, if it *had* been published—let's say at least a few hundred copies—and lots of people had read it, *then* maybe I could take what it says at face value. But I think all it proves is that there were people at the time who hated Sharaku's work.

"On the other hand, the writer Shikitei Samba talks about Sharaku as a great artist. And in one of Jippensha Ikku's books there's an illustration of a child flying a kite decorated with a picture by Sharaku. I don't think Ikku just made that up. If Sharaku's pictures appeared on toys he *really* must have been popular; kids know what they like when they see it. When you think about it, there is something *manga*-esque about Sharaku's style, so maybe children were a big part of his fan-base. Maybe adults couldn't stand seeing his work slapped on all sorts of merchandise and were relieved when he suddenly disappeared. That would explain the criticism of Sharaku's work in *Ukiyo-e Ruiko* and why Tsutaya didn't have him do erotica or pictures of courtesans: that's not what kids were interested in. Just like the pop duo Pink Lady didn't sing adult songs because they were essentially a teenybopper band."

"I doubt Sharaku would appreciate getting lumped together with Pink Lady!" exclaimed Saeko laughing. "Anyhow, that's a pretty bold thesis you've got there." She breathed out deeply, clearly impressed.

"Well, I could never write that in a scholarly article," said Ryohei. "But there's other evidence Sharaku was a big hit at the time. If you examine his work closely, you'll notice the same picture often appears again and again, only the colors of the clothes have been changed or the lines are slightly different. This is especially true of his earlier work, printed with mica. I haven't actually studied this myself, but Segi Shin'ichi, who proposed the Sharaku workshop hypothesis, has counted seven or eight versions of one print alone. You know, the famous one of the actor Ichikawa Ebizo playing the role of Takemura Sadanoshin which the post office put on a stamp. Scholars refer to these as either 'subsequent imprints' or 'variants'—what we call a 'reprinting' in the trade now. If Sharaku was as unpopular as people say, these simply wouldn't exist."

"Why's that?"

"You see, with woodblock prints, a publisher would order an initial print run of about two hundred copies. If those sold well, a second print run would be ordered using the same blocks. Depending on what dyes the printer had ready for use—or if the publisher wanted to save money by using cheaper dyes—the colors might be changed. That's a 'subsequent imprint.' With each reprinting the blocks cracked a little bit until eventually they were unusable. Minor cracks could be filled in, but if the cracks were deep or spread across the entire surface, a new block had to be cut. That means the lines of the picture will be a little bit thicker or thinner in places, or slightly out of position. Since these later reprintings were made from an entirely different block than the original, scholars call them 'variants.' Now, there are seven or eight color versions of Sharaku's print of Takemura Sadanoshin, which means—"

"There were seven or eight printings," said Saeko, finishing his sentence.

"Exactly. Besides Sharaku, I can only think of a few other artists whose work went through so many reprintings. In short, Sharaku was big—really big. It shouldn't be surprising that people wrote nasty things about him, simply out of spite," concluded Ryohei.

"Which means," said Saeko, with a dazed look on her face, "we have to look at the problem of Sharaku's identity in a completely different way."

"Correct. Sharaku *wanted* to remain anonymous. He needed an escape route in case his work was a flop—like a writer who uses a penname. Long ago there were even singers who debuted on stage wearing a mask; if they were a hit they'd always remove the mask at the end of the show. Everyone wants to be famous—it's failure they're afraid of. Therefore, we can rule out Hokusai, Choki, Kiyomasa, and Toyokuni—who weren't well known at that time—plus the Sharaku workshop and the 'Apprentice of Iizuka Toyo' hypotheses. If any of them had been Sharaku we would know about it because it would have been a huge boost to their careers, so you can be sure they would have owned up to it. Likewise, we can eliminate Kyoden, Sogai, Buncho, Hoitsu, and Okyo because they were already successful. If Sharaku had been a flop they would have kept quiet, but he wasn't. There's no shame in being famous. You also have to consider Tsutaya's nature. If he'd been able to get Kyoden or any of the others to work for him, he certainly wouldn't have concealed the fact. No, there seem to be only two possible explanations for why Tsutaya would have been so secretive about Sharaku's identity: either there was no point in revealing his real name because he wasn't someone anyone had heard of, or else for some reason the consequences of doing so were so serious Tsutaya could have been put out of business. Sharaku's work didn't break any laws or anything, so even if someone very respectable like Hoitsu or Sogai was behind it, they had no reason to remain anonymous."

"I see," agreed Saeko. "You make it sound so simple, Ryohei."

"But this line of argument doesn't work if Tsutaya or Ubasoku was Sharaku. In Tsutaya's case, the more successful Sharaku became the greater the disadvantages of revealing the truth; the public would quickly lose interest in Sharaku if they found out he was really just a merchant with no formal artistic training. Plus, from a business perspective it was better for Tsutaya if Sharaku's identity remained a mystery. As for Ubasoku... well, he's a more difficult case; we only have one book of his to go on."

"But Ryohei, can't you eliminate him the same way you ruled out Hokusai, Choki, and the other up-and-coming artists?"

"No. The thing is, Hokusai and Choki were active for years, decades even, after Sharaku disappeared. If either of them was Sharaku, why didn't they exploit his fame? But we don't know what happened to Ubasoku. Maybe he died—and Sharaku along with him—in which case he couldn't have exploited Sharaku's fame even if he'd wanted to."

"Okay. But what about the possibility you mentioned earlier: that Ubasoku was really Kitao Shigenobu?"

"It's very likely," agreed Ryohei. "But it doesn't necessarily follow from that that Shigemasa was Sharaku. If scholars operated on assumptions there wouldn't be any point in doing research. Without facts capable of convincing a third party, Ubasoku will just have to remain Ubasoku. That's only fair."

"I see what you mean," conceded Saeko. "But then his identity's a mystery and there's nothing we do about it. Personally, Ryohei, if you believe Shigemasa was Ubasoku, that's good enough for me..."

"If only everyone were like you, Saeko," Ryohei said with a rueful smile. "But if you consider Tsutaya's personality, it seems unlikely Ubasoku was Sharaku."

"So he'll just have to remain Ubasoku?"

"I'm afraid so. Look, Ubasoku illustrated just one book for Tsutaya in the spring of 1793. After that, nothing. If Tsutaya thought Ubasoku's talent was worth exploiting commercially, why would he have waited a full year-and-a-half before publishing him as Sharaku? Isn't that odd? Tsutaya was the top publisher in Edo. Why didn't he ask Ubasoku to illustrate more books for him? One could argue Tsutaya was nurturing Ubasoku, having decided to publish him as Sharaku, but that theory doesn't hold water. It's generally accepted the emergence of Toyokuni in 1793 was the impetus for Tsutaya to publish Sharaku's work. So why would he allow himself to fall so far behind Toyokuni by waiting eighteen months if he already had Ubasoku under his wing? In other words, one has to conclude Tsutaya was never all that impressed with Ubasoku."

"And Tsutaya didn't bet on artists he didn't think had talent, right? But was Ubasoku a good illustrator?"

"One of the best. There's no way he could have failed to impress Tsutaya. That's why some people think he was Shigemasa. Shigemasa illustrated over forty books for Tsutaya. Plus, like Ubasoku, he lived in Negishi at the time. But Shigemasa was a leading figure in ukiyo-e circles. Not only was he Kyoden's teacher but he also had a huge influence on Utamaro and Hokusai. Without some particularly compelling reason, the chances he was Sharaku are pretty small. Tsutaya might have let him illustrate one book under the name Ubasoku, but he never would have agreed to publish over a hundred prints by Shigemasa under an assumed name."

As Saeko remained silent, Ryohei said, "Now, this probably has nothing to do with Sharaku's identity, but it's interesting Shigemasa's name should come up. Let's see, now... If we also include Kokan, who was overshadowed by Choki..." Ryohei opened his notebook and started to sketch something.

Staring at the notebook, Saeko asked, "What's that?"

"A diagram of the relationships between various literati of the period. A line indicates a close link: a teacher and an apprentice, for example, or close friends. The box in the middle is Shigemasa. Shigemasa studied Danrin poetry with Sogai and illustrated several collections of his work. Adding Shigemasa makes the diagram complete. Plus, if you assume Shigemasa was Ubasoku, this covers just about all the possible candidates for Sharaku."

Saeko looked at the diagram.

```
Tsutaya ------ Kyoden-------[ ? ]--------Sogai
     Buncho-------Hoitsu------Hokusai
     So Shiseki-------Gennai------Kokan
```

"Hoitsu moved to within a stone's throw of Shigemasa's house in Negishi, though not until much later," explained Ryohei. "It might just have been a coincidence, but this diagram suggests there was more to it. This was Tsutaya's circle, so to speak. Even if they didn't have direct contact with one another, I think they regarded each other as associates."

Saeko waited for Ryohei to continue.

He went on, "If one of these individuals was Sharaku, it'd be natural to assume the others knew about it."

"One would think so," said Saeko.

"But none of them ever mentions Sharaku—not even once. Kyoden wrote a postscript to *Ukiyo-e Ruiko* but says nothing about Sharaku in it. Were they all sworn to secrecy or something? Was it that big a deal? It makes an intriguing mystery, but is it realistic? That's why I'm basically not all that interested in the question of Sharaku's identity."

Saeko laughed. "You seem pretty interested to me!"

"All I've done is summarize the existing research for my own benefit. After all, as an art historian working on ukiyo-e it's not a question I can avoid. But after reading all the scholarly literature on the subject, I was forced to conclude Sharaku was just Sharaku, some second-rate artist no one paid much attention to. Tsutaya used his business savvy to turn him into a big sensation. Then for some reason, after ten months, it all came to an end. Sharaku stopped making woodblock prints. My guess is he died. That's it—end of mystery."

"So basically," said Saeko, "you agree with Professor Nishijima!"

"Not at all. The professor's view is it doesn't matter who Sharaku was. He could be Hoitsu or Tsutaya for all he cares. It wouldn't alter his appraisal of Sharaku's work. That's not *my* position. I don't think Sharaku was any of the candidates who have been proposed but instead some unknown artist. That's completely different."

"Doesn't that leave us right back where we started? Maybe Sharaku really *was* a Noh actor from Awa? It would explain why he was unknown. After all, there must be some basis for that old claim."

"But there's no evidence Saito Jurobei painted anything or even that such a person ever existed. The sole 'basis' for the claim is *Ukiyo-e Ruiko*, which is only a copy of an old manuscript. Unless some heretofore unknown painting by Saito-slash-Sharaku emerges—which seems unlikely—that line of inquiry seems hopeless."

"That means Sharaku was someone no one's thought of before. But if he was some obscure artist, won't it be extremely hard to track him down? And there I was thinking we'd be able to link him to Shoei just like that," said Saeko with a sigh. "That's looking pretty unlikely now."

"Actually, I think the possibility is extremely good," responded Ryohei. "First, Shoei was unknown. Second, we have evidence he painted, well enough to have been Sharaku. Third, since he knew Kokan he had a connection—however tenuous—to Tsutaya. Fourth, his pseudonym suggests an association with ukiyo-e. Fifth, in the 1790s he left Edo and returned to Akita. He meets all the criteria. And here's the most crucial piece of evidence: in at least one instance, he refers to himself as Sharaku."

"It seems to be an open-and-shut case. So why are you still so hesitant?" asked Saeko.

"All our evidence so far is circumstantial. How well did Shoei really know Tsutaya? When was he in Tokyo, and when did he return to Akita? Why did he abandon ukiyo-e? Unless we can get some hard answers to these questions, our argument won't fly. Just because we've eliminated all the other suspects doesn't mean Shoei's our man. Unfortunately, he's not mentioned in any known historical documents. That's why I've been tearing my hair out. With just the painting catalogue as evidence, all we've done is add one more inconclusive theory to the pile."

"But Professor Nishijima thinks it's promising, right?"

"Promising, yes—but not convincing," said Ryohei. "Scholarship's not that simple."

On that note, Ryohei brought the discussion to an end.

All the other customers had left the café; Ryohei and Saeko had been so engrossed in their conversation that neither had noticed. Ryohei looked at his watch. It was already ten o'clock. They had to leave the hotel at nine thirty the next morning. The two stood up and returned to their respective rooms. Ryohei's voice sounded a bit hoarse from having talked so much.

4

The Akita School

November 1

"WHAT a beautiful day!"

The sky was blue as could be. Saeko stretched out her arms as she came out of the hotel. It was unusually warm for November.

"We better get going or we'll be late."

"What time is our train?"

"9:38."

"What? We've only got ten minutes! Are we going back to the same station as yesterday?"

"No. To get to Kosaka we have to take a private line. The train leaves from a different station. According to Kudo it's not so far."

The two broke into a run.

"What a tiny station," Saeko whispered in Ryohei's ear as they took their seats in the waiting area. There was still some time to go before the train was due to depart. The waiting area was hardly more than three hundred square feet. A stove sat in the middle of the room, a small fire burning inside and only five other people were waiting.

Soon the station attendant appeared and announced that the ticket gate had opened. The two got up and followed the rest of the passengers out toward the platform.

"What in the world...?" Ryohei blurted out. There, in the middle of the long platform, a one-car red-and-yellow train was waiting.

"A one-car train—how romantic!" said Saeko. "Hey, look. That's the man who punched our tickets just now." She pointed in surprise at the train driver, who had just gotten onto the train behind the other passengers.

The train threaded its way through the folds in the mountains. Along the way it made several stops where passengers got on and off, but the number of people inside the car never exceeded about ten. All of them sat next to a window alone, staring out at the passing scenery.

On the surrounding hillsides, the autumn foliage was at its peak. The trees spread their luxuriant branches over the single-track line, the bright colors of their leaves shining into the car and occasionally falling onto Saeko's cheek, coloring it by turns red or yellow or orange.

As they emerged from the last of three long tunnels, the landscape suddenly opened out in front of them and they saw the tiny village of Kosaka nestled against the foot of the mountain. Bathed in a warm gentle light, it looked as pretty as a postcard. Ryohei had a feeling it was going to be a good day for research.

As they emerged from the station onto the street he heard a voice call out, "Ryohei Tsuda?" A black two-door Nissan Skyline was parked at the curb in front of the station. Beside it stood a young man, who bowed to them. He appeared to be in his early twenties. He had a black leather jacket on—unzipped and not on quite straight—and tight-fitting blue jeans. Like most men his age, his hair was cut short.

"I got a call from Kudo…"

"You must be his friend, Nara Yoshiaki."

"That's correct," the young man replied politely. He walked over to them. Ryohei and Saeko introduced themselves.

"I hear you two are here on important business. Kudo tells me Kosaka's gonna to be famous. 'Least you can do,' he says, 'is take the day off and show them around.'"

"But I thought today was your day off anyway…" said Saeko in surprise.

"Don't mention it. I owe him one—don't know how many times he's done the same for me over in Odate," replied Nara, casting aside her concerns. "Now, where do you two want to go? It's a small place, so there's not much to see," he said with an affable smile, opening the door of the sports car for them. The two climbed inside.

"I hear you work at the mine," asked Ryohei.

"Yeah. Not exactly office work."

"Is there some sort of company archives room there?"

"A reference room? You want to know something about the mine?"

"Not exactly—just about its history."

"Can't help you there. Not much interested in history myself. Anyway, I don't think there's anything like that at the mine."

"I see…" mumbled Ryohei, disappointed.

"But there *is* a brand new local history museum in town. It's not only about the mine though…"

"Really? That's perfect. Could we go there first?" asked Ryohei, surprised at their luck.

The local history museum was about a five-minute drive from the station. A smart redbrick building, it looked more like a church than a museum.

The three went inside.

On the front wall of the entrance lobby hung an enormous photograph mounted on a panel; at least, that's what Ryohei thought it was at first. But as he drew near, he realized it was made up of numerous white tiles, each about eight inches square, onto which pieces of a photograph had been developed before being assembled. The photograph, which showed Kosaka as it looked long ago, was sepia-toned, giving it an old-fashioned feel. One could clearly make out figures walking along the street. Smoke billowed from a large smokestack, practically filling the sky; clearly the mine was thriving.

"This must have been taken around the time Sato Masakichi lived here," mumbled Saeko, reading a plaque next to the panel.

"1913… about seven years after he died," said Ryohei, passing his eyes over the text. "Before coming here I read somewhere that Kosaka was the first town in Tohoku to get electric lighting."

"Really? Because of the mine?"

"Uh-huh. Even though it was a small town, it was way ahead of the rest of the region, culturally speaking. It even had a kabuki theater with a revolving stage."

"No kidding? Maybe that's why Kiyochika came here," said Saeko, turning her attention back to the photograph.

After a few moments, the three climbed the stairs to the exhibition rooms on the second floor. Contrary to what Ryohei had been expecting, most of the items on exhibit were related to local life and customs.

"This isn't much help," said Nara, who seemed to have figured out what Ryohei was looking for.

"I can't say I'm all that surprised. It's not like Sato was famous or anything," said Ryohei. "But I thought there might be some record of the 1907 flood."

"Wait a minute," said Nara. "I know someone who works here. I'll go ask him." He disappeared downstairs.

After a while, a voice called to Ryohei from downstairs. He and Saeko returned to the lobby to find Nara seated on a bench talking to an older man. Ryohei and Saeko bowed and sat down beside them.

"My name is Chiba," said the man, making a slight bow. He was thin and small in stature. "What is it you're looking for?" he asked, removing his glasses and wiping them with a cloth.

"I'm trying to find out about a man who lived here in the early 1900s."

"I see… What's his name?"

"Sato Masakichi."

"Hmm… he lived in Kosaka, you say?"

"Yes. Probably from about 1902 to 1907."

"Did he work at the mine?"

"I'm not sure."

Ryohei took a photocopy of the catalogue of Sato's painting collection out of his bag and handed Chiba the page containing Kiyochika's preface. The man lit a cigarette and ran his eyes over the words.

"I see," he said after a few moments. "So he died in the flood of 1907. Then he must have worked at the mine. The town was mostly unaffected when the Oyu River flooded that year."

"What, *that* little stream?" asked Nara.

"Yes. It runs past the mine. Long ago there used to be a dam upstream with a hydroelectric plant. The heavy rains burst the dam and all the houses up on Mt. Gen were washed away. If I'm not mistaken over fifty people were killed," Chiba explained.

"Is that so? The mine where *I* work is on Mt. Gen," Nara said, surprised.

"But it's odd…" said Chiba, tilting his head to one side. "This Sato must have been pretty well-to-do to collect paintings. But Mt. Gen was where the unskilled laborers lived. I wonder what he was doing up there?"

"Maybe he just happened to be visiting the mine," suggested Nara. "When he heard about the flood he would have gone to help, then got swept away in the waters himself."

"Hmm… I suppose it's possible," said Chiba, nodding.

"I thought Sato's house was swept away in the flood too," said Saeko.

"Kiyochika's preface says nothing about his house," replied Ryohei. "Only that his paintings were spared. But now it's starting to make sense. I always thought it was a bit strange that only Sato should have died in the flood while the rest of his family survived."

"Yes I see," said Saeko. "That's a good point."

"But if Sato didn't live on the mountain then where might he have lived?" Ryohei asked Chiba.

"Perhaps on the hill just above the town," replied Chiba. "It's a bit far from the mine, but that's where the company houses for all the managers were."

"Are any of the old houses still standing there?" asked Ryohei excitedly, sensing a glimmer of hope.

"Not one, I should think. They've built a housing complex for the miners there now."

Ryohei could not help feeling disappointed.

"How would one go about finding out about the people who died in the flood?" Saeko asked Chiba, noting the disappointment on Ryohei's face.

"Let's see now… There are no records like that here at the museum. I imagine they'd be pretty hard to track down. In the old days, a mining town was a strange place—lots of people from outside came looking for work. No one bothered much about names," said Chiba. "Of course, things are different now," he added, looking at Nara.

"Isn't there a memorial to the victims?"

"Not as far as I'm aware. All I know is that a lot of people died."

"But Sato Masakichi wasn't just *any* mineworker," persisted Saeko.

"I suppose the town hall might have something. But he was from Shizuoka, right? His family register is probably there. I doubt he would have brought it with him."

"Meaning?"

"Without a family register, a death can't be recorded. Even if he died here in Kosaka, it'd be up to the town hall that holds his family register to remove his name from it."

Of course, thought Ryohei. *Why didn't I think of that?*

"In those days it wasn't as easy to change one's permanent residence as it is now. Or you might say that back then, people didn't worry so much about bureaucratic procedures. Anyway, how about going over to the town hall and checking there?" Chiba's patience seemed to be wearing thin.

"Could I just ask one more thing?" Ryohei was not ready to give up just yet. "Would you happen to know anything about a painter named Chikamatsu Shoei? He belonged to the Akita School."

"The Akita School? You should check out the public library next door. They have a reference room devoted to local history. You can probably find out something there." Chiba pointed to a building visible from the window.

Thanking Chiba for his help, the three left the museum and headed over to the library.

Although not a large building, the library was quite impressive for a small town. On the left as they entered, there was a long hallway leading to the main reading room. Halfway down the hall on the right was the local history reference room. Entering, they found a small room about twelve feet square lined with bookcases. In the middle there were four tables. No one was in the room, although apparently visitors were free to browse at their leisure.

The shelves were filled with books about Akita and bound volumes of official reports and local literary magazines.

"Wow, I never even knew this place existed," exclaimed Nara, gazing at the bookshelves.

"Where should we begin?" asked Saeko enthusiastically.

"Let's see," said Ryohei. "Why don't you go through all the books on art that look as though they might have anything to do with the Akita School. I'll look through historical materials."

He began scanning the bookshelves from left to right. *The Land and Climate of Akita, Akita Fief and Kubota Castle, History of Kosaka...* Whenever his eyes lighted on something promising, he opened the book and scanned the table of contents. There wasn't time to sit down and study each one properly. He remained standing by the bookshelves and quickly flipped through their pages, his hand reaching for one volume after another.

Saeko pulled down several large art books and painting catalogues from the shelves, piled them up on one of the tables, and began looking through them. Nara, somewhat at a loss, picked a book at random off the nearest shelf and began browsing through it.

Ryohei kept his eyes open for any mention of Sato Masakichi, Chikamatsu Shoei, or the Akita School. He found nothing. He did come across a few accounts of the 1907 flood—including one in a multi-volume work whose title proclaimed it part of *The Local Historical Documents Series*—but none mentioned the names of anyone who had died. Finally, having exhausted everything else, he turned his attention to the various local literary magazines and municipal reports, thinking one of the town elders might have written something of relevance to their quest. They had wasted an hour in the room already. Ryohei was growing impatient.

Suddenly Saeko cried, "I found something!"

"What is it?" asked Ryohei, trying not to get his hopes up.

"A painting catalogue—I should have looked at it to begin with." She passed the book to Ryohei, her finger sandwiched between the pages to mark her place.

Painters and Calligraphers of Akita, edited by Takaaki Inoue, 1981—published by a local press. It was an impressive tome of over three hundred pages giving detailed information about over three hundred Akita-born painters and calligraphers from the early Edo period to the present. Ryohei opened it to the page Saeko had indicated and read:

Chikamatsu Shoei—Painter. Born in Akita. Vassal of Lord Satake. Flourished circa Bunsei era (1818–1830) [Masu.]

"Is that it?" asked Ryohei, sounding disappointed. Of all the entries in the book, it was by far the shortest. There were three pages of description on Odano Naotake alone, plus four plates showing examples of his work. Needless to say, there were no illustrations of Shoei's work.

"Yes… But this establishes that Shoei was a samurai from Akita, doesn't it?" replied Saeko. She sounded somewhat put out by Ryohei's response.

"The bio in Sato's painting catalogue is better than this. And what does 'Masu.' mean, anyway?"

"Let me see," said Saeko, taking the book from Ryohei and opening it to the front. "There seems to be a bibliography. Ah, here it is: 'Masu.' stands for 'Masuya Terumizu, *Directory of Samurai Families in Dewa Province* (original manuscript copy by the late Toyosawa Takezo, 1914).' Look, all the entries that cite the same reference are as brief as Shoei's. It must have been some sort of personal notebook."

"You're probably right. I suppose it was the editor's sole source of information on Shoei." Flipping through the book, Ryohei found several more entries on other artists citing the same source. All of them were brief and without illustration:

Hasegawa Choshu—Painter. Born in Akita city. Real name Hasegawa Hobin. Southern School. [Masu.]
Miura Bunkei—Painter. Born in Kazuno. Real name Miura Fusaku. Studied painting under Bunryo. [Masu.]

"Well, at least it appears Shoei wasn't an exception. It must just have been the author's personal style."

Nevertheless, Ryohei could not help feeling disappointed. Whoever Masuya Terumizu was, he must have seen Shoei's paintings in person. Otherwise he could hardly have included him in his notebook, as apparently no other sources of information on Shoei existed. The same must be true for the other artists, all of whom were described in the same confident, declarative style.

Couldn't he have provided a little more detail? thought Ryohei.

The same could be said for the biography of Shoei in Sato's painting catalogue. Professor Nishijima had thought it was probably based on an old manuscript or else the label on the box in which the scroll had been stored. Either way, if only the biography of Shoei in the catalogue had been more thorough, Ryohei might have been saved the trouble of coming all the way to Kosaka.

Perhaps this Masuya guy was accustomed to writing in classical Chinese and believed brevity was a virtue, thought Ryohei, annoyed.

"There's also an artist named Chikamatsu Eiwa listed here," Saeko said with curiosity as she perused the table of contents.

"Is that so?"

"But he seems to have lived during the Meiji period."

"That's no good to us."

Ignoring Ryohei's remark, Saeko turned to the page listed in the table of contents and began reading.

"Hey," she said. "He was an Akita samurai too and he was born in the Edo period." She passed the open book back to Ryohei. This entry was much longer than the one on Shoei and included a plate with illustrations.

Chikamatsu Eiwa—1821–1889. Painter. Real name: Endo Shoeki. Sobriquet: Setsuo, a.k.a. Tokugien. Father's name: Eisho. Served as tea master to Satake Nanka—castellan of Yuzawa Castle—also acting as artist-in-residence. During the time of the young Satake Yoshinari (15th lord of Yuzawa) a "dark cloud" descended over the castle. Constant in-fighting among the lord's vassals erupted into a bitter dispute between the two chief clans, the Yamagata and the Harada, which became known as the Yuzawa Incident. Caught in the middle, Chikamatsu took a position critical of the Haradas. He made a painting showing a samurai wearing the Harada crest beneath a satirical poem which read: "The world today is

like a carriage full of women—there's no shortage of idiots."
This led to his being censured and having to flee to Edo.
He later returned to Akita and found a position as artist-
in-residence in the Yajima region (perhaps in the vicinity of
present-day Mizugami). It was at this time that he took the
name Chikamatsu.

"Hmm…" mused Ryohei.

The illustration beside the entry was of a vertical painting
depicting a hawk perched on the branch of a pine tree, resting its
wings. The hawk had an imposing presence and the style of the
painting was extremely accomplished.

"This painting reminds me of one by Naotake," said Saeko,
peering over Ryohei's shoulder.

"Which one?"

"Let's see. I just saw it a second ago…" Saeko opened one of
the books lying on the table and began leafing through it. "Here it
is—aren't they similar?"

The plate she showed Ryohei was also a vertical painting of a
hawk perched on the branch of a pine tree. Apart from the fact
that the bird's eyes were looking in the opposite direction, the two
paintings were nearly identical.

"They *are* similar," agreed Nara, who had come over and was
standing beside Saeko. "Now that's what *I* call art."

"But Eiwa wasn't an Akita School painter," said Ryohei.
"Granted, his style is very similar."

"So I guess this isn't enough to go on?" said Saeko crestfallen.

"I'm afraid not. But what intrigues me is why he took the name
Chikamatsu after returning from Edo. Whereabouts in Akita is
Yajima, I wonder?"

Ryohei got out his map of Akita and began pouring over it.

"Yajima? I think it's near Honjo," said Nara helpfully.

"Honjo?"

"Yeah. I've got some relatives who live over that way."

Ryohei looked surprised.

"Isn't Honjo where Shoei lived according to the biography in
Sato's painting catalogue?" asked Saeko.

"You're right. He did live in Honjo. No mistake about it," said Ryohei, nodding.

They checked the map and found there was just one Honjo in Akita Prefecture. It was only about twelve miles from Yajima, quarter of an hour by car.

"He must have been a protégé of Shoei's," said Ryohei, looking up from the map.

"Or at least if he didn't actually study under Shoei himself, he was influenced by his work, or perhaps studied painting from one of Shoei's apprentices. Then there's his name: Eiwa."

"What about it?" asked Saeko.

"Well, it doesn't say so here, but I suspect he borrowed the Chinese character '*ei*' at the beginning of his name from 'Shoei.' Just like most of Toyokuni's apprentices took the character '*kuni*' as part of their names: Kunisada, Kuniyoshi, Kunimasa, etc. It was a tradition among ukiyo-e artists for students to adopt the second character of their teacher's name as the first character of their own name."

"Is that so?"

"Eiwa started out as a tea master and eventually became an in-house artist to the Akita daimyo, right? Someone of his stature wouldn't have studied painting under some local town artisan. Shoei was also from a respected and well-established Akita samurai family, so for that reason alone there's a good chance the two were connected. When Eiwa moved to Yajima he must have met Shoei or learned of his reputation and decided to adopt the name Chikamatsu Eiwa."

Saeko asked, "So it couldn't be a simple coincidence?"

"Unlikely. Painters don't change their names lightly. It's not as though there could have been many artists in a rural place like this. No, Eiwa knew Shoei. They must have been connected in some way for him to take the name Chikamatsu. If he wasn't a protégé, then perhaps he married Shoei's daughter or granddaughter. That could explain why he took his name."

Saeko nodded.

"Anyway," Ryohei went on, "this corroborates the information in Sato's catalogue that Shoei lived in Honjo. That's extremely important."

Ryohei took a number of books up to the library information desk and asked the librarian to make copies of several pages relating to Shoei, Eiwa, and the flood of 1907. Then they left the library.

"I'm famished," said Saeko, "It's already one o'clock."

Ryohei suddenly felt a pang of hunger too. "Is there any place to get something to eat around here?" he asked Nara.

"Only a greasy spoon or two… If you want a decent restaurant we'll have to drive some distance."

"COULD I ASK you something?" Nara, looking rather serious, said to Ryohei once they had sat down and ordered their food. "Excuse me for my ignorance, but what is the Akita School anyway?"

"How shall I put it?" replied Ryohei. "I guess you could say it was the first concerted effort to apply Western painting techniques to depict Japanese subject matter." He went on to elaborate: "The Akita School was founded in 1773 when Hiraga Gennai arrived in Akita. This was a time when the central government in Edo was under the control of Tanuma Okitsugu. The daimyo of Akita fief, Satake Yoshiatsu, a.k.a. Shozan, had asked Gennai—one of the foremost mining experts of the day—to come to Akita to provide technical advice on increasing the output of the domain's copper mines. Gennai was widely recognized as the brains behind Tanuma's policies, and some have speculated that Shozan hoped to use Gennai to curry favor with Tanuma. At any rate, on Tanuma's orders, Gennai set off for the Ani copper mine in Akita. Along the way he stopped off at the castle town of Kakunodate.

It was in Kakunodate that Gennai made the acquaintance of Odano Naotake. Naotake was a vassal of Satake Yoshimi and an extremely talented artist. It's unclear exactly how Gennai and Naotake met, but since Naotake was a household name in Kakunodate and Gennai was interested in painting, someone probably introduced the two. There is a famous anecdote that goes something like this: Gennai told Naotake, "Paint a picture of a *kagami-mochi* viewed from above." Naotake went home and, with great difficulty, managed to produce something like the New Year's decoration of two rice cakes, one small and one large, with a bitter orange on top. He took it to show Gennai who took one look at it and said, "I can't tell if this is a rice cake or a plate!" Then he picked up a brush and shaded the picture around the edges. Suddenly it looked like a rice cake. "This is how they paint in the West," Gennai said. Naotake realized he had at last found someone worthy of calling "master" and prostrated himself at Gennai's feet. The story is most likely apocryphal, but given Gennai's penchant for mocking people, there is probably some kernel of truth to it.

For his part, Gennai was quite taken with Naotake. Once he had completed his work at the copper mine, he was given an audience with Shozan. Though there's no record of the meeting, it's thought Gennai took the opportunity to praise Naotake's skill as an artist. Shortly after Gennai returned to Edo, Naotake followed him there in the official capacity of "inspector of mine production." It seems Shozan's real intention in sending Naotake to Edo was to have him learn Western painting techniques from Gennai. Shozan himself had been trained in the Kano School of painting and was a strong proponent of Naturalism. But he had a political motive as well, for Gennai held the backdoor into Tanuma's inner circle open. As daimyo of Akita, Shozan knew it could not hurt to have one of his own samurai among the ranks of Gennai's apprentices.

Once in Edo, Naotake took up residence in Gennai's house in Yamatocho in Kanda. Gennai took every opportunity to show off his protégé's paintings to other people. Within a year, Naotake's name was known throughout Edo on account of his illustrations for Sugita Genpaku's *New Anatomy*. The choice of Naotake as illustrator was largely thanks to Gennai's friendship with Genpaku. Be that as it may, the young man from Akita was more than up to the task. The detail and precision of his anatomical illustrations made Genpaku's *New Anatomy* a phenomenal success and catapulted Naotake to fame. He was twenty-six.

In 1777, Naotake left Edo, having spent the better part of five years there, and returned to Akita. He was by this time thoroughly steeped in the techniques of Western painting, as taught to him by Gennai. Most likely he had had also studied with So Shiseki, who was a friend of Gennai's. Shiseki was a Naturalist in the tradition of the Chinese painter Chen Nanpin, having mastered the so-called "boneless" style of painting that eschewed outlines in favor of shading. It was not quite Western style painting, but the basic tenets were the same. Drawn to Shiseki's style, Gennai asked him to illustrate a book he was writing called *Things and Their Properties*. This work best exemplifies Gennai's unique genius as a natural historian. Published in five volumes, *Things and Their Properties* is a kind of illustrated encyclopedia of rare plants, minerals, and various products from across Japan. Gennai needed someone who could render objects from the natural world with a high degree of precision and detail, and Shiseki was just the man for the job.

Meanwhile, not long after Naotake returned home to Kakunodate, he received an unexpected summons: he was to report at once to Kubota Castle (in Akita city, the feudal seat) and assume his new post as personal assistant to the daimyo. It was an unprecedented appointment for someone so young. Naotake picked up his belongings and moved to Akita, where he began instructing Satake Shozan in the techniques of Western painting. Shozan, who already had a solid grasp of the fundamentals of Japanese painting, proved a quick study. Thus, the Akita School was born. If painting was good enough for their lord, it was good enough for the samurai of Akita. Naotake must have quailed beneath the deluge of applicants seeking his tutelage.

One year later, in October 1778, Naotake returned to Edo, this time in the company of his lord, Shozan, who was required to reside in the shogun's capital during alternate years. As soon as Naotake arrived, he went to see Gennai to pay his respects to his teacher and excitedly informed him of the sudden success of the Akita School. Gennai could not have been more pleased. The two men toasted their reunion and talked of the future of Western painting in Japan.

It was at this time that Shiba Kokan, an apprentice of So Shiseki, began to frequent Gennai's house and to study Western painting with Naotake. But although the future looked bright, a cloud was about to descend on Naotake's world. Gennai's mental state began to deteriorate. He would get into heated arguments with publishers and patrons over the slightest things, and he barred his apprentices from his rooms, fearful lest they steal his work. When word of this leaked out, some within the Akita clan began to criticize Naotake for his affiliation with Gennai, even though the latter still enjoyed Tanuma's favor.

Then, in November 1779, Gennai was imprisoned for murder. Though the details are foggy, according to one account, a protégé of Gennai's came to see him one day; finding his master out, he entered his rooms without thinking and picked up some interesting looking book that happened to be lying about. When Gennai returned, the story goes, he found the man engrossed in the book, flew into a rage, drew his sword, and struck him dead. Anyway, whatever really happened, it dealt Naotake and the Akita School a decisive blow. Later that month, Akita officials decided to 'censure' Naotake, although the reason is not recorded in the official clan register. Though this may not sound like much, it meant that Naotake was obliged to return to Akita and was effectively placed under house arrest. It also severed all relations between Gennai—a branded criminal—and the Akita clan. To Naotake, it must have felt as though he had been thrown into an abyss.

Returning to Kakunodate in disgrace, Naotake sank deeper and deeper into despair. On May 17, 1780, he died. He was only thirty-two. It is variously rumored that he committed seppuku, swallowed poison, or simply died of insanity. The death registry at the temple of Shoanji in Kakunodate where he was laid to rest simply mentions Naotake's posthumous Buddhist name, "Zetsugaku Genshin died May 1780, son of Odano Heishichi." His real name is not mentioned. The shame he had brought on himself and his family persisted long after he was gone.

With Naotake's passing, the Akita School too died out. It had not lasted even ten years.

"IN OTHER WORDS," said Ryohei, summing up, "Gennai was responsible for the birth of the Akita School as well as its death."

They had finished eating lunch and were seated around the table drinking coffee.

"So who was the first artist in Japan to do oil paintings?" asked Nara.

"That's not entirely clear. It's commonly believed to be Gennai, but there are oil paintings that predate him."

"But who did Gennai learn oil painting from?" asked Saeko.

"It's said he studied it in Nagasaki, but there's no proof of that. He probably just taught himself."

"Taught himself?"

"There were lots of Western oil paintings coming into Japan through Nagasaki around that time. He probably just saw some and copied them. You know that painting said to be by Gennai called *Portrait of a Western Lady*? The original it's based on is still in Nagasaki today."

"He must have been extremely talented," observed Saeko.

"Stubborn is more like it," said Ryohei, smiling. "That's what drove him to make his electrostatic generator and thermometer. He wanted to prove everyone who said Japan wasn't as good as the West wrong."

"I've heard of Gennai's electrostatic generator, but what's this about a thermometer?"

"Well, apparently the first time Gennai was shown a Western thermometer by his Dutch interpreter in Nagasaki, he immediately grasped the principle of how it worked. He even boasted to his friends that he could make his own in a couple of days. It was several years before he made good on his boast."

"Why's that?"

"He said it was pointless. In the middle of summer when it's blazing hot, what good is it to know exactly how hot it is? It won't make it any cooler. That was his view anyway."

"How true," said Saeko, smiling. "But it sounds to me like he was just making excuses."

"That's exactly what his friends said. Finally, a few years later, Gennai had some time on his hands so he made a thermometer and showed it to them. It took him more than just a couple of days— a week, apparently."

"Not bad," said Saeko, impressed.

"In fact, he made two. One he gave to Tanuma; the other he presented to the daimyo of Takamatsu, where he was born."

"That's what I call one smart guy," said Nara, shaking his head emphatically.

"That's why I say he probably figured out how to make oil paintings—the techniques, the materials—just by looking at one.

Problem was, he wasn't a very good artist. So he started looking around for people who were. He wanted to popularize oil painting."

"And that's when he happened to meet Naotake, is it?"

"That's right. Naotake was exactly the kind of person Gennai was looking for—young, bursting with curiosity…"

"But how in the world did he get hold of oil paints in Akita?" Nara asked skeptically.

"He didn't. Akita School artists didn't actually paint with oils. You're right; they *were* hard to get hold of. Instead, they painted Western-style pictures using Japanese watercolors. When they were done, they slapped something called 'chian turpentine'—what we might call varnish—over the canvas with a brush to create the effect of an oil painting."

"*What* turpentine?" asked Saeko.

"Chian—it's a substance made by diluting resin obtained from pine trees."

"Wow, Gennai thought of everything, didn't he?"

"It didn't do any good knowing how to make oil paints, since the ingredients weren't available in Akita. So instead he figured out a way to make watercolors *look* like oil paints. I suspect it was his idea to use chian turpentine—all smoke and mirrors, very typical of Gennai."

"Style and no substance, is that what you mean?" said Saeko, grinning. "So Kokan's Western-style paintings weren't really oil paintings either?"

"They came quite a bit later. By that time Kokan was able to get hold of proper oil paints. Only he didn't call his pictures 'oil paintings'—he called them 'wax paintings.'"

"Wax?" asked Saeko. "As in candles?"

"Yes. But it didn't really have anything to do with wax. It was all a question of image. If he used the word 'oil painting,' Kokan thought people would confuse it with the oil they used to fill their lanterns."

"When you say 'quite a bit later,' how much later do you mean?"

"Not until around 1790. He probably painted one or two oil paintings before that, but most of the ones I know of are from the 1790s onward."

"The 1790s—that's Sharaku's time period."

"Right; which, incidentally, was about ten years after Gennai and Naotake died."

"*That* much later? So the story about Kokan studying Western painting techniques from Naotake is made up?"

"No, it's true all right. Only, Naotake taught him *Western* painting, not *oil* painting. Kokan did make a number of Akita-style paintings using watercolors in the 1780s. You must have come across them in the library. He collaborated with Shozan on several works."

"Oh, like that one where Kokan painted the human figures and Shozan did the background?"

"That's right, that's one of Kokan's early works. It's a watercolor painting."

"When was that, roughly?"

"Let's see… Shozan died in 1785, so the earliest it could have been was around 1783."

"But wait a minute… that was *after* Naotake died, wasn't it?"

"The picture's not dated, so it's impossible to say, but that's what scholars of Kokan's work believe."

"So Shozan pursued Western painting even *after* Naotake's death."

"Well, not with the same passion as before. Apparently when Shozan heard Naotake had died, he swore he'd never pick up a brush again."

"I wonder how Kokan got to know Shozan."

"I think Kokan sought Shozan out. It was around the time Kokan pioneered copperplate printing in Japan, and he was riding high. His timing was perfect too—by then, the excitement over the Gennai affair had pretty much died down and clan officials had relaxed their vigilance."

"Did Kokan want Shozan's patronage?"

"No doubt that was part of it. Kokan was a pretty shrewd operator, he knew how to get ahead. He was probably in and out of Shozan's Edo residence all the time. I bet that's how he met Shoei."

Saeko added, "Since Naotake was no longer around to introduce them."

"Right. And Shoei didn't become Naotake's apprentice until after Naotake returned to Akita just before he died. By that time

Kokan was already one of Edo's brightest lights. When Shoei found out that Kokan had also studied under Naotake, he probably felt drawn to him."

"I wonder what Kokan thought of Shoei," mused Saeko.

"I doubt he gave him much thought either way. But since Shoei was one of Shozan's vassals, Kokan wouldn't have snubbed him. In fact, knowing Kokan, he probably made a pretense of doting on the young man."

"Kokan doesn't seem a terribly nice person."

"What do you expect? According to Sato's catalogue, Shoei was born in 1762. That means he was only about twenty-two at the time. Having just arrived in Edo from Akita, he must have seemed a country bumpkin to someone as urbane and sophisticated as Kokan. Kokan was in his mid-thirties and thought of himself as avant-garde. He wasn't the sentimental type; he wouldn't embrace Shoei as a kindred spirit just because they'd both studied Western painting under Naotake. I doubt he even thought of Shoei as a fellow apprentice, let alone a colleague."

"Yeah, 'cause we're just a bunch of hillbillies up here," Nara suddenly chimed in, breaking his long silence. He gave an embarrassed smile.

"Er... that's not exactly what I meant."

Ryohei had forgotten he was not in Tokyo any longer.

"No good," said Ryohei as he opened the car door.

He had just returned from the town hall. Nara and Saeko were waiting in the car.

Ryohei continued: "They don't know any more about the flood than we were able to find out at the library. Turns out the materials we were looking at over there used to be kept here. So now we're right back where we started—with no leads at all on Sato Masakichi. The girl working inside asked me, 'Have you tried the local history museum?' She didn't have a clue where to begin. She disappeared into the back for half an hour only to return saying she'd been unable to find out anything. I guess I'll have to make a trip to Shizuoka. Apparently most of the mine supervisors around that time came from Tokyo or the Kanto area. 'There's no record here even of their *names*,' said the girl, clearly implying: How in the world do you expect me to find out anything about some guy named Sato Masakichi?"

Ryohei smiled wryly as he lit a cigarette. The strong smell of burning tobacco wafted through the car.

"Well, don't get too upset about it," consoled Saeko. "After all, it's not as though *he* was Sharaku."

"That's true!" Ryohei gave a loud laugh.

BY THE TIME Nara had finished showing Ryohei and Saeko around Kosaka and dropped them off at their hotel in Odate, it was well past six in the evening.

"Why the long face?" asked Saeko as she took a bite of her chicken sauté. They were seated in the hotel restaurant just like the previous night.

"I was going over my notes in my room just now when it suddenly struck me how unproductive this trip has been."

"Really? I thought we'd make good progress."

"Huh?"

"You said it yourself, Ryohei: Eiwa's existence confirms Shoei lived in Honjo, just as Sato's book says, right? It also tells us Shoei was an artist of considerable standing. To be honest, at first I didn't believe Sharaku would have chosen to leave Edo and come to live up here in the middle of nowhere. But finding out about Eiwa has put those worries to rest. I can see now he might have wanted to live out the remainder of his life in peace and tranquility."

Ryohei replied, "But that doesn't get us anywhere."

"But it proves the biography of Shoei is accurate. Of course, just because part of it is true doesn't mean it all is. But you know what it says about him knowing Kokan? That seems plausible too. On the whole I think it's factual, including the part about Shoei returning to Akita in the 1790s."

"True enough. I guess it is still possible Shoei was Sharaku." Ryohei's expression brightened at last. "Which means Shoei lived in Odate at some point... I wonder if there are any clues here..." Ryohei and Saeko turned their heads simultaneously and gazed out the window at the cityscape around them.

Again Ryohei was struck by a thought. Was Sharaku here, in this very city, at a different point in history?

Saeko interrupted his reverie. "I wonder if Sato acquired that painting by Shoei here in Odate?" she mused out loud. "The railway line between here and Kosaka had been built then, right?"

"No. It didn't open until 1909. But it's no distance at all from here to Kosaka. People were probably going back and forth all the time. After all, the Ou Main Line to Aomori stopped here. Kiyochika would have gotten off the train here in Odate when he went to visit Sato in Kosaka."

"On the other hand, Kakunodate is really far from Kosaka," pointed out Saeko. "In the Meiji period it must have been a huge trek. And Honjo is on the other side of the prefecture. So Odate is the only place Sato could have acquired the painting."

"Good point," agreed Ryohei. "Shoei's painting is dated 1798, when he was living in Kakunodate."

"So when did he come to Odate, I wonder?" mumbled Saeko, almost to herself.

"Ah, there's the rub," said Ryohei with a deep sigh. "That's what I'd like to know."

Half an hour later, Ryohei left Saeko and returned to his room. He had just begun summarizing in his notebook what they had learned that day when the telephone rang.

"It's me."

The voice on the other end of the line was Yosuke's.

"I just got a call from Saeko," he said. "Sounds like you're really onto something. So you found a protégé of Shoei's?"

"Well, possibly."

"Always Mr. Cautious, aren't you?" laughed Yosuke. "Saeko says the problem now is figuring out when Shoei was in Odate."

"Yeah, our information's inconclusive…"

"Actually, that's why I called. I think I found the answer—by chance of course."

"You're kidding!" said Ryohei in disbelief. How had Yosuke, sitting in Tokyo, managed to find out what had eluded them? He pressed his friend to explain.

"It was nothing really," replied Yosuke. "At first when Saeko mentioned Odate the name didn't mean anything to me, but after hanging up I checked my encyclopedia of Japanese place names. You know, one of those Sanseido pocket editions. Hold on a sec— let me read it to you: 'Odate: central city in the Odate Basin on the upper reaches of the Yoneshiro River. Population: 77,664. Seat of the Asari clan during the Muromachi period. In 1602, the Satake clan was put in charge of Odate Castle and unified the Hinai-Ani region. In 1795, the daimyo of Akita established a district magistrate's office there.'"

"1795!" Ryohei could hardly believe his ears.

"Exactly—the year Sharaku disappeared."

"But how does that connect him to Shoei?"

"Shoei left Edo and returned to Akita, right? Well, I don't think he simply quit his job and returned home; he was *sent* there to take up a new post in the district magistrate's office in Odate. I bet it had something to do with the Ani copper mine. It says here the Ani region had been placed under Odate's jurisdiction, right? Well, while I was at it, I did some research and found out that, in its heyday, over twenty thousand people lived in Ani. That appears to have been after Gennai had left the mine. In other words, in the 1790s the mine was just reaching its peak, which is why the district magistrate's office was moved there. Riots are common in mining towns, the authorities must have been short-staffed and sent to Edo for extra help."

"Speaking of the Ani mine, wasn't Naotake's job—"

"Inspector of mine production?"

"Exactly."

"Akita clan officials wanted to give Naotake a reason—other than studying painting—for being in Edo. Therefore, can't we assume the same must have been true for his protégé Shoei?"

"Particularly because Shoei probably wasn't nearly so famous in Akita as Naotake."

"Which means it's possible that when Shoei was sent to Edo he was also given a job dealing with mine production. And when mine production took off, a new district magistrate's office was set up, and they needed people to run it…"

"Hmm… It's quite possible," Ryohei admitted. "The bio of Shoei in Sato's catalogue only says he was a samurai—it doesn't say he was an official painter."

"So have I convinced Mr. Cautious?" asked Yosuke.

"Hey, cut me slack; it's just the way I am."

Yosuke gave a big laugh.

Ryohei went on, "But one thing's got me a bit worried."

"What's that?"

"Well, if Shoei left Edo in 1795, the possibility he was Sharaku seems pretty good. 1795 was perhaps the most important year in Sharaku's life. But to be honest—I know this sounds strange coming from me—somehow it doesn't seem quite real."

"That's because you're the one who discovered Sato's book. What would your opinion be if this were someone else's theory?"

"Well… it's still not clear what was Shoei's connection to Tsutaya. But I guess I'd say it seems fairly convincing."

"Is that it? What am I going to do with you?" exclaimed Yosuke. "But I suppose it's a good thing to be cautious. As for Tsutaya, I think I might be able to come up with something."

"You think so?" asked Ryohei.

"Hey, I haven't exactly been sitting around twiddling my thumbs. Anyway, I'll get everything straightened out by the time you get back to Tokyo."

"You mean your research materials?"

"No, my thoughts. I've read so many articles about Sharaku lately my head is still a bit of a jumble." Then, with affected seriousness, Yosuke told Ryohei to give Saeko his regards and rang off.

1795… Odate… Shoei… Sharaku…

The same words kept flashing over and over again through Ryohei's mind.

5
Tsutaya's Revenge

November 2

WITH KUDO DRIVING, Ryohei and Saeko managed to reach Kakunodate before noon. They had left Odate before nine o'clock that morning and had been on the road for about two-and-a-half hours. They booked rooms in a hotel downtown that Kudo had recommended. As it was still too early to check in, they deposited their bags at the front desk. Ryohei then invited Kudo to join them in the hotel restaurant on the second floor.

"I'm having udon," said Saeko, not even bothering to look at the plastic food models in the showcase at the entrance to the restaurant. Ryohei wondered if she was tired of all the rich food they had been eating. He and Kudo both ordered the deep-fried breaded pork filet.

"Same as yesterday," remarked Saeko, with an amazed look on her face. "I'm surprised you don't get tired of it."

The restaurant was empty. The three of them sat down at a table next to a window with a view of the town.

"Look, that's the man I saw last night," said Saeko, staring down at the parking lot.

"What man? Saw where?"

"That man walking in our direction. He was staying at our hotel in Odate last night."

Ryohei scooted over next to Saeko and looked down into the parking lot. A tall thin man in his mid-thirties was walking toward the hotel and looking up in their direction. A staircase led from the parking lot directly to the restaurant. The man headed for it. He must have known there was a restaurant upstairs.

"What's *he* doing here?" muttered Ryohei.

"You know him?" asked Saeko.

"He owns an antique shop in Morioka. I go there a lot."

"Really? He was watching us."

"Watching us—when?"

"Last night, when we were in the restaurant. Oh, that's right. You were facing the other way. He was seated in the back of the restaurant the whole time, drinking a beer by himself."

"Really?"

"He'd occasionally look over and stare in our direction—it gave me the creeps."

"He was probably drunk. I'm sure he couldn't resist your beauty."

"Cut it out. It wasn't *that* kind of look," Saeko said, with a shy smile.

The man entered the restaurant and sat down at a table not far away. Ryohei looked at him. For a moment their eyes met. Ryohei instinctively nodded his head. The man seemed a bit taken aback but mumbled some form of greeting. He seemed to have recognized Ryohei.

"Ah, I thought it was you." The man stood up again and walked over to their table with a smile on his face. "I'm sorry. I've forgotten your name," he said, scratching the back of his head in embarrassment.

"Tsuda," Ryohei replied.

"Ah, that's it. I though you looked familiar when I saw you last night but I couldn't remember your name. That's why I didn't come over and say hello."

"You mean in the restaurant?" asked Ryohei.

"Oh, you saw me then? My, aren't you the sly one. You should have said something!"

"No, my friend here only just told me." Ryohei introduced Saeko.

"Pleased to meet you. My name is Kato," the man said, a smile still pasted on his face. "Proprietor of Kozukata Antiques in Morioka."

"Kozukata? How do you write that in Chinese characters?" asked Saeko.

"Here, let me give you my card," replied the man, reaching into his pocket. "So I take it you don't hail from Morioka then?"

"No," Ryohei answered for her, "Okayama."

"I thought so. Everyone in Morioka's heard of Kozukata Castle. It once belonged to the daimyo of Nambu," explained Kato.

Saeko nodded. Kato moved over to their table and took the seat next to Saeko.

"By the way, you haven't dropped by my shop lately," Kato said to Ryohei, lighting a cigarette.

"That's because I haven't been back home to Morioka lately."

"Ah, that's right. You live in Tokyo."

"Yes. So how's business? You seem to be keeping busy."

"Lousy. You know what they say—'No rest for the weary.' I'm here on a buying trip, but there's not much on the market these days."

"Seen any woodblock prints?"

"Afraid not. All the good stuff winds up in Tokyo. The best I can manage is a Kunisada."

Though Kato's shop specialized mainly in Japanese swords, he also sold ukiyo-e prints. Whenever Ryohei was home visiting his parents in Morioka, he always popped in at least once or twice. But Kato was normally quite taciturn and until now their discussions had been confined strictly to business. Ryohei wasn't surprised Kato hadn't remembered his name.

"Do you often come to Akita to buy antiques?"

"Yeah. If I don't change my merchandise every six months or so my customers get bored. This time I'm visiting Odate, Kakunodate, and Yokote."

"Did you have any luck in Odate?" asked Ryohei. It suddenly occurred to him that since Kato's business took him around lots of antiques shops, he was the perfect person to hit up for information about Shoei.

"Nothing worth mentioning. If it's woodblock prints you're after, you'll find portraits of samurai and that sort of thing around here, but not much else."

"How about the Akita School?"

"Western-style paintings? Do you collect those now too?"

"No, I'm just doing a bit of research. That's why I've come to Akita."

"I see. Well, I can't think of anything offhand. I've only seen two or three Akita School paintings since I went into business. I'm afraid all the good ones have already been snapped up."

"Is that so?"

"Yeah. Even though Kakunodate's the birthplace of the Akita School, you won't find any of their paintings here—not even in the local museum," Kato added. "You have to go to Akita city if you want to see some."

"Oh, I don't want to *see* any," said Ryohei. "I'm just trying to find out about a painter."

"Which one? Shozan? Naotake?"

"A protégé of Naotake's—someone named Chikamatsu Shoei."

"Chikamatsu Shoei? Never heard of him."

"He lived in Odate at one time."

"Really? Imagine a Western-style painter in little town like that! On second thoughts, though, perhaps it's not all that surprising—it *is* Akita, after all."

"I think he made a fairly large number of paintings."

"Is that so? Well, there are only about four or five artists with any real commercial value." Kato proceeded to rattle off a list of names: "Shozan, Naotake, Satake Yoshimi, Unbo... Then there's Dokugensai—not quite as valuable, but if one of his paintings came up for sale it would cause quite a stir."

"And how about Yoshimi's son, Yoshifumi?" asked Ryohei.

"He was a bit of a dilettante. Still, I suppose his work would fetch a pretty good price."

"So none of the other Akita School painters have any value?"

"It's not that they don't have any value. It's just that their works hardly ever come up for sale, so it's hard to put a price on them. Rumor has it that just before the war the market was flooded with forgeries, so there are quite a few fake Shozans and Naotakes floating around out there."

"You mean out-and-out forgeries?" asked Saeko.

"Usually there's just a forged signature, typically on a painting that's not been signed. But there have been cases where someone has actually cut off the original signature and faked another one."

"And these are being bought and sold?" asked Saeko incredulously.

"I see quite a lot of them I'm afraid. A signature is often the only thing that separates something worthless from something valuable. It's not just the Akita School either. Western-style paintings in general were mostly copies to begin with, so it can be hard to tell the best artists from the second-rate ones. In that sense they're easy to forge."

"I see. So even one of Shoei's paintings might be…"

"If it's been in the hands of a collector for a long time, that's a different matter. But if it's been in circulation for a while, there's a good chance someone's tampered with it."

Ryohei looked at Kato in disbelief.

"Was this Shoei a good artist?" asked the antiques dealer.

Ryohei nodded emphatically.

"It that case, the chances are pretty high. I doubt anyone would try to pass him off as Naotake… Yoshimi more likely."

Of all the stupid—! Even if Shoei was Sharaku we might never know!

"But…" Ryohei was about to say something to this effect, then stopped himself. He didn't want to raise the issue of Sharaku with Kato just yet. Instead he said, "What happens if you discover you've bought a forgery?"

"What happens? If it's a bad one there's not much one can do about it. But if it's good I let it go. In this business, your eyes are your livelihood—nobody wants to admit they've been duped."

"You mean you'd sell something knowing it's a forgery?" Saeko asked in an accusing tone.

"If I know for sure it's a forgery, I wouldn't sell it to a customer. But I'd put it up for sale at a dealers-only auction. It's like that card game Old Maid. You know—whoever gets stuck with the Queen loses. Only in this case, the dealer with the worst eye gets stuck with the forgery. After that, it's out of my hands."

"That's awful!" said Saeko, looking to Ryohei for confirmation.

"What goes around comes around," replied Kato. "It's happened to me several times. At first, you feel like cursing the bastard who sold it to you. But if you think of it as a learning experience it helps to ease the pain. That's how you develop your eye as an antiques dealer."

Kato's narrow lips broke into a smile.

"But since no one ever buys something *knowing* it's a fake," said Saeko, "it follows that sometimes a dealer might unknowingly pass a fake on to a customer, right?"

"Naturally," replied Kato.

"But doesn't that lead to problems?"

"Why should it? The dealer sold the piece believing it was genuine; he didn't intend to deceive his customer. He never would have sold it if he'd known it was a forgery. In this business, trust is everything. A dealer would never risk losing the trust of customers he had spent years cultivating just to turn a quick profit."

"I see," said Saeko. She sounded somewhat mollified.

"If a customer realizes later he's bought a fake, most dealers will agree to take it back and refund his money."

"Then what?" asked Ryohei curiously.

"Say nothing and sell it at auction. Once you admit it's a fake, no one will buy it. Works can travel around the country like that for years, passing from one dealer to another. Eventually it winds up in the hands of the least discerning dealer in Japan, and that's the end of it," said Kato with evident delight.

"What a racket!" exclaimed Saeko.

"That's the art world for you. Show me twenty pictures by Yokoyama Taikan, and I'll bet you nineteen of them are fakes. In this business if you don't know your stuff backwards and forwards you'll soon get taken to the cleaners. Oh, the stories I could tell… For example, I know this dealer who bought a hanging scroll by a big-name artist. If it'd been genuine, a scroll like that'd sell for three or four million yen. This guy got it for just seven hundred thousand. No one else was willing to touch it. He was sure it was the real thing though. He took it home and hung it in his shop, but none of his customers was interested. They didn't simply ignore it; even worse, they'd take a long hard look at it, then shake their heads and walk away. You see, the painting was *too* good. The artist in question is famous for haiga—the paintings made to accompany haiku—which people praise for their rough, carefree quality. But this painting was too clean and neat. No one came right out and *said* to the dealer's face it was a forgery, but they steered clear of it. He eventually gave up and put it up for sale at the next the dealers' auction, but he didn't find any takers. In the end, what do you suppose he did?"

Ryohei, Saeko and Kudo indicated they didn't have the faintest idea.

Kato laughed. "He cut off the signature!"

The three stared at him in disbelief.

"That's right—snipped it right off and had the scroll remounted. Then he took it to the big trade show in Tokyo. He bet the painting could stand on its own. Sure enough, he ended up getting a cool two million for it."

"You're kidding!" exclaimed Saeko.

"Wait—there's more," Kato continued. "Some years later, the dealer was talking to a man who collected the same artist's work. With great gusto, he related what had happened—leaving out the part about snipping off the signature, of course. The collector became very interested and asked him who'd bought the painting in the end. The dealer replied he didn't know since it'd sold at auction. He took out a photograph of the painting and showed it to the collector. The man took one look at it and gasped. It turned out it was genuine after all! Not only that, but it dated to the best period of the artist's career. If the dealer could track it down, the collector said, he'd give him eight million for it."

Ryohei, Saeko and Kudo involuntarily gasped in unison.

Kato summed up his story: "The dealer had taken a genuine masterpiece and turned it into what amounted to a fake. It'd be laughable if it weren't so tragic. No one will buy a painting if it's bad, but they won't buy it if it's too good either. What a way to make a living!" concluded Kato, smiling all the same.

"What you said just now about the dealer having a photograph of the painting," said Ryohei, "Was that by chance?"

"No, lots of us keep photos of what we sell—for our own reference, not as a memento, you understand. It's useful to have something you can carry around and show to customers, to get a sense of what they're after. Since Polaroids came along, more and more dealers are doing it."

"So a dealer who specializes in the Akita School might have photographs of every painting he's ever sold?"

"I expect so... Ah, I get it. You want to look for works by Shoei, is that it?"

Ryohei nodded.

"The only problem," Kato went on, "is that even if a dealer has photos, he might not be willing to show them to you. Dealers often jot down critical information on them, such as how much the work sold for."

"How complicated," sighed Ryohei.

"Unless you were a trusted customer or..." Kato paused for a moment, contemplating the downcast expression on Ryohei's face. "Okay," he said at last. "I'll see what I can find—seeing as I'll be making the rounds of the antiques shops in Kakunodate anyway. I'm also going to visit a major art dealer in Yokote. He might well have some Akita School paintings. I'll be back home in Morioka the day after tomorrow, so give me a ring then."

"Thank you very much." Ryohei gave Kato a deep bow.

"WHAT A STRANGE GUY," whispered Saeko to Ryohei as they waved goodbye to Kato.

"You thought so? Seems fairly normal to me."

"I couldn't decide if he's good or bad," said Saeko. "But I guess you have to be that way to make it in this business."

"Exactly. Even though he's the youngest antiques dealer in Morioka he's already made quite a name for himself. He's got a sharp eye."

"I bet he does. Imagine running your own business at his age."

"Is Kozukata Antiques that big shop near the park?" asked Kudo.

"That's the one. Kato's not originally from Morioka—Yamagata or someplace like that, I think. So it's not like he simply inherited his business from his father. He's pretty impressive. Until now we've never spoken much. I don't know whether it's just his reserved nature or whether he sized me up as not much of a business prospect. Anyway, he's usually a bit aloof."

"He seemed pretty friendly just now," observed Saeko. Kudo seconded this view.

"I think he's got the hots for you," said Ryohei, chuckling. "He's single, after all."

"A dandy like that? No way!" said Saeko. She made a disparaging remark about the thin red scarf Kato had been wearing around his neck. "It suited him," she said, "but I didn't like the way he acted as though he *knew* it suited him."

"I'll never understand women," said Ryohei, though he sounded strangely relieved. Then he said, "Anyway, we learned something really important."

"You mean that Shoei's paintings might have been altered to pass them off as someone else's?"

"Exactly. If that's the case then our search is hopeless. Shoei might have signed all his paintings 'the artist formerly known as Sharaku' and we'd never know because some dealer cut the signatures off."

"No one would do *that*, would they?"

"Well, let's hope not. But Shoei's lion painting is extremely good, plus it's a copy of a copperplate engraving. If a dealer took it into his head to forge Naotake's signature on it, no one would know the difference."

"But surely no one would cut off *Sharaku*'s signature."

"Remember, up until the late 1930s everyone believed Sharaku was Saito Jurobei, a Noh actor from Awa province. Think of the story Kato told us. The problem wasn't the painting, it was the signature. Someone from Awa couldn't have painted an Akita School painting, people would say. Look in any standard reference work from the time; they all say the same thing. Even *I* would have concluded Shoei's lion was a fake. No, unless Shoei's works have been kept in private hands all this time—instead of being put up for sale long ago—there's a good chance they've been altered."

"Hmm, I wonder."

"Look, we can assume that not long after Sato Masakichi died his collection was sold off. After all, there wouldn't have been much of a market for Akita School paintings in Shizuoka. No, however you look at it, things don't seem promising."

"But if we could find photographs of the unaltered works, that would constitute proof, wouldn't it?" asked Saeko.

"That's not what bothers me," replied Ryohei in a desultory tone. "It's the thought of Shoei's paintings floating around the country, all evidence linking them to Sharaku erased, but failing to

pass as authentic Shozans or Naotakes, or whatever forged signature they now bear. A moment ago I was hoping Kato might turn up some photographs we can identify as Shoei's paintings, but now I pray he doesn't. It would be too depressing." Ryohei paused for a moment. "Plus," he continued, "while I was talking to Kato I remembered something else: there's evidence to suggest Sharaku painted with oils."

"You're kidding!"

"A long time ago, a scholar named Inoue Kazuo published a book citing an alternate text of *Ukiyo-e Ruiko* that apparently states, under the entry on Sharaku, 'Also an accomplished oil painter; used the sobriquet 'Yurin.'"

"*Apparently* states?" queried Saeko.

"I haven't actually seen this alternate text myself. Recent scholars have dismissed Inoue's theory. Today, it's pretty much ignored.

"Do you mean we have to add another name to the list of Sharaku suspects?"

"The trouble is Inoue wrote his book before the war when it was believed Sharaku and the Noh actor Saito Jurobei were one and the same. So what Inoue actually says in his book is Saito Jurobei was an oil painter. Later, when the Saito Jurobei hypothesis collapsed, it took Inoue's theory down with it. The modern print edition of *Ukiyo-e Ruiko*, published by Iwanami Bunko, contains no reference to Sharaku's oil paintings or, for that matter, to the existence of an alternate text. That's not surprising. It appears the editor—one Nakata Katsunosuke—never believed what was written in Inoue's alternate text. These days, no art historian does. It's simply been written off as impossible."

"But if Shoei was Sharaku, then Inoue's theory…"

"Might be correct. Exactly. I should have thought of it sooner. But neither the professor nor Yosuke brought it up. It goes to show how ignored Inoue's theory is these days. *Ukiyo-e Ruiko* is so closely associated with the Saito Jurobei hypothesis, it hadn't occurred to me to use it to establish Shoei's connection to Sharaku. It's quite possible whoever added the information about oil painting to the entry on Sharaku in Inoue's version of *Ukiyo-e Ruiko* did so after seeing a painting by Shoei made

after he'd returned to Akita but *before* he changed his name to Chikamatsu—in other words, when he was still using the name Sharaku. Inoue must have read it and concluded Saito Jurobei had made oil paintings. You can't blame him. At that time, Sharaku and Saito Jurobei were synonymous. If Sharaku painted oils, that meant Jurobei painted oils."

Saeko looked puzzled.

"You see, this has nothing to do with the Saito Jurobei hypothesis. The entry doesn't say, 'Saito Jurobei painted oils.' All it says is, 'Sharaku painted oils.' Inoue went and conflated the two."

"In other words, Sharaku was an accomplished oil painter—is that it?"

"Yes, but it meant about Shoei!" said Ryohei, his voice rising in excitement.

"What made you think of it only now?"

"I was musing about Shoei's paintings floating around the country as forged Shozans or Naotakes. That got me wondering: what would have happened to them before Western-style painting became popular with collectors? From the early Meiji period until World War Two, Sharaku's signature on a Western-style painting would have actually *hurt* its value. But before the 1870s, there was no market for Western-style paintings of any kind, period. It wouldn't have been worth altering one of Sharaku's works unless there was lots of money to be made, would it? So perhaps there were paintings in circulation at that time with his name on them. Of course, they wouldn't have fetched much money. That's when I suddenly remembered Inoue's book."

"I see."

"Then it hit me: if the Saito Jurobei hypothesis hadn't gone unquestioned for so long, the mystery of Sharaku's identity would probably have been solved long ago. Even Kurth, in rehabilitating Sharaku, took *Ukiyo-e Ruiko* at face value. It would have been next to impossible for anyone to contradict the Jurobei Hypothesis. Come to think of it, that may be why Kiyochika never wrote anything about Sharaku after Sato's catalogue was published. Yosuke speculated it was because he hadn't noticed the signature on Shoei's painting, but I think even if he had he would have dismissed it as absurd. That was a time when people talked about Saito Jurobei being Sharaku as though it were a historical fact."

"A slip-up in the initial stage of the investigation…"

"Exactly. One that's led to forty years of wasted effort. In the meantime, Sharaku's paintings have been tampered with and scattered across the country," said Ryohei, biting his lip in frustration.

"I understand how you feel," said Saeko, "but we don't know for sure that's what happened. There's still a chance they've survived intact."

"I hope so. But I think it's more likely the signatures have been altered, as Kato says. Shoei was a great painter, but from a purely commercial standpoint, he's just not famous enough."

"And Sharaku's signature is even more of a liability. What a bizarre situation," murmured Saeko.

"In the antiques business it's not what's real that matters, it's whether you can convince people it's real."

"And people will never be convinced Sharaku painted oils."

"This is giving me a headache," groaned Ryohei. "At this rate, I think we'll have to write off Kakunodate too. Maybe we better just stick to sightseeing," he said with uncharacteristic sarcasm.

"But, Ryohei, it was nothing short of a miracle you found that signature in Sato's catalogue. I don't think anyone else would have noticed it. You must be channeling Sharaku or something," said Saeko, smiling at him.

"I'm starting to wish someone else had noticed it," replied Ryohei managing to return her smile.

OUTSIDE THE HOTEL, Ryohei and Saeko said goodbye to Kudo, who was going to take advantage of the long holiday weekend to make a long overdue trip to Morioka to visit his parents. Then the two headed straight for the local folklore museum.

Kakunodate's folklore museum was located on an old street lined with former samurai mansions. It was only a short walk from their hotel. The historic center of the town was divided into two parts: Uchimachi, where the samurai once lived, and Sotomachi, which was the merchants' quarter. Their hotel stood on the border between the two, facing an open space known as "Firebreak Square" because that was where, in Edo times, there had been an area of land left vacant to prevent fires from spreading from one side of town to the other.

Across the square, a wide straight avenue stretched away from their hotel. It was lined on both sides with Edo-period samurai mansions shielded by high black wooden fences. From behind these fences, the long willowy branches of hundreds of large weeping cherry trees hung down over the street, their branches shimmering as they swayed in the autumn breeze. The Japanese government had designated them a national monument. There was not a soul anywhere to be seen.

"What a beautiful, quiet place!" Saeko exclaimed as she strolled along, gazing up at the enormous trees.

"Try coming here in the springtime. This street will be chockablock with tourists."

"Cherry-blossom viewing?"

"Yes, it's incredible. Like a tunnel of pink-and-white blossoms."

Saeko nodded.

Dubbed the "Little Kyoto of the North," Kakunodate is now a popular tourist destination, but until a few years ago it was little more than a sleepy rural town. Then in 1976, NHK chose it as the setting for its latest serialized television novel, *Carpet of Clouds*. Tourists began arriving in droves. Such fads usually fizzle out after two or three years, but Kakunodate proved to have considerable staying power. Though there was little to recommend the town apart from its old samurai houses, it succeeded in marketing that period charm for all it was worth. The town council put great effort into preserving not only the old houses themselves but also their natural surroundings. New buildings had to be designed so as not to clash with the town's carefully cultivated image.

Unlike Morioka—another, much larger, old castle town—where one occasionally runs across a historic building buried amidst urban sprawl, modern Kakunodate has grown up around its well-preserved old quarter. Everyone who visits goes away vowing to return. It is one of the rare Japanese cities that has that effect on people.

The folklore museum though of recent construction, had been designed to blend harmoniously with the samurai houses surrounding it. With attractive features such as a traditional hip-and-gable roof on the main building and an adjoining earthen-walled storehouse housing a small archive, the museum had a relaxed sort of beauty. Inside one could see exhibits and watch demonstrations of the local craft of fashioning wooden containers out of cherry bark, known as *kaba-zaiku*. But while it had plenty to offer the casual tourist, unfortunately, the museum was less of interest to the historian. Despite Kakunodate's being the birthplace of the Akita School, the museum had virtually nothing related to Western-style painting.

Having visited the folklore museum several times before, Ryohei knew all this. He had already decided that, for research purposes, it was not worth another visit. But as soon as they reached Kakunodate he changed his mind. Inside the museum there was a large souvenir shop. Ryohei realized he had been keeping Saeko's nose pressed to the grindstone, preventing her from indulging her taste for such pleasures. His instinct was confirmed as he watched Saeko happily browsing the merchandise on offer. Soon she had selected a number of kaba-zaiku pendants and key chains, presumably as gifts for her friends and colleagues.

Telling Saeko he would meet her in half an hour in the café on the second floor, Ryohei made his way to the staff office. As long as he was in Kakunodate he thought he might as well try to see where Odano Naotake was buried. Opening the door, he found a clerk in his forties seated alone at a desk, hard at work. In a few words, Ryohei stated his business, whereupon the man politely took out a map and explained what Ryohei wanted to know.

"On the way here I passed a house with a plaque by the entrance that said, 'Odano residence.' Is that where Naotake was born, by any chance?" Ryohei asked.

"No, that house belonged to one of his relatives," the man replied.

"So where would I find Naotake's birthplace?"

"The house where he was born was not located on the main street. It doesn't exist any longer, I'm afraid."

Ryohei nodded.

"But if you're interested in Akita School painters, have you been to the municipal art museum?"

Ryohei shook his head.

"Right now it's got something else showing, but in the past there have been a number of exhibits on the Akita School. Just a moment…" Turning, the man pulled a catalogue off the bookcase behind him and handed it to Ryohei.

According to the cover, the catalogue was published in 1980 to mark the fifth anniversary of the opening of the Kakunodate Museum of Art. Flipping through it, Ryohei saw it contained many deluxe color plates, among which he recognized several works by Naotake. Towards the back of the catalogue there was a list of all the exhibits held at the museum during those five years, including the titles of all the works exhibited. It even went so far as to provide the date and dimensions of each painting and a brief profile of the artist. Three of the exhibits had been on Western-style painting.

"What a beautiful catalogue," said Ryohei. He really meant it.

Ryohei was sitting in the café perusing the catalogue. The clerk had let him borrow it, saying he could return it on his way out.

"Have you been waiting long?"

Holding a shopping bag in her hand, Saeko sat down across from him.

"I don't mind waiting if you want to do some more shopping," replied Ryohei.

"I think I've got everything I need," Saeko said, smiling as she tapped the side of the paper bag. "What're you looking at?"

"This—" Ryohei said, handing her the catalogue. "I borrowed it from the office downstairs. It's a catalogue from the local art museum. They've done several exhibits on the Akita School."

"You're right. Here's a painting by Naotake," said Saeko, looking through the catalogue.

"I thought we might head over and have a look."

"Do they have an exhibit right now?"

"Not at the moment. But the clerk downstairs says he'll introduce me to one of the curators there. I thought he might know something."

The waitress came over to take Saeko's order. She pondered for a moment and then asked for tea with lemon.

"Kakunodate really takes its culture pretty seriously, doesn't it?" remarked Saeko. "Not many towns of this size have their own art museum. And I have to say, I'm very taken with this folklore museum. I'm seeing Kakunodate in a whole new light."

"Hey, did you read this?" asked Saeko, looking up from the catalogue. "This part about Satake Yoshimi…"

"No. What does it say?"

"It says he was a protégé of Tani Sogai."

"What! Yoshimi? Really?" Ryohei hurriedly scanned the page Saeko was pointing to with her finger. It was part of the section at the back that provided profiles of the various artists in the catalogue.

Satake Yoshimi—1749–1800. Head of the northern branch of the Satake clan and thirteenth lord of Kakunodate Castle. Born Yoshihiro. Sobriquets: Koshosanjin, Sessho, Ikkentei. Studied painting from Naotake. Protégé of Sogai. Also known as a poet of linked verse in the Edo Danrin style.

"Could it be a coincidence?"

"Well, Sogai *did* count many daimyo among his students, so it wouldn't be all that surprising. But both Shoei and Naotake started out as vassals of Yoshimi, so it would be a bit strange if Yoshimi turned out to be a protégé of Sogai's."

"You mean because of that fan painting?"

"Uh-huh. It means we can link Shoei to that as well. We still don't know exactly what the painting means, but the old man pictured in it might well be Sogai. This is evidence that Shoei must have known Sogai. By the way, I didn't mention this before, but there's another interesting theory about who that old man might be."

"You mean besides Tsutaya or Toyokuni?"

"Yes… Shiba Kokan!"

"Really?"

"It bears a close resemblance to Kokan's self-portrait. The age is not quite right, but there's anecdotal evidence Kokan shaved his head to make himself appear older than he really was."

"Hmm. Sogai or Kokan? Both of them—"

"Were connected to Shoei," Ryohei said slowly, finishing her sentence.

LEAVING THE TOWN behind, Ryohei and Saeko's taxi sped over a large bridge and emerged into the suburbs of Kakunodate. After they had gone some distance, a large building appeared ahead of them.

"That's the art museum. It used to be a bowling alley," the driver explained with a smile. The taxi pulled up and stopped in front of a large entranceway.

"Wow—this place is enormous!" Saeko exclaimed once they were inside.

The museum was indeed enormous. It seemed all the more so for, having once been a bowling alley, there was not a single pillar anywhere to be seen. It was well-lit and had an immaculate look to it.

"Ah, yes. We were told to expect you." When Ryohei presented himself at the information desk, the receptionist immediately recognized his name and ushered him and Saeko through a door to a small waiting room. Within a few minutes a man appeared. He was about thirty and smartly dressed in a suit and tie. A number of veins stood out on his forehead, giving him an intense look, but he proved quite affable. He bowed politely and presented his card to Ryohei. The name "Konno" was printed on it.

"So I hear you're doing research on the Akita School?"

Ryohei nodded and asked if he could see some paintings.

"We have photographs of every work that's been exhibited here at the museum. I'll go get them," Konno said as he left the room. When he returned, his arms were full of almost more photo albums than he could carry.

Ryohei and Saeko began going through the albums one by one looking for Akita School paintings. They found forty or fifty, but none signed by Shoei. Nor did they see a single one that looked like it might be a painting of his that had been altered.

Ryohei was disappointed but also somewhat relieved.

"Shoei? Can't say I've ever heard of him." Konno, who had been listening to their conversation, had a dubious look on his face.

Ryohei explained.

"You say he's listed in *Painters and Calligraphers of Akita*?" Konno left the room and returned shortly carrying the book in question.

"Ah, here he is. But it doesn't say anything about him being part of the Akita School."

Ryohei told Konno about finding Sato's catalogue. Of course, he left out the part about Sharaku.

"He painted *that* many works, did he? Living in Kakunodate, I really should have heard of him before," said Konno with a self-deprecating smile.

Ryohei questioned Konno about the profile of Yoshimi printed in the museum catalogue.

"Yes, I wrote that. Most of the information about Akita-related painters in the catalogue comes from this book," he replied, indicating *Painters and Calligraphers of Akita*. "It contains all the major cultural figures of the time. It's been tremendously useful to me."

"Besides Yoshimi, were there other apprentices of Sogai here in Akita?" Ryohei asked.

"Oh, yes, many. During Lord Shozan and Lord Yoshimi's time—the 1770s and '80s—the arts flourished throughout Akita. People were into everything; not just Western-style painting but also comic *kyoka* poetry, haiku, linked verse... you name it. But Shozan and Yoshimi don't deserve all the credit. The Akita clan was struggling to get back on its feet financially in the 1790s, and the chamberlains in charge of running the clan's Edo estate—men like Sato Bantoku and Tegara Okamochi—were great connoisseurs. That rubbed off on Shozan and Yoshimi."

"Tegara Okamochi—as in Hoseido Kisanji, the writer?"

"Yes. That was his penname."

This piece of information surprised Ryohei. Kisanji had been one of the brains behind Tsutaya's success. Tsutaya had published several of his books.

"Bantoku isn't as famous as Okamochi," continued Konno, "but he was a real *bon vivant*—so much so it was said under his administration much of the clan's business was conducted in the Yoshiwara, the red-light district in Edo. He also wrote fiction and composed poetry. He even taught Sakai Hoitsu how to write haiku and was best friends with Tani Sogai. In terms of the scale of his activities, Okamochi didn't even come close."

Ryohei was speechless.

In modern terms, a clan chamberlain was akin to a foreign minister or secretary of state. In feudal times, every fief ran its own independent economy, and the chamberlain in Edo was responsible for representing the daimyo in business dealings with the central government and the private sector. Shozan was daimyo of Akita during the administration of Tanuma Okitsugu, which was infamous for its corrupt practices. Every ten years or so, the shogun undertook a major renovation of Edo Castle. The work—performing maintenance and repairs to the castle, rebuilding bridges, and so on—was divided up among the various clans. It was possible for a skillful chamberlain to negotiate an assignment that did not place a heavy financial burden on the clan. In this sense, having a chamberlain such as Bantoku or Okamochi, who knew how to game the system, was essential to the clan's long-term survival.

Of course, the Akita clan! Now why didn't I…

So caught up had Ryohei been in his pursuit of Akita School painters that he had failed to consider the context of the times. Ryohei felt like kicking himself for his obtuseness. At the same time he couldn't suppress a feeling of astonishment at the huge cultural influence the Akita clan had exerted in the late eighteenth-century.

"This links Shoei to both Tsutaya and Hoitsu!" said Saeko, flabbergasted.

Ryohei tried to remain calm as he asked Konno where he had come across this information.

"It's all here in this book," said Konno, opening *Painters and Calligraphers of Akita* and showing Ryohei the entries on Bantoku and Okamochi.

"Where can I buy a copy?" asked Ryohei. He wanted to read it cover to cover.

"Any local bookstore will have it," Konno replied matter-of-factly.

RYOHEI AND SAEKO caught a taxi back to town.

It was already past three. They would need to hurry if they wanted to see Naotake's grave. Their taxi passed in front of their hotel, sped through Sotomachi—the old merchant quarter—and turned left in the direction of Kakunodate Station. Then it came to a halt. Without saying a word, the driver pushed a switch, opening the automatic rear door. The two got out. Right in front of them, they saw the gate of an old temple. On it, a sign read, "Shoan Temple." It was smaller than Ryohei had imagined.

Immediately to their right as they passed through the gate stood a six-and-a-half-foot high stone slab in the shape of a leaf. On it, in thick bold characters, was carved, "In Memory of Odano Naotake."

Ryohei took a picture of the front of the monument and then walked around behind it. On the back was another inscription carved in smaller, more closely spaced characters. Ryohei raised his camera and pressed the shutter button several times, trying his best to avoid the glare of the winter sun, which shone in his direction.

"'Born the eldest son of Odano Naokatsu in Kakunodate on December 11, 1749, Naotake had a prodigious talent for painting...'" read Saeko. "It says this monument was erected in 1936."

"That recently, huh?"

"Hey, according to Kato, wasn't that around the time Akita School painting became very popular with collectors?"

Ryohei nodded.

Turning away from the monument, the two stood facing the main hall of the temple and bowed. Then they made their way around behind the temple to the place where Naotake's grave was located.

They came to a small cemetery. Here, in an area of about a tenth of an acre, closed in by houses on either side, several hundred tombstones stood in neat rows. Though they had thought Naotake's grave would be easy to find, they looked for some time without success.

"Perhaps it would be faster if we asked someone," suggested Saeko to Ryohei, who was some way off, as she walked around peering at the tombstones.

"Yeah. Let's do that," replied Ryohei, giving up and turning back towards the main hall.

Just then, Saeko called out, "Wait—I think I found it."

Naotake's tombstone stood practically hidden behind another grave.

It was small—only about four inches thick and sixteen inches high. The lower half had turned black, suggesting it had been partially buried in the ground for a long time, and there was a long crack running diagonally through it where it seemed to have broken in two at some point and the pieces been joined back together using cement. It was a sorry sight. The two stared silently at it for some time. If it had not been for a small signpost next to it that read "Naotake's Tomb," no one would have imagined that beneath it lay the illustrator of Sugita Genpaku's *New Anatomy*.

"It looks like a child's grave," Saeko said sadly as she compared it to those around it.

"It's almost like it's been tucked away behind this other one so no one will find it," said Ryohei. "There's hardly even any room to leave flowers."

"Wait a sec. I'll go buy some." Saeko turned on her heel and dashed off in the direction of the main hall.

As Ryohei stood in front of Naotake's tomb, eyes closed and palms pressed together in prayer, the sound of Saeko's shoes clicking over the cobblestone pathway receded into the distance.

Zetsugaku Genshin—"*Seeker after Supreme Learning and the Source of Truth*."

Naotake's posthumous Buddhist name popped into Ryohei's head. It felt as though a force beyond the grave was rejecting his prayers.

It's not just me. He refuses everyone…

As the sky clouded over, Ryohei felt a melancholy mood descend on him.

THE LIGHTS of Kakunodate glimmered silently outside the restaurant window.

It didn't even take twenty minutes to cross from one side to the other of the old town, which straggled along the main thoroughfare.

How many times had they crossed it that day? After leaving the temple, Ryohei—wanting to walk the same streets Shoei had walked and see the same places Naotake had seen—had spent two hours with Saeko traipsing up and down back streets, from one side of the main thoroughfare to the other.

Though physically exhausted, Ryohei was satisfied he had now become one with Shoei and Naotake. There was no doubt in his mind that if Shoei had arrived in Kakunodate, Naotake would have welcomed him into his home with open arms. It was the sort of friendly, laidback small town that naturally fostered such free and easy connections between human beings.

"What are you thinking?" asked Saeko, following the direction of his gaze.

"Just that I'm glad we came…"

At that moment, the bottle of wine they had ordered arrived at their table.

"Let's make a toast," said Ryohei, filling Saeko's glass. "To our trip—it wouldn't have been the same without you." He really meant it. "You must be dead tired—we walked for hours today."

"A little bit… But it was fun, so I don't mind." Saeko smiled as she raised her glass. "Now getting back to what you were saying earlier," she continued, visibly more relaxed.

"About the Akita clan?"

"Yeah. I think you touched on some really important points."

As they explored the town on foot, Ryohei had been talking passionately about the profound impact the Akita clan had had on Edo culture.

"I don't know where Tsutaya got the idea of using Shoei to create Sharaku's prints," said Saeko, "but it seems pretty certain the publisher knew him."

"Providing Okamochi—Kisanji, that is—and Shoei were close friends, which is likely, since they both lived at the Akita clan's Edo residence. Kisanji was also friends with Ota Nampo. Like Kisanji, Nampo was one of the brains behind Tsutaya's success. Anyway, I think if we look hard enough we'll find a connection."

"Hasn't anyone else noted the connection between the Akita clan and Tsutaya?"

"No. But who could have imagined that a place like Akita way up in the sticks could have exerted such an influence on cultural life in the capital Edo? On the other hand, Tsutaya published several books by Kisanji, so it wouldn't have been all that surprising if someone had put two and two together by now. That said, Kisanji was actually from Edo; although his wife's family—which had adopted him because they had no male heir of their own—came from Akita. Other scholars might have assumed his connection to Akita was irrelevant."

"How curious."

"Just now, back in my room, I was trying to piece together what we know…"

"What is it? Not another diagram…"

With an apologetic smile, Ryohei reached into his pocket and took out a piece of paper folded into quarters. He opened it up and spread it out on the table.

"This shows the connections between the Akita clan and various other important figures."

"This one is a lot more complex," observed Saeko, looking at the diagram in surprise.

Tanuma
Yoshimi—Shozan—Gennai—Naotake
Sogai—Bantoku—Kisanji—Nampo—Kokan
Shigemasa—Hoitsu—Buncho—Shoei
Kyoden—Tsutaya

"In addition, the Akita clan had an official painter in Edo named Sugawara Dosai, who was married to Tani Buncho's younger sister. The two had a son who married one of Buncho's daughters."

"You found that in *Painters and Calligraphers of Akita*?" asked Saeko, staring at Ryohei incredulously.

"Hard to believe, isn't it?" laughed Ryohei. "But the diagram is still not complete. I think further research will turn up more connections. Edo might have been a small world, but even so, this seems unusual. I'm starting to get the feeling Shozan was the biggest patron of the day. He was a far cry from your average daimyo who dabbled in the arts."

Saeko said nothing.

Ryohei continued: "This is just a hunch, but I think Sharaku might have been Tanuma's love child, in a manner of speaking."

"Love child? How so?"

"Tanuma's rise and fall seems to have had a profound impact on the fortunes of Tsutaya and the Akita clan. If Tanuma's administration had lasted longer, we might never have had Sharaku. The fall of Tanuma's regime laid the groundwork for Sharaku's appearance."

"You've discovered something, haven't you?" said Saeko, who had gotten good at reading between the lines of Ryohei's speech. She beamed at him.

"It's just a suggestion. I'll have to do some careful research once I get back to Tokyo. But I *can* say this much: Shozan fell ill and died right around the time Tanuma fell from power. He was only thirty-eight. I'm beginning to think he might have been murdered for political reasons."

"By who?"

"His chief vassals. They saw Shozan had become too close to Tanuma, and after he fell they were afraid he'd bring the clan down with them, so getting rid of Shozan was the only solution. Just as they were quick to discard Naotake earlier over the Gennai affair."

"But wait a minute. This is different; Shozan was the daimyo," Saeko said, looking at Ryohei in disbelief.

"In 1784, the whole house of cards started to collapse on the all-powerful Tanuma's head. His son, Okitomo, was cut down in Edo castle itself. It was an extreme act of protest against Tanuma's administration. It's said the murderer, a shogunal vassal, or *hatamoto*, by the name of Sano Zenzaemon, was widely hailed as the 'Great Reformer.' The incident made it abundantly clear to everyone Tanuma's days were numbered. Shozan died in June the following year. Then, in 1786, just as everyone had expected, Tanuma resigned from the shogun's senior council on the pretext of ill health, undoubtedly having come to the realization his power was dwindling. Tanuma was replaced as Chief Senior Councilor by Matsudaira Sadanobu, who proceeded to purge the government of

Tanuma's supporters. Akita clan officials only escaped getting the axe because Shozan *just happened* to have died the previous year. It's the timing of Shozan's death that's so suspicious; it was just a little *too* convenient."

Saeko was listening attentively.

"Meanwhile, there are hints Tsutaya benefitted substantially from his ties to the Akita clan."

"So you were right."

"Yes. Tsutaya went into publishing in a big way after getting to know Kisanji in 1776. His business grew rapidly over the next ten years; by 1789 it was the largest publishing house in Edo. Now—this is the critical part—of the hundred or so titles Tsutaya published between 1776 and 1786, about seventy percent were either books of popular fiction written by Kisanji or collections of comic verse. Now, none of those poetry books are directly attributed to Kisanji, but we know Tsutaya gained entrée to Edo poetry circles through Kisanji. In other words, after meeting Kisanji, Tsutaya's business suddenly took off. It's even possible that Kisanji was funneling money to Tsutaya's business on behalf of the Akita clan."

"Why do you say that?"

"Tsutaya was undoubtedly a brilliant businessman, but publishing requires huge sums of capital. Sound business sense only gets you so far. To have grown so big, so fast, Tsutaya must have had a patron. Now, I haven't come across any evidence for this theory just yet, but when you consider the timing, it doesn't seem farfetched to suppose the Akita clan recognized Tsutaya's ability and decided to back him. In those days, it wasn't unusual for a clan to run its own publishing house. Tsutaya had a little bookshop just outside the Yoshiwara, and he must have seen Bantoku and Kisanji coming and going on a daily basis. Tsutaya probably latched onto them as his ticket to success."

"Tsutaya's shop was near the Yoshiwara, was it?"

"Uh-huh. He started out selling guidebooks beside the main gate."

"What kind of guidebooks?"

"To the brothels. They ranked them by class and gave the names of the prostitutes, where they were from, how much they cost... just about anything a customer might want to know."

"Is that so? I never knew such things existed."

"They were called *saiken*. Apparently it was quite profitable but the bottom of the barrel as far as publishing went. If Tsutaya had wanted to branch out into other genres, he would have had to join a different publishers' guild, and that was very expensive. In 1776, he at last managed to join the prestigious Kabuki Script Publishers' Guild. That gave him the foothold he needed to grow his business."

"1776? Wasn't that—"

"The year he met Kisanji? Correct."

Saeko appeared convinced. "I don't think there's any doubt," she said. "The Akita clan must have been backing Tsutaya financially."

"So you agree?"

"Like you said, from the point of view of the big publishing houses, Tsutaya was just some two-bit publisher of whorehouse guidebooks; not a respectable line of work, no matter how profitable it was. It would have taken more than money to turn his little shop into a publishing empire. I don't think he could have done it without some influential backer."

"Right," said Ryohei. "The Akita clan's patronage would have meant money *and* prestige."

Saeko nodded vigorously.

Ryohei went on: "If Tanuma had held onto power, the Akita clan's position would have remained secure and Tsutaya's business would have continued to thrive. But when Tanuma resigned in 1786, things became difficult for Tsutaya. Fortunately, the solid foundation he had built over the previous decade got him through the next few years. But then he was slapped with his first fine."

"His *first*?"

"Kyoden's arrest in 1791 was the fourth time Tsutaya had a run in with the authorities. The first was for something Kisanji wrote."

"Really? Kisanji too?"

"In 1788, he wrote a book called *Sifting Through the Arts of War and Peace* which poked fun at Matsudaira Sadanobu's Kansei Reforms. The upshot was Kisanji was banned from writing fiction."

"That's harsh."

"And in 1789, two more books Tsutaya published were banned, both of them political satires."

"Then in 1791, Kyoden cost Tsutaya half his fortune, right?" said Saeko. "Following on the heels of the freewheeling Tanuma years, when his business took off, I can imagine Matsudaira's draconian reforms weren't much fun for Tsutaya. But I guess both Tsutaya and the government went a bit too far."

"Yeah. By that time, Tsutaya was getting slapped with fines almost every year. But Kyoden hadn't even criticized the government. You have to feel kind of sorry for Tsutaya—Matsudaira seems to have been punishing him for his ties to Tanuma, finding fault anywhere he could just to run him out of business. That would explain why Tsutaya was singled out for punishment while other publishers were left alone."

"He must have felt he'd get into hot water no matter what he did."

"In 1788, Tsutaya's output took a nose dive. He managed to keep things afloat by rereleasing some old favorites, but the number of new titles he brought out fell by more than half of what it had been. It wasn't until 1793 that he got back on his feet again—the same year Sadanobu fell from grace. The following year Sharaku made his appearance... When you look at it this way, it can't have been a coincidence Sharaku came along when he did. You might even say Sharaku was a kind of victory dance by Tsutaya and Tanuma's other supporters who had suffered under the Kansei Reforms. Tsutaya couldn't have done it all on his own. He must have had help from many quarters—from Kisanji and Kyoden, for one, whose works were banned by the government; from Kokan, for another, who ran afoul of Sadanobu; and, finally, from the late Shozan's vassals."

"But why?"

"Pride, plain and simple. Tsutaya's comeback essentially undid much of what the Kansei Reforms had tried to accomplish. Sharaku was their way of thumbing their nose at Sadanobu for everything he'd done to them."

"But what was the point? Sadanobu had already left office by that time."

"Sadanobu's resignation was different from Tanuma's. He was still a daimyo. Plus, even though he retired from the shogun's senior council, most of those who took over after he left were his cronies. He merely resigned his leadership role in the face of mounting criticism over the government's draconian policies. His influence over politics remained undiminished."

"In that case, weren't they taking a big risk?"

"Like I said, it comes down to pride. It was the only way left for the Tanuma crowd to flex their muscles."

"But why did they chose Sharaku? Why not come out and criticize Matsudaira openly?"

"If they had attacked Matsudaira head on they'd have been crushed. No, they needed to make Tsutaya a force to be reckoned with again without running afoul of the law. The others probably provided the money and the manpower and left the rest to Tsutaya. Thus Sharaku was born. The idea was to take a complete nobody, lavish money on him, and turn him into the most celebrated artist in all of Edo. If Tsutaya pulled it off, his fame would be unrivalled— that would show Sadanobu! But the plan would only work if he used someone who wasn't already famous. Tsutaya had to prove his influence alone had made Sharaku what he was."

Ryohei paused to catch his breath.

"I see," said Saeko. "So that's why it had to be an unknown artist." She seemed deep in thought.

"Anyone could have sold Utamaro's work. Tsutaya could hardly have claimed that a personal success. He needed an artist no other publisher would have touched with a ten-foot pole. In that sense, Shoei was perfect: he was knocking around at Kokan's house, still bitter over the way his master had been bumped off (incidentally, there must be some story behind why he left the clan after Shozan's death—perhaps he was drummed out because he'd belonged to Shozan's clique); he wasn't an ukiyo-e-style painter, but as one can clearly see from Sato's catalogue, he had tremendous talent; and he was unknown as a woodblock printmaker. Given all this it's not surprising Tsutaya chose him."

"But Tsutaya had to keep Sharaku's identity a secret—"

"Or Sadanobu would have known the Tanuma crowd was behind it!" said Ryohei, finishing Saeko's sentence.

The two laughed and congratulated themselves with a handshake.

"All the pieces of the puzzle are in place, aren't they?" said Saeko. "We know what Tsutaya's connection was to Shoei and why he kept Sharaku's identity a secret; we have proof he painted; we know the reason he suddenly abandoned Edo in 1795 and returned to Odate, and… let's see… Oh, how about his name? Why 'Toshusai Sharaku'?"

"We know that too."

"Huh? We do?"

"*Toshu* is obvious, right? 'The Lands of the East'—or as we would say today, Tohoku. In Genpaku's *New Anatomy* Naotake signs himself 'Odano Naotake of Akita in the East.' In other words, *Toshu* refers to Akita. As for *Sharaku*, the standard reading of that is 'one who likes to sketch'—sketching from life was the basic tenet of the Akita School."

"One from Tohoku who likes to sketch…"

Saeko repeated the words quietly to herself.

After saying goodnight to Saeko, Ryohei returned to his room and opened a can of beer. He wasn't in the habit of having a nightcap, but for some reason he felt like drinking tonight.

What should he say to Yosuke and Professor Nishijima when he returned to Tokyo? As he pondered this, Ryohei's cheeks began to feel flushed. He sat down in a chair by the window and opened it a crack. A gust of cold air blew into the room.

I've solved the mystery everyone thought was unsolvable. I know who Sharaku was…

Slowly, without his even being aware of it, a smile rose to Ryohei's face.

As he gazed out into the darkness, the town of Kakunodate, where Sharaku once lived, quietly settled down for the night.

6
Farewell

November 4
AS THEIR RESEARCH was at an end, Saeko headed back to Sendai.

Ryohei remained behind in Morioka after seeing her off at the train station. Now he made his way to Kato's antique shop near Iwate Park. He had already made up his mind about Sharaku's true identity, but he had promised to call on the art dealer before returning to Tokyo and he did not want to go back on his word. As he sauntered through the streets, Ryohei's mind was already back in Tokyo.

"Ah, I wasn't expecting you so early."

Kato looked up with a smile as Ryohei entered the shop. Though it was almost noon, it seemed Kato had just opened up for the day and he still looked sleepy.

"Had a bit too much to drink last night," he explained, filling a teapot with hot water. "It was already late when I returned to Morioka and then I had to go straight out, so by the time I got back here to the shop it was three in the morning... Before I forget, I've got something to show you." Placing a steaming cup of tea in front of Ryohei, Kato disappeared into a room at the back of the shop.

It was a relatively large shop—a good 350 square feet. In the middle was a row of five neatly aligned display cases stuffed with all manner of old pots and swords. The surrounding walls were hung with many scrolls and ukiyo-e prints, so there was hardly space in between.

"I found a lot of Western-style paintings in Akita," said Kato, returning with a thick stack of photocopies and taking a seat across from Ryohei. "Most of these are from a dealer in Yokote."

Flipping through the pages Kato handed him, Ryohei was astonished. Each sheet had five or six paintings on it, all were part of some sort of album, over thirty pages in all. Ryohei recognized a number of the paintings by Naotake from various books he had seen.

"All of these paintings passed through the dealer's hands?" he asked.

"So it seems," replied Kato. "He said this is everything he's sold from before the war right up to the present, he deals a lot with museums."

"I'm surprised he was willing to show you all this."

"Well, he's a good friend of mine," Kato said. "Of course, I didn't actually make the copies myself. A girl in the shop did it for me. You'll notice the prices and such have been removed."

Beneath many of the pictures were thick black lines made by a magic marker. Presumably that was what Kato was referring to.

"I'm afraid I've put you to a lot of trouble," Ryohei said apologetically.

"Don't mention it. The owner loves me—when I told him I was interested in learning something about the Akita School, he was very eager to help," Kato replied nonchalantly.

"Ah-ha!" exclaimed Ryohei, his eyes growing wide.

"What is it? Did you find something?"

"Yes. There are two paintings on this page right next to each other that look a lot like Shoei's work."

"Look like?"

"The signature reads, 'Tashiro Unmu.'" Ryohei reached into his bag and pulled out his copy of Sato's painting catalogue, which he opened and placed alongside Kato's album.

"Ah, this is the one."

Ryohei removed a page from each set of photocopies and handed them to Kato.

"Hmm, they *are* similar," mumbled Kato as he glanced back and forth, comparing the two photocopies. "If you cut off the part with Shoei's signature it's an exact match—see, this is the same."

"What is it?"

"Do you see this little bird perched on the branch of this pine tree right above Shoei's signature?"

"Yes…"

"Look at this other painting. There's something protruding up here in the corner, right at the edge— the tip of the bird's tail."

There certainly *was* something protruding into the painting at the top left-hand edge, where the painting was cut off.

"No one would paint a painting like this. It's obviously been tampered with—Shoei's signature has been removed," declared Kato.

Ryohei was dumbfounded. "When do you suppose this painting came on the market?" he asked once he had collected himself.

"Let's see. I suppose I could call up the dealer and find out." Kato reached for the telephone and began dialing a number. "Well, well… if it isn't just as I predicted," he said with a smug look on his face.

You wouldn't be so nonchalant about it if you knew that Shoei was Sharaku, thought Ryohei, feeling slightly annoyed.

"Hi, it's me," said Kato. "It was nice seeing you yesterday… Yes, thanks—you were a great help… Actually, that's why I'm calling. I wanted to ask you about a couple of those paintings…"

Kato took the photocopies from Ryohei.

"Let's see… There's no page number or anything, but it's the page with a painting of a small fish in the upper left—it's by Naotake. Sure, I'll wait… He's going to take a look now," Kato said to Ryohei, covering the receiver with his hand.

"Are you there? Yes, that's the one. Now, below it are two paintings by someone called Unmu. Would you happen to know when you sold those?"

Ryohei could feel his heart begin to beat faster.

"1937–38? Right before the war then… Oh, nothing special. It's just that I have a customer who's been doing some research on Unmu, that's all."

Kato grinned and looked at Ryohei.

"He happened to stop by this morning and we got to talking about your album. I was just wondering where those paintings might have ended up… Well, if you don't mind. Hold on a second… He says he wants to talk to you about it," Kato said, handing the receiver to Ryohei. Then he whispered, "Just pretend you know something about Unmu."

Ryohei repeated the question Kato had asked earlier.

"Well, I don't know where they are now," the voice on the other end replied. "These were paintings my father sold. The one above it by Naotake went to a museum in Akita in '37, so those other two must have sold just after that."

"Do you think they might have been sold to a museum too?"

"If they were, I'd have a record of it—sales like that are good for drumming up business." The man gave a gruff laugh. Ryohei thought he sounded about fifty.

"In the run-up to the war we used to get a lot of other dealers coming in here—the two paintings you're asking about were probably sold around that time. Wait, there might be something written on the back…"

There was a pause on the other end of the line. Ryohei could hear the sound of something being peeled away.

"Just as I thought," the man said, picking up the receiver again. "It was 1937. No record of who bought it though."

"I see," Ryohei said disappointedly.

"My father often used to jot things down on the backs of his photographs and I thought that just maybe… We bought both paintings from a dealer in Odate. He's no longer alive though."

Why am I not surprised? thought Ryohei.

"By the way, do you know if Unmu had any connection to Nagatoro?" asked the man suddenly.

"Nagatoro?" asked Ryohei.

"It's a little village near Kakunodate. It seems the man my father bought these paintings from also offered to sell him a third by Unmu—a landscape scene painted in Nagatoro. My father noted here that he didn't buy it."

Ryohei replied that he had never heard of Nagatoro.

"Unmu was born and raised in Akita city," the man went on. "So it *is* a bit strange he painted such a picture. Still, I suppose he happened to pass through the village on one of his visits to Kakunodate to see Naotake…"

Ryohei made a vague reply. In reality he knew very little about Unmu. He was beginning to get worried their little deception would be found out and that it would reflect badly on Kato. Ryohei made a sign with his eyes and the dealer quickly took the phone from him, thanked the man on the other end and rang off.

Ryohei explained that the man had started asking him about Unmu and he hadn't known what to say.

"I suppose that third painting purported to be by Unmu was in fact also by Shoei," mused Kato.

Ryohei nodded.

"He must have had a relative or something in Nagatoro. I doubt he'd have made a special trip there just to paint a picture."

"True. If it was painted near Kakunodate it's safe to assume it was by Shoei."

"Well, in that case, the painting traveled around quite a bit. 1937... that was just before the war. I wouldn't be surprised if it was destroyed in the bombings."

Ryohei nodded with disappointment.

November 6

TOKYO WAS SLIGHTLY WARMER than when Ryohei had left. He noticed the subtle change in the weather returning from chilly Tohoku.

Ryohei got off the train in Shinjuku and began walking through the underground passageway toward Kinokuniya Books. On the ground floor of the building next to the bookstore was a café where he had arranged to meet Yosuke.

The large café was nearly full. Ryohei looked around for his friend.

"Over here!" called Yosuke, spotting Ryohei and waving.

"The Shinkansen is great, isn't it? You can leave Morioka in the morning and still get to Tokyo before lunch," said Ryohei, glancing at his watch.

"I hear your trip was quite a success. Saeko sounded very excited."

"Yes, I've got enough information to write an article now."

Ryohei spread his research materials out on the table and began going over everything. Yosuke listened attentively, asking questions from time to time.

An hour passed.

"Well, that settles it—you've got enough evidence to convince anyone," said Yosuke as he lit a cigarette, his skeptical expression finally softening. "The connection between the Akita clan and Tsutaya is fascinating—that's a real breakthrough. What I found out pales in comparison."

"You found something too?"

"I was trying to link Tsutaya and Shoei in a completely different way."

"And did you?"

"Uh-huh. Ever heard of Hezutsu Tosaku?"

"The kyoka poet?"

"That's the one—very popular, though he was ultimately overshadowed by Ota Nampo and Karakomoro Kisshu, who like him were pupils of Uchiyama Gatei. Tosaku was the oldest of the three. They launched the first comic poetry competitions in Edo together in 1770, setting the stage for the kyoka boom of the 1780s. Nampo—widely regarded as the most brilliant of the three—shot to fame, but he couldn't have done it without Tosaku. In 1669, at the age of just nineteen, Nampo had published his first kyoka collection, *The Collected Works of Master Groggy*, under the penname 'Shokusanjin.' Tosaku got none other than Hiraga Gennai to write the introduction."

"No kidding!"

"Tosaku and Gennai were close friends. At Tosaku's behest, Gennai introduced Nampo to Suharaya Ichibei, the publisher who had handled most of Gennai's own books, and he agreed to publish *Master Groggy*. Without Gennai's introduction and backing, a complete unknown like Nampo who was still a teenager could never have published a book."

"True."

"From that point on, Nampo became Gennai's protégé, in a manner of speaking. It's said that when Gennai was working on a play, he'd ask Nampo to write the tricky historical parts. That's how much he trusted him."

"I didn't know that."

"Nampo even modeled his *nom de plume*, 'Furin-sanjin,' on Gennai's, which was—"

"Furai-sanjin!" exclaimed Ryohei, remembering the correct answer.

"Correct. Anyway, even though Nampo was more popular than Tosaku as a poet, Tosaku's friendship with Gennai gave him greater cachet. You might say he was the kingmaker of the kyoka world. Plus Tosaku seems to have been close to Tsuchiyama Sojiro, an important figure in Tanuma's administration, which meant he wielded a lot of financial clout."

"Wasn't Tsuchiyama the finance minister indicted for corruption and put to death in 1787 during the Tanuma purges?" asked Ryohei.

"That's him. He was beheaded for embezzling three thousand ryo from the shogun's coffers; in fact he probably took much more than that. He was famous for his extravagance—once he supposedly spent twelve hundred ryo, or over fifty million yen in today's money, to buy a geisha's freedom. On most nights of the week, Nampo, Kisshu, Akera Kanko and the other famous kyoka poets could be found in the Yoshiwara living it up on Tsuchiyama's dime. It's largely thanks to Tsuchiyama that kyoka became all the rage in the pleasure quarters."

"I see… and Hoseido Kisanji?"

"No doubt he was close to Tsuchiyama too. It stands to reason, given their common interest in kyoka as well as Kisanji's official role as Lord Satake's chamberlain," replied Yosuke.

"This is getting interesting!" exclaimed Ryohei.

"Now, this is where Tsutaya comes into the picture," went on Yosuke. "He bet his whole future on wooing Tosaku. If he could work his way into Tosaku's entourage, he'd be able to get Nampo and the other kyoka poets to join his stable of writers. Plus, through Tsuchiyama, Tosaku could provide Tsutaya with an entrée to Tanuma's inner circle, giving him access to Gennai, the most popular writer of the day. Winning over Tosaku wouldn't just be like killing two birds with one stone, it'd be like killing dozens of birds with one stone! Fortunately, Tosaku wasn't like Nampo and other samurai. In addition to his literary activities he ran a tobacco shop in Shinjuku. He was even rumored to dabble in financial speculation. In short, for a commoner like Tsutaya, Tosaku was very approachable."

"You're right about Tsutaya considering Tosaku one of his most important writers," added Ryohei. "When Tsutaya started publishing kyoka books in 1783, he asked Tosaku to write *Who's Who in Kyoka*, which came out later that year."

"Uh-huh. And did you know it lists Tosaku in the top rank of kyoka poets."

"No, I hadn't realized that."

"Making friends with all the important kyoka poets of the day was what launched Tsutaya's success: Kisanji, Nampo, Koikawa Harumachi... even Santo Kyoden, who wrote kyoka under the penname Migaru Orisuke... not to mention Torai Sanna, a student of Nampo's who became indispensable to Tsutaya in the 1780s as a writer of popular fiction... Tosaku opened lots of doors for Tsutaya. It was only because of him that Tsutaya became Edo's leading publisher."

"And Tosaku had connections to Gennai and Tsuchiyama, Tanuma's inner circle. He was *the* man to know," said Ryohei.

"*All* the kyoka poets of the day were probably part of Tanuma's clique. In fact, most of those who ran afoul of the Kansei Reforms of the 1790s had some connection or other to kyoka."

"You're right!" exclaimed Ryohei. "Nampo, Sanna, Kyoden, Kisanji... They were all kyoka poets. And didn't Harumachi commit suicide over something he published which displeased the authorities?"

"Yes, and what's more, Tsutaya published *all* of them," said Yosuke. "A blow to Tsutaya was a blow to the kyoka crowd, and cracking down on kyoka was an attack on Tsutaya's influence. His closeness with Tosaku essentially made him a member of Tanuma's clique."

"But how was it that Kisshu alone managed to escape punishment? He was one of the leading poets."

"Kisshu was a member of the Tayasu house, one of the three junior branches of the Tokugawa clan, meaning he was a vassal of Matsudaira Sadanobu's."

"Is that so?" said Ryohei, surprised.

"Around the time Tanuma fell from power and Sadanobu became chief senior councilor," explained Yosuke, "Kisshu and

Nampo had a falling out for some reason and Kisshu broke from the group. Now, this might be reading too much into it, but I can't help feeling the political rivalry between the ancien régime and the new order were at play."

"That makes perfect sense," admitted Ryohei. "There's no question Tsutaya was part of the Tanuma clique. I've been pursuing the problem from the Akita angle, but in the end it all comes down to Tanuma."

"Tosaku was a frequent visitor to Gennai's house, so he must have been friendly with Naotake, who'd taken up residence there. It's easy to imagine that Shoei, having heard about Tosaku from Naotake, would have gone to see him when he arrived in Edo. Through him, he could have met Tsutaya. At least, that's the way I was looking at it. But you're right. It's more likely Shoei met Tsutaya on the basis of his Akita connections alone."

"I wouldn't go that far," said Ryohei. "The fact both were involved only helps prove our theory that Shoei was Sharaku."

"Maybe you're right," conceded Yosuke." When you look at it that way, it's easier to believe Sharaku was a plan hatched by Tanuma's clique. In 1789 Tsutaya more or less stopped publishing kyoka books; or rather, he was forced to. The kyoka poets' resentment of Sadanobu, plus the enmity of Shoei and others in the Akita clan, combined to create the perfect storm. Like kyoka, Sharaku's ukiyo-e prints were very satirical—that's why Tsutaya couldn't reveal his true identity. If Sadanobu had known the Akita clan was behind it... No, wild horses couldn't have dragged the truth out of Tsutaya."

Yosuke seemed to be trying to convince himself more than Ryohei.

"You know," he went on, "there's a legend that Gennai didn't actually die in jail like everyone believed, but went to live in Shizuoka, Tanuma's home fief, for a number of years."

"Really?"

"Tanuma was at the height of his power at the time, so he could have easily pulled something like that off—that is, substituting someone else's body for Gennai's and whisking him away to Shizuoka. It's said when Gennai died in jail he'd been on a hunger strike for almost three weeks, but some people think that was just a ruse to alter his appearance and provide a pretext for his supposed death. How else to explain someone in perfect health dying suddenly like that? Supposedly, later, when Tanuma fell from power, Gennai fled up north to Dewa province—modern-day Akita and Yamagata prefectures—and lived well on into the 1800s. Apparently there's a tombstone up there just a line from one of Gennai's puppet plays with no name on it."

"Sounds pretty far-fetched to me," replied Ryohei skeptically.

"What's more far-fetched is the story that someone as important to Tanuma's regime as Gennai died in jail for killing one of his apprentices. Any tyrant worth his salt could have quashed so minor a scandal, and Tanuma was certainly a tyrant. I used to think the Gennai legend was idle speculation—but if one can accept the theory Sharaku was an obscure painter from Akita, then it's hard to rule out the possibility Gennai might have lived to a ripe old age."

"So what are you saying?" Ryohei asked.

"Simply this: the reason Tsutaya took such pains to hide Sharaku's true identity was that if anyone found out who Sharaku was, it might lead them to Gennai."

Ryohei remained silent.

"The Tanuma clique knew Gennai was alive," went on Yosuke. "But after Tanuma was deposed in 1786 they had to make sure no one else found out about it. If word got out, they'd all lose their heads. It would have been the perfect excuse for Sadanobu to crush the Tanuma faction once and for all. It was a terrible secret each of them had to guard with their lives. Then they spent a fortune turning an unknown artist into an overnight sensation. It was a stroke of genius worthy of a modern marketing guru. Tsutaya was a brilliant businessman, but could he really have hatched such a stratagem? No, I think this has Gennai's fingerprints all over it. After all, he's the one who supposedly advised Tanuma to open up trade with Russia—national pride be damned. He's the one who made his patented ivory combs all the rage in Edo by handing them out to high-class geishas to wear. Only he could have come up with something so counterintuitive."

Ryohei was listening intently, hanging on Yosuke's every word.

After a short pause Yosuke resumed his story:

"Shoei's surname was Chikamatsu, right. Well, right around the time Tsutaya was publishing Sharaku's prints, the writer Jippensha Ikku was living at Tsutaya's house."

"So?"

"So it's possible Ikku knew who Sharaku was. That much is fairly common knowledge, but do you know what name Ikku used when he was writing puppet plays?"

"Remind me."

"Chikamatsu Yoshichi."

"No kidding!"

"It might just be a coincidence but... Shoei didn't start out life with the name Chikamatsu. Assuming he adopted it after leaving Edo and returning to Akita, I think he might have borrowed it from Ikku... Then there's the question of Sharaku's picture of that boy sumo wrestler."

"You mean Daidoyama?" asked Ryohei.

"That's the one. I've always thought it strange Sharaku should have made that print, but I think it could have something to do with—"

"Dewa?" Seeing where Yosuke's train of thought was heading, Ryohei gave a wry smile. Daidoyama was from Dewa province, and Dewa was where Gennai had supposedly fled. "Isn't that a bit of a stretch?" he asked.

"Did you think I was talking about Gennai? Hardly. I was thinking of Nagatoro."

"That village near Kakunodate?"

"No, that's written with different Chinese character. I mean the one near Yamagata city. That's where Daidoyama came from."

"Is it?"

"C'mon, get with it. It says so right on Sharaku's print. Shoei must have had some connection to the other Nagatoro, the one you're talking about. Then along comes this seven-year-old sumo prodigy from a place with the same name—which is not far away actually—and becomes a sensation in Edo. It's not surprising he caught Sharaku's attention."

Ryohei realized Yosuke was onto something.

"Remember your theory about how Sharaku was especially popular with children?" asked Yosuke. "This fits perfectly. Sharaku drew Daidoyama to appeal to children, not adults. I'm sure of it."

"Yes. You must be right. Daidoyama was a hero to children in Edo. This clinches it—Shoei *was* Sharaku!" exclaimed Ryohei loudly. The other customers seated nearby in the café looked at the two men in surprise.

"Yes. Shoei was Sharaku," repeated Yosuke. "And you're the one who figured it all out."

Yosuke chuckled as he contemplated the look of childish glee on Ryohei's face.

November 8

"IT MAKES PERFECT SENSE—I don't see any room for doubt."

Nishijima folded his arms and let out a deep sigh. It had already been two hours since Ryohei had arrived at his house carrying an armful of research materials. Ryohei was dripping with sweat. The professor's study was climate controlled to protect all his many books and warm air filled the room.

"This is enough to convince most scholars," went on Nishijima. "It's a major discovery. Your theory that Sharaku was an offshoot of the Tanuma regime is a bit radical, but it's true some considerable forces must have been at play to bring Sharaku into existence. I think you've got ample evidence Tsutaya had connections within the Akita clan. Now it's just a question of how you want to unveil your theory to the world."

There was a strange glint in Nishijima's eyes.

"Do you want to write something for Geichosha's journal," he continued, "or announce it to the media first and then follow it up with an article in *The Edo Art Association Journal*? Our annual general meeting is coming up next month, so you should probably give a presentation. Anyway, whatever you chose to do, you don't want it to come across as the latest in a long list of theories. You need to present it in such a way that everyone will have to accept it. After all," Nishijima said with a hearty laugh, "you've got an iron-clad case. But don't worry about all that now—the first thing you need to do is write up your results. In the meantime, leave Sato's catalogue with me; I'll decide the best way to proceed. The sooner we act the better. But remember," Nishijima concluded, emphasizing his point, "don't say anything to Iwakoshi or the others. I don't know what the Ukiyo-e Connoisseurship Society crowd might do if they got wind of this. Let's just keep it between you and me for the time being."

"So you convinced the professor?" Yosuke, on the other end of the receiver, said in surprise. "I thought he was a bit more cautious than that. I mean, not that anyone could fail to be convinced."

He gave a gleeful laugh.

"But," Yosuke went on, "I don't know why he had to bring the UCS into the discussion. That seems to be going a bit far. After all, without Sato's catalogue as evidence there's not much they can do."

"I thought it was a bit strange too," conceded Ryohei.

"It's a good sign that he asked you not to talk to anyone about it. That means he's hooked. You've scored a rare coup."

"Speaking of which, you don't think the professor might be thinking of trying to pass the theory off as his own, do you?" asked Ryohei.

"You must be kidding! Stealing his own student's work? Not even the professor would stoop *that* low."

"But somehow I got that impression. Not that I'd really mind all that much."

"What!" exclaimed Yosuke. "How can you say that?"

"What I mean is, the theory's just not as persuasive coming from me," explained Ryohei. "Everyone would accept it at face value if the professor presented it as his own. In the end, that would be better for Sharaku."

"Did you tell the professor that?" asked Yosuke.

"No, not yet."

"Well, don't. You can't always be Mr. Nice Guy, Ryohei. Academia's a dog-eat-dog world. What was the point of going to Akita unless you're going to get credit for your own work? It's got nothing to do with the professor. Just don't say anything. As long as you don't bring it up, I'm sure the professor wouldn't think of it. Anyway, just think how upset Saeko would be if that happened."

Ryohei was taken aback. But Yosuke was right. The theory belonged to Saeko too. "Got it," he said. "I'll do my best."

With that, Ryohei rang off.

November 12
IN THE AFTERNOON, Ryohei set out for his university in Kichijoji.

While at the art history department he'd received a call from Yoshimura asking if he could meet at a café. When he arrived, Yoshimura had already finished his first cup of coffee. Ryohei sat down and Yoshimura ordered two more cups.

"Last night I went over to the professor's house," began Yoshimura, looking grave. "He showed me your paper."

"I see…"

Yesterday afternoon Ryohei had taken the seventy-page paper he had just finished writing over to Nishijima's house.

"To be honest, I'm a bit annoyed with the professor," continued Yoshimura, bitterly. "He never said a word to me about what you were working on."

"Well… at first it wasn't clear whether it would lead anywhere," mumbled Ryohei.

He couldn't help wondering why Yoshimura had asked to meet him. *Surely not just to make catty remarks*, he thought gloomily.

"I find your theory about Shoei entirely convincing," said Yoshimura. "I've got no complaint with *that*. Sato's catalogue is irrefutable."

What's this?

Yoshimura had never spoken to Ryohei like this before.

"That said, I don't think it will sound quite so convincing coming from you."

Ah, I should have known.

There had been something about Professor Nishijima's attitude yesterday that had given Ryohei pause. The professor had repeatedly said he would need to "pave the way" for Shoei's introduction to the world. Ryohei had ignored the remark and left without saying anything more. Afterward the professor must have called up Yoshimura and asked him to come over.

"Think of it this way," Yoshimura went on. "It's like a child with a toy water pistol—no matter how much he pulls the trigger he can't hurt anyone. Now, the professor's behind you one hundred percent. But his support won't carry as much weight as it should because you're his student. People will think he's only doing it out of a sense of duty. The UCS crowd will say he doesn't really buy your theory and is only backing you out of obligation."

It's not the message, it's the messenger—is that the problem?

Ryohei had not fully considered this possibility.

"If that happens," went on Yoshimura, "your great discovery will come to nothing—the Shoei hypothesis will be written off as just hot air. We can't let that happen. That's how strongly the professor believes in your theory."

Ryohei said nothing.

"Even if you *weren't* his student he'd be just as supportive, but people will think… Anyway, the professor's quite worried."

"I'm sorry," Ryohei mumbled.

"There's no need to apologize. It can't be helped. But I'm sure you understand how the professor feels. He loves Sharaku more than anyone. It must be awful for him to think that now, finally, we know who Sharaku really was, but people will dismiss it as just another crackpot theory. He has no problem with you presenting your paper. But if it results in Sharaku's true identity being ignored, it will be your own fault."

"How so?" Ryohei shot back.

"You're still young—a mere child in academic terms. There aren't many people who would listen seriously to what you have to say. They'll tear your theory apart. Not only that, but they'll find fault with things that have nothing to do with it. There are plenty in the Ukiyo-e Connoisseurship Society crowd who are old hands at doing just that. To make matters worse, you're the professor's student. They'll go after you for that reason alone. If Sharaku's identity gets lost for reasons that have nothing to do with the theory itself, you'll have no one to blame but yourself."

As much as Ryohei hated to admit it, Yoshimura had a valid point. It was precisely because the same thought had occurred to Ryohei that he had been inclined to let Nishijima take the credit for his work in the first place. He began to waver. It pained him to think his theory might be dismissed for such petty reasons.

"Look, even if *I* had made the discovery it would still be an uphill battle," continued Yoshimura. "People envy the professor because he's powerful. The UCS gang will use every trick in the book to try to crush me and discredit the theory. They don't care who Sharaku really was."

"Really? I wouldn't go *that* far," countered Ryohei. "Anyway, I'm sure people would listen to *you*."

"No, they wouldn't. Sharaku's too hot a topic even for *me*," retorted Yoshimura.

His insinuation was clear.

"In short," he added, cutting to the chase. "At this point only the professor is powerful enough to publish this theory."

"What's your goal?" asked Yoshimura, his tone suddenly softening. "Or perhaps I should say, what's your goal *as a scholar*? I'm sure you want to leave your mark on the world and all that. But scholarship is not like politics. The purpose isn't to become rich or powerful— it's to see your ideas become acknowledged by the world at large in one way or another. Isn't that the true joy of scholarship?"

Ryohei understood all this, but he'd never expected to hear such sentiments coming from Yoshimura. After all, this was a guy who made no bones about wanting to get ahead in the world and had gone to work for a museum straight out of university.

"You've made a major discovery," Yoshimura went on. "None of us in Professor Nishijima's inner circle would deny that. All the more reason why we don't want to see your theory destroyed. As a scholar, it's incumbent upon you to ensure the world at large acknowledges your work, even if that means letting someone else take the credit. Now, if you choose to do it yourself the professor and I will back you all the way. But that will take years. You'll need to start slowly and gradually build consensus for your theory. You'll have to be low-key about it at first and… well, not to put too fine a point on it, it would simply take too long. Leave everything to me. In less than six months I'll see to it that your theory is accepted by everyone in the field."

"You have some sort of plan?" asked Ryohei.

"Early next month—at the latest—we'll publish your paper under the professor's name, in both Japanese and English. Then I'll fly to Europe and the US with the paper and visit all the scholars I know over there. I'll try to persuade them to attend the EAA's annual meeting here in Tokyo on the twenty-first of next month. We'll invite people from all the major newspapers, magazines, and journals to attend and hand out copies of the paper to everyone at the meeting. Then, after the professor delivers his talk, we'll have some foreign scholars get up and endorse the theory. By the end of the meeting it will have the backing of the entire EAA. The art journals are already on our side, so they're not going to raise any objections. Finally, in about March, the professor will publish a book with Shoei's paintings and Sharaku's prints side by side one another."

They've thought that far ahead.

Ryohei was dumbfounded.

"You'll have to keep a low profile for a while," Yoshimura went on. "But your name will be on the book as the professor's collaborator when it comes out in the spring. There's really no downside for you. If you tried to do it all on your own you'd never get half that far. So, what do you think? Are you with us?" Yoshimura stared at Ryohei.

"So you mean the professor will be addressing the meeting alone…"

"I'm afraid so. It has to be that way. It's got to look like the professor's discovery. That's the only way to get the media's attention. But look at it this way—the Shoei hypothesis will become the dominant theory in the field. That's what you want, isn't it?"

"Yes, but…"

"By the way, I hear the professor's decided to send you to Boston."

"Uh-huh…."

"See—that shows how much confidence he has in you. He'll do everything in his power to promote your theory."

Why bring Boston into it all of a sudden?

Ryohei started to feel uncomfortable.

"You'll get much better treatment over in the States if you go as the professor's collaborator on a major new discovery," Yoshimura went on, "rather than as the lone proponent of an unproven theory. That's another reason not to waste any time."

Of all the devious…

"And if by some chance the theory should come unraveled," added Yoshimura ominously, "then your trip to Boston won't be the only thing to suffer."

November 13

YOSUKE STARED into his glass and watched the ice cubes melting. One of the cubes burst with a loud *crack!*

He and Ryohei were sitting in *More*, Yosuke's neighborhood bar.

"So, in the end you agreed to let Yoshimura handle everything?" he asked Ryohei, flabbergasted.

"I'm sorry…" replied Ryohei apologetically. "I know it was selfish of me…"

"Well, after what Yoshimura said, I can't exactly blame you. I didn't know about the Boston trip. I can understand you wouldn't want to jeopardize it."

"Actually, it had nothing to do with Boston. That came up way before this whole Sharaku thing."

"But in the end it comes down to that. If you'd kicked up a fuss the professor might have decided not to send you to Boston. You agreed to go, right? They knew you wanted it and used it to blackmail you to get what they wanted."

"I suppose you're right. But that's not what mattered most to me," replied Ryohei feebly. "It was more a question of whether I'd be able to convince people of the theory on my own. I was furious at Yoshimura for saying I couldn't, but I knew in my mind he was right. I'm just no match for the professor."

"Yoshimura's just using you. If that's going to be your attitude, people like Yoshimura will walk all over you. I can understand you want the Shoei hypothesis to be accepted, but I wonder if it was really necessary to hand it to the professor on a silver platter."

"But in academia it's more or less common knowledge professors often publish their students' work as their own."

"Yes, but there are limits. This was your big chance to make a name for yourself. A more ambitious person would've taken credit for it himself, whatever the consequences. You can be sure of one thing: Yoshimura would have. That's how important this discovery is."

"I'm sorry," said Ryohei contritely, bowing his head. "I just don't have the clout to pull it off."

"Clout, huh? Is that what everything in this world comes down to?" muttered Yosuke. "Two people say the same thing but the rest of us only listen to one of them." His tone was one of resignation.

"I *do* feel bad for Saeko…"

"Don't worry, I'll try to explain things to her," said Yosuke. "Although I'm sure she'll accuse us of being spineless. She doesn't understand how academia works. Anyway, as far as I'm concerned this proves once and for all the professor's washed up. He hasn't published anything new for over a decade, but at least he still has his reputation. But if he could stoop to stealing his own student's work he doesn't deserve to call himself a scholar."

"But," objected Ryohei, "it might all be Yoshimura's idea."

"You're not serious, are you? I wouldn't put it past him, that's for sure. But that greedy fool doesn't do anything unless there's something in it for him. He wouldn't have taken the trouble of talking to you unless the professor had put him up to it. He's just toadying to the professor. Part of his reward is no doubt this trip abroad he mentioned."

"Maybe you're right."

"Take my word for it, he's just trying to milk this for all its worth. Plus, he'd rather have the professor take the credit than see someone younger than him basking in the limelight. That way he saves face. As for his promise that your name will appear on the professor's book, I'm pretty dubious about that. You'd be a fool to take it at face value."

"I don't care," persisted Ryohei. "Just so long as the theory is accepted."

"How can you be so…" Yosuke's voice trailed off. "Oh, I give up," he muttered, refilling Ryohei's glass. Then, his expression indicating he'd reached some sort of decision, he at last he continued, "Well, it's clear you've decided to throw in the towel. But I won't stand idly by and let the professor get away with this. Once your theory's been accepted and all the excitement's died down, I'll find a way of exposing him for what he really is. To be perfectly honest, this isn't the first time the professor's done something like this. Only this time, I'm not going to stand for it. If he get can away with this it defeats the whole point of research. I won't allow that."

"But what will you…" Ryohei stammered nervously, taken aback by Yosuke's angry tone.

"I've got a plan," replied Yosuke, a smile rising to his lips. "Don't worry," he added, seeing the worried look on Ryohei's face. "I won't make trouble for you." He gave his friend a pat on the shoulder. "It's out of your hands now. This is between me and the professor. You just do whatever you have to. Anyway, it's all up to the professor now. If he keeps his word and gives you equal credit on his book, I won't lift a finger. But if there's any funny business from him or Yoshimura, they're finished. I swear I'll bury them…"

Staring into his glass, Yosuke chuckled.

Ryohei felt a chill run down his spine.

December 15

ALMOST A MONTH had passed since Ryohei's conversation with Yosuke at *More*.

Ryohei had been idle during that time. His research paper was out of his hands. Yoshimura had moved on to phase two of his plan, shutting out Ryohei completely. Even though Yoshimura had explained beforehand that until the meeting was over they would have to proceed as though the professor was acting alone, Ryohei couldn't help feeling left out. But since he had given the plan his blessing, he was in no position to complain. He tried to accept the situation, telling himself he should have foreseen from the beginning this was what would happen.

Ryohei had seen Yosuke and Saeko several times since then, but something had changed. The laughter had gone out of their conversations. He tried to put the whole episode behind him, telling himself he had simply been outgunned, but he could not shake the feeling he had been a coward.

On the other hand, thought Ryohei, *if he had rejected Yoshimura's offer he would have been run out of academia.*

I can't turn my back on ukiyo-e the way Yosuke has. If I could, I'd never have spent all those years as the professor's research assistant. I won't give up on ukiyo-e and my research. But I'll do things my way, not the professor's.

That was why compromise had been unavoidable he told himself.

Meanwhile, preparations for unveiling the Shoei hypothesis were proceeding smoothly. Yoshimura had gone abroad with the English translation of Ryohei's paper and, with just a week left before the Edo Art Association's annual meeting, four foreign scholars—all internationally recognized Sharaku experts—had agreed to attend. Iwakoshi and the professor's other present and former students were busy round the clock booking hotel rooms and preparing lecture slides.

Ryohei alone remained behind at the university, teaching the professor's classes for him whenever he was absent, as he often was.

For his part, Professor Nishijima spent most of his time in meetings discussing preparations for the meeting and lobbying other members of the EAA's executive committee. His students also began meeting more and more frequently to discuss the upcoming event, but Ryohei was never invited. This was all Yoshimura's doing. The other students never doubted for a moment that the Shoei hypothesis was the professor's own work. If they had known it was actually Ryohei's, the mood of excitement swelling around the announcement would have fizzled. Not even Iwakoshi, whom Ryohei saw practically every day, had any inkling the paper propounding the Shoei hypothesis had been written not by Professor Nishijima but Ryohei.

"Look out world, here we come!" exclaimed Iwakoshi gleefully, walking into Ryohei's office one day. "Geichosha's going to devote the entire February issue of *Art Currents* to the Shoei hypothesis."

"Are you serious?" Ryohei's heart leapt. As removed as he was from events, he couldn't help feeling happy.

"Last night Yamashita dropped by *Sakamoto* to give the professor the good news. He was going on about how this is the biggest discovery to hit the art world in decades."

Art Currents was a general arts magazine, not a coterie journal for ukiyo-e enthusiasts. The fact that it had decided to do a special issue on the new theory meant that its acceptance was virtually guaranteed.

"The professor was ecstatic," continued Iwakoshi. "His own publisher, Shugakusha, now plans to publish a special volume on the Shoei hypothesis as the centerpiece of their forthcoming anthology of the professor's work. Plus, word has it he's going to be nominated as the Edo Art Association's next executive director at the general meeting. He'll take over from the current director, who'll become chairman, and Yoshimura will assume the professor's current seat on the executive board. So there you have it. In both name and reality, Professor Nishijima will be the most powerful figure in the ukiyo-e world."

Iwakoshi laughed loudly.

"We're going to be *really* busy from now on," he added. "After the meeting the professor's going abroad. Lecture invitations are already flooding in. And I'll be going to Akita with Yamashita."

"Akita?" said Ryohei in surprise.

"Yoshimura's already been up there once it seems. This time Yamashita's going to take photographs for the magazine and I've been chosen to go with him.

"Yoshimura went to Akita, you say?"

"Well, who do you *think* the professor sent to do the research for his paper?" replied Iwakoshi, astonished at Ryohei's ignorance.

"I'm afraid it just turned out that way," said Yoshimura apologetically. He had telephoned Ryohei within a few hours of Iwakoshi's departure. Iwakoshi must have reported back to him on his conversation with Ryohei.

"It was unavoidable," he continued. "The professor hasn't been out of Tokyo for weeks, so he can't claim to have gone to Akita. That's why we have to say I did the research."

Ryohei remained silent.

Yoshimura continued: "The question came up unexpectedly when the professor and I were meeting with the EAA's executive director—the answer just popped out of my mouth. I apologize. Anyway, do us a favor and let's just leave it at that. The story's already got legs. At this point it would be awkward to turn around and say you did the research."

"But that's not what we agreed," protested Ryohei.

"I'm aware of that. But if we change our story now everything will be ruined. I'm sorry, I really am. But please understand, for the professor's sake."

Though Yoshimura's words were conciliatory, his tone was forceful and left no room for argument.

Ryohei gave up. Ultimately, it was his fault for being so naïve not to have seen this coming. If he kicked up a fuss now he'd not only jeopardize the Shoei hypothesis but create trouble for everyone. There was no telling how the meeting would play out. It was a long time since Professor Nishijima had come out with a new theory and the eyes of the media would be riveted on him.

As soon as it gets around that Yoshimura has taken credit for my research, there will be no question of my name appearing on the professor's book.

Once someone is forced on the defensive there's no turning back. Ryohei realized Yoshimura had set an ingenious trap. Had he really had no choice but to accept it all "for the sake of the theory?"

I've been a coward.

For the first time, Ryohei was wracked with remorse. Deep down he felt the stirrings of an ambition he had hardly been aware of. The memory of the three days in Akita with Saeko came back to him like a long-forgotten dream.

I not only betrayed myself, I betrayed Saeko.

In the gathering darkness of the professor's office, Ryohei felt utterly alone.

December 21

RYOHEI ARRIVED at the Kudan Kaikan hotel shortly before one o'clock in the afternoon.

The Edo Art Association's general meeting started at two and he had come to help everyone set up. Not that his assistance was really needed. However, the previous evening Yoshimura had called and made him promise to come one hour early. Even Yoshimura seemed to think it would look bad to shut Ryohei out of the preparations completely.

When he entered the building, Ryohei found that Iwakoshi and the professor's other students were already busy setting up.

"Ah, Ryohei. You're here."

From across the room, Uchida Yumi, wearing a frilly white blouse and a dark blue suit, spotted Ryohei and came running over. She was a junior at Musashino University and the only woman in the professor's seminar. Ryohei, used to seeing Yumi in jeans, recoiled slightly at the sight of the undergraduate dressed to the nines. Noticing his reaction, Yumi giggled.

"You've been assigned to the welcome desk too, right?"

"Yeah, um, I got a call from Yoshimura…" Ryohei mumbled in reply.

Why do I feel so awkward all of a sudden?

In his mind, Ryohei played back the previous evening's conversation with Yoshimura.

"I know it's a bit late to mention this now, but the professor's been saying he'd feel more comfortable if you weren't in the room when he gave his lecture. I have to say, I understand how he feels. He'll be reading *your* paper, after all."

Ryohei could not see Yoshimura's face, but the voice on the other end of the line sounded grave.

"You're saying you don't want me to come to the meeting?"

Personally, Ryohei had not been all that eager to go in the first place, so it actually came as something of a relief.

"On the contrary, the others might think it odd if you weren't there. As it is, you already seem to have made Iwakoshi suspicious."

Of all the nerve! What have I done to make anyone suspicious?

The casualness of Yoshimura's tone made Ryohei furious.

"In fact, if you don't go to the meeting at all," Yoshimura went on, "it might create problems."

"So what should I do?" Ryohei asked irritably. "The professor says he doesn't want me there."

"Now don't get all huffy. This is my problem too. I'm sorry to ask you to do this, but do you think you could be in charge of the check-in table tomorrow?"

"The welcome desk!" said Ryohei sullenly.

"Just so the professor doesn't see you until *after* he's given his talk. I understand how you feel, but that's the best plan I could come up with on the spot. Please. Everything's riding on tomorrow."

"Has something happened between you and the professor?" Yumi quietly asked Ryohei.

"What do you mean?"

"Just that I heard Iwakoshi saying you'd been excluded from this event."

"Not at all. I'm here now, aren't I?"

"True. I guess it was silly of me to be worried," said Yumi, smiling cheerfully. "Anyway, isn't this amazing? I hear there are going to be TV cameras! I wonder if we'll be on TV too."

"TV, huh?"

"There are reporters from several networks here already—and lots of journalists, of course. I didn't realize the professor was *this* famous!"

Ryohei had mixed feelings about it all.

A bundle of programs arrived at the check-in table.

On the front was printed the name of the Edo Art Association and the words, *Annual General Meeting*. Below was written: *To Be Preceded by a Special Lecture by Professor Nishijima Shunsaku to Announce His Latest Research*. Yoshimura was going to give a supplemental lecture entitled, "Western Painting in Japan and the Akita Clan." There followed the names of four foreign scholars. Though the subject of their talks had been left blank, they undoubtedly would be speaking in support of the Shoei hypothesis.

Of course, the theory would not be put to any sort of up or down vote by the entire assembly. But during the general meeting that followed the lectures, Professor Nishijima's name would be put forward as the next executive director and, if approved, it would amount to an official endorsement by the EAA of his new theory.

While the participants might not see the two as being connected in any way, the rest of the world would not make such subtle distinctions.

It's nothing short of brilliant.

The sheer brazenness of the professor's plan left Ryohei speechless.

"Hello." Yamashita approached the check-in table. "Not much longer now," he said. "Our photographer should be here by now—seen him?"

"You're from Geichosha, right?" said Yumi with mock seriousness.

"Get a load of this chick!" replied Yamashita, giving Yumi a nudge on the forehead. She burst into giggles. "Hey, look, TV cameras! By the way, you know who else is getting on my nerves? The professor. He still hasn't let us take those photos."

"Which photos are those?" asked Ryohei.

"The ones for the magazine. He won't show us that painting album of his—says the light will damage it. He told us to use the slides Yoshimura and the others have already made, but those guys don't know jack when it comes to photography."

"But surely they're in black-and-white," said Ryohei.

"Well, I'll have a look at them today. I've agreed to use them as long as they're not out of focus. Anyway, the professor's guarding that album as greedily as a lioness watching over her cubs."

"He probably wants to keep it safe until a high-quality reproduction can be made," Ryohei suggested helpfully.

"Is that what he said?" asked Yamashita.

"Apparently it's supposed to be published as a supplement to his book on Shoei next year."

"I see. Well, I guess you can't blame him then." With a wave of his hand, Yamashita headed into the main hall.

The Hon. Yokoyama Shuzo, member of the Japanese House of Representatives, approached the check-in table. He was widely known to be a long-time connoisseur of ukiyo-e and acted as an adviser to the Edo Art Association.

As Yumi handed the politician a program, a barrage of flashbulbs went off. She could hear the sound of a video camera churning away as it recorded the event. She blushed bright red, her face fixed in a permanent smile. Bathed in the bright light of the cameras, Ryohei cringed. The thought occurred to him that Saeko would probably see all this on the TV news and it made him depressed.

"The meeting's started," an undergraduate named Ota, who was in Yumi's class, came to inform them. He was one of those helping out inside the hall.

Ryohei showed no sign of leaving the check-in table.

"Aren't you coming?" Ota asked him with a puzzled expression.

"Someone's supposed to stay here... Yumi, you go ahead without me," replied Ryohei.

Yumi gave an apologetic bow and followed Ota into the main hall.

Ninety minutes passed. Ryohei waited impatiently. From time to time, a clamor of voices arose in the hall and spilled through the closed doors. Each time this happened, Ryohei's heart began to beat faster. The only thought in his head now was that it didn't matter to him who announced his theory, so long as the world accepted it.

Ripples of applause reached his ears. It seemed that Professor Nishijima had finished his lecture. Suddenly the noise grew into a crescendo as a young man emerged from the hall. He wore a press badge around his arm.

"Where's the telephone?" he asked Ryohei arrogantly.

Ryohei pointed to a red payphone just behind the check-in table.

"Do you mind?" The man gestured with his chin to Yumi's empty chair and sat down without waiting for Ryohei's answer. "It's me... Yes, it just ended. Incredible! I'm planning to interview the professor now and ask him a few more questions. What a lecture! The evidence is overwhelming. He even showed a slide of a painting with Sharaku's signature on it... A fake? Not a chance. It's from a book published in 1907. That's before Kurth, it seems... You know, Julius Kurth, that German guy. Look, I'll explain everything when I get back to the office. Anyway, I want my article to appear in the Metro section, not Arts. This is *big*.

It's about more than art; it's got roots in all the sociopolitical intrigues of the Edo period. Fascinating stuff. Tanuma Okitsugu's name came up quite a lot… Yes, really. Apparently, Sharaku was part of his clique. That's the theory anyway… See, I told you it was good… Of course, I'll check all that thoroughly. I think we should run a series on this before one of the weeklies comes out with something on it. Anyway, let's take things one step at a time. I'll figure the rest out once I've interviewed the professor. Just make sure you leave plenty of room for my piece. Don't worry, I'll deliver the goods."

The man slammed down the receiver. Then, as though noticing Ryohei for the first time, he asked:

"You a member of the EAA?"

"Uh-huh," answered Ryohei, looking down at the floor.

"Happen to know Professor Nishijima?"

"Actually, I'm one of his research assistants."

"Really? What luck running into you."

The man hurriedly stood up and handed Ryohei his card.

"Sorry to keep you waiting," Yumi said, returning from the hall. "I'll take over now." Ryohei breathed a sigh of relief.

"This gentleman is from a newspaper," said Ryohei. "He says he has some questions about the professor."

"Is that so?" The information seemed to arouse Yumi's interest. She bowed her head politely. Ryohei introduced her to the journalist and then stood up and gave her his seat.

Instead of going into the hall, Ryohei went downstairs to a café located in the basement. It was empty. After ordering a coffee he closed his eyes.

It's all over. I thought I didn't care who got the credit as long as people accepted my theory, but now… I wish I hadn't overheard that journalist's conversation.

A feeling of melancholy washed over Ryohei. It was he, not the professor, that journalist should have been talking about. Right now there was nothing he wanted more than to get as far away from there as possible, but if he left now there would have been no point coming in the first place.

Ryohei stared blankly into space thinking of Saeko.

December 22

RYOHEI finally crawled out of his futon and went to the front
door to get the newspaper, then he lit the kerosene space heater.
His head felt as though it were about to burst. He had a hangover.
Last night he'd done something he hadn't done for a long time:
gotten drunk alone.

He stared fixedly at the newspaper lying on the table, afraid to
open it. *This is ridiculous*, he thought, but still his hand would not
move. Finally, resigning himself to the inevitable, he reached for the
newspaper.

Ryohei's heart leapt into his throat as he opened it. There,
staring out at him, was Shoei's lion painting and next to it a large
photograph of Professor Nishijima. Ryohei began to devour the
article.

New Theory Links Sharaku to Hiraga Gennai!
Ukiyo-e Artist the Creation of Tanuma Okitsugu?

DECEMBER 22—A two-hundred-year-old mystery has
been solved: the true identity of the celebrated ukiyo-e artist
Toshusai Sharaku. According to one scholar's theory, Sharaku's
real name was Chikamatsu Shoei, a minor samurai from Akita
fief who studied Western-style painting from a protégé of
Hiraga Gennai, the great Renaissance man of the Edo period.
The theory also elucidates the formative influence the Akita
clan exercised over the culture of the time by patronizing
artists and currying favor with the shogun's Chief Senior
Councilor, Tanuma Okitsugu…

The article was simply a summary of Ryohei's paper; nothing new
had been added. At the end of the main text, which explained the
Shoei hypothesis in some detail, appeared a profile of Professor
Nishijima:

Nishijima Shunsaku, the originator of this groundbreaking
new theory which has shaken up the world of art history, is
a professor at Musashino University and a world-renowned

expert on ukiyo-e. After delivering a lecture at the annual general meeting of the Edo Art Association to announce his theory, he was unanimously elected that organization's new executive director. The move means that the newly christened Shoei hypothesis will almost certainly be accepted by ukiyo-e experts around the world. Since unveiling his theory, Prof. Nishijima has been besieged with requests for books and articles from publishers and magazines, as well as invitations to speak overseas. He gleefully complains that his schedule promises to be extremely busy heading into the New Year, and says that in the future he hopes to uncover more paintings by Shoei, which he believes have found their way unrecognized onto the art market over the years.

Though it pleased Ryohei to see that his Shoei hypothesis was getting the attention it deserved, at the same time he couldn't help feeling upset.

Fortunately, the day before yesterday the university had gone on winter break, so for the time being Ryohei would not have to go in to the art history department. That was one small blessing. He decided he needed to get away from Tokyo for a while, at least until his anger subsided. He would return home to Morioka. It was not as though the professor would be likely to miss him or wonder where he'd gone. On the contrary, Nishijima would probably be relieved to have him out of the way. Ryohei could never have imagined that in the short space of one month, he and the professor would have become so estranged from one another.

December 24

"WELL, AREN'T YOU the sly one!" burst out Kato the moment he saw Ryohei. The antiques dealer was alone in his shop polishing a sword.

"I'm sorry," mumbled Ryohei. "I was planning to tell you everything but…"

"I *thought* it was odd you should go all the way to Akita on account of some no-name artist I've never heard of."

A thin smile played about the corners of Kato's mouth as he returned the sword to its display case.

"But what a discovery!" he went on. "It created quite a stir around here. My customers have been talking about nothing else for the past couple of days. I hear that dealers up in Akita are rushing around frantically searching for hidden Shoeis."

"Already? I didn't think—"

"But I wouldn't hold my breath if I were you. They don't even know how to recognize his style. Not unless his signature is actually on the painting. But my guess is most of them have been altered."

"You're probably right." Ryohei nodded.

"By the way," said Kato, glancing up at Ryohei. "That catalogue you showed me on your last visit—the one causing all the fuss. Do you still have a copy?"

"Yes. I brought it to Morioka with me in fact."

"I see… Would you mind if I had another look at it?"

"Not at all," Ryohei replied without hesitation. It was the least he could do under the circumstances.

"Thanks. I appreciate it. The newspaper only printed the one painting of the lion. No one's seen anything else by Shoei. If I could get a look at some of his other works, it would help me, you know…"

The art dealer smiled.

"I'll make a copy and bring it in," said Ryohei. "I don't have the original, of course, so the quality won't be all that great, I'm afraid."

"That'll do just fine. I'll reimburse you for the copies."

"Would tomorrow be soon enough?"

"Perfect. I really appreciate it."

"It seems the catalogue is going to be published sometime early next year, so after that I guess you won't be needing the copies anyway."

"Is that so? So where's the original now?"

"Professor Nishijima has it. I hear he keeps it locked away in a safe in his study. Apparently he won't take it out to show to anyone—says the light could damage it." Ryohei chuckled. Come to think of it, he hadn't actually lent it to the professor. He'd been duped into handing it over.

I haven't seen Mizuno since the book fair. He must be fuming right now.

It was Mizuno who had given Ryohei the book in the first place. But as things stood now, meeting him might be awkward. Ryohei cringed to think of how many people's trust he had betrayed.

"When exactly do you suppose the catalogue will be published?" Kato asked curiously.

He must want to know how much time he's got to make use of the photocopies. Knowing him, he probably has some sort of deal in the works already.

"April at the earliest is what I hear," replied Ryohei.

"April, huh? I suppose the professor hasn't gotten around to photographing it yet."

"I think that will be impossible before mid-January. Until the end of the year the professor will be busy taking over his new duties at the EAA and all that. Then there's New Year's, or course. Don't worry, you've got a good three months."

"Oh! I didn't mean…"

Kato gave an embarrassed smile.

January 3

RYOHEI'S ALARM CLOCK went off. The ringing continued intermittently. From the depths of his warm futon, Ryohei stretched out a hand toward the alarm clock next to his pillow. But his alarm clock wasn't there. The noise continued.

Eventually, Ryohei realized he wasn't in his apartment in Tokyo but his parents' house in Morioka, and the ringing he was hearing wasn't his alarm clock but the downstairs telephone. Squinting, he poked his head out from beneath his futon cover. The sun was already high in the sky. His mother began calling him from downstairs. It was Iwakoshi on the phone.

Ryohei hurriedly threw a cardigan on over his pajamas and raced downstairs.

"I'm sorry. I had a late night last night," apologized Ryohei, speaking into the receiver.

"I thought I'd find you there," said Iwakoshi. "I tried your apartment but when no one answered, I wondered if maybe…"

Iwakoshi sounded even graver than usual.

"Is it something urgent?" Iwakoshi had never telephoned Ryohei in Morioka before. Ryohei had a vague sense of foreboding.

"The professor's dead…"

"Huh?"

"Professor Nishijima was found dead this morning," repeated Iwakoshi, practically shouting.

Ryohei felt his knees go weak.

"Wh… what happened?" he asked, once he had collected himself.

"A fire at his house," said Iwakoshi, choking on the words. "They found his body after it had been put out."

Professor Nishijima had been at home alone, according to Iwakoshi. The rest of the family was safe, having left for Hakone the night before. Every year, on the day after New Year's, all of Nishijima's current and former students were invited his house for an all-day party which went on in to the evening. When it was over, the professor always went away with his family for several days to a hot springs resort. But this year he had stayed behind because he had some magazine interviews lined up starting on the fifth.

Iwakoshi had been at the party. Nishijima had apparently been in high spirits, talking animatedly about Sharaku with Yoshimura, Iwashita, and the others. By the time everyone left, the professor had been quite drunk.

"Around eight o'clock, after cleaning up after the party, it seems his wife left with the children… Once they were gone, the professor probably went to his study to work… The fire broke out around midnight. His body was discovered on a daybed next to his desk where he took naps, so the fire department believes he probably started the fire by accident—a lighted cigarette falling onto a pile of papers, or something like that. He must have fallen asleep and been overcome by the smoke before he could escape," explained Iwakoshi sadly.

The suddenness of it all left Ryohei speechless.

Iwakoshi burst into tears. "Of all the idiotic things!" he shouted. "Why did this have to happen now, just when things were getting started! What in the world are we going to do?"

A memorial service was to be held the following day. Promising to be there, Ryohei rang off. He returned to his room and lay down on his futon. Tears began to flow freely. Ryohei felt a strange mix of emotions. He had hated the professor—hadn't he?

That was precisely what made it all so unbearable. Ryohei was not sure exactly how he felt. He owed the professor a lot—there was no denying it. Even if Yosuke were right and Nishijima *had* lost his direction as a scholar, if not for him, Ryohei would never have come to appreciate the wonders of ukiyo-e. He had not wanted to part from the professor on bad terms. That was why he had left Tokyo.

Why did you have to go and die on me?

Ryohei felt angry at Nishijima's selfishness.

7
The Artist's Alibi

January 7

THE FUNERAL RITES for Nishijima Shunsaku were held at Somon-ji in Tokyo's Nakano ward starting at 1 p.m. The Hon.Yokoyama Shuzo of the Japanese House of Representatives acted as chief mourner. Over 700 people came to pay their last respects. Tables were set up to receive the mourners, and Ryohei and Yumi were put in charge of one of these. Members of the Edo Art Association's administrative staff also took turns helping out.

It couldn't be more different from Mr. Saga's funeral!

The temple had received hundreds of floral wreaths, so many sthey did not all fit in the courtyard and some had to be placed on the street outside the main gate. The Japanese Minister of Education was scheduled to deliver the eulogy. Only now did Ryohei become aware of just how powerful Professor Nishijima had been.

"Ryohei!" someone behind him called out in a low voice. It was one of the professor's seminar students. "Yoshimura wants to see you in the waiting room."

As a member of the funeral committee, Yoshimura was serving as an usher, greeting guests and showing them to their seats in the temple's main hall. Though Nishijima's death initially seemed to have come as a severe blow to him, as the days passed, he had gradually regained his usual good humor.

As soon as Ryohei reached the waiting room, Yoshimura came out and beckoned him into another room.

The room was empty. Ryohei couldn't imagine what Yoshimura's intention could be in sending for him.

"An editor from Osaki Arts has just arrived," began Yoshimura. Osaki Arts was the publishing house that had been planning to publish the professor's book on Shoei. "I'm in a real mess," Yoshimura continued. "Fortunately I have a copy of the professor's paper and the negatives of the slides Iwakoshi and the others took of Shoei's paintings, but I don't have Kiyochika's preface or his biography of Shoei. We've been planning all along to reprint the entire catalogue as an appendix to the professor's book, but I never thought something like this might happen."

"What do you mean?"

"The original has been destroyed."

Ryohei had forgotten about the original.

"Apparently the editor was planning to start photographing the catalogue tomorrow. He says a photocopy will be good enough for the parts that are merely text. I remembered you had made a copy for yourself, so I went ahead and told him he could use it."

That's taking quite a bit for granted, isn't it?

Ryohei was indignant. "What! You mean *you* didn't make a copy?"

"Don't be ridiculous. How could I? The professor told me it could wait until after the Shoei hypothesis had been announced. There was no need to make another copy—more to the point, he wouldn't let it out of his sight."

Ryohei said nothing.

"C'mon, let me borrow your copy. Please," Yoshimura begged. "Without it we won't be able to reprint the catalogue. Think of it as a final tribute to the professor." Uncharacteristically, Yoshimura bowed his head.

A tribute to the professor, my foot! Now that he's dead, Yoshimura plans to take his place!

"I left it in Morioka," Ryohei replied bluntly, intending his words as a refusal.

"Okay. Pick it up anytime you like. Naturally, I'll pay your expenses."

Yoshimura's superciliousness took Ryohei by surprise.

"Let me think about it. The professor's only just died. It's quite a lot to process right now."

"Sure. Take your time. We'll talk about it again soon," said Yoshimura nodding. He seemed to have decided things could get messy if he pushed Ryohei too far.

When Ryohei returned to the reception table, he saw an unexpected face waiting there.

"Hey, long time no see!" the man greeted him.

"Inspector Onodera... What are you doing here?"

"Just popped in for a look... Say, isn't this some funeral! Leave it to the professor to draw a crowd," said the policeman, casting an amiable smile in Yumi's direction. Then in a low voice he said, "There are a few things I'd like to ask you later... Do you mind?"

After the funeral was over, an elaborate memorial service was to be held in the temple's annex. Ryohei had not been invited. As soon as it started, Ryohei slipped away with Onodera. Ryohei had already removed his necktie and since he was wearing an overcoat he didn't stand out as being dressed for a funeral. After walking for five minutes they came to a restaurant. Without saying a word, Onodera pushed open the door and went inside.

"You know," Onodera began, sipping a glass of tomato juice, "I saw Mizuno at the funeral."

"Oh?" replied Ryohei. "I didn't notice him come in." He felt a twinge of guilt. After all this time, he still hadn't spoken to the book dealer.

"He said he was returning the favor you did by coming to his brother-in-law's funeral."

"Is that so?"

"But it's a shame, isn't it? First Saga, now Professor Nishijima... In a matter of two short months, the ukiyo-e world has lost its two leading scholars," Onodera said, giving Ryohei a meaningful look.

Grasping the detective's implication, Ryohei gave a start.

Is that it? Is that why he's come today?

When one paused to think about it, it *was* a strange coincidence—though a coincidence it certainly was. In the space of two months, both the Edo Art Association and the Ukiyo-e Connoisseurship Society had lost their central figures. What's more, the two men had known each other—indeed, had once been friends—for decades. One didn't have to be a detective to find it all just a bit suspicious.

I wonder why it never struck us as strange?

No one in Nishijima's inner circle had thought to draw any connection between Saga Atsushi's death and the professor's. It just went to show how remote a figure Saga had been to them. While outsiders would have looked at Saga and Nishijima and seen two ukiyo-e scholars, to those on the inside the two men seemed to belong to different worlds.

"Was there anything suspicious about the professor's death?" asked Ryohei, jumping to the crux of the matter.

"Well, right now it's hard to say." Onodera gave a wry smile.

"Hard to say?"

So the fire didn't start by accident?

Ryohei leaned forward in his chair.

"The thing is," Onodera went on, "we haven't been able to determine the cause of the fire—all we know is it started in his study. You see, there were so many books, it's hard to pin down exactly *how* it started. But it seems now the local police are treating it as arson."

"Arson!" exclaimed Ryohei. That meant murder. He probed the detective for more information.

"At this point it's just a hunch; one death coming right after the other and all. Anyway, that's what the inspector in charge of the case seems to think. He rang our office up to ask whether there was anything suspicious about Saga's death."

Ryohei said nothing.

"Since I was in charge of the Saga investigation," Onodera went on, "I came down to Tokyo to talk to him. I explained 'til I was blue in the face that Saga's death's has nothing to do with this, but he wouldn't listen—says it's too easy to dismiss it as mere coincidence."

The detective smiled.

"So he thinks Mr. Saga's death wasn't a suicide, and the professor's wasn't an accident, is that right?" asked Ryohei.

"That's about it."

"But why would someone have wanted to murder them? It's true Mr. Saga and the professor were friends once, but they had hardly spoken to each other for years."

"True, it's hard to imagine they were both killed for the same reason. But I suppose it's conceivable someone killed Nishijima as revenge for Saga's death."

"So you still think the professor might have somehow driven Mr. Saga to commit suicide?"

"No, I was just kidding. What I meant was there's no other way to explain their deaths."

Ryohei looked confused.

"At any rate, I intend to investigate this until I'm satisfied I've got the answer. Ultimately I think we'll decide one was a suicide and the other was an accident. But there *is* one thing that's been bothering me..." Onodera hesitated before continuing.

"What's that?" Ryohei prompted him.

"Have you seen Yosuke Kokufu recently?"

"No—that is, not since before New Year," Ryohei replied. Then he quickly added, "Why, what's *he* got to do with this?"

"Well, a witness has reported seeing someone matching his description near the scene of the incident on the night Professor Nishijima died."

"You're kidding!"

"The clerk at the neighborhood liquor store has stated that when he stepped outside around nine in the evening to lower the store's shutters, he saw someone who looked like Yosuke walking toward the professor's house. It seems Yosuke had bought alcohol at the shop on numerous occasions when visiting the professor in the past, so the clerk recognized him; only he can't say for sure it was Yosuke because he didn't actually exchange greetings or anything with him. Still, it's been nagging me a bit."

"The professor's house... Yosuke?" Ryohei couldn't believe it. But then he realized it *was* possible. There was no denying Yosuke had been thinking of doing something about the whole Shoei affair. But Ryohei wasn't about to say as much to the detective. Not only would it cast suspicion on Yosuke but Ryohei would then be obliged to relate the painful story of how Professor Nishijima had stolen his research. Otherwise, Onodera wouldn't understand why Yosuke had been so upset at the professor.

"Now, I understand Yosuke had been expelled, as it were, from Nishijima's inner circle," said the detective.

Ryohei said nothing.

"Some people might consider that suspicious," went on Onodera, lighting a cigarette. "However, there's too big a gap between nine in the evening and midnight, which was when the fire broke out. So at this stage I don't think Yosuke can be linked directly to the fire. But if it *is* determined to be arson then the question of motive…"

"But what about Mr. Saga's death? Yosuke would never—"

"I know. But the police on the case don't know Yosuke. They're just grasping at straws. I know he's not the type of person who would do that kind of thing. This is just my own hunch, but I don't think it was arson at all." Onodera smiled, trying to cheer Ryohei up. "Don't worry, I'll figure something out before Yosuke gets dragged into this mess. I just wanted to let you know… confidentially."

With that, he ended the conversation.

Outside the restaurant, the two men parted and walked away in opposite directions. After a while Onodera checked to make sure Ryohei was out of sight. Then he returned to the restaurant.

"Good work," said a young detective, sitting just behind where Ryohei had been seated. Without attempting to hide his displeasure, the detective sat down across from him.

"There, I told him."

"I'm sorry to have put you through that," the man apologized.

"I just think this is going a bit too far—Yosuke Kokufu has nothing to do with this case."

"But that's all we've got to go on for now… Anyway, there's Yoshimura's testimony."

"That's just a malicious accusation. Is this how Tokyo cops always operate?" Onodera asked sarcastically.

"C'mon. Look, wasn't it *you* who was saying there was something fishy about two ukiyo-e experts dying one right after the other?"

"That's true. But I never said Kokufu had anything to do with it."

"Yeah. But right now we don't have any other leads to go on. At least if we find out he's not involved then we'll have gotten somewhere. Just bear with me a bit," the younger man said, bowing his head repeatedly.

"Anyway, what makes you think Tsuda will say anything to Kokufu? He claims he hasn't seen him for a while."

"Maybe, but at least I've done what I can, so the chief can't complain." The younger man paused thoughtfully for a moment before adding: "Let's see what Kokufu does if and when Tsuda talks to him. Then we'll know what our next move should be."

When Ryohei returned to the temple the memorial service had just ended and mourners were pouring out through the main gate. Breaking into a jog, he hurried over to the reception table but it had already been cleared away. Iwakoshi and the professor's other students stood huddled around a small stove taking a break.

"Did you hear about Yoshimura?" Iwakoshi asked abruptly when Ryohei appeared. "Seems he's going to start teaching at Musashino in the spring."

"Yoshimura?"

"The president of the university was at the memorial service— apparently he formally extended an offer which Yoshimura eagerly accepted. Isn't that a laugh?"

"What about his job at the museum?" asked Ryohei.

"The teaching position's only part-time, for now he'll get to keep his fingers in both pies. He'll be taking over the professor's classes."

"Really?"

"Is that all you can say?" asked Iwakoshi. "Aren't you mad? I mean, what are we, chopped liver? We've been his teaching assistants all these years. Yoshimura's perfectly aware of how we'd feel about this. Just because the president of the university asked him personally doesn't mean he had to go and accept the offer right off bat. He should have talked to us first. That's common sense."

All the others nodded in agreement. Most of them were undergraduates in the professor's seminar and knew Iwakoshi and Ryohei much better than Yoshimura.

"That snake!" continued Iwakoshi. "Who would've thought he had designs on becoming a professor?"

"It seems he's the *only* one who's benefitted from the professor's death," said Yumi. Her words took everyone by surprise.

"Now that you mention it," said Iwakoshi angrily, "it looks like he's getting ready to take over the professor's research on Shoei."

"That reminds me, Ryohei," said Yumi. "A man named Mizuno was looking for you a little while ago."

"Is that so?" Ryohei replied nonchalantly.

"He asked if you wouldn't mind calling him tomorrow at this number." She reached into her pocket, took out a piece of notepaper and handed it to Ryohei.

I bet he's annoyed at me—I haven't seen him since he gave me the catalogue.

The day had been one long ordeal.

Thanking Yumi, Ryohei sank deep into thought.

"WHAT DO YOU MEAN you're quitting? You can't just give up on ukiyo-e!" exclaimed Yosuke, staring at Ryohei in utter disbelief.

The two friends were seated in a sushi restaurant in Jimbocho in downtown Tokyo. After the funeral Ryohei had called Yosuke at his office and suggested they get together for a drink.

"I've had enough. I'm fed up," complained Ryohei, looking serious. "The professor's dead, and now there's talk of Yoshimura coming to Musashino this spring to teach. Suddenly I feel like I don't have the strength to go on."

"But what about Boston?" asked Yosuke.

"That probably won't happen now. The ministry's request was actually made to the EAA, not the professor, so now that he's gone…"

"I see… What a mess!"

"It's my own fault. I was too easy-going. I should have listened to you in the beginning and stuck up for myself more."

Yosuke was silent for a while. At last he asked, "So what do you plan to do after you quit?"

"I haven't figured that out yet. I guess I'll go back to Morioka and talk it over with my parents. I'll probably look for a job there. Anyway, I have a while to think things over. I have to stay at the university until the end of March to teach the professor's class."

"So now *you're* throwing in the towel, too?" Yosuke muttered sadly. "It looks like the only person to come out of all this smelling like roses is Yoshimura. So he fancies himself a professor, does he? What cheek!"

Ryohei was in a dilemma. Should he tell Yosuke what Inspector Onodera had said to him? He still hadn't made up his mind.

Yosuke continued: "I was furious when I saw that article on Shoei in the newspaper. But now the professor's dead, it all seems so silly. At least he was a worthy opponent, but Yoshimura!" He smiled ruefully. "As a matter of fact," he added, "I went to see the professor the night he died…"

A shiver ran down Ryohei's spine.

"I must not have been thinking straight," Yosuke went on. "I got off the train and walked all the way to his house before I remembered the professor always goes to Hakone right after New Year's, so I turned around and went home. I was shocked when I heard about his death on the news the next morning. To think he'd been home after all! I have to admit, I couldn't help feeling sad. I mean, I'd known the guy for over ten years—ever since I was in college. It hit me like a ton of bricks."

Ryohei breathed a sigh of relief. Now he could tell Yosuke what Onodera had said. He proceeded to do so, leaving out the part about the cloud of suspicion hanging over his friend's head.

"Arson! You're kidding!" exclaimed Yosuke, his eyes growing wide.

"But Onodera himself says he thinks it was an accident," added Ryohei.

"Hmm… I wonder. Why do you someone would want to kill the professor?"

"A random act of violence perhaps?"

"Now *that's* farfetched. If it *was* arson, it can't be a coincidence. No, someone wanted the professor dead. So who benefits? Yoshimura for one, but I don't think he's got the guts to pull it off. So far he's been lucky things have gone his way, but I don't think he could have seen this far ahead. Anyway, he still needed the professor. That leaves only one logical conclusion: the only people who had a motive for wanting the professor out of the way are you and me."

Ryohei was flabbergasted.

"As soon as the police start digging around for anything that suggests arson," continued Yosuke, "Yoshimura and the others are bound to point them in our direction. After all, they know we both had an axe to grind with the professor... Oh, wait a minute... You don't need to worry after all."

"Why's that?" asked Ryohei.

"Because Yoshimura won't dare drag you into it. If he mentions his suspicions of you to the police he'll first have to admit he stole your research. He'd be digging his own grave. I'm the one who's going to bear the brunt of their attack."

"C'mon. You're being paranoid."

"Not at all. I wouldn't be surprised if Yoshimura's already talked to the police about me. Perhaps that's the reason for Onodera's visit to Tokyo."

Ryohei said nothing.

"In which case," Yosuke went on, "my little visit to the professor's house that night could prove a tad inconvenient..."

Yosuke gave Ryohei a wry smile.

January 8

THE NEXT DAY, Ryohei dialed the number Onodera had given him and asked to speak to the detective.

"Is that right?" Onodera said cheerfully when Ryohei was done speaking. "So he realized the professor wasn't there and went home? I figured as much."

"He mentioned this without any prompting from me, you understand," Ryohei hastened to explain. "It just came out naturally when we were talking about the professor. I'm positive he's telling the truth."

When he had finished speaking to Onodera, Ryohei gave Mizuno a call. It was a call he dreaded making. He had no one to blame for that but himself.

Mizuno answered the phone right away.

"Nice to hear from you. I'm sorry I missed you yesterday," he said in a surprisingly cheerful voice. Ryohei breathed a sigh of relief.

"I'm very sorry about the painting catalogue," Ryohei said, beginning with an apology.

"Huh? Oh, there's no need to apologize," responded Mizuno. "I gave it to you with no strings attached. I was only hoping it might be of some use to you."

Mizuno laughed.

"I must admit," he went on. "I was pretty surprised when I saw that newspaper article. Sharaku—imagine! I have to hand it to you art historians. That's a fine bit of research."

Ryohei was at a loss for what to say.

"So anyway, where are you now?" asked Mizuno.

Ryohei arranged to meet Mizuno in a café near the west exit of Shinjuku Station. He said he had a favor to ask Ryohei and there was someone he wanted him to meet. He didn't give a name. As Ryohei couldn't very well refuse, he set out for Shinjuku. He arrived at the café a little past the specified time. Mizuno was already seated inside, engrossed in conversation with another man.

"Ah, there you are."

Smiling, Mizuno beckoned Ryohei to sit beside him. Ryohei and the other man exchanged greetings.

He looks vaguely familiar.

The man was perhaps a little over forty. He wore thick glasses and had flecks of gray, but his long hair and stylish jacket made him appear considerably younger.

"This is Minegishi Takashi," said Mizuno.

Of course...

Minegishi was a leading member of the Ukiyo-e Connoisseurship Society. He was especially close to the late Saga Atsushi. Though he hadn't officially been Saga's protégé, everyone treated him as such. Mizuno must have thought Ryohei might not want to meet Minegishi if he mentioned his name. Ryohei had seen Minegishi's photograph several times in magazines but never met him.

"Takashi has been very eager to meet you," said Mizuno, looking somewhat at a loss for how to explain the reason for the introduction.

"The truth is," volunteered Minegishi, "Keiji here was telling me how he'd given you that painting catalogue. That's when I started pestering him to introduce us."

"He seems interested in finding out something," said Mizuno smiling. "He has a bee in his bonnet when it comes to Kiyochika."

Ryohei finally put two and two together.

Ah, that's right. Minegishi's an expert on Kiyochika.

"You see, I've been out of the country since last fall," explained Minegishi. "So I only just found out about the catalogue."

"Yes. Now, if you'd been *here* I'd have shown it to you straight away," said Mizuno defensively. "Bad timing, that's all."

Minegishi looked at Mizuno and scowled. How could you give a perfect stranger a book you knew I'd kill to get my hands on, his look seemed to say.

Minegishi was a professional photographer, specializing mostly in nature photography—landscapes and that sort of thing. That was how he had become interested in ukiyo-e. He had even written an article on the use of light in Kiyochika's woodblock prints. One could argue he was Japan's foremost expert on Kiyochika's work.

"And now Professor Nishijima is dead... Is it true Sato's catalogue was destroyed in the fire?" Minegishi asked Ryohei.

"I'm afraid so," answered Ryohei. "I'm very sorry."

"Now, about that," chimed in Mizuno. "You didn't happen to make a copy, did you? The newspaper mentioned Kiyochika's preface in the article but it didn't quote any of it. I *told* Takashi there was nothing interesting in it, but he wouldn't give up... he kept harping on about how he wanted to see it for himself. By accident I went and mentioned you might have a copy, and this is what happened!"

Mizuno gave a quizzical smile and looked at Minegishi.

"I know it's probably nothing, but I just can't stop thinking about it. I'm sorry for being so pushy," Minegishi apologized.

"As a matter of fact, I do have a copy," replied Ryohei. "It's not here with me in Tokyo but I can bring it next time if you like."

"You can?" exclaimed Mizuno. "Thank goodness! Now I can get him off my back."

"So what was it about Kiyochika that you were most interested in finding out?" Ryohei asked Minegishi.

"Well, I just happen to be in the process of writing a chronology of Kiyochika's life, and I haven't been able to find out very much about the period he spent in Tohoku. I wondered if he mentioned anything about it in his preface to Sato's catalogue."

Ryohei nodded. He knew exactly how Minegishi felt.

"The problem is, Mr. Mizuno is right—the preface is just a *fomulaic* sort of thing. It really says very little," said Ryohei.

"I see…"

Minegishi looked disappointed.

"I suppose the only piece of information it contains is the date he visited Kosaka."

"Really? It gives a date?"

"Yes. Sometime in late November 1906, if I'm not mistaken."

"Is that right? Even that much is a great help," replied Minegishi delightedly.

"But if your copy's not here in Tokyo then where is it?" asked Mizuno, as though struck by a sudden thought.

"At my parents' place in Morioka."

"Morioka? I go there all the time," said Minegishi. "For work, usually, but I also go twice a year to trace the route Kiyochika walked on his way to Tohoku: Sendai, Morioka, Aomori, Hirosaki…"

"Now that you mention it, Kiyochika *did* spend quite a bit of time in Morioka," said Ryohei.

"A lot of his nikuhitsu-ga are still floating around up there," said Minegishi. "Whenever I go I always stop at the antiques shops and ask them to keep an eye open for his paintings and give me a call if anything turns up."

"Ever heard of Kozukata Antiques?" asked Ryohei, referring to Kato's shop.

"Kozukata—you mean that one just near the park?"

"That's it."

"It specializes in woodblock prints, if I'm not mistaken," said Minegishi, searching his memory.

In the end, Minegishi arranged to meet Ryohei in Morioka the next time Ryohei was there. Besides being eager to see Kiyochika's preface, Minegishi was already planning to go to Aomori soon to take a look at a sketchbook by Kiyochika which a dealer had found for him. He said on the way back he would stop off in Morioka and give Ryohei a call. Ryohei, of course, had no objection to the plan.

January 14

MORIOKA was in the midst of a blizzard.

Unusually, this year there had been no snow at New Year. Then, as though trying to make up for it, snow had started falling heavily on the tenth and hadn't let up. Now even the roads were covered in several inches of densely packed snow.

Ryohei had arrived home on the eleventh. Tonight he had gone into town after receiving a call from Minegishi. Downtown there were two large bookstores on opposite sides of the main street from one another. On the phone Minegishi said he would be waiting for Ryohei in the café on the second floor of one of them. Before leaving the house Ryohei telephoned Kato to invite him along. The antiques dealer remembered Minegishi well, he told him to give him a call the next time he came to Morioka. Since Kato's shop was not far from the bookstore, he would definitely be there when Ryohei arrived.

"Ah, there he is," called Minegishi, waving to Ryohei.

Kato was sitting across from Minegishi. The two men were engrossed in an animated conversation.

"Now this is what I call a blizzard!" said Kato, smiling as he offered Ryohei the seat next to him. "Mr. Minegishi was showing me a sketchbook by Kiyochika."

"The one from Aomori?" asked Ryohei, taking off his coat.

"Yes. It's a real find if you ask me," said Kato.

The sketchbook wrapped in a *furoshiki* sat on the table.

"Do you mind?" Ryohei asked Minegishi.

Minegishi nodded. Ryohei removed the square of cloth and opened the book. Pasted onto the pages were over twenty hand-painted sketches of flowers and other still lives. The colors were calm and subdued, even understated, and the tone completely different from Kiyochika's landscapes, demonstrating superb draftsmanship.

"Amazing!" exclaimed Ryohei.

As he flipped through the pages Kato looked on, marveling at each one.

"Apparently he painted these while staying at a ryokan right here in Morioka," muttered Kato, chagrinned.

"Is that so? That *would* be frustrating," said Ryohei.

"I wonder how that dealer up in Aomori got hold of it?" mused Kato.

"If it's any consolation, I think it found its way to Aomori a long time ago," said Minegishi soothingly. "I knew the moment I saw it that it was a real find, but I thought the dealer was asking too much. So I was planning to just photograph it, but when I noticed it was signed, dated and everything, it was irresistible."

Minegishi couldn't help gloating.

"Here, I photocopied this for you," said Ryohei, handing Minegishi a copy of Sato's catalogue as he wrapped the sketchbook back in its cloth.

"Thanks," Minegishi said gratefully. "Sorry to have dragged you out just for this." He set to reading Kiyochika's preface.

Ryohei wondered if he would find anything of interest in it. *The greater the expectation, the greater the disappointment*, he thought as he watched Minegishi's detached expression.

"Ah-hah!" exclaimed the photographer as his eyes came to rest on something. Suddenly he went pale and a strange look appeared on his face.

"Are you okay?" asked Ryohei in alarm.

"Uh-huh…"

Minegishi was sunk deep in thought.

"I've been duped," he said at last. "This sketchbook… is a fake!"

He thumped the book in annoyance.

"What makes you say that?" asked Ryohei. There'd been nothing to suggest it was a forgery. He was by no means an expert on Kiyochika, but the brushwork and signature looked perfectly authentic.

"Look at the date!" exclaimed Minegishi. "The date!"

He opened the sketchbook again and showed Ryohei and Kato the last illustration. Running down the left-hand side in Kiyochika's handwriting was an inscription: *I compiled this sketchbook while convalescing at the Taiseikan in Morioka from November 20th to 25th of this year.*

"The Taiseikan… Is there such a ryokan in Morioka?" asked Minegishi.

The other two men replied they had never heard of it.

"Just as I thought. Whoever forged this sketchbook used Morioka instead of Aomori so it would be harder to verify."

Minegishi cradled his head in his hands.

"Maybe it's simply gone out of business," suggested Ryohei. "That doesn't necessarily mean the sketchbook's a forgery." He couldn't see what Minegishi was making such a fuss about.

"Kiyochika came to Tohoku from July 1906 to May 1907," explained Minegishi.

Ryohei was aware of this.

"Which means we can assume that by 'this year' he means 1906." Ryohei nodded.

"But in the preface to Sato's catalogue Kiyochika states he was visiting his friend Sato in Kosaka from November 23rd to 28th."

Minegishi spread the photocopies Ryohei had given him out on the table.

"Now, if he was in Morioka compiling this sketchbook until the 25th —and *convalescing* from an illness—how could he have traveled to Kosaka on the twenty-third?"

"I see…" mumbled Ryohei.

Now it was his and Kato's turn to be surprised.

"That dealer must have figured I was an easy target, always rattling on about Kiyochika," bemoaned Minegishi, biting his lip hard. "There are lots of Kiyochika forgeries floating around up here in Tohoku—I should have done my homework more carefully. I have to say, though, whoever painted this did a damned good job. I didn't suspect a thing."

"Absolutely. *Anyone* would think it was by Kiyochika," said Ryohei consolingly. He picked up the sketchbook and turned it over and over in his hands. "Doesn't the binding look old to you?" he asked Kato.

"Yes," replied the art dealer, "but bindings aren't really important. I wonder if someone added the inscription later."

"But that goes without saying. After all it's a fake," said Minegishi despondently.

"No, I mean, perhaps the sketches *are* by Kiyochika and the inscription was simply added later."

"Oh, I see what you're saying," said Minegishi. "Well, it's certainly possible. These sketches sure *do* look like Kiyochika's handiwork. And his handwriting is very distinctive too. Whoever faked this inscription has imitated it perfectly," said Minegishi.

"There's no doubt about the sketches, so all the more reason to suspect the inscription's a fake—I see it all the time," said Kato emphatically.

Minegishi nodded. "I suppose you're right. It's not as though Kiyochika could have gotten the dates wrong in his preface," he said, starting to relax a bit.

Ryohei was suddenly struck by a disturbing thought.

No, it couldn't be...

But once planted, the seed of doubt began to grow in Ryohei's mind.

Returning home after saying goodbye to Minegishi and Kato, Ryohei removed his copy of Sato's catalogue from its envelope. He photocopied the entire book from cover to cover, including the front and back. Now, once again, he began inspecting it from the beginning, scouring every inch. But nothing in particular caught his eye.

It's just your imagination.

Ryohei had a hunch the sketchbook of Kiyochika's which Minegishi had purchased in Aomori was in fact the genuine article. Since Kiyochika couldn't have been in both Kosaka and Morioka at the same time, this cast doubt on the authenticity of Sato's catalogue.

But scour as he might, Ryohei could find nothing amiss. On the other hand, there was no reason to suspect the catalogue was a forgery. A forged sketchbook by a famous artist could fetch a tidy sum—but a painting catalogue was a different matter entirely. No matter how rare, an old book couldn't compete with an actual painting in price. Moreover, Ryohei had acquired the catalogue in question for next to nothing. What motive, then, could someone have had for forging? If, at the book exhibition, Ryohei's eye had not fallen on it, the catalogue might still be passing from one rare book dealer to another. Ryohei laid his suspicions to rest.

But just as he was about to put the photocopies back in the envelope, a postcard fell out. It had been tucked inside the original catalogue. It was now, in a manner of speaking, the only souvenir of it he had left.

Looking at it now Ryohei felt a surge of emotion.

On the front was a photograph of a mountain hot springs resort, probably taken shortly before the war. In the foreground was a long suspension bridge spanning a ravine. On it stood two women, dressed up as geisha, smiling into the camera. Beyond them in the distance clouds of steam rose from a town clustered around the hot springs. The whole scene conveyed a sense of peace and calm.

Ryohei stared absentmindedly at the photograph for some time. In the bottom right-hand corner was written "Naruko Onsen."

The postcard was addressed to someone in Yokohama. It had probably been sent by a guest at the resort to a friend back home.

Naruko—that's near Sendai. Speaking of which, I wonder how Saeko's doing.

Ryohei suddenly felt a strong urge to see her.

January 17

"I'M OFF to London later this month," Kato said excitedly as Ryohei sat down.

It had been some time since he last stepped into Kozukata Antiques. When he arrived, Kato was talking to an elderly gentleman whom Ryohei had seen there several times before. His name was Senda and he taught history at a local junior college in Morioka. He was interested in rare books and often visited Kato's shop. Ryohei sat down next to Senda and joined the conversation.

"Vacation?" asked Ryohei.

"Not exactly—I'm going with some friends." Kato rattled off the names of two or three other art dealers who all had shops in Morioka.

"A business trip then?"

"Sotheby's is our main objective," said Kato, his eyes twinkling.

Every year some of the world's most valuable art passed through the doors of Sotheby's, the world's largest auction house. Museums and gallery owners from around the world flocked to its periodic public auctions. The prices fetched at Sotheby's established benchmarks for the global art market in any given year. Though anyone could attend, the objects on offer were not ones people could afford. It was a Mecca for art dealers, and Japanese travel agencies even organized tours. Kato explained he had signed up for one such tour.

"Not that I can afford to buy anything," he laughed. "I'll just be window shopping—there's a lot of Asian art coming up for auction this time. February is always slow around here anyway. For ages my friends have been trying to convince me to go, but this year I finally decided to take the plunge. It's something I've always wanted to do before I die."

"Like a child in a candy store!" laughed Senda.

"There *was* once a ryokan called the Taiseikan in Morioka," remembered Senda. "It was behind the Hachiman Shrine, very famous in its day. I think there's an office building there now."

Ryohei and Kato listened attentively. Ryohei had begun the conversation by bringing up the subject of Minegishi and the sketchbook he had bought the other day.

"Anyway," concluded Senda, "it went bust before the war."

"Then it's not surprising we hadn't heard of it," said Kato nodding.

"Once it was a first-class establishment," Senda went on. "But in the 1930s it went downhill and became the sort of place where geisha entertained their clients."

"Well, times change," said Kato triumphantly.

"So Minegishi's sketchbook…" prompted Ryohei.

"It means the forger did his homework. Anyone could have found out about the Taiseikan simply by asking someone who's old enough to have been around before the war. No forger worth his salt would make such a rookie mistake."

Ryohei looked puzzled.

"In other words, all we've succeeded in establishing is that the Taiseikan actually existed," explained Kato. He was convinced the inscription in the sketchbook was a forgery.

But if the forger did his homework, why not choose the name of an old reputable inn that's still around? Why a geisha house? That would just

be likely to arouse suspicion. It's not as though the guestbook would have
survived from the turn of the century. Another inn would have been better.
Ryohei wasn't that convinced.

That night Ryohei telephoned Yosuke.

"So you think the sketchbook's genuine?"

"Well, I…" Ryohei faltered. When asked point blank, he wasn't prepared to go that far. After all, both Minegishi and Kato thought it was a forgery, and *they* were the experts. "I'm pretty sure the illustrations are genuine, but the other two say the inscription was probably added later."

"Does Minegishi agree about the illustrations?"

"More or less."

"Well, he's the leading expert on Kiyochika in Japan. If *he* is convinced they're genuine, what's the problem? I mean, why would someone have felt the need to forge the inscription if the sketchbook was the real deal?"

"According to Kato, originally the sketchbook probably contained more pages but someone broke it up and rebound them into several smaller volumes. Since those were unsigned, the forged inscription and signature were added."

"Hmm… a clever theory. I suppose it's possible. Not having seen the inscription I can't say, but if it *is* genuine then the dates in Sato's catalogue must be wrong."

"Precisely. And what does *that* mean?" asked Ryohei, wondering what Yosuke might make of it all.

"What does it mean? Well, Kiyochika might have remembered the dates incorrectly or it could be a misprint… or maybe…"

"What?"

"Well, maybe the preface itself is a forgery."

Ryohei sighed. The same thought had occurred to him.

"It's pretty unlikely," said Yosuke, "that Kiyochika made a mistake. He's always very specific when it comes to dates. He probably looked it up in his diary. As for a misprint, that's unlikely too—there's not much text in the catalogue to begin with. One can't rule it out entirely, of course, but the chances the editor happened to screw up the dates seem pretty slim."

Ryohei said nothing.

"So if the sketchbook and the inscription are genuine, then Kiyochika's preface must be a forgery," concluded Yosuke.

Ryohei broke into a cold sweat. "But why in the world would someone want to forge it?" he countered. "Someone somewhere must have had something to gain from it. Behind every forgery there's a profit motive. In this case, however, no one's profited so far except us."

"And Yoshimura. He's moving up in the world!" laughed Yosuke.

"Assuming the catalogue was published with the intention of increasing the value of Shoei's work," said Ryohei, "then by now his name should be more widely known. "But it's not. He's still a nobody. No one had even *seen* the catalogue up until now, not even experts on Western-style painting, let alone ukiyo-e scholars. Very few copies must have been published. So who profited?"

"Yeah," agreed Yosuke. "If anything, unscrupulous art dealers would have *removed* Shoei's signature before selling his paintings," observed Yosuke.

"Right. So if Kiyochika's preface was forged, it seems the forgery was a failure."

"I agree with you entirely," Yosuke said to Ryohei's surprise. "So what does it all mean?" he asked puzzled.

"I suppose it means the inscription in the sketchbook *is* a forgery after all," replied Ryohei.

"I guess that's the only possible conclusion based on what you've said… Anyway, until I've seen the sketchbook I can't say either way. By the way, what has Minegishi done with it?"

"Well, since the illustrations appear to be genuine, he's gone ahead and taken it home," said Ryohei.

"So it's in Tokyo. Good. I'll contact him and ask to see it—I met him at Mr. Saga's house a number of times."

"Thanks, Yosuke. I appreciate it."

"Don't mention it. I'm curious to see it too. Oh, by the way, I wonder if you could send me a copy of Sato's catalogue?"

"Of course. The whole thing?"

"Yes. The front and back cover, too, if you don't mind."

"Got it. I'll also send you a copy of the postcard."

"What postcard?"

Ryohei explained. Would Yosuke mind looking up the address in Yokohama for him, he asked. Now that he'd begun to have his doubts about the catalogue, Ryohei said he didn't want to leave any stone unturned. Yosuke was intrigued. "I wish you'd shown it to me earlier," he said reproachfully.

"I forgot all about it until now."

"Well, anyway, it's probably nothing."

Yosuke hung up the phone with a laugh.

January 29

YOSUKE was walking through Tsurumi ward, an old quarter of Yokohama.

In his hand he held a photocopy of a small-scale prewar map. He had circled one area on the map in red. He knew Tsurumi had been bombed heavily during the war and most of its houses destroyed, but as he walked he noticed the layout of the streets had changed very little. As he approached his destination, what he saw matched almost exactly what was on the map. This neighborhood seemed to have been spared the bombing. *What luck*, he thought.

It must be just about here...

Yosuke came to a stop and looked around. It was a hilly neighborhood. He was breathing heavily.

He walked from house to house peering at the nameplates on each one. Being broad daylight, he felt a bit uncomfortable. Passersby, who took him for a door-to-door salesman, steered clear.

"Ah-hah!"

He came to a nameplate that read "Matsushita." It was an old house. Yosuke double-checked his map. No mistake about it—the house corresponded to the address on his map. He couldn't help feeling a bit disappointed at how easy it was to find. He had felt sure the house would have been destroyed long ago.

Mustering his resolve, Yosuke slid open the glass-paned wooden door. A bell sounded automatically.

A voice called out, "Who is it?"

An elderly woman appeared from inside the house and peered suspiciously at Yosuke, but she seemed to relax once she had taken in his appearance. She politely asked what he wanted. Yosuke explained the reason for his visit.

"Yes, we *have* lived here since before the war," she said. "Why do you ask?"

"I was looking for a Mr. Matsushita Yuji…"

"That would be my grandfather… He's no longer alive, of course."

From his pocket Yosuke removed a copy of the postcard Ryohei had sent him from Morioka and unfolded it. It was addressed to *Matsushita Yuji, Tsurumi, Yokohama*, followed by the house number. He showed it to the woman.

"My! This was sent to my grandfather. Where did you get it?"

"It was inside an old book I came across while doing some research."

"Is that so? Well, thank you for taking the trouble to show it to me." The woman seemed to have mistaken Yosuke for a public servant. She didn't bother to ask him what his "research" entailed. Yosuke decided to say nothing. "But that book has nothing to do with him," she added. "I gave this postcard away after my grandfather died."

"Gave away?"

"Everything of any sentimental value that belonged to him I gave away to friends and family. Now, let's see… Who was it I give all those postcards to? Some of them were quite rare. I seem to recall putting them together and giving them to someone."

The woman asked Yosuke to wait a moment and disappeared into the house. Yosuke waited anxiously.

"I found it."

The woman returned carrying an old notebook. Apparently she kept a record of everything of her grandfather's she had given away.

"Ah, that's right. I gave them to one of my nephews. His hobby was collecting stamps at the time and he begged me to let him have them."

"When was that?" asked Yosuke.

"Let's see. Grandfather died six years ago…"

"That recently?"

"I wouldn't call that recent. My nephew's in college now."

Yosuke was dumbfounded. Because the postcard was very old, he'd been assuming all this must have happened long ago.

The young man's name was Matsushita Yoshitake. After getting his address and telephone number, Yosuke left.

The address the woman had given him was somewhere in Gotanda in Tokyo, which happened to be on his way home. He called the number from a pay phone at Tsurumi station. Despite being a Saturday, the nephew was at home.

"Yes, this is Yoshitake..." the young man said, a note of caution creeping into his voice when he realized the call was from a total stranger. But as Yosuke explained his business he could hear the young man's tone relax.

"Oh, no!" he said, "So my aunt knows!" He laughed unapologetically.

At Yosuke's request, Yoshitake readily agreed to meet at a café outside Gotanda Station in one hour so Yosuke could ask him some more questions. Yosuke told the young man he would be able to recognize him by his green Burberry trench coat.

"Shall I wear a red carnation in my lapel?" Yoshitake responded with a laugh.

"He's just finished making a phone call. Now he's buying a ticket. Okay... Talk to you later."

The man hurriedly hung up the phone and, trying hard to look innocent, began tailing Yosuke. He followed him to the station and upstairs to the train platform.

It was the young detective Onodera had met at the restaurant near the temple on the day of Professor Nishijima's funeral.

"Mr. Kokufu?" a young man sporting a pompadour called out to Yosuke as he entered the café. He was not very tall.

"You must be Yoshitake," replied Yosuke.

The young man nodded, sucking on a straw. He wore a black leather jacket and baggy black trousers, with only a tee-shirt underneath his jacket. He was drinking a cream soda.

"Thanks for meeting me," began Yosuke, sitting down across the table from Yoshitake.

"No problem. Gave me an excuse to get out of the house."

"Meaning?"

"My mom... she's a real hard-ass. Told me I was grounded today," laughed Yoshitake. "I crashed my friend's wheels the other day. When you called I was sure it was the cops."

Yoshitake scratched his head in embarrassment.

"Let's see now," said Yoshitake, searching his memory in response to Yosuke's question. "Sometime last spring, I think it was. I was in desperate need of cash so I sold the postcards along with my stamp collection. It was really traumatic—I'd slaved to scrape together that collection since I was in elementary school."

Yosuke had trouble picturing someone like Yoshitake pouring over a beloved stamp collection day after day.

"What with one thing and another, I only got about a hundred thousand for the whole lot."

"A hundred thousand yen—that's incredible!"

"You gotta be kidding. The retail value of the stamps *alone* was well over *seven* hundred grand," said Yoshitake. "But the old man who ran the shop was giving me a lot of grief about them being in bad condition. It pissed me off but I was in a hurry to get my hands on the dough, so... I still get mad just thinking about it," he grumbled.

"How many postcards were there?"

"About three hundred."

"Wow, impressive."

"People would give them to me when they heard I was collecting stamps. None of them was all that rare or anything, but in a shop they'd still fetch about three hundred yen each. Even at a hundred a pop, conservatively speaking, that comes to thirty thousand yen. And that jerk only gave me five thousand... What a slime ball," complained Yoshitake as he ordered a glass of tomato juice from the waitress. "Anyway, now I'm screwed—it was supposed to be a secret. I never thought my aunt would find out."

"I'm sorry. It just came up in the course of something I've been investigating."

"Smells like foul play if you ask me," joked Yoshitake.

Yosuke laughed. "By the way," he asked. "Do you remember the name of the shop where you sold them?"

Yoshitake gave him the name of a place in Shinjuku. Yosuke knew it. It was small but advertised extensively in collector's magazines.

"Just mention my name—they'll know me. I've bought a lot of stuff from them over the years," Yoshitake added as Yosuke was leaving.

All in all, a decent young man, thought Yosuke.

Yoshitake remained behind in the café, saying he was going to meet some friends.

It was getting on for six o'clock when Yosuke walked out of Shinjuku Station. He'd left his office at twelve—over five hours ago—and his stomach was growling, but he wanted to wind up his investigation as quickly as possible. The stamp shop Yoshitake had mentioned was on a back street behind the Mitsukoshi department store. Yosuke quickened his pace.

He had no trouble finding the shop. As Yosuke entered, the owner, a fat man in his fifties, greeted him affably. There were no other customers. Yosuke briefly stated his business. When he realized Yosuke had not come to buy anything the owner looked put out, but he listened to what Yosuke had to say without interrupting him.

"Ah, yes… him." The fat man remembered Yoshitake well. "Now that you mention it, he hasn't been here lately."

"I think he's given up stamp collecting."

"That was wise—won't get anywhere if you go about it half-assed like he was." The man gave a loud laugh.

"Now, about this postcard…" said Yosuke, ignoring the man's remark and handing him a photocopy of the postcard addressed to Yoshitake's grandfather. The owner stared at it for a while.

"Beats me. I *did* buy a bunch of postcards from him, but I don't remember every single one. Anyway, it's not like this is rare or anything. I probably just stuck it in with a bunch of other cheap ones and sold them as a set.

Against the left-hand wall of the shop there stood a row of divided shelves filled with bundles of postcards held together with rubber bands, each containing several dozen postcards and labeled with titles such as "Trolley Cars of the '30s and '40s,"

"Japanese Volcanoes," and "National Parks." Then there were single cards encased individually in cellophane sleeves. Yosuke was astonished at the prices. There were even several dating to the late nineteenth century showing scenes of Asakusa.

"Now if it'd been something like *this*," said the owner, indicting a Meiji-era postcard of Tokyo's first "skyscraper," the famous Asakusa Twelve-Stories, "I might remember it but…"

"So you've no recollection of it at all?" Yosuke pressed him. If he gave up now all his efforts would have been for nothing. "What title might you have categorized it under?" he asked, trying to jog the man's memory.

"Let's see… 'Hot Springs Resorts,' I suppose," replied the owner.

On Yosuke's photocopy of the postcard the caption in the bottom right-hand corner was illegible. "Apparently it's a photograph of Naruko Onsen," he explained.

"Is it? That's near Sendai… Wait a minute," said the owner, searching his memory. "Maybe it was *him*…"

"Have you remembered something?"

"No, it's just… I can't say with absolute certainty, but last summer there was a guy who came in here regularly. He said he was looking for scenes of famous places in Tohoku. I can't remember selling him this one, but he did buy a number of others, better than this of course, much older… of Matsushima and Hirosaki Castle and such; mostly late-nineteenth century."

"What was this man like?"

"Oh, I don't know… just an ordinary guy. Let's see, I think I have his business card here somewhere. Hold on a sec, it should be in this drawer…"

The man rummaged around in a drawer below the cash register. Yosuke's heart began to pound.

"Ah, here it is! See, on the back it says 'Looking for Tohoku postcards.' I wrote that to myself as a reminder."

The owner handed Yosuke the card. He took one look at it and caught his breath.

Him! But why? What did it mean? Yosuke began to feel dizzy. "Are you *sure* you don't remember selling this postcard to this man?" he persisted. Everything now hinged on the man's answer.

"Well, if it's *that* important…" the owner folded his arms across his chest and tried to remember.

Just then a woman's voice called out from the doorway at the back of the shop.

"I'm back!"

Looking relieved, the owner called the woman's name. She came out wearing a blue smock. The owner explained why Yosuke had come and showed her his photocopy of the postcard.

"I think I bundled it together with some other postcards of hot springs resorts," he added.

"Was it that bunch labeled 'Postcards from Tohoku,' I wonder?" the woman said.

"That's it!"

"In that case, it was definitely *that* gentleman who bought it," the woman said emphatically. "He came in once while you were out—asked me to reduce the price because he wasn't interested in two-thirds of them. But I said I couldn't do that without asking you first. In the end he caved in and bought the whole lot and left."

"Ah, is that what happened?" said the owner.

"When was that?" asked Yosuke, flustered.

"Must've been sometime last October. It was a bit cold that day but we hadn't gotten around to turning on the heat yet…"

Around the time Sato's catalogue turned up, thought Yosuke.

He stood there for a long time, silently contemplating the significance of what he had just learned. He completely forgot that he still hadn't eaten anything.

"I'm not sure. Right now he's at a ramen shop in front of Fuchu Station. So far I haven't observed anything suspicious. I followed him to a café in Gotanda where he had a long conversation with some punk who looks like he's in a motorcycle gang, but being on my own I couldn't get close enough to overhear what they were saying… Yeah, that stamp shop in Shinjuku will be closed by now but I'll check it out first thing tomorrow. Anyway, seeing as I've been following Yosuke Kokufu all this time and turned up nothing, I guess he must be innocent after all. I expect he'll head straight home now. Is it okay if I knock off after that?… Right, got it."

With a relieved look, the young detective put down the telephone.

January 31

A CALL CAME for Inspector Onodera. It was from Tokyo.

"I see... nothing suspicious, huh?"

Onodera heaved a sigh of relief.

"You're right. It's probably got nothing to do with the case. Maybe some work-related errand... A postcard, you say? No, haven't got a clue. What's that? He's looking for the person who bought it?"

The voice on the other end of the line rattled off a name.

"Oh, I see..."

Suddenly the information sunk in.

"W... wait a minute!" he stammered. "What was that name again?"

The voice repeated it.

What the hell? What's he *got to do with this?* he wondered.

Onodera was stumped.

February 1

RETURNING to his office after lunch, Yosuke found a note on his desk. On it were written Minegishi's name and telephone number.

So he's finally back, thought Yosuke. He'd been trying to call Minegishi for days, but the photographer had gone to Kyushu for work and had not been at home. Yosuke immediately dialed the number.

"Hi there, I heard you called a number of times while I was away," said Minegishi, picking up the phone right away. The number Yosuke had dialed was for the apartment in Yotsuya which Minegishi used as his office. Yosuke asked if he could see the sketchbook.

"Boy, word travels fast. Who told you about it?" asked Minegishi suspiciously.

Yosuke mentioned Ryohei's name.

"I see. That's right, I'd forgotten you were also one of Professor Nishijima's students." Minegishi laughed. His confusion was understandable given he had only ever met Yosuke at Saga's house. "Well, actually I'm in the middle of photographing it now. I have it right here." He invited Yosuke to come by and see it.

The company where Yosuke worked was in Kanda, less than twenty minutes away by taxi. Asking one of his colleagues to cover for him, he ducked out of the office with an apologetic bow.

"As far as I can tell it looks genuine," said Minegishi as he brewed a pot of black tea.

Yosuke was hunched over the sketchbook. "It's certainly a fine work of art," he said.

"I meant the inscription, not the sketches."

"Are you sure?" asked Yosuke.

"Uh-huh. I compared it to other samples of Kiyochika's writing and couldn't find anything wrong with it," said Minegishi. "Now, I don't claim to be a handwriting expert or anything, but I photographed dozens of examples of his signature from paintings he made around the same time and blew them all up to the same size. I noticed a few minor discrepancies in the spacing of the characters, but the balance of the strokes matches perfectly. Boy, though, did it give me a headache!"

"Wow, that sure beats anything any of us could do hands down."

"All in a day's work. It's my bread and butter, after all," said Minegishi, looking rather pleased with himself. "Anyway, what do *you* think?" he asked Yosuke.

"Well, if the inscription *is* authentic…"

"Who would have thought it? Two works by Kiyochika fall into our laps and we don't know which to believe. In fact, it only confuses the situation even more."

Yosuke said nothing.

"Incidentally," continued Minegishi, changing the subject, "I stopped at Kosai and Miho on my way back from Kyushu."

"You mean in Shizuoka?"

"Yes. Kiyochika spent two years there in service to Tokugawa Yoshinobu. I thought I might find out something about Sato Masakichi there."

Kiyochika had been a vassal of the shogun. After the Meiji Restoration, the last shogun, Yoshinobu, was sent back home to Shizuoka accompanied by many of his vassals.

"Learn anything?" asked Yosuke.

"Not a thing. Kosai is really just a municipal district made up of various towns and villages, so it has virtually no records of its own. I had my hopes pinned on Miho but that turned out to be in vain too. But now that I think about it, Kiyochika wrote that he met Sato *in* Shizuoka; he never said Sato was *from* Shizuoka. I guess it was naïve of me to suppose I could trace him so easily. If they really were such close friends then at the very least Sato's name should have turned up in the scholarly literature on Kiyochika by now."

Yosuke and Minegishi both sighed.

"I guess there was nothing in Akita either?" asked Minegishi.

"On Sato? Apparently not."

"I wonder if Yoshimura really looked very hard," said Minegishi, unaware it was really Ryohei who had gone to Akita.

"Why do you say that?"

"Well, I assume he was focused more on Shoei than on Kiyochika…"

"Yes, but he searched the public archives and the historical society for information on Sato," Yosuke explained on Ryohei's behalf.

"But why didn't Yoshimura go to Shizuoka?"

"I suppose there was no need to. Sato was just an art collector who happened to take an interest in Shoei's work. If nothing had turned up on Shoei in Akita then a trip to Shizuoka might have been necessary, but something *did* turn up—the mystery of Sharaku was solved. Sato became irrelevant."

"I see. I always suspected scholars simply ignored anything that didn't fit their preconceived theories; now I'm convinced of it!" said Minegishi with a forced smile. Then he added, "Personally, *I* still think Kiyochika is more important as an artist."

"By the way," said Yosuke, remembering something he had wanted to ask the photographer. "Albumen printing was still being used in 1907, wasn't it?"

"Albumen printing? Oh, you mean for photography," replied Minegishi, a bit surprised at the abruptness of Yosuke's question. "Yes, at that time the photographic plates used in magazine and book publishing were mostly albumen prints."

"But the plates in Sato's catalogue weren't what I typically think of as albumen prints—the paper was thick and kind of shiny. I wonder what sort of technique they were using in Akita around then?"

"But albumen printing has nothing to do with the type of paper," said Minegishi.

"It doesn't?"

"They're just called albumen prints because they use albumen—egg white, that is—to bind the photographic chemicals to the base."

"So the thickness and color of the paper doesn't matter?"

"No. Publishers generally opt for thinner paper to cut costs. But in theory they could use any type of paper. Plus, unlike bromide paper or gaslight paper, which we typically use today, albumen prints use photosensitive paper. So there's no need for a dark room. It's really quite a simple process."

"Photosensitive paper?" asked Yosuke.

"You know, like those pinhole cameras you must have played with as a child—they use photosensitive paper."

It was all starting to make sense to Yosuke.

"In those days, for the most part publishers used albumen printing to save money," went on Minegishi. "Of course, even in a place like Akita, fancier methods would have been available at, say, any local portrait studio."

"I see," said Yosuke. "It was just something that had been bothering me, but I guess that pretty much explains it."

"But more to the point," puzzled Minegishi, "are you sure the plates weren't printed onto the pages in halftone or collotype?"

"No. They were definitely photographs pasted directly into the book."

"Hmm… that's interesting," said Minegishi, looking surprised. "Having only seen slides and photocopies of the catalogue, that hadn't occurred to me."

"Don't forget we're talking about photographs of *paintings*," said Yosuke. "The publisher must have thought that using photographic plates would ensure the highest quality reproduction."

"Hmm… amazing…" murmured Minegishi, shaking his head.

"Is something wrong?" inquired Yosuke.

"No, not wrong. I was just thinking the whole thing must have cost a lot of money. I wonder how many copies were printed?"

"Good question. At least fifty I'd guess."

"Sounds about right; certainly no more than that. In those days photography wasn't something affordable to the masses like it is today. That catalogue must have cost a small fortune to produce. How many plates were there again? About seventy, wasn't it? In today's money that would probably come to over a hundred thousand yen a copy."

"That much? You're kidding!" exclaimed Yosuke in disbelief.

"That is, unless Sato owned his own camera or had a relative who ran a portrait studio. But if he had to hire a professional photographer that's about what it would have cost." Minegishi chuckled. "In those days it cost about one yen to hire a professional photographer to take a photograph. One yen might not seem like much, but consider that back then a cup of coffee cost three sen. One sen was a hundredth of a yen, and a movie ticket about twenty sen. One yen was a lot of money—the equivalent of about ten thousand yen today. And let's say it cost twenty sen to develop a photograph. Assuming fifty copies of the catalogue were published, that puts the cost at eleven yen per painting: one yen for actually taking the photograph plus ten yen for developing. With seventy paintings in the catalogue, that puts the cost for all the plates at nearly eight hundred yen."

"Eight hundred yen… that's about eight million yen in today's money!" exclaimed Yosuke.

"Don't forget the cost of printing and binding. Put it all together and that comes to about a thousand yen. That's twenty yen per copy—nearly two hundred thousand yen today—a good chunk of change in those days. Back then for a thousand yen you could have built a pretty nice house. I'd say Sato must have been a very rich man indeed," murmured Minegishi enviously.

On the way home Yosuke caught the Chuo Line from Yotsuya.

Things are starting to come together.

Holding onto a strap as he stood in the crowded train, Yosuke mulled over his conversation with Minegishi.

Even if I don't figure it out, Ryohei or Minegishi will.

But Yosuke had no intention of turning the riddle over to someone else to solve. This was his problem. He had to find the solution himself.

This calls for drastic action.

Yosuke thoughts turned to the man whose name was on the business card the stamp dealer had shown him.

8
The Encaustic Lion

**Elusive Sharaku Brought to Light
Sotheby's Auction Yields Groundbreaking Discovery!!**

FEBRUARY 3—Two days ago, a heretofore unknown painting by the artist Sharaku (a.k.a. Chikamatsu Shoei)— the longstanding mystery of whose identity has only recently been solved—was discovered by a Japanese man at Sotheby's auction house in London. The painting was part of a collection of "Oriental Art" put up for public auction. The auctioneers were apparently entirely unaware of its true significance until it was pointed out to them. The instigator of the groundbreaking discovery is an art dealer from Morioka city in Iwate Prefecture by the name of Kato Tetsuo. Mr. Kato had arrived in London a few days earlier with a group of fellow art dealers from Morioka for the express purpose of attending the auction.

At first, said Mr. Kato, he did not realize the painting was by Sharaku. But upon second inspection he remembered having seen a reproduction of the very same painting in a catalogue of works by Shoei shown to him by a friend. Though the signature on the painting was that of the Akita School painter Satake Yoshifumi (eldest son of Satake Yoshiatsu), Mr. Kato could clearly identify where the original signature (presumably Shoei's) had been cut away. Mr. Kato's excitement at the discovery drew the attention of other art dealers and collectors attending the viewing, and the painting became the principal subject of discussion the following day when the collection came up for auction. Ultimately, the painting was acquired by a private American art museum for eighty-two million yen—the highest sum ever paid for a work by Sharaku—sending shockwaves through the art world.

Mr. Kato, together with his companions, remained in the bidding until the very end. "I very much wish I could have taken it back to Japan with me," he said, unable to conceal his disappointment upon finally losing out to the Americans.

A PAINTING by Shoei! Discovered by Kato, no less!

Holding the newspaper, Ryohei's hands trembled.

Could it be a coincidence? His head reeled.

If Sotheby's hadn't realized the painting was by Sharaku, Ryohei reasoned, it must not be one of the ones featured in the recent spate of newspaper and magazine articles. In which case only someone familiar with Shoei's work from having seen either Sato's catalogue or a copy of it could have recognized the painting. To the best of Ryohei's knowledge, apart from his colleagues, that included only a handful of people. What were the chances of one of them happening to go to Sotheby's and making the discovery? And on Kato's very first visit! Feeling there was more to this than met the eye, Ryohei turned his attention back to the newspaper.

I wonder why Kato made such a fuss about his discovery?

Ryohei could understand the art dealer's excitement at coming across an unknown Sharaku. But he was a professional; undoubtedly it wasn't the first time he had made such a discovery. If he had kept his cool and said nothing he could have bid on the painting, and he very likely would have won. It was very unprofessional of him to have gotten excited and driven up the price like that. That wasn't the Kato whom Ryohei knew.

It was Kato who suggested somebody might have forged the inscription in Kiyochika's sketchbook after Minegishi noticed the discrepancy with the dates.

The more Ryohei thought about it, the more suspicious Kato's behavior began to seem.

But if the sketchbook is genuine, that means the preface to Sato's catalogue is a fake. And if the preface is a fake, then maybe Shoei…

Ryohei blanched.

Maybe Shoei—is a fabrication!

Then again, nowhere in Sato's catalogue did it actually *say* Shoei and Sharaku were one and the same. It was Ryohei who had made the connection. Based on what? On just *one* inconspicuous reference to Sharaku in *one* inscription on *one* painting of a lion. If someone *had* forged that signature, why not make the connection a bit more obvious? It had taken a trained art historian to prove beyond a reasonable doubt that Shoei was Sharaku, and even then only after extensive research. What if Ryohei *hadn't* happened to stumble upon the album? And what were the chances of him, or *any* art historian for that matter, noticing one tiny signature? One in a million perhaps. If that were true, the forger had taken quite a gamble! If someone with a trained eye hadn't noticed the inscription, all his efforts would have been in vain.

No, it was simply too farfetched. The paintings must be real—it was Kiyochika's preface that was forged.

Ryohei's head was beginning to ache.

But why forge the preface? It made no sense. If Sato had been alive at the time the catalogue was published, then one could imagine he forged the preface in order to associate himself with a famous artist like Kiyochika. But he'd died in the flood before it was ever published. Would his widow really have lied on his behalf? It seemed highly unlikely.

No, if the catalogue really was published in 1907, Kiyochika's preface must be genuine.

Ryohei had reached a conclusion.

On the other hand, this meant the converse was also true: assuming the dates given in the preface were *not* simply a misprint and that the preface itself had been forged, then the catalogue couldn't have been published in 1907.

If so, when might it have been made? Sometime before 1937—that much is clear. The photo album belonging to the art dealer in Yokote proved that the two paintings from the catalogue had been sold as works by Tashiro Unmu around that time. Obviously, the photographs in the catalogue must have been taken before Shoei's signature was removed and Unmu's added.

But in those days no one questioned the conventional wisdom that Sharaku had been a Noh actor from Awa. Alternate theories of his identity had yet to be proposed. In which case, even if the catalogue was *not* published in 1907, then *at least* the pictures must be genuine. Before 1937 there would have been no reason to forge Sharaku's signature on a painting by Shoei since no one would have believed for a second that Shoei was Sharaku. According to popular belief Sharaku was from Awa, not Akita. Any forger would have understood that.

Therefore, as Ryohei had said to Yosuke before, if the catalogue *was* a fake then it must have been made in order to bring Shoei to the attention of the art world. Ryohei knew there were plenty of art collectors out there who published deluxe catalogues of their collections in an attempt to inflate their market value.

In the end, it seemed to Ryohei this was the only possible explanation.

And yet if the forger's plan in creating the preface had been to make people think that Kiyochika had been an admirer of Shoei's work, it had failed spectacularly. Today, even in Akita, Shoei was all but unknown. The art world, it seemed, was not so gullible after all.

At last Ryohei was satisfied.

I bet it was Kato who found that work by Shoei. He probably planned the whole thing—got one of his companions to put it up for auction and then made a fuss about it.

Anybody could sell a painting through Sotheby's. The auction house only made a cursory appraisal to make sure the work was reasonably respectable before putting it up for auction. Then they collected a certain percentage of the selling price as their fee. Of course, as in this case, Sotheby's occasionally mounted auctions on a particular theme—such as "Oriental Art"—using works they had acquired themselves. But presumably they accepted outside works provided they would fit the general theme of the auction. Kato had seized this opportunity. The dealers and collectors at the auction were all devotees of Asian art. If anyone was going to pay a record-breaking price for a Sharaku it was one of them. Sotheby's was an art dealer's dream.

I wonder if he found it in Yokote?

It was quite possible. Kato had been on his way to Yokote the time Ryohei had run into him in Kakunodate. Kato had probably tracked it down after talking to Ryohei.

Of all the sneaky…

The least Kato could have done was to show it to Ryohei before putting it up for auction. After all, Ryohei was the one who had given the art dealer a copy of Sato's catalogue in the first place. He felt miffed.

Toward evening Ryohei received a telephone call.

"It's me—Onodera."

Ryohei was taken aback.

"I'm in Morioka," the detective went on. "Do you mind if I stop by for a minute?"

Ryohei asked Onodera what he wanted to talk about.

"I can't… not over the phone…"

After asking the detective where he was, Ryohei said he would come to meet him. He didn't want to worry his mother by having a detective dropping by the house.

"Any idea where Yosuke might be?" Onodera asked as soon as he saw Ryohei.

"Has something happened?"

"He's vanished."

"Huh?"

"He didn't show up at his office yesterday morning. It seems he went out somewhere the night before. He's not at his apartment either."

"How do you know?" asked Ryohei.

"I got a message from the officer assigned to the case."

So, they've been trailing Yosuke all this time!

Ryohei was dumbfounded.

"Did you check to see if he was at his parents' house in Okayama, or his sister Saeko's apartment in Sendai?" asked Ryohei.

"Yeah, neither. I've tried everywhere I could think of. You were my last hope," replied the detective with a worried look on his face.

"Are you afraid he's gone on the run?" Ryohei asked sarcastically.

"No, that's the least of my worries…"

"But you *do* think he set fire to the professor's house."

"No, no. We've ruled that out. Now I'm just following a hunch."

"A hunch?"

"I can't say anything for sure. I've just got a feeling something bad is going to happen. Did you know Yosuke's been going around asking questions about some old postcard?"

"Yes. I asked him to."

"What!" Onodera's face lighted up. He pressed Ryohei to explain. Ryohei decided he might as well tell the detective the whole story.

Upon hearing it was Ryohei who had discovered Sato's catalogue and not Professor Nishijima, Onodera grunted but said nothing. Ryohei calmly related what the professor had done after learning about the catalogue. When he came to the part about the postcard which he had found inside, Onodera finally spoke:

"Hmm… Presumably somebody put it there as a bookmark. In other words, whoever owned the postcard also owned the catalogue," the detective said ponderously.

Ryohei nodded. That was why he had asked Yosuke to check out the address on the postcard.

"Well, your friend Yosuke tracked him down."

"What?" This time it was Ryohei's turn to be surprised. "Who was it?"

"Fujimura Genzo," replied Onodera.

"Fujimura… Should I know him?" asked Ryohei.

"He owns a rare book shop in Sendai. Saga Atsushi was about to mail a book to him just before he died. *That* Fujimura…"

Ryohei said nothing.

"What do you suppose it means?" mused Onodera. "Is there a connection between Yosuke's disappearance and Fujimura's owning the catalogue? All this time I've been thinking Saga's suicide was unrelated—that it was just a random coincidence."

"Perhaps…" Ryohei muttered to himself. "Perhaps it *is* connected to Mr. Saga."

"You mean the catalogue?" asked Onodera.

"Yes. You see, it was given me by his brother-in-law, Mr. Mizuno."

"But then—" the detective paused mid-sentence, his mouth still open. "Then there's a good chance Mizuno knows Fujimura," he said thoughtfully. "Funny he didn't say so when I talked to him at the funeral. I showed him the envelope with Fujimura's name and address on it to confirm it was in Saga's handwriting."

"Perhaps he was too upset at the time to notice?"

"Impossible. I asked him more than once if he had ever heard of Fujimura's bookshop. He said no."

"So that means—"

"Mizuno was lying," said Onodera, finishing Ryohei's sentence. "Now listen to this: the day before yesterday when I got a call from Tokyo and Fujimura's name came up, I was sure Yosuke had uncovered something to do with Saga's death. So I immediately made a call to Sendai and had them make some enquiries about Fujimura's movements."

"What did you find out?"

"On October ninth—the day of Saga died—Fujimura was attending a rare book exhibition at a Sendai department store. From lunchtime onward he didn't step foot outside the store. A number of other book dealers have confirmed this."

"So Mr. Saga's death—"

"Even if it *was* murder, Fujimura wasn't involved. So I suppose he isn't connected to Yosuke's disappearance either."

Ryohei said nothing.

"Since then, Fujimura's been keeping a low profile, just minding his shop as usual. Though, come to think of it, he did close up and go off to London for one week last month."

"London!" exclaimed Ryohei. "When exactly?"

"From the 20th to the 27th."

It can't be a coincidence.

"Didn't you read today's news about that Sharaku painting?" Ryohei asked Onodera.

"Yeah. That was London, was it?"

"Yes. And I think Fujimura took it there."

Ryohei told the detective about the conclusion he had reached that morning. "Yosuke knew the discovery of Kiyochika's sketchbook made it likely the preface to Sato's catalogue was a fake," he said. "So once he learned Fujimura was involved…"

"Yes, it all fits. That means Kato's probably mixed up in it too. I wonder if he really found that painting up in Yokote?"

"That's the key. It's also possible Fujimura had it all along…"

"Right. We'll have to verify that," said Onodera.

"But how?"

"Simple. I'll just ring up all the art dealers in Yokote. If that *is* where Kato found the painting, someone up there must know about it."

"True," agreed Ryohei. "Damn! I wish I'd thought to ask the name of that shop in Yokote whose owner I spoke to on the phone."

"I'll ask about that too. I'm sure we can find out."

Onodera got up and rushed off to find the nearest telephone.

Ryohei's pulse quickened at this unexpected turn of events.

"How strange," said Onodera returning to the table after some time. He had a puzzled look on his face. "I called all the art dealers in the phone book but no one knows anything about the painting. And no one recalls lending Kato any photo album or speaking to you on the telephone."

"What?" exclaimed Ryohei. "Do you think someone's hiding something?"

"This is what I found out: First, Akita School paintings *never* turn up in Yokote; all the dealers I spoke to were unanimous on that point. Second, if *anything* of museum quality had been bought or sold there recently, they would know about it. And, last but not least, they say it's unlikely anyone, even in Akita city, keeps an album devoted exclusively to Akita School paintings."

"But," Ryohei objected, "I talked to a dealer there who—"

"That's what Kato *told* you," the detective shot back. "How do you know he was really an art dealer?"

Ryohei felt as though he had been slapped in the face.

"But if he wasn't a dealer—"

"Kato conned you," said the policeman.

"You mean the photo album is a fake too?"

"Assuming no one in Yokote is lying to me," said Onodera, nodding confidently.

"But," said Ryohei, "if you're right about Kato… if that photo album *isn't* for real, then…"

"Then what?" asked Onodera.

"Well," replied Ryohei, "then not only is Chikamatsu's preface probably a forgery but Kato's story about a dealer selling two of Shoei's paintings in 1937 is also false. In other words, it's possible Sato's catalogue was created out of whole cloth sometime in the past year."

"How so?"

Onodera still hadn't grasped the significance of this new set of facts. Ryohei felt irritated at the detective's obtuseness. "Don't you see?" he said. "The photo album Kato showed me which contains photographs of Unmu's work gave Sato's catalogue an alibi, so to speak. It proved it had to have been published before 1937. *That's* why I couldn't understand how anyone could have forged it, since up until then no one would have believed for a second that Shoei had been Sharaku. But if the photo album is a hoax, then Sato's catalogue could have been made *anytime*—last year even. In which case there *is* a motive for forging it because nowadays there is a lot of controversy over Sharaku's identity, so one stands to profit by convincing people that Sharaku and Shoei were one and the same."

Ryohei explained the current situation in the world of ukiyo-e.

"Therefore," he continued, "if the catalogue dated to before 1937, Shoei's paintings could still be genuine even if the preface were a fake, because back then everyone believed Sharaku was a Noh actor from Awa. It wasn't until *after* the war that alternative theories about his identity began cropping up. On the other hand, if it was made recently, it's likely that both the preface and the paintings are forgeries, because if someone *really* owned a painting of a lion with Sharaku's signature on it, the logical thing would be to show it to an expert. Given all the theories about Sharaku's identity floating around these days, any expert would give it a serious look and not just reject it out of hand. Ergo, the fact that someone went to the trouble of making the catalogue must mean Sharaku's signature on that painting is forged."

"Hmm. I see what you mean," replied Onodera, at last sounding convinced.

"The catalogue's a fake," Ryohei went on. "And if it *was* Fujimura who took it to London, that supposed dealer I spoke to on the phone—"

"—was probably Fujimura, too," said Onodera, finishing his sentence. Then in utter amazement he added, "I'll be damned... It's sheer brilliance! Not just anyone could have pulled this stunt off."

"It'd be impossible without first doing extensive research on ukiyo-e," Ryohei added. Just then, a name popped into Ryohei's head.

"I wonder," mused the detective, as though reading Ryohei's mind, "whether Saga Atsushi was mixed up in it. After all, if Mizuno was involved it's natural to assume he went to his brother-in-law for help."

"But," Ryohei objected, "do you really think Mr. Saga would have agreed?" Somehow he just couldn't bring himself to believe it.

"Ah, that's right." The detective nodded to himself, as though realizing something. "It wouldn't make sense. He and Professor Nishijima were the two leading experts on Sharaku."

"So?"

"So why go to the trouble of fabricating a catalogue when you can simply come right out and announce that Shoei was Sharaku? Everyone would have believed him, right? The same holds true even if Mizuno put him up to it. No, Saga wasn't involved. In fact, it's more likely he figured out what Mizuno and the others were up to."

"And that's why he committed suicide?" asked Ryohei. "To atone for his brother-in-law's crime?"

"In that case he would have left some kind of suicide note. No," declared the detective, "I think they killed him."

"Okay, let's review," said Onodera, noting the dubious expression on Ryohei's face. "Mizuno and Fujimura knew each other. But they were more than just casual acquaintances; that follows from the fact they forged Sato's catalogue. So there's no reason for Saga to have killed himself... Look, we've been assuming Saga committed suicide over the book he stole from Fujimura's shop. Now, according to Yosuke, bibliophiles like Saga have a compulsion to show off every new acquisition. Saga would naturally have shown the book to Mizuno, not thinking of the possible consequences. When Mizuno, being a book dealer himself, learned of the theft, he would have known immediately Saga was the culprit—it's not like Koetsu books are available on every street corner. As soon as Fujimura put the advertisement in the trade journal, Mizuno would have acted to prevent disgrace falling on his brother-in-law and found a way to resolve the situation quietly. Therefore there would have been no reason for Saga to commit suicide."

Onodera paused for breath.

"That's why I can't believe Saga stole the book," he continued. "Given Mizuno's relationship to Fujimura, one would expect him to have acted *before* Fujimura placed the advertisement. But the fact is the ad *was* placed. I think it was a trick to create a motive for Saga's suicide. They knew the police would launch an investigation if Saga turned up dead without any plausible motive for committing suicide, so they created one. That includes planting the parcel containing the book addressed to Fujimura in Saga's handwriting. No, Mizuno and Fujimura killed Saga—that's for sure. Their motive was that Saga was on to their forgery. Anyway, that' the way I see it."

"But Mizuno and Fujimura both have alibis," Ryohei pointed out.

Onodera looked at him blankly for a moment.

"Mizuno was with Yosuke the whole time," Ryohei went on. "He told me so himself."

"Then it must have been Kato," responded the detective. "Morioka is hardly any distance from Cape Kitayama. It's the *only* possible explanation!" he concluded, his voice rising shrilly.

WHEN THEY WERE FINISHED at the café the two men headed straight over to Kato's antique shop. Of course, they weren't going to meet Kato, who had not yet returned from London, but to check out Kato's alibi for the day of Saga's murder, October ninth. Kato was a bachelor and had no employees, so if he had gone to Cape Kitayama that day he would have had to close up his shop at least for the afternoon. It took five hours to go there and back, even in a hurry.

The two men split up and walked around the neighborhood making inquiries. October tenth had been a Sunday and the eleventh happened to have been a national holiday, so there was a good chance one of the nearby shopkeepers would remember if Kato had closed his shop the day before. However, Kato's alibi turned out to be airtight. The local merchants' association held a five-day bargain sale over the holiday weekend—that is, from October ninth to the thirteenth. In fact, it had all been Kato's idea, and he had kept his shop open throughout the event.

"Why am I not surprised it was Kato's idea?" muttered Onodera bitterly.

The two men gave up and went to a nearby restaurant. It was already past seven in the evening and both of them were hungry.

"Perhaps Mr. Saga was killed somewhere else?" suggested Ryohei.

"Unlikely," replied Onodera. He proceeded to give Ryohei a detailed account of Saga's movements on the day in question.

"On the night of the eighth he boarded a train in Tokyo," he said. "We don't have any witnesses, but since we know he arrived at Hachinohe Station around ten o'clock the next morning, that's the only explanation. Now, we're no longer sure if he took the 10:46 train bound for Fudai because we were basing that assumption on the package we found on the train. Be that as it may, he must have reached his cottage around three in the afternoon, because when Yosuke went to the cottage later he saw Saga's bag there. Based on his stomach contents, the coroner puts the time of death around five p.m.—not enough time for Kato to get back to Morioka, or for Fujimura to return to Sendai.

"Do you have witnesses who saw Mr. Saga in Hachinohe?" asked Ryohei.

"No, but he made two phone calls from the station, one to the Fuchu public library and one to Mizuno."

"Ah, that's right," remembered Ryohei. "But are you sure he really made the calls from Hachinohe?"

"He must have—the timing fits perfectly. Let's see…" said Onodera, taking out his notebook. "Saga would have caught the 11:50 Towada Express No. 5 from Tokyo on the night of the eighth, which gets in to Hachinohe at 10:13 the next morning," he explained. "He called the library at about 10:40 a.m. The librarian asked him where he was calling from but Saga didn't answer. Then the librarian happened to overhear an announcement in the background."

Ryohei leaned forward in his seat.

"The announcement," Onodera went on, "said that the Kurikoma No. 1 train due in at 10:42 that morning was running five minutes late and had just left Sannohe Station, the stop before Hachinohe. Of course, the librarian didn't actually remember all that—he just remembered hearing the name Hachinohe and that a train was going to be five minutes late, and I looked into it and figured out the rest."

"Do you think it could have been a tape recording or something?" asked Ryohei.

"Impossible," said the detective. "You can't predict when a train is going to be late. And even if it *was*, Fujimura or Kato couldn't have gone to Hachinohe that day. I don't know about Mizuno, but at the estimated time of Saga's death he was in Tokyo."

"What about the call Mizuno received?"

"Well, we only have his word that Saga actually called him, but all he says is that his brother-in-law sounded very depressed and he got worried and went to his apartment to check up on him. Finding he wasn't home he started looking for him everywhere he could think of before remembering it was the day Saga's book club met at the library. There he ran into your friend Yosuke, who told him he'd gotten a call from the librarian saying the meeting was cancelled. The two went to talk to the librarian and that's when they found out Saga had called from Hachinohe. Mizuno had a feeling his brother-in-law had been on his way to his vacation cottage near Fudai and he said he was going to drive up there right away. And that's how Yosuke ended up going along."

"Hmm… Well, if it wasn't a tape, maybe someone else placed that call from Hachinohe—that announcement in the background giving away his location is just too good to be true," insisted Ryohei.

"But who?" asked Onodera. "We're talking about murder, remember. They'd be taking a big risk bringing in another accomplice—three's about the limit, I'd say."

"How about Mizuno? After all, he's close in age and would sound a bit like Mr. Saga."

"Well, I suppose he *could* have been in Hachinohe at that time, but like I said before, he was in Tokyo when Saga died."

"How can the coroner be so certain about the time of death? Wasn't Mr. Saga's body only found days later?" asked Ryohei.

"When he reached his cottage Saga ate a box lunch from the Ko'uta Sushi store in Hachinohe Station—we found the empty tray on the table in the cottage with a label confirming the date of manufacture," explained Onodera. "The coroner calculated how long he'd been dead based on the state of digestion of his stomach contents. Now if he was in Hachinohe Station at 10:30 a.m. and caught a train from there to Kitayama, he couldn't have gotten to his cottage until past two o'clock. Since he ate his lunch at the cottage, he must have eaten sometime after that. According the autopsy Saga died within three hours of his last meal—in other words, sometime around five in the evening. Plus we found a copy of that day's *Eastern Tohoku News* in his bag. So whether or not it was murder one thing's for sure: he didn't die anywhere else. Even the water in his lungs matches the seawater off Cape Kitayama. In short," the detective concluded, practically spitting out the words, "even if Mizuno somehow faked the telephone call from Hachinohe, there's no way we can get him for murder."

"Why not?" asked Ryohei.

"Why? Because… of the sushi tray and the newspaper, which place Saga at the cottage—"

"But wait—that doesn't make sense," interrupted Ryohei. "Surely if Mizuno faked the telephone call he could also have bought the newspaper and the sushi!"

Inspector Onodera said nothing.

"Aren't you just *assuming* Mr. Saga died at Cape Kitayama because that's where the body was found?" asked Ryohei. "Admittedly, *I'm* suspicious because I think Mizuno is guilty…"

"Okay. But then how do you explain the newspaper and the sushi tray?"

"Simple. Mizuno drove to the cottage later with Yosuke, right? He could have planted them there when Yosuke wasn't looking."

"Hmm..." Onodera lit a cigarette and inhaled deeply. His cheeks were becoming flushed.

"I see... Mizuno places the call to the library in Tokyo from Hachinohe in the morning, buys the newspaper and the sushi, and returns straight to Tokyo; then he kills Saga after getting him to eat the sushi... It's possible. Let's see, Mizuno went to the library in Tokyo at..." Onodera consulted his notebook, "...about four p.m. After leaving the library with Yosuke he returned home alone, having arranged to meet up again with Yosuke later. So he has no alibi for around five p.m., the estimated time of death. The question is whether there's some way he could actually have left Hachinohe at ten in the morning and still gotten back to Tokyo by about three in the afternoon." Onodera paused. "Rest assured, I'll get to the bottom of it," he said, his eyes flashing. "Now then... next he killed Saga—I'm guessing at the apartment he uses as an office—then stuffed the body into the trunk of his car and went off to meet Yosuke. Then he left Tokyo in his car with Yosuke somewhere around six and drove up to Iwate."

"So you're saying Yosuke was in the car with Mr. Saga's body the whole time?" asked Ryohei.

"Must've been. Mizuno didn't leave Kitayama from the time he reached the cottage until the body was discovered. There was no time to return to Tokyo to collect it."

Looking pleased with himself, Onodera snapped his notebook shut and mumbled something about starting his investigation over from scratch. Then, pursing his lips, he fell silent.

DESPITE this breakthrough in the case, the two were still no closer to finding out what had happened to Yosuke. Still harboring a sense of unease, Ryohei said goodbye to Inspector Onodera and returned home.

But he did not have to wait very long. News of Yosuke's whereabouts came that very night. As Ryohei was heading back to his room after his evening bath, Onodera called again. As he gripped the receiver, Ryohei felt the room begin to spin.

Yosuke had been taken to Sendai Municipal Hospital, having been hit by a car, and was in critical condition.

"What about Saeko?"

"We've contacted her," said the detective. "She's already at the hospital."

"What happened?" cried Ryohei.

"A hit-and-run. We have witnesses. Someone got the license plate number and we've traced the owner—the car belongs to Fujimura Genzo."

"So it was Fujimura! Where is he now?"

"He reported the car stolen this afternoon. He must have thought he could get away with it thinking we weren't onto him. What a fool! Now we've got them."

"And Yosuke?"

"I don't know yet. I'm about to head over to Sendai now and check on him."

"Take me with you," said Ryohei.

"That's why I called," replied Onodera, sounding tense.

"Even monkeys fall from trees," said Onodera from behind the wheel as they drove to Sendai. Ryohei, who was seated in the passenger seat, smoked a cigarette but said nothing. "It just goes to show Fujimura and Mizuno were starting to panic," the detective continued. "Of course, we should have been more vigilant—if we'd been keeping closer tabs on Fujimura this probably wouldn't have happened."

"But how did you hear about Yosuke's accident?" asked Ryohei.

"The day before yesterday I rang up the Sendai police to make some inquiries about Fujimura, so when the accident happened one of their men contacted me, thinking it might have something to do with the case. That was after they'd learned the car was registered to Fujimura. I tell you, my heart nearly stopped when I heard Yosuke was the victim."

"So Yosuke was on to Fujimura then?"

"Mizuno's alibi was that he was with Yosuke at the time of Saga's death, and Kato was out of the country. So he must have narrowed it down to Fujimura. I had a *feeling* Yosuke was trying to track down Saga's murderer. But I wonder why he chose to do it alone. If only he'd said something to me…"

Onodera's voice trailed off in a tone of regret.

Finally he said, "We blew it when we checked out Fujimura and concluded he'd had nothing to do with Saga's death. I take full responsibility for that. If something should happen to Yosuke…"

Ryohei made no reply.

Onodera and Ryohei's car pulled up to the hospital a little after one o'clock in the morning. When they entered the lobby they found a man waiting for them.

"Inspector Onodera, Kuji Police," said Onodera, introducing himself.

The other man did likewise. He was from the Sendai Police Department.

"What's Mr. Kokufu's condition?" asked Onodera.

"He's lost a lot of blood. He's in the intensive care unit right now. By the way, what exactly is going on? Is this connected to a case?"

"How about the owner of the car?" asked Onodera, ignoring the question.

"Mr. Fujimura came by a little while ago to check on the patient. Even though the car was stolen, he apologized to Mr. Kokufu's sister, saying he felt bad about it all the same."

"That idiot! Does he think he can play us for fools?"

The other policeman was taken aback by anger on Onodera's face.

Ryohei left Onodera and headed for Yosuke's room. Inside it was quiet. Through the door he could hear only the hushed voices of what he took to be nurses. He knocked and was startled at how loudly the sound echoed through the corridor. A nurse opened the door and Ryohei gave her his name. At the sound of his voice, Saeko rushed out into the corridor. Her face appeared to have gotten thinner in the month since he had last seen her. She peered into his face as though making sure it was really him. Then, as though the floodgates had opened, she burst into tears and flung herself on his shoulder. Drawing her tightly to him, Ryohei gently began stroking her back.

"How's Yosuke?" he asked once Saeko had regained her composure.

"As soon as I got here, the doctor told me I'd better call our parents in Okayama and tell them to come…"

Ryohei probed no further.

The muffled sound of footsteps could be heard approaching along the corridor and Onodera appeared.

"Thank you for your phone call," said Saeko as soon as the detective had introduced himself.

"Ryohei, could you spare a moment?" Onodera said in a low voice.

Ryohei followed the detective down the corridor to a small smoking area set up to one side. Saeko returned to Yosuke's room.

"That damned Fujimura's got an alibi," said Onodera, taking a pack of cigarettes out of his pocket. Then, realizing it was empty, he threw it in annoyance into the nearest wastepaper basket. Ryohei took out his own cigarettes. Thanking him, Onodera removed one from the pack and lit it.

"He claims he was playing mahjong with some colleagues. Come to think of it, since he only reported the car stolen this afternoon, he must have planned it all well in advance. No doubt he arranged his alibi ahead of time."

"So you think Mizuno was driving the car?"

Onodera nodded.

"Kato's out of the country; that much is certain. The accident seems to have occurred just before nine o'clock, so if Mizuno is headed back to Tokyo he won't have gotten home yet. I'm tempted to phone his house to see if he's there—if it were the middle of the day and he answered I could invent a pretext for calling, but at this late hour…" the detective muttered sadly. "I wouldn't want to jump the gun and tip him off to the fact that we're onto him."

"Good point. And at this rate I wouldn't be surprised if Mizuno—"

"Of course. I'm sure he's got his alibi all prepared. But now things are different; we've got our man. He won't pull the wool over our eyes this time. I'll pick apart his alibi, just you wait. Still, Mizuno probably isn't expecting me to have heard about Yosuke's accident already. I wouldn't have, in fact, if I hadn't thought to check up on Fujimura. Now we'll be able to get one step ahead of him."

"If they were willing to go *this* far, maybe they were behind the professor's death, too," said Ryohei.

"I don't know if we can say that just yet," replied Onodera. "I don't see they had much of a motive for wanting Nishijima dead."

"But what if their aim wasn't murder but arson?"

"What are you getting at?"

"It only occurred to me just now: if they forged Sato's catalogue then maybe they were trying to destroy the evidence."

Onodera said nothing.

"They knew," continued Ryohei, "that the catalogue was going to be photographed sometime after the tenth of January. They were probably worried what might happen once the catalogue was studied carefully."

Ryohei suddenly remembered how Kato had seemed unusually interested in the fact that the catalogue was going to be photographed. He related this to Onodera.

"I see," said the detective. "If the catalogue was revealed to be a fake their whole plan would collapse. In other words, it was good enough to fool us and Nishijima—who wasn't a rare book expert after all—but it would have been risky to allow a high-quality reproduction to be subjected to the scrutiny of the whole world. Is that it?"

The detective seemed to find Ryohei's argument convincing.

"It's certainly possible," Onodera went on. "After all, the professor wasn't physically disabled or anything. If they'd wanted to kill him they could have found a method with a higher probability of success. I agree it makes sense that their real motive was destroying the book. Assuming the professor didn't accidentally start the fire himself, it's seeming more and more likely Mizuno and his pals did. That means they've committed two murders. Say, do you suppose Yosuke knew that?"

"He's a very smart guy," replied Ryohei. "I imagine he'd figured out a lot of what was going on. But unless he'd found solid evidence the catalogue was an out-and-out forgery, it might not have occurred to him they'd killed the professor."

"True. If the catalogue were genuine there'd be no need to burn down his house. So it's probably safe to assume Yosuke didn't know. Plus, if he'd realized they'd committed murder, I doubt he'd have risked going after them on his own."

Ryohei and Onodera nodded in mutual agreement.

"Yosuke was probably pursing Fujimura simply because the postcard had aroused his suspicious," added Onodera, "without realizing he and Mizuno would have viewed him as a serious threat. And since they'd killed twice already, one more murder would've seemed no big deal to them."

"But I wonder how they knew Yosuke was on to them?" puzzled Ryohei.

This seemed to stump Onodera.

"Is one of you Mr. Tsuda?" asked a nurse, hurrying up to them. Noticing the tense look on her face, Ryohei stood up.

"Has something happened to Yosuke?"

"Please come quickly."

Ryohei and Onodera turned and started toward Yosuke's room

The door to the room was open and from the corridor they could see inside. Saeko clung to Yosuke, crying. For some time, Ryohei stood frozen near the threshold, too astonished to speak.

Just then a young doctor, having given some instructions to the nurse, came out of the room. "I'm very sorry…" he said in a low voice, bowing his head as he passed Ryohei. Onodera turned to follow him and headed off down the corridor. Ryohei could still not bring himself to enter the room.

Suddenly everything seemed to close in on him.

This is a dream—this is all a bad dream.

Yosuke appeared to be asleep. Gazing at his profile from a distance, Ryohei felt his body stiffen.

The calm, slow movements of the nurse as she removed the intravenous needles from Yosuke's arm gave Ryohei a sense of unreality.

He no longer noticed the coldness of the corridor.

Outside the window, in the darkness of the night, it was snowing steadily, white flakes glistening in the light as they drifted to the ground.

February 4

TOWARD NOON, when Yosuke and Saeko's parents arrived from Okayama, Saeko at last seemed to regain her composure. "I've got to try to be strong… for them," she said to Ryohei, forcing a little smile. It made Ryohei incredibly sad. After greeting the parents he left the hospital so Saeko could be alone with them.

Putting in a call to the Sendai Police Department, Ryohei asked Onodera if he had found out anything since he last saw him. They arranged to meet in a café near the hospital.

"No doubt about it. I put in a call to Tokyo this morning to see if I could turn up anything new on the Nishijima case. Turns out one of Mizuno's professional acquaintances happened to see someone he thought was him hanging around in the vicinity of the professor's house on the day of the incident. The Tokyo police hadn't taken much notice of it since he wasn't on their list of suspects, but this clinches it," said Onodera. He was so excited he hadn't even touched his coffee yet.

"They've got his home and office staked out right now," the detective continued. "So far he hasn't shown up at either. As it turns out, he *wasn't* in Tokyo last night after all—I called his house this morning and was told he'd gone to Fukushima. So that seals it."

"If it *was* Mizuno who set fire to the professor's house, maybe he saw Yosuke there that day. That must be what drew his attention to Yosuke's activities," said Ryohei.

"Yeah. Knowing he and the professor had had a falling out, Mizuno would've found it strange that Yosuke was coming to see Nishijima. So while Yosuke thought he was pursuing Fujimura, Mizuno was actually pursuing *him*. When you consider that the attack on Yosuke occurred just two days after he left Tokyo, that much seems almost certain."

Nodding to himself, Onodera reached out for his cup of coffee, which by now had become cold.

"They're a clever bunch, I'll give them that," he continued. "If Minegishi hadn't stumbled on that sketchbook by Kiyochika we wouldn't have known Sato's catalogue was a fake. And it wasn't until we'd figured out it was a fake that we realized their motive for setting fire to Nishijima's house. We never could have solved this on our own."

"We never suspected them because it seemed that Mizuno had no known connection whatsoever to Professor Nishijima," added Ryohei. "That goes for Fujimura and Kato, too."

"The same is true of Saga's death," replied Onodera. "Mizuno owed his business success to his brother-in-law. If not for the catalogue we'd never have thought to pin the murder on him. And to think that at the funeral he looked like he'd lost his best friend!"

A look of anger crossed the detective's face.

"The more I think about it, all this is my fault," said Ryohei. "If I hadn't been taken in by that catalogue, Yosuke would still—"

"That's not true. Look, Professor Nishijima and lots of other scholars were fooled as well. It could have happened to anyone," said Onodera consolingly. "What we need to do now is break down Mizuno's alibi. Now we know he's the culprit it shouldn't be hard. I'll do whatever it takes. Never underestimate the power of the police; we're not like those bumbling cops on TV. Oh, I almost forgot… I've figured out a way Mizuno could have gone to Hachinohe Station in the morning and gotten back to Tokyo by three in the afternoon."

Onodera took out his notebook and showed Ryohei a timeline of events:

<u>Going</u>
(TDA flight 221)
Tokyo----------------------Misawa
7:45   9:00

(Hatsukari No. 6)
Misawa--------------------Hachinohe
10:11   10:28

At Hachinohe Station
10:40 M. places call to Fuchu Library
10:46 M. leaves parcel on train bound for Fudai
(Buys box lunch from Ko'uta Sushi and newspaper)

Return
(TDA flight 224)
Misawa----------------------Tokyo
11:55   1:10

"We've confirmed that Mizuno was out drinking with some business associates until after two in the morning of the ninth, so he couldn't have taken an overnight train," the detective explained. "Well, I'm sure he did that on purpose to give himself an alibi. As far as I can tell, that makes this the only possibility—time-wise, it works out perfectly. The 10:46 train to Fudai would have been packed with young sightseers since the following day was the start of a two-day holiday. It's unlikely anyone would have noticed Mizuno leaving the parcel containing the Koetsu book on the train's overhead luggage rack. That enabled him to two birds with one stone: making it look like Saga had been on the train and creating a motive for his suicide. Also, Hachinohe and Misawa are close enough that he could have taken a taxi and had plenty of time to catch his flight back to Tokyo."

"I see," said Ryohei. "If he landed at Haneda Airport at 1:10 in the afternoon he could definitely have gotten to the library in Tokyo by four."

"With time to spare. He probably used the time in between to get Saga to eat the sushi he'd bought from Hachinohe—what we don't know is Saga's exact condition at the time."

Ryohei was silent.

"Right now," Onodera continued, "I'm having someone check the airplane passenger list and call all the taxi companies operating around Hachinohe Station. No doubt Mizuno gave a fake name when he checked in, but since we know exactly how many people were on the flight I'm sure we can track down everyone in less than ten days. As long as something turns up, he won't be able to wriggle out of this one. Don't worry," the detective said emphatically, stubbing out his cigarette. "I won't let Yosuke's death go unpunished."

February 10
THE PAST WEEK had been hectic.

Yesterday Ryohei had returned to his apartment in Kunitachi after a long absence. Instead of returning to Morioka he had decided to stay in Tokyo on his way back from Okayama after attending Yosuke's funeral.

Inspector Onodera also happened to be in Tokyo.

Saeko, having gone to Yosuke's apartment on the evening of the seventh to retrieve his address book, found that his room had been ransacked. She reported it to Onodera.

Ryohei went in to the university for the first time in nearly three weeks and gave notice at the personnel office that he would be quitting at the end of March. Then he put in a call to Onodera at the Fuchu Police Department.

"Any word yet?" he asked the detective.

"It's just a matter of time. We haven't heard back from the taxi companies yet, but as for the airplane passenger list, we've narrowed it down to three names. It hasn't been easy though—you'd be surprised how many people don't write down their addresses properly when they check in. By the way, how was the funeral? I'm sorry I couldn't go."

"Everything went off well. Saeko said to send you her regards. Speaking of which, any leads yet on who ransacked Yosuke's apartment?" asked Ryohei.

"We figure Mizuno did it on his way back from Sendai. But as to the reason… When Saeko gets back to Tokyo we'll have ask her if she notices anything missing. So far we haven't found any fingerprints that match Mizuno's."

"Well, those guys don't seem to make many mistakes."

"Tell me about it—it's driving me crazy," said the detective. "I'd be able to haul them in if only we had proof they forged the catalogue. Anyway, I don't suppose you've got any ideas?" the policeman asked, turning the question around.

"How about leaning on Kato a bit? After all, he lied to me about that supposed dealer in Yokote," suggested Ryohei.

"On suspicion of what? It's not like lying is a crime."

"Fujimura then?"

"He has a rock-solid alibi for all three murders; the postcard alone isn't enough to link him to the crime."

"How about Sotheby's? Fujimura gave them the painting to sell."

"That's true, but we'd need proof it was a forgery."

Ryohei said nothing.

"We can't do anything until we've got proof they were in cahoots with Mizuno," said Onodera.

Resignedly, Ryohei hung up the phone.

We've come this far, and yet we don't have any proof.

Of course, the story that Mizuno had been in Fukushima on the night of the third was a complete fabrication. Be that as it may, without proof their hands were tied. Mizuno had no idea they knew as much as they did. That was why they had to leave him alone until they had solid proof. If Mizuno flew the coop at this point everything would be ruined.

If we could just find those paintings.

Ryohei was sure that Mizuno had the other fifty Shoei paintings pictured in Sato's catalogue stashed away somewhere. If they could just find them, that would be all the proof they needed.

Ryohei couldn't wait to get started.

February 12

SAEKO CALLED Ryohei at his apartment early in the morning. Since he had no telephone in his room, he rushed downstairs to the building manager's office to take the call outside in the corridor.

Saeko seemed almost her normal self again.

When he heard what she was calling about, he couldn't believe his ears. Saeko said a letter had turned up that Yosuke had written before he died.

"A letter? You mean like a suicide note?"

"Something like that. I haven't read it yet. I thought it might be best if you went and had a look at it first."

"Wait a minute. Go where? Who has it?"

"Someone at the company where my brother worked. I saw him at the funeral and we got talking about what to do with his personal effects which he'd left at the office. Then he asked me what I wanted to do about the private files my brother had been keeping on his work computer."

"Private files?"

"It seems my brother sometimes used his computer at the office for typing up notes and stuff to do with outside research he'd been working on."

"Is that so?"

"Each file has a name, so apparently that's how the man knew what they were. I said I'd be willing to pay if he'd send me the... What was it he called them—floppies? Apparently they're a bit like little LP records or something. Anyway, he said he couldn't do that because there was work-related stuff on them too. Plus he said I wouldn't be able to read them unless I had the right sort of computer and software. But apparently if I just want the documents themselves he can print them out and send them to me."

"I see."

"So he asked me if it was okay to print them out and erase the files afterward, and I said that was fine. Then last night he calls and says he found something that looks like a suicide note."

"Hmm... strange."

"It is strange, isn't it? He seemed quite concerned... said your name was mentioned in it. As a matter of fact, it seems to be addressed to you."

"What! Really?"

"He said he could send it to me, but I thought maybe it'd be better if you went over and took a look at it."

As surprised as Ryohei was to hear that the letter was addressed to him, his first instinct was to rush over and take a look at it. He knew where Yosuke's company was located. Telling Saeko he would call them up later that morning, he hung up the phone.

"All this!" blurted out Ryohei in astonishment when he saw the thick stack of typed documents Yosuke's colleague produced. There must have been over three hundred pages of A4-sized paper—just part of the research Yosuke had diligently been plugging away at over the years.

"Most of it's stuff related to ukiyo-e, but then there was this…"

The young man took out another envelope.

"This appears to be different. Not that I've read it or anything… I just glanced at the beginning. As soon as I saw your name on it I contacted Yosuke's sister. It looks like it might be a draft of a short story or something, so I thought I'd better…"

The man checked to make sure the contents were correct and handed the envelope to Ryohei.

It was certainly very long for a letter—over twenty pages. It wasn't surprising Yosuke's colleague thought it might be a short story.

What on earth could have prompted him to write all this?

Thanking the man, Ryohei left the office cradling the documents in his arms and ducked into a nearby café, too impatient to wait until he got home to read them. He hesitated for a moment before plunging in. To calm his nerves he lit a cigarette.

The first page was covered with black ink in that impersonal way printed documents always have. Ryohei glanced at the first line of text. The words "I'm catching a train for Sendai tomorrow morning" caught his eye.

Ryohei stiffened.

Yosuke went on to explain his reasons for doing what he had done.

IT'S NOW eight o'clock at night. I'm catching a train for Sendai tomorrow morning. I have to resolve this myself. If you're reading this, it means I didn't make it back. In case that happens, I thought it best to write down what I know. I want to explain why I've decided to go to Sendai alone.

This series of events is all my doing. The anger, resentment, and jealousy lurking deep in my subconscious have propelled events in a direction I hadn't foreseen. It's fair to say this is all my fault—ultimately, it was my resentment that killed the professor.

I knew Sato's catalogue was a fake before you even showed it to me. If only I'd told you, none of this would have happened. Instead I said nothing. I'll explain why later.

If Yoshimura or someone rather than you had discovered the catalogue I think things might have turned out differently. Probably I... No, I won't say anything more about that. At this point anything I say would just sound like empty excuses.

This is going to take a while. But the night is still young. I should be able to get through it all by morning.

I have here with me one of Mr. Saga's notebooks. That night after I went drinking with you and Onodera I found it tucked inside the slipcover of one of his books on ukiyo-e, which I took down from my bookshelf that night out of a sense of nostalgia. He gave me the book in person several days before he died. Perhaps if I'd discovered the notebook sooner his death could have been avoided.

I've read that book of his so many times I've practically got it memorized. For me it was sort of an introduction to the world of ukiyo-e. He knew that, and that's why he went to the trouble of giving me a signed edition. After showing me the inscription he put the book back into its slipcover and handed it to me. Then I put it on my bookshelf and forgot about it until that day. Perhaps he chose to give me that particular book because he knew I'd read it many times already. He must have foreseen that I'd put it away and not look at it. It's strange when one comes to think of it—the first time I met Mr. Saga I talked to him about that book. Then he forgot about it for two years until one day when he suddenly decided to give me a copy. It was stupid of me not to have realized he was trying to tell me something.

That night I read the notebook. I was dumbfounded by the extraordinary nature of what it contained and I had no idea what it meant.

It was an unbelievable confession given that I had only just been persuaded earlier the same night by Onodera's explanation of the motive for Mr. Saga's suicide.

In the notebook Mr. Saga wrote that he had committed a crime which, if it were to become known, would have shaken the ukiyo-e world to its very core. What's more, its sole purpose was to bring about the downfall of Professor Nishijima.

I could only think that Mr. Saga had gone mad. At the same time, I felt a loathing for the professor, who had driven him to that point. To be perfectly honest, this is how I still feel right now. In my opinion Mr. Saga was one of the most brilliant scholars of ukiyo-e Japan has ever had, one who always had the best interests of ukiyo-e at heart. To a true scholar like Mr. Saga, Professor Nishijima was the very epitome of everything he despised. This wasn't some personal grudge but a reflection of the righteous indignation everyone who loves ukiyo-e felt toward the professor. How many young scholars' careers had he nipped in the bud? How much new research had he stifled? Mr. Saga's anger and my disappointment were two sides of the same coin.

Mr. Saga was involved in the controversy surrounding the construction of a national ukiyo-e museum. Though I never told you, this was a major cause of my falling out with the professor.

It happened about eight years ago, while I was still in college. The Ministry of Education had sounded the professor out about the construction of the museum. Apparently, they asked him to draw up a budget and an exhibition plan. The professor was thrilled and discussed his hopes for the project's success with us, his students. He said it heralded a reappraisal of ukiyo-e in Japan—he gave us impassioned pep talks about it on almost a daily basis. For our part, we wanted nothing more than for the museum to become a reality. We were prepared to move heaven and earth to help the professor. Those were heady days for all of us. There wasn't a single scholar in the field who wasn't following every new development with bated breath.

Then, one day, Yoshimura got wind of a startling rumor—namely, that the idea for a national ukiyo-e museum had originated with the Ukiyo-e Connoisseurship Society. Someone from the UCS—so the rumor went—had gone to some bureaucrat at the Ministry of Education and passionately explained the need for such a museum. Moved by this impassioned plea, the bureaucrat had made a report to his superiors, who in turn had decided to sound out Professor Nishijima. The feeling at the ministry seemed to be that provided the Edo Art Association gave its approval for the idea, they would go ahead and start working out a budget.

When Professor Nishijima heard this he was outraged. His words still ring in my ears: "If this was all the UCS's idea I'll make sure it never sees the light of day! I'm not their lackey!" From that day forward, the professor ranted about how the museum was all a dirty plot by the UCS and twisting other scholars' arms to get them to oppose the idea. When he was done, he submitted a report to the Ministry of Education on behalf of the EAA in which he dismissed the plan to build a national ukiyo-e museum as "premature."

As a result, the whole thing fell through. I've never felt so dejected in my entire life as I did at the moment. If the matter of the UCS had never come up, the museum would have been built for sure. At first I detested the UCS as much as everyone around me, but I quickly realized I had been wrong. The museum—in one shape or another—was the shared dream of everyone who loved ukiyo-e. There was no room for personal egos. But the professor had gone and smashed the dreams of the entire ukiyo-e world to smithereens—and after holding forth so passionately to us about the need for just such a museum! My despair knew no bounds.

Why were we studying ukiyo-e? The only thing that kept us going was the conviction that someday ukiyo-e would become important to the world at large. But the professor wasn't thinking about the future of ukiyo-e. All he cared about was the present and himself. Otherwise, how could he have quashed the plan to build an ukiyo-e museum? The museum was key to ukiyo-e's—nay, to our—very future. I began to doubt the professor. Maybe he didn't give a damn about ukiyo-e after all? Harboring such doubts, I couldn't stand being around the professor any longer. I abandoned the idea of staying on after graduation as his research assistant and instead took a job that had nothing to do with ukiyo-e.

For these reasons, I understood Mr. Saga's anger all too well. It was he who had taken the idea for the museum to the Ministry of Education. But he didn't have the clout to galvanize support among other scholars. That's when he hit upon the idea of enlisting his former colleague's—the professor's—support for the plan. He understood that what was important was not who got the museum built, but that it got built at all. Never in a million years did he think that the professor would sabotage the plan.

When he found out, Mr. Saga cursed the professor.

So long as the professor's supremacy over the ukiyo-e world remained unchallenged, he would continue to twist it to his own benefit. But the professor's power was too great for Mr. Saga to do anything about. Newspapers, magazines, journals, museums—there was hardly any aspect of ukiyo-e in Japan into which Professor Nishijima's tentacles did not extend. If Mr. Saga were to butt heads with the professor in the name of the UCS, he would only end up endangering its own existence. And as its principal member, that was something Mr. Saga could not do.

So Mr. Saga resolved to take on the professor on his own. Only now do I realize that the reason Mr. Saga showed me such special favor was because the professor had expelled me from his inner circle. Mr. Saga was like a tiger preparing to pounce—watching and waiting for the perfect opportunity to destroy the professor.

That chance finally came.

One day Mr. Saga was shown over fifty Akita School paintings. All of them were unsigned. His brother-in-law, Mizuno Keiji, had brought them to him to have them appraised on behalf of a Tohoku art dealer.

At first Mr. Saga had had no intention of doing what he did. But as he gazed at the paintings Mizuno had left with him, a plan gradually began to come together in his mind.

In his notebook, Mr. Saga says the first thing that popped into his head was the Shunpoan forgery affair of 1934. It occurred to him he could replicate the same method to lay a trap for Nishijima and bring about his downfall. But the professor wouldn't be lured into the trap just by some very nice paintings. After all, his disdain for nikuhitsu-ga was legendary. Mr. Saga set to work on a plan at once. The important thing was to approach it the way a scholar would. His plan must be capable of fooling even himself. At last, he hit upon a ruse he was confident would succeed—Sato's painting catalogue.

While, on the one hand, the professor disdained nikuhitsu-ga, on the other he had a weakness for anything printed. Mr. Saga realized he could exploit this weakness to draw Nishijima into his trap. Compared to a handwritten manuscript, a typeset book inspires confidence due to the huge expenditure of time and money that goes into producing it. There's a universal tendency to think that something must be true if it's printed in black and white. This is true even for a nikuhitsu-ga—once it's printed in a book we cease to think of it as a painting. This was the crux of Mr. Saga's strategy. And, more importantly, to fool one person it was only necessary to print one copy of the catalogue. Books are always printed in large numbers. If you come across a book you immediately assume there are hundreds more just like it. Who could think otherwise? It would never occur to you that no one else had ever seen it before.

Even now I have to take my hat off to Mr. Saga—it was a brilliant idea. If the catalogue had been a simple handmade album with photographs *pasted into it, it undoubtedly wouldn't have been enough to deceive the professor, however much he hungered for fame and fortune. Only a printed book could have caused him to cast aside any doubts he might have.*

Once Mr. Saga had perfected his plan he went to talk to his brother-in-law about it. Not surprisingly, Mizuno at first seems to have hesitated to sign up. But his own dealings with Nishijima over the years had left a bitter taste in his mouth, and in the end he was won over. It was really when Mr. Saga explained the part about the catalogue that Mizuno began to believe the plan would work. Mizuno had a very high opinion of Mr. Saga as a scholar. He promised his full cooperation. But the fifty paintings did not belong to him. Should they buy all of them or explain their plan to the dealer and try to bring him on board? It had to be one or the other. Mizuno opted for the latter.

Thus they set to work creating Sato's catalogue. Of course, Mr. Saga didn't just make up the name Shoei out of thin air; he came across it in a book. The catalogue wouldn't have been credible if they had invented a completely fictitious painter whose identity couldn't be confirmed.

In his notebook Mr. Saga doesn't say exactly where he found the name Shoei, but I've no doubt it was in Painters and Calligraphers of Akita, which you came across in the course of your research. The prerequisites for choosing an artist were, one, that his name could be verified from historical sources, two, that he have a strong connection to Akita, and three, that none of his paintings should have survived. After eliminating several possible candidates, Mr. Saga finally settled on Chikamatsu Shoei.

Next, the key was crafting a plausible biography for Shoei. If they made it too perfect it might arouse suspicion. The important thing was to make Nishijima believe he had reached the conclusion about Shoei's identity through his own research. Only a scholar could have come up with such a brilliant ploy. Mr. Saga agonized over finding just the right balance. Everything hinged on how accurately he estimated his adversary's scholarly abilities. It would be pointless hiding clues only to find out they were too subtle for Nishijima's powers of observation.

But there was another problem that needed to be solved—how to draw the professor's attention to the catalogue in the first place. That was where Kiyochika's preface came in. The preface served two purposes. First, of course, it would attract Nishijima's attention to the catalogue. Second, it provided *eyewitness testimony for the existence of Sato Masakichi, the collector of Shoei's paintings.*

Kiyochika had actually been in Tohoku at that time. This was something most ukiyo-e scholars would be aware of. There was nothing unusual about Kiyochika having written such a preface. The preface provided evidence for the existence of Sato Masakichi, and as soon as one accepted Sato's existence, one accepted the fact that the album had been published in 1907. For a scholar like the professor, Kiyochika was a more immediate and believable presence; the mere mention of his name would imbue the album with an air of reality.

In his notebook Mr. Saga doesn't mention Sharaku's name even once, instead referring only to "a certain well-known artist." I think that was probably a matter of pride. At any rate, he added the "certain well-known artist's" name to only one of the paintings—all of the others he signed simply "Shoei." In this regard his skill as a calligrapher came in very handy.

It seems Mr. Saga was tempted to sign the "certain well-known artist's" name to several more of the paintings out of fear that Nishijima might not notice it, but in the end he decided that would seem unnatural. Mr. Saga was hanging his hopes on the fact that the professor still had a modicum of scholarly ability left.

For the plates, Mr. Saga decided to paste photographs directly into the album to ensure that the inscriptions on the paintings would be legible. While halftone printing would have provided the perfect finishing touch, it seems Mr. Saga was afraid the most crucial part might be lost.

For the text, Mr. Saga says they took an old book from the period, cut out all the Chinese characters they needed one by one, pasted them onto mounts and made up the printing plates directly from that, presumably using offset printing. This explains why the catalogue had so little text in it.

It was Mizuno who was mainly in charge of aging the pages and giving them a suitably musty, mildewy smell. Mr. Saga doesn't say exactly how Mizuno did it but he probably steeped them in black tea or fumigated them by burning peanut shells—both are old book forger's tricks. To give them a mildewy smell all he had to do was hang them in a damp place and leave them there for a while. If he were a perfectionist he might have inserted each sheet between the pages of a genuinely mildewed old book.

Mr. Saga says that when the catalogue was finished even he was surprised at how convincing it looked. All they had to do now was to casually dangle the bait in front of Nishijima's nose.

Once his curiosity was aroused, Nishijima would almost certainly send one of his minions to Akita to conduct further research. Mr. Saga came up with another plan in case this happened: he would position someone on the ground to move things along if necessary. If everything went as Mr. Saga predicted that person wouldn't need to do anything. But if the professor's proxy ran up against a brick wall, Mr. Saga's agent would casually appear and provide a clue. Once the desired conclusion had been reached, Nishijima would be notified of the result.

From that point forward it was easy to predict what action Nishijima would take: he would use all the influence at his disposal to bring his momentous discovery to the attention of the world. That would be Nishijima's undoing as a scholar.

In anticipation of this moment, Mr. Saga had inserted various clues in the catalogue that he could point to later to prove it was a fake. Once these were brought to light, Nishijima would find himself in a very tenuous position. What's more, these clues, while showing beyond a doubt that the catalogue was a fake, had been specifically designed so no one would be able to trace the forgery back to Mr. Saga and his associates. Mr. Saga would be able to point these out without having to worry about drawing suspicion to himself.

Mr. Saga's plan had almost reached its final phase. But just as Mr. Saga was about to deliver the coup de grace, he found himself in an unforeseen situation.

No doubt it all began when Mizuno and the other conspirators—amazed at the brilliance of Mr. Saga's plan to engineer Nishijima's downfall—began to get greedy. They seem to have decided on their own that if the professor determined the catalogue was genuine, there was no need for them to point out that it was a forgery. It's not surprising really. Even if the catalogue were revealed to be a fake and the professor's career destroyed, they didn't stand to profit one yen. But the moment Nishijima's discovery was announced to the world, their horde of Akita School paintings would be worth a fortune overnight. Just imagine—fifty Sharaku nikuhitsu-ga backed by the full faith and credit of the international art market! If they played their cards right the paintings might fetch more than 300 million yen.

Mr. Saga believed it was at this point that Mizuno's resolve began to waver, but I think he probably had it in mind as a possibility all along, from the very moment Mr. Saga told him about his plan. Mr. Saga's righteous indignation alone was not enough to muster the human and financial resources needed to create the catalogue. From the very beginning, Mizuno and the others had no interest in unmasking the catalogue as a fake. So they used Mr. Saga for their own ends.

Sooner or later, Mr. Saga realized what his accomplices intended to do. But it was already too late. The catalogue was finished and out of his hands.

Mizuno and the others threatened Mr. Saga, saying they would go and confess everything to the police if he made a fuss about the catalogue's authenticity after Nishijima had announced his "discovery." Mr. Saga had fallen into a trap of his own making. If his role in the forgery were revealed, the reputation of not only Professor Nishijima but the entire ukiyo-e establishment would be destroyed. The revelation of personal self-interest and petty grievances behind the UCS and EAA's factional rivalry would raise grave doubts in society at large about the credibility of the ukiyo-e establishment. However much Mr. Saga insisted he had acted out of righteous indignation, the general public simply wouldn't understand. On the contrary, once people learned why Mr. Saga was so upset at the professor, they would take an even dimmer view of the ukiyo-e world. The scandal would leave a wound which would take decades to heal. After all, the fallout from the Shunpoan forgery affair of 1934 has still not completely settled after all this time. Mr. Saga despaired. He had been trying to help ukiyo-e but instead he had gone and made things worse. It was all simply too horrible.

For the sake of ukiyo-e's future Mr. Saga had no choice but to keep his mouth shut. But the idea that the catalogue would be accepted as authentic went against everything he stood for as a scholar. What made it all the more unbearable was the possibility that this "discovery" would only enhance Nishijima's influence. That was one thing Mr. Saga could not allow.

At this point, suicide must have seemed like the easiest way out. Once he was dead, there would be no reason for Mizuno and the others to go and spill everything to the police. The crime would be theirs and theirs alone. They might try to claim that Mr. Saga had made the catalogue but they would have no proof. The month before he died, Mr. Saga seems to have become consumed with thoughts of suicide.

Mr. Saga's death would solve everything—everything, that is, except for the question of Nishijima. That's when Mr. Saga thought of me. He must have known I detested the professor. He decided to reveal everything to me and let me decide what to do. Once the catalogue came to light I could choose to warn the professor or try to carry out his original plan—the decision was up to me. However, whatever I chose to do, it must be in the best interests of ukiyo-e. With that he concluded his notebook.

I wept. I grieved. I was furious.

Many times I was tempted to thrust the notebook in the professor's face saying, "Here, read this!" Mr. Saga was innocent. It was the professor who was to blame. At that moment, I swore to avenge Mr. Saga's death. I chose to finish what he had begun.

However, at this point something happened which I hadn't expected.

You, of all people, discovered the catalogue. Of course, this must have been an eventuality Mr. Saga foresaw. He had a high opinion of your abilities. What's more, Sharaku was your specialty. And being the professor's research assistant, your time was more or less at your disposal. Of all of Nishijima's students, you were the perfect person to find the catalogue.

As it turns out, Kiyochika's preface and Shoei's biography were written with you in mind—this is how you would respond to this piece of information, interpret this word, this place name... Mr. Saga went over and over your thought patterns in his mind. As his guide he no doubt referred to your recently published paper, "Sharaku: The State of the Debate."

The forgers had had you in their sights for several months.

Their plan to lure you to the rare book sale by sending out a catalogue listing a large number of titles on ukiyo-e worked like a charm. If you hadn't returned the postcard asking to reserve one of the books listed in the catalogue they would have waited for their next opportunity. The books sale is held several times each month—there would have been other chances. Perhaps they had tried several times before already. Once you returned the postcard, all Mizuno had to do was contact you to say your name had been chosen; that would be enough to ensure you came.

When you arrived at the book sale Mizuno casually approached you. All he had to do was get you interested in Sato's catalogue and their work would be half done. After that, if you hadn't taken any action within a few days, Mizuno probably would have contacted you and somehow drawn your attention to the painting with Sharaku's name on it, but fortunately you noticed it straight away. In that regard, you behaved exactly as Mr. Saga had expected. His estimation of your abilities had been exactly right.

You were completely convinced that you had discovered the catalogue all by yourself. If Mizuno had just brought it to you and said, "Here, take a look at this," you wouldn't have been inclined to accept the authenticity of Sharaku's lion painting so readily—Professor Nishijima even less so. It was crucial to their plan that you thought you had stumbled upon the catalogue by chance. If I hadn't already read Mr. Saga's notebook when you told me about how you had discovered the catalogue, I probably would have believed it was pure chance too.

I was flabbergasted.

Until you showed it to me, it hadn't occurred to me that you might be the one who discovered the catalogue. What's more, you told me you had already shown it to the professor and he had deemed that it "had possibilities."

But I didn't want you getting mixed up in this affair. When you showed me the catalogue, all the while I was looking at it I was trying to think of a way to explain to you it was a forgery. The easiest thing would have been to have you read Mr. Saga's notebook, but I didn't want to do that. For one thing, it might bring dishonor on Mr. Saga's memory. "C'mon, there must be a way I can let him know it's a fake without telling him about Mr. Saga," I thought desperately. Just then my finger happened to rub against the inside of one of the uncut double-leaved pages. Suddenly I understood why they had had to print the book using this traditional Japanese method. There were two reasons. One was that in order to give the pages the patina of old age it had been necessary to take the book apart, hang up the pages separately and reassemble them. That would have been difficult with a Western-style binding. But with a traditional Japanese-style binding, the pages could just be sewn back together after they'd been artificially aged. The second reason was to conceal the fact that they had used offset printing, as Mr. Saga implies in his notebook.

The main difference between offset and letterpress printing is that with the latter the pressure of the type makes a strong impression on the page—with offset printing there is virtually none. When printing on thin paper using letterpress printing, the impression of the type will show through on the back of the page, and punctuation marks will sometimes even leave a hole in the paper. But the backs of the uncut pages in the catalogue were smooth. That's a sure sign offset printing was used. To conceal this they used double-leaved pages. That way no one would be able to see the backs of the pages.

It was ingenious, but it had its drawbacks.

Though lithography existed in Japan in the early 1900s offset printing did not. Therefore, anyone familiar with the history of printing in Japan would have immediately realized the catalogue was a fake. I was about to say as much to you when all of a sudden the desire for revenge welled up inside me again. The professor had told you that the catalogue "had possibilities." At this rate, it looked like he would fall into Mr. Saga's trap. Moreover, the question of the impression made by the type—or lack thereof—which I had noticed was really a very simple thing. If I were to point it out later, publicly, there would be no way to trace the forgery back to Mr. Saga. I could destroy the professor's career without having to use Mr. Saga's notebook as evidence. This thought made me ecstatic. I could bury the professor without causing trouble for anyone else.

Also, I had a strong urge to understand the scholarly underpinnings of this catalogue Mr. Saga had labored over so obsessively. I knew it wouldn't be possible for you to base an entire theory solely on the evidence in the catalogue. Mr. Saga had put all of his considerable scholarly ability into crafting his plan. I was sure he had devised it in such a way that some crucial bit of evidence would emerge in the course of research. For the record I'd like to say that more than the desire for revenge, it was my own scholarly curiosity that caused me to pursue this course and delay my revenge.

There would be time later to think things through carefully. For the time being, I decided to say nothing to you.

You went off to Akita to pursue your research. While you were away I did some research of my own on Sharaku. I learned all about Hiraga Gennai and the comic poets of the period, and for the first time in ages I felt fulfilled. "What a fascinating subject!" I thought, envying you for having continued your study of ukiyo-e.

It was just chance that I looked up Odate in my encyclopedia of Japanese place names when I heard you were staying there. Even now I don't know why I thought of it. I wonder if Mr. Saga was really reading that far ahead when he chose to make Odate the place where Shoei lived. But knowing him, he probably was. He probably realized that sooner or later someone would discover what I did—in 1795 the daimyo of Akita established a district magistrate's office in Odate. His plan was worked out brilliantly. I've never been so surprised in my life as I was at that moment.

Meanwhile, in Akita, you dug up some information about Shoei yourself. You'd even uncovered a possible apprentice by the name of Eiwa who lived very close to Honjo, the town Shoei supposedly had moved to when he retired. For a moment I even forgot the catalogue was a fake and became convinced that Shoei had been Sharaku.

I think you found out more than Mr. Saga ever imagined. Of course, since Shoei was a samurai from Akita it wasn't surprising you should have delved into the Akita clan. But I don't think even Mr. Saga could have predicted your theory about the connection between Tanuma Okitsugu and Tsutaya Juzaburo, and the Akita clan's central role in shaping late-eighteenth-century Edo culture. I think Mr. Saga had picked up on the relationship between Tsutaya and the Akita clan chamberlain Tegara Okamochi (a.k.a Hoseido Kisanji), but he probably thought the mere fact that Shoei was a Western-style painter from Akita who was in Edo when Sharaku was active and who returned to Odate in 1795 would be enough to get Nishijima to take the bait. Once Shoei's bona fides had been accepted, everything else came down to the catalogue's supposed date of publication—1907. Who in the world would dare question the authenticity of a painting signed by Sharaku that had appeared in a book published before Julius Kurth?

You returned from Akita. I was bowled over when you explained your theory to me. I had never thought you would be able to connect Sharaku to Shoei so perfectly. Not only that, but you had found incontrovertible evidence that Shoei's works had found their way onto the art market by the early 1930s. You said that Shoei's signature would have been removed and replaced by that of some other artist. If one didn't know that the catalogue was a fake, one would have to say that you proved your case decisively. But that was impossible. The catalogue of Shoei's paintings had been created out of whole cloth by Mr. Saga only recently. There was no way one of the paintings could have been sold by a dealer in Yokote in 1937.

At first I thought this too was all part of Mr. Saga's intricately devised plan. And how ingenious it was! It meant that if one of Shoei's paintings were to come on the market now no one would be able to claim it was a forgery.

With today's technology, no matter how skillfully forged a signature might be it can't stand up to careful scientific scrutiny. If the forgers had simply tried to sell one of Shoei's paintings as is on the open market, the forgery would undoubtedly have been uncovered in less than a month.

But what if the paintings were to appear on the market bearing the signature of some other artist? Thanks to the catalogue it would already have been established that the paintings had originally been signed by Shoei. In other words, everyone would immediately know that Shoei's signature had been removed and that of the other artist had been added recently. Subjecting the signature to scientific analysis would only confirm what everyone already knew—that the signature was recent.

Therefore, Shoei's signature could only exist on the painting in the context of the catalogue. No amount of modern technology could determine the age of a signature on a painting in a photograph. All the forgers had to do was remove Shoei's signatures from the paintings and add those of some other artist. Then no one in the world would be able to say they were fakes. It was truly the perfect crime.

As I was thinking all this through, I had a flash of insight: Mr. Saga would never have faked the evidence from the dealer up in Yokote. All he wanted to do was use the catalogue to destroy the professor's career. No, this must have been Mizuno's idea. That meant you must have encountered one of his associates on your recent research trip to Akita. I casually asked Saeko about it. When I heard her answer, the first thing I thought was that Kato must be one of Mizuno's associates. But according to her, it had been your idea to ask Kato to search for photographs of Akita School paintings. But there's simply no way Mizuno could have prepared the photographs in advance knowing you would ask such a question on your own. I was perplexed. The dealer in Yokote had definitely said 1937. I began to suspect him of being part of the plot too, but if Kato wasn't in league with Mizuno after all, that would mean it was pure chance he had put you in touch with the dealer in Yokote. I was thoroughly confused.

A few days later I figured out their scheme. Kato was Mizuno's associate and the dealer in Yokote was a fiction. But the idea to remove Shoei's signatures from the paintings occurred to them only after talking to you. They hadn't thought so far ahead. Something you said must have made Kato realize that doing so would be greatly to their advantage.

I think Kato must have been trailing you from the time you arrived at Kosaka. But then Saeko spotted him in Kakunodate and, knowing he'd been recognized, he decided to approach you. As he was chatting with you, you happened to say something about how it might be helpful if you could track down some photographs of Akita School paintings. It must have struck him as an intriguing idea. After you two parted he immediately telephoned Mizuno, who was enthusiastic about the idea. He went and removed Shoei's signature from the paintings, replaced it with that of Tashiro Unmu and took some Polaroids. It was probably Mizuno who took the Polaroids to Morioka to give to Kato.

Meanwhile, Kato had been scraping together any images he could find of Akita School paintings in order to make an album. He told you the Yokote dealer had sold many of the works to museums, but in fact he made that up—he just took images from museum catalogues to forge a catalogue of a collection, which lent an air of legitimacy to his fictional art dealer friend up in Yokote. Then he put these into an album together with the Polaroids which Mizuno had taken and photocopied it. This way he was able to disguise the fact that they were Polaroids and images cut out of museum catalogues. Then Kato sat back and waited.

When you turned up at his shop Kato put on an innocent look and showed you the album. You of course discovered the works by Shoei right away and asked him where he had got the album. Then Kato called another of his accomplices. The dealer in Yokote was of course a complete fabrication. But it wasn't Mizuno. You had met Mizuno. They weren't ones to take such a risk. Anyway, the man on the telephone explained to you that the paintings had been sold in 1937. Then he casually proffered the information about Nagatoro. At this point, anyone would have been hooked.

In this way Mizuno and his associates succeeded both in fabricating evidence that Sato's catalogue was indeed very old and, at the same time, convincing the world of the convenient "fact" that Shoei's paintings were now circulating in the art market under another artist's forged signature— Tashiro Unmu's.

This doesn't mean I blame you. It was simply your passion for Shoei that gave rise to the album. It's not your fault.

But this "fact" made the assertion that Shoei was Sharaku irrefutable. For any doubters who might have wondered why Shoei hadn't been recognized until now, this provided the answer. Everyone in the world would accept the Shoei hypothesis as true. So long as I kept my mouth shut it would become the prevailing theory. Now everything depended on me.

At this point I found myself in a dilemma. Should I unmask the catalogue as a fake or not? My indecision made Sharaku's supposed relationship to Tanuma seem all the more intriguing—for the first time Sharaku began to feel like a real person to me. I don't think Mr. Saga had gotten as far as Tanuma in his thought process. But while talking to you I began to think maybe Sharaku really had been an Akita School painter—perhaps not Shoei but someone else, it didn't matter if it wasn't Shoei, your theory was still valid. How else could one explain the fact that you had managed to uncover such a convincing web of human relationships? Mr. Saga had set out to create a forgery, but what if he had stumbled upon the truth? No, there could be no doubt—Sharaku was from Akita. You'd been chasing a lie but had ended up solving mystery of Sharaku at least in part. Of this I was now convinced.

So what to do? If I unmasked the catalogue as a forgery I'd destroy the basis of the very theory I believed was true. From a scholarly perspective what was the right thing to do? If I wanted to keep the Shoei/Akita School hypothesis alive I couldn't come out and say the catalogue was a fake.

Then again, this was a question the world should decide on its own. Your theory was too compelling to simply sink back into obscurity.

I decided to do nothing. Mr. Saga's plan had taken on a life of its own. This was now your discovery. I had no right to destroy it.

But there was still one thing that worried me, and that was what the professor might do. Knowing him, I'd a strong feeling he wouldn't leave it all in your hands. If the professor tried to pass off your work as his own... At that point, I wouldn't hesitate to act. If he would stoop so low as to nip the career of a promising young scholar like yourself in the bud, then he no longer deserved to be allowed to preside over the ukiyo-e establishment. I wouldn't regret seeing the Akita School hypothesis ruined in exchange for destroying the professor. But at the same time, deep down, part of me still wanted to trust the professor. I couldn't bring myself to believe he would really rob one of his own students of such a momentous discovery.

But, as you know, that wasn't the way things turned out. At the EAA's general meeting on December 21, the professor made his position perfectly clear.

I was dumbstruck. It pained me terribly to think of how you must feel. I decided to act. But before I did, I wanted to let the professor know what I thought of him. If, as a scholar, he agreed to do the right thing and come out and repudiate the catalogue as a fake, he could spare the ukiyo-e establishment any trouble. If he did that, I wouldn't pursue the matter any future. Because, somewhere inside me, I didn't want to completely give up on the professor.

On the night of January 1 I telephoned the professor. I said I had something very important to discuss with him regarding the catalogue and asked when it would be convenient to see him. He said to come the following night. He would be at home alone. From the tone of my voice, he must have realized it was something serious.

The next night I went to the professor's house just after nine o'clock.

I didn't show him Mr. Saga's notebook. I told him only that the catalogue was a forgery. He didn't believe me. I pointed out that the catalogue seemed to have been printed using offset printing. When he heard that the professor suddenly went as white as a sheet. He jumped up, removed the catalogue from the safe and began pouring over it. The look on his face at that moment is burned into my memory: it became all contorted, like he was about to burst into tears. Then he hit me—he had understood.

For a while after that the professor stood stock-still. Then he took out a lighter and moved it toward the catalogue as though to light it. If the catalogue were destroyed, the evidence that it had been printed using offset printing would be lost. No one would be able to prove it had been a forgery. Understanding what the professor intended to do, I lunged and grabbed the catalogue away from him. The professor leaped on top of me. But I was stronger. I pinned him to the ground and scolded him for his despicable conduct. Suddenly, he began bawling like a baby. It was all so sad and pathetic. Unable to stand it any longer, I rushed out of the house, leaving the catalogue behind. As I fled, I could still hear him sobbing.

The next morning the professor was found dead. I figured he must have taken his own life, unable to bring himself to come out and announce that the catalogue was a fake. This whole torrid affair had begun with Mr. Saga's suicide and ended with the professor's.

If I had found Mr. Saga's notebook earlier I might have been able to prevent his death. And if I had simply told you that the catalogue was a fake as soon as you found it, the professor wouldn't have had to die either. Without intending to, I had caused the deaths of two people. This sense of responsibility was hard for me to bear.

I had killed the professor—or so I thought. But just then you gave me some startling news: someone had set fire to the professor's house and he had died before he could escape.

My head was in a tumult. Hadn't the professor committed suicide? If not, who would have wanted to kill him? I thought of Mizuno. But that was inconceivable. He and his associates still needed the professor. They needed him to publish his paper and the catalogue so that the Shoei Hypothesis would become unassailable. Until then he was indispensible to them. I still haven't figured out the answer to this riddle.

Then Minegishi discovered Kiyochika's sketchbook.

The discovery of the sketchbook brought about a whole new development. You and Minegishi began to have doubts about the authenticity of Kiyochika's preface to Sato's catalogue. No doubt Mizuno was just as surprised by this development as I was. Then when I heard it was Mizuno who had introduced the two of you, I was astonished at his recklessness. Was he as confident as that? Granted, at that point, no one could have foreseen that the sketchbook would be discovered.

If doubts hadn't arisen about the authenticity of Kiyochika's preface, Mizuno and his associates would probably still be sitting on their paintings, biding their time. They probably planned to wait two or three years to let things cool down before unveiling their "discovery." Having come this far, it would be fatal for them to do anything out of the ordinary. But now the situation had changed.

No doubt they've realized that sooner or later you and Minegishi will uncover proof the preface is a fake. Though they won't be able to predict how things will play out once that happens, one thing is certain—now they'll be trying to sell the paintings in a hurry.

I'd been planning to wait until that happened to put an end to this in my own way, but before I could, I discovered something unexpected.

For the past few days, as you asked me to, I've been trying to trace that postcard you found tucked away inside the catalogue. It's not a very important clue. At least, that's what I thought at first. But curiously it began to intrigue me. What was written on the card seemed to have no particular significance. So I traced the person whom it was addressed to, which led me to a stamp dealer in Shinjuku, where I found out the name of the last person to own it. The dealer showed me a business card given to him by the man who purchased it. On it was a name that took me by surprise: Fujimura Genzo, the rare book dealer to whom Mr. Saga, on the day he died, had been trying to return the book he had stolen.

A coincidence perhaps?

No, that was too farfetched. Even assuming Mizuno purchased the postcard from Fujimura and just happened to leave it inside the catalogue, the chances that Mr. Saga just happened to steal a book from the same man were virtually nil. It was more logical to suppose that Mr. Saga had stolen the postcard along with the book, but why? It made no sense. It wasn't rare—the stamp dealer had been adamant about that.

There was only one explanation: Fujimura was in cahoots with Mizuno. He was probably the person you spoke to on the phone believing he was an art dealer in Yokote.

But if Fujimura was one of the forgers, something didn't quite add up. Why didn't Mr. Saga simply return the book to him directly? Why did Fujimura claim he didn't know Mr. Saga? Why didn't Mizuno bat an eyelash when Inspector Onodera asked him about Fujimura? Doubts flashed through my mind in quick succession.

Mr. Saga must have been murdered.

However much I thought about it, I couldn't find any plausible reason why Mr. Saga should have gone to all the trouble of trying to return a book to Fujimura just before he died. The parcel must have been a trick to make his death look like suicide. So I concluded.

I don't know who exactly killed Mr. Saga. But I know either Mizuno, Kato, or Fujimura is the culprit. It must have seemed to them that Mr. Saga was on the verge of revealing the catalogue was a forgery, so they decided to kill him first.

I was in a quandary.

I had read Mr. Saga's diary. He had committed suicide. Or so I had believed. Because of that I had been blind to what they were up to, even though I knew the catalogue was a fake. I thought they had only been after money. I pitied them but it did not make me angry. But I had underestimated them. They were murderers. And I had allowed them to remain at large because of my own hatred and envy of the professor.

Once I realized this I began to suspect they had killed the professor too. At that moment my despair knew no bounds.

I decided to hunt down the killer, or killers, on my own. This had all been my fault. I had to make amends.

Today I made two copies of Mr. Saga's notebook, one for Mizuno and one for Fujimura. Mizuno's already received his. I stuffed it in his mailbox this morning. Tomorrow I'll take the other copy to Sendai and do the same for Fujimura. They're sure to contact each other. Then all I have to do is keep an eye on them and wait for them to make a mistake. They'll dig their own graves. If I'm lucky, I might find out where they've got the paintings stashed—if I can produce any with Shoei's forged signature still on they won't be able to talk their way out of it. I'll leave the rest to Onodera. We're talking about murder after all. I'd like to settle this without dragging ukiyo-e into it. But that might be unavoidable.

It's almost dawn. I have to go now. Mr. Saga's notebook is still sitting on my bookshelf inside the slipcover of his book. I don't want to have to use it. Even without it I hope to be able to prove they murdered Mr. Saga and the professor—though now the catalogue has been destroyed, it'll be difficult to prove it was a fake. If I could just figure out those clues Mr. Saga hid inside the catalogue to trip up Nishijima—so far that's eluded me.

I guess I better be going

I'm sorry for causing you so much trouble. Look after Saeko for me.

RYOHEI could not bring himself to shed a tear.

He knew it was a fake all along. He knew Shoei wasn't real.

Even though he held the proof in his hands, Ryohei could hardly believe it. Deep in his heart he still believed he and Yosuke had solved the mystery of Sharaku's identity together.

How could he do it! How could he have been so selfish!

All of a sudden, Ryohei was consumed by an irrepressible rage.

Do you think dying absolves you of responsibility? Does that make everything better? Sure, the professor behaved badly. But Mr. Saga... He went too far! How could you say he loved ukiyo-e? If he'd loved ukiyo-e he wouldn't have gone and written Sharaku's name on someone else's painting. Don't you understand that? It wasn't me who was used by Mr. Saga—it was you, Yosuke! He put the future of ukiyo-e in your hands. The burden was too much for him so he foisted it off onto you. And then, satisfied with himself, he went and died... In the end, everyone was thinking about themselves; no one gave a damn about us, the ones who'll have to live with this.

Saga and Yosuke had been willing to risk their lives to defend ukiyo-e, but they had ended by dragging it through the mud.

How full of ourselves we've all been—imagining ukiyo-e needed us to prove its relevance to the world. What conceit! Ukiyo-e's not some poor cousin who'll starve without our help. It's better than that. If ukiyo-e could be destroyed by one selfish whim of the professor's, then good riddance to it—we can live without it. But ukiyo-e will go on. Mr. Saga and the professor may be gone, but ukiyo-e will thrive. As far as ukiyo-e's concerned, we're just strangers passing in the night. Ukiyo-e doesn't need us. It can survive all on its own.

For the first time, tears welled up in Ryohei's eyes.

After all was said and done, what was left? All Ryohei could think of now was that three people had died in vain. Yosuke's death, in particular, left a void in his life that could never be filled.

Seated in a corner of the café, Ryohei continued to cry, mourning the loss of his friend.

TO HELL with ukiyo-e! I'd rather Yosuke were still alive. I'd sooner destroy what Yosuke and Mr. Saga died trying to protect then allow Mizuno and the others to get away with this.

Having made up his mind, Ryohei put in a call to the Fuchu Police Department and asked to speak to Onodera. Mizuno must have ransacked Yosuke's apartment looking for the notebook. Once the police got their hands on it they would be able to arrest Mizuno. Once they had conclusive proof the catalogue was a fake, they would have Mizuno and his cronies right where they wanted them.

It didn't bother Ryohei in the least that Saga's act of forgery and the professor's unbridled arrogance might be revealed in the process. He was convinced ukiyo-e was strong enough to survive any such scandal.

When the detective picked up the telephone, Ryohei gave him the titles of four books. Ryohei knew these were the only books Saga had written that had been published with slipcases. If Mizuno hadn't already found it, the notebook would be inside one of them.

Saying he would telephone Saeko immediately to get her permission to search Yosuke's apartment, Onodera rung off in high spirits.

February 20

IT WAS all over.

Onodera had found Saga's notebook, exactly as Ryohei had said, inside one of the slipcases where it had escaped Mizuno's notice. Based on this piece of evidence, the detective took Mizuno into the police station for voluntary questioning on suspicion of fraud. Kato, who had recently returned from London, and Fujimura were picked up for questioning by police in Morioka and Sendai, respectively.

It was Mizuno who had committed all three murders.

Kato and Fujimura proved surprisingly easy to make talk. When they realized the fraud had been discovered they tried to foist all of the blame onto Mizuno. They claimed they only had been acting on Mizuno's instructions and had been thoroughly convinced the catalogue was original.

Mizuno proved a tougher nut to crack, but once Onodera had the flight passenger list analyzed and confirmed that one of the names was in his handwriting, he eventually caved in. Once he had made one confession the rest came spilling from his mouth like an avalanche.

Just as Onodera had deduced, Mizuno had murdered Saga at his office, drowning him in a bucket of seawater collected off Cape

Kitayama which he had brought back with him to Tokyo several days ahead of time.

Mizuno was formally arrested on suspicion of murder just three days after he was taken in for questioning.

Nearly fifty hanging scrolls bearing Shoei's forged signature were found in the storeroom attached to Fujimura's shop in Sendai. Each was carefully wrapped up in wax paper and tightly sealed. Just as Yosuke had imagined, if Kiyochika's sketchbook had not surfaced, they had planned to sit on them for a least three years.

Also discovered was the painting bearing Sharaku's signature. This work, dubbed the "Encaustic Lion," would later appear splashed across the pages of newspapers and magazines throughout Japan and come to symbolize the entire affair. The painting—the artist of which has yet to be identified—will no doubt remain etched into the minds of many people for years to come.

The case had been solved.

"They had it all planned out perfectly."

Inspector Onodera was seated in a café beneath Ueno Station talking to Ryohei, who had come to see him off.

"About a week before Saga died it appears Fujimura and Kato had been taking turns making threatening phone calls to his apartment—even hinting they might kill him," said the detective. "Not surprisingly Saga began to feel paranoid. That was why he turned his notebook over the Yosuke. Mizuno denied Fujimura and Kato would go that far, but he managed to convince Saga to move someplace safer."

"Someplace safer?"

"The rented apartment Mizuno used as his office and storeroom. He probably convinced Saga it was safer because no one ever came there… safer to commit murder too." Onodera clenched his fist. "It had a bathroom, a shower, a bed and everything—a perfect place for someone to hide out for a few days. Saga felt reassured and moved in there on the night of the eighth. Of course, he took an overnight bag packed with a change of clothes and assorted toiletries."

Ryohei said nothing.

"In the meantime, Mizuno promised Saga he would smooth things over with the other two up in Tohoku. But he warned

Saga he couldn't let up his guard until everything was settled. Both Fujimura and Kato knew the address and phone number of Mizuno's office, after all, so he was told not to go outside or answer the phone under any circumstances, just in case."

"Hmm. It's no wonder Mr. Saga trusted him," said Ryohei.

"If he'd been staying anywhere else, Saga would probably have thought Mizuno was just being paranoid," continued Onodera. "Anyway, with that warning Mizuno set off on the morning of the ninth for Hachinohe, saying he was going to talk to the other two."

"I see. And Mr. Saga just sat tight and waited."

"Yeah. Waited to be murdered," said Onodera. "It makes you sick, doesn't it? Listening to Mizuno's confession I wanted to lean over and slug him. Saga just sat tight and waited for Mizuno to return, convinced Mizuno had seen the error of his ways. He came back that afternoon carrying two boxes of sushi from Hachinohe. Saga, who hadn't had anything to eat since morning, tucked in without suspecting a thing. While they were eating, Mizuno grilled Saga about what he'd done while he was gone. Had he gone out? Had anyone come by? Had anyone telephoned? Had he called anyone? Since Saga wasn't supposed to be in Tokyo, Mizuno's plan would have been ruined if anyone noticed anything suspicious. Mizuno was very savvy about things like that. He said he was prepared to postpone Saga's murder if anything seemed out of place."

Ryohei was astounded by Mizuno's meticulousness.

"Once he had confirmed to his satisfaction that everything was as it should be," went on Onodera, "Mizuno told Saga that Fujimura had come to Tokyo to go talk to him, and he went out again. Saga was surprised to learn of this new development. This was also part of Mizuno's plan. With this piece of information, Saga wouldn't dare go out for several hours. Mizuno hurried over to the library. The rest happened just as we imagined. Having established his alibi, Mizuno returned to the apartment to kill Saga. A big guy like that wouldn't have had any trouble drowning a pipsqueak like Saga in a bucket of water."

"So Mr. Saga's body *was* in the car when Mizuno and Yosuke…"

Nodding gloomily, Onodera wiped his forehead.

"Mizuno told me he never expected Yosuke to come along—but it gave him an airtight alibi. When they reached Saga's cottage, Mizuno and Yosuke split up and searched the house. Having never been there before, Yosuke didn't know his way around and Mizuno says he used the extra time to plant Saga's overnight bag and leave the newspaper and empty sushi tray on the table. Then he made sure Yosuke discovered them. He's a real sly one, that Mizuno."

"You can say that again," said Ryohei. "No wonder even Yosuke fell for it."

"After that he disposed of the body. He drove Yosuke out to Cape Kitayama to make a show of looking for Saga. Once he was sure Yosuke had headed off in the direction of the restaurant, Mizuno returned to the car, hauled the body out of the trunk and… hurled it into the dark sea."

"Didn't it make a noise?" asked Ryohei.

"There was a fierce wind that night apparently—perfect conditions for disposing of a body. Mizuno says he went back several times to make sure the body had sunk out of sight. Seems he was worried since it was so dark."

"And Professor Nishijima? Was that Mizuno too?"

"Yeah. He confessed to setting the fire, though he denies he intended to kill the professor… By the way, you were right—Mizuno saw Yosuke going into the professor's house that night and thought it strange, knowing they had had a falling out. He hid beneath the study window and eavesdropped on their conversation. Apparently when he heard Yosuke tell the professor the catalogue was a fake he thought the game was up. But it seemed Yosuke didn't know about Mizuno and his associates. He'd only detected the forgery because of the offset printing, and Mizuno breathed a sigh of relief. Then he waited for things to quiet down, and when he thought the professor had gone to sleep he started the fire. He said he never dreamed Nishijima would be sleeping on the daybed in his study. But even if he'd been asleep in another room there's still a possibility he wouldn't be able to escape in time, so our reading of it is Mizuno acted with the intent to commit murder."

Ryohei nodded.

"For that point on," Onodera continued, "Mizuno keep an eye on Yosuke's activities. Even though the evidence of the forgery had been destroyed, Yosuke still posed a threat. Then, when Saga's notebook appeared in his mailbox, he immediately knew it was Yosuke's handiwork. It seems he decided he had no other choice now but to kill Yosuke. Because of the postcard, Mizuno figured Yosuke would turn up sooner or later at Fujimura's shop, so he set off for Sendai to get there first. When Yosuke arrived in Sendai, Mizuno already had him marked. He waited until Yosuke was alone on the street and ran him down in Fujimura's car. Yosuke must never have suspected *they* would be trailing *him* or he would have been more careful," Onodera said with a shudder. "Yosuke only found out about Fujimura's role because of the postcard. Otherwise he might still be alive. By Mizuno's own confession, it was only once Yosuke had traced the postcard that he started to panic, thinking Yosuke would figure everything out. You see, the postcard was never part of Saga's original plan…"

"So it wasn't Mizuno's idea?" asked Ryohei.

"No, Fujimura's. They stuck it in the catalogue at the last minute to convince people the album was old, but Mizuno regretted it immediately. At first nobody took any notice of the postcard, but wouldn't you know it, in the end that one stupid mistake proved fatal…"

Ryohei said nothing.

Fatal for Yosuke, that is—if only I hadn't asked him to…

The thought was almost too much for Ryohei to bear.

"If only Yosuke had waited a bit longer," went on Onodera. "At least until the Shoei painting had surfaced at Sotheby's. Perhaps then he wouldn't have been so foolish as to chase after that gang all on his own. Just one more day… If he'd known they'd gone and sold one of the paintings, surely even Yosuke would've given up and come to talk the situation over with you or me."

"But the catalogue had been destroyed," said Ryohei. "And besides, Yosuke wanted to keep Mr. Saga's notebook a secret at all costs."

"Hmm. I can't really speak to that," replied Onodera. "By the way, what about those clues Saga supposedly hid in the catalogue— did they really exist?"

"I've poured over my copy but I can't come up with anything—except for what Yosuke pointed out about the offset printing."

"I see," replied the detective. "But that's strange, isn't it? That means Saga would actually have to see the catalogue again in the flesh, so to speak, in order to point the problem out. He wouldn't be able to claim he figured it out from a picture in the newspaper. And what guarantee did he have that Professor Nishijima would be willing to show it to him?"

"Hmm…"

Onodera was right. From what he knew of Saga and the professor's relationship, Ryohei had to admit that was out of the question.

"It had to be something one could have figured out without seeing the original."

"You're right."

"No, the clue must be something else," the detective said flatly. "But if Yosuke couldn't find it and *you* can't find it, then probably no one will. When you think about it Saga was a scary guy… and I don't just mean because he was so damn smart."

Ryohei agreed.

Mr. Saga had been obsessed—obsessed with the professor. The catalogue was the fruit of that obsession.

Ryohei suddenly felt sad. If the ukiyo-e establishment had not been split into two rival factions, Saga and the professor could have pursued their research together, as friends, and this whole incident would never have happened. But in the wake of the murders, that rift, far from mending itself, only seemed to be getting wider.

Even though he had already decided to quit academia, this was one thing that still weighed on Ryohei's mind. There was no guarantee that some day another incident would not arise from this rift. In that sense, the affair had not been laid to rest. It never would, so long as the rivalry between the Ukiyo-e Connoisseurship Society and the Edo Art Association continued. Ryohei trembled with a sense of dread.

The fallout from the scandal had also destroyed Yoshimura's career, and Musashino University had cancelled all it courses on ukiyo-e. Like Ryohei, Iwakoshi was planning to return to his hometown. Nishijima's current and former students had all gone their separate ways.

In the end Mr. Saga won—it all turned out just as he planned.

Ryohei looked around, imagining for a moment he could hear the sound of Saga laughing. Suddenly the voices of the other travelers around him seemed very loud.

"Is something wrong?" Smiling, Onodera looked at Ryohei. Then, changing the subject, he said, "Now about the Akita School hypothesis… It took me several days, but I finally finished reading your paper. Yosuke was right—you're definitely onto something. Now, I don't know anything about painting, but looking at it as a criminal investigation, I agree entirely with your conclusion. Your theory is rock solid. It's a pity you don't have any proof, but in my line of work that's what we call 'instinct.' From now on I can tell people Sharaku was actually a painter from Akita. Don't worry, sooner or later you'll find the evidence you're looking for," Onodera said encouragingly. "Don't give up on ukiyo-e. Stick with your research."

Ryohei felt a warm feeling rise within his breast.

"Thanks to you, I'm beginning to like ukiyo-e," the detective went on. "I haven't learned much yet, but at least I can tell the difference between a Sharaku and an Utamaro."

Onodera's body shook as he laughed. The detective's smile lifted Ryohei's spirits for the first time since the case had ended.

The two men laughed together.

Epilogue

TWO YEARS had passed.

Ryohei was now teaching Japanese history at a private middle school in Morioka. Though popular with his students, he had a reputation for being a bit on the quiet side. Several times each year, however, when the class came to a unit on ukiyo-e, their teacher's eyes would suddenly light up as though he had awakened from a long sleep.

One day, needing to look something up, Ryohei made his way to the prefectural library, which has an extensive reference collection.

The objective of Ryohei's search was the origin of an old place name in Iwate Prefecture. Heading straight for the reference section, his hand reached for the "Tohoku" volume of *The Geographical Encyclopedia of Japan*, edited by Yoshida Togo. First published in 1899, the encyclopedia runs to seven volumes and over five thousand pages, and remains today the best source of information about the history and origins of Japanese place names.

Unfortunately, Ryohei was unable to find the name he was looking for. He put the "Tohoku" volume back where he had found it and pulled the supplementary index off the shelf.

Opening it at the front, he saw the first hundred pages consisted of testimonials about the encyclopedia by twenty-five prominent individuals. Intrigued, Ryohei began flipping through the pages. Most of the great intellectuals of the late nineteenth century were represented. Among them Ryohei noted the names of Tsubouchi Shoyo, Shibusawa Eiichi, Okuma Shigenobu, and Hara Takashi.

Wow, an all-star lineup!

Ryohei was suitably impressed. Though he often used the encyclopedia, he had never noticed these testimonials. Selecting one interesting-looking section at random, Ryohei began reading:

In these flourishing times there is no shortage of books, and each passing month brings more and more. But most of these are aimed at appealing to popular tastes and passing fancies. They are mere trifles... This is something intellectuals like myself greatly bemoan.

As his eyes took in the old-fashioned sounding prose, something clicked in the back of Ryohei's mind—he had come across the same passage somewhere before. The author of the article was someone by the name of Kano Jigoro. Ryohei seemed to recall that he was the founder of the modern sport of judo.

Ignoring the nagging feeling at the back of his mind, Ryohei turned the page:

He grew up in a small village in the mountains and at one time aspired to make his name in the world as a scholar. But due to circumstances beyond his control he was forced to abandon his formal education without finishing middle school... When he came of age he had to make his own way in the world, again for family reasons. He eventually found his way to Hokkaido...

Ryohei stopped reading and stared at the page. Now he remembered. It was a passage from Kiyochika's preface to Sato's catalogue, the part where he talked about the life of Sato Masakichi. The phrase, "when he came of age he had to make his own way in the world" had stuck in Ryohei's mind because it was so old-fashioned sounding. Apart from the fact that "Hokkaido" had been changed to "Akita," the two were identical. This section had been written by one Ichijima Kenkichi.

Of course! And the earlier one too...

Ryohei turned back to the previous page—it was the first paragraph of Kiyochika's preface.

What does it mean?

For a moment, Ryohei couldn't make sense of it. Then a light bulb went off in his head.

This is it! This is the clue! Mr. Saga lifted Kiyochika's preface from this encyclopedia on purpose!

A scholar of Saga's caliber could easily have written Kiyochika's preface in convincing period style if he had wanted to. Instead, he had chosen to steal it verbatim from Yoshida Togo's *Geographical Encyclopedia* as evidence that the catalogue was a fake. Ryohei felt as though the wind had been knocked out of him.

He excitedly began flipping through the pages, scanning the various testimonials. He came across a couple more passages that matched Kiyochika's preface exactly.

In the end, Ryohei determined that Saga had pieced together Kiyochika's preface using excerpts from four of the testimonials in the encyclopedia.

Ryohei checked the date of publication of that particular edition: October 13, 1907. The same year as the catalogue.

Mr. Saga must have used this to piece together Shoei's biography too. He says in his notebook that he cut the words out of a book from the same period. This must be the one he was referring to.

The *Geographical Encyclopedia* would have been the easiest place for Saga to find unusual place names such as "Odate" and "Honjo" which appeared in Shoei's biography.

Ryohei's head began to reel.

Once Professor Nishijima had unveiled the Shoei Hypothesis to the world, all Saga had to do was trot out the encyclopedia and point out the plagiarized passages. That's all there was to it. People would begin to doubt the authenticity of the catalogue. Then Saga would go on the attack.

His heart pounding, Ryohei dashed out of the library. He started running in the direction of his apartment. He had to tell her.

If only I'd known… If I'd only noticed it then…

Ryohei continued running.

Ryohei clattered up the stairs to his apartment, threw open the front door and dove inside.

Startled by the sound, Saeko, wiping her hands on her apron, hurriedly emerged from the kitchen. Ryohei slumped down on the floor clutching his chest.

"I did it—I finally found it!" he blurted out, still short of breath. Saeko stood frozen.

"If only I'd known then… Yosuke would still be alive… He wouldn't have had to die," said Ryohei, choking back tears.

Saeko only nodded.

A cool breeze blew through the room rustling her silky hair, which she had let grow long.